YEARNING TO LOVE, LEARNING TO LOVE

She made the mistake of glancing at him again and caught him staring at her mouth. The stillness, the fascination, the hunger in him stopped her heart for one long, dizzy second. But afterward, he made no move toward her, didn't try to touch her. The yearning silence deepened.

Had she been wrong? After all, what did he know of kisses? But she was making too much of it. All of this unbearable tension must be coming from her, not him. He was only sitting there, gazing off to the side now, his dark, clear-cut profile beautiful in the dusk. Breathless with daring, she leaned toward him and pressed her lips to his hard cheek.

He sat perfectly still, his only movement the rapid blinking of his eyelashes. The smell of him was soap and pine and man. "Thank you," she murmured and laid her cheek lightly against his. Her heart was pounding hard and fast. He wouldn't even look at her. She touched his arm.

It was trembling, the muscles corded and rock-hard. Then she saw his fingers gripping the edge of the iron bench between them, the tough tendons flexing in the back of his hand.

She stood up quickly, awkwardly. It was absurd to be afraid of Michael, and yet fear was what she felt. Sharp, panicky fear of something wild and dark, unpredictable, and held in check by a white-knuckled control she had no idea she could trust.

PATRICIA GAFFNEY

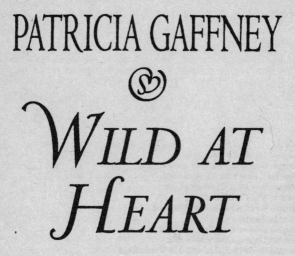

WILD AT HEART

A TOPAZ BOOK

TOPAZ
Published by the Penguin Group
Penguin Books USA Inc., 375 Hudson Street,
New York, New York 10014, U.S.A.
Penguin Books Ltd, 27 Wrights Lane,
London W8 5TZ, England
Penguin Books Australia Ltd, Ringwood,
Victoria, Australia
Penguin Books Canada Ltd, 10 Alcorn Avenue,
Toronto, Ontario, Canada M4V 3B2
Penguin Books (N.Z.) Ltd, 182–190 Wairau Road,
Auckland 10, New Zealand

Penguin Books Ltd, Registered Offices:
Harmondsworth, Middlesex, England

First published by Topaz, an imprint of Dutton Signet,
a division of Penguin Books USA Inc.

First Printing, January, 1997
10 9 8 7 6 5 4 3 2 1

For the amazing Audrey LaFehr

I

Sunfall. Shadows moving slow across the bar on the window. Wooden bar. The guard nailed it there, the day after he tried to escape.

Escape. Run fast and quiet, like a wolf. Run home.

The professor said he must think in words, not pictures. Sunfall, wolf, home. Bar.

Room. This was his room. The square in the wall was a painting. At first it looked like nothing to him, colors jumping, lines twisting in front of his eyes. But now he could make it hold still. It was people eating food outside on the grass. There were trees, and a white thing on the ground covered with apples and plates and things he didn't have names for. All the people looked happy and safe. He stared at the painting, because there was nothing else in his room to look at. He liked the yellow-haired lady and the little boy. The boy had his head on the lady's legs, and she was resting herself against a tree, smiling with her mouth closed, and her body curved like an S.

He knew *S* from his book. He knew all the letters. But most of the words made no sense to him now. *While visiting in your host's drawing room, do not shift your feet, drum your fingers, or play with tassels or knobs. Cultivate repose.*

The sound of laughter came into his room on the breeze. A man's laughter, then a woman's under it, softer. What was the word he had used for *laugh* before he had learned it again? He'd already forgotten. It wasn't a word, anyway; it was a thought in his head, not spoken. And smells and sounds and tastes—they all had words that went with them, and Dr. Winter wanted him to say them out loud.

But he would be one of them if he talked out loud. He would be a man.

The wind died. He smelled the odor of dead meat from the plate the guard, O'Fallon, had left on his table. "This is beef," Professor Winter said. "You must eat it like this, cooked." Now he could take a little bit and not get sick, but it still tasted like ashes, like dirt. He had stopped eating insects, even when no one was looking. But nothing could make him eat those yellow sticks or those dark green stalks, "vegetables," hot and still smoking, soft and slimy and disgusting. His stomach rolled at the thought.

Quiet now. Before, a sound had come from the big house, and he knew what it was but he couldn't capture the word. M. Like water flowing through his head, through his blood. He had jumped up and walked from the door to the window fast, back and forth, holding his ears to keep the noise out at first, but then letting it in as his fear went away. The sound tickled his chest and made him feel crazy, even though it was beautiful. What was it? M.

Night coming. Birds going to sleep. He could smell the water, heavy and dark. "The lake," Professor Winter called it. Not like the water at home, which was bright and light and full of fish to eat. At home, the days would be getting longer. Leaves would be making the forest dark, and the birds would be looking for partners. Food would be easy to find, and he would get fat and lie on a hill with the old wolf, watching the sun slide down the sky.

A memory floated just out of reach, something about the grass, the smell of it now, just cut. "New-mown grass." How did he know that saying? Something old, old, before the boat in the water, something he didn't even know he knew. He closed his eyes to breathe in the sweet green smell of the grass, stalky and raw—and when he opened his eyes, a white angel was floating toward him through the trees, filling the night with her soft laughter.

"Come for a walk with me, Sydney."

Sydney Darrow looked up from the cards in her hand, avoiding her brother's eye. Just last night Philip had pointed out to her, "Charles is always ordering you around, Syd. Why do you put up with it?"

"Come, Sydney. While the sun's going down over the lake. Shall we?"

There, she thought, *he asked me, he didn't order me.* "You don't mind, do you?" She smiled at Sam, her other brother. "You've already won all my money, plus a note for all the money I'll ever have for the rest of my life."

Sam grinned in triumph, showing the hole where his last baby tooth used to be. "I beat you, Sydney," he crowed, "I won and you lost."

"Don't gloat, Samuel," Aunt Estelle reproved from her terrace chair a good thirty feet away. "It's vulgar."

Sydney, Philip, and Sam made identical silent grimaces at each other, a family gesture that meant, *How could she possibly have heard that*?

Sydney stood, and Charles put his hand on the small of her back, pressing firmly to get her going. "I'll play Flinch with you when we come back," she promised Sam over her shoulder.

"Dinner is in twenty minutes," Aunt Estelle said dampeningly, not looking up from her needlepoint. She didn't have to; she had eyes not only in the back but also the sides of her head. "You and Mr. West won't want to be late."

Out of sight of the house, presumably out of earshot, Sydney moaned, "Lord, she's *still* chaperoning me. She did it all over Europe."

"Ha. And did you need chaperoning?"

She slipped her hand through Charles's arm, pleased to think he might be jealous. "Oh my, yes, the men were everywhere, it was hard to walk in a straight line. In Rome we had to take hansoms, because the sidewalks

were littered with the bodies of all my conquests." Finally
he laughed, realizing she was teasing; sometimes her
jokes were lost on Charles. "Aunt Estelle even chaperones
me in church, you know. You'd think I was eighteen
years old, innocent as a maid." Not a twenty-three-year-
old widow, with so little interest in the attentions of the
opposite sex it was laughable.

"I'm glad you're back, Sydney. I missed you."

"That's nice." She smiled, patting his arm.

"You seem happier." He put his head back and stared at
her through the lower half of his bifocals. "Not quite so
sad."

"Oh, we had a wonderful trip. Just what the doctor
ordered."

Just what Aunt Estelle had ordered, anyway. "A year is
long enough for a young woman to mourn a loved one,"
she'd decreed three months ago. "Continued moping beyond that point is not only unhealthy, it's unseemly."

Their trip, designed to cheer Sydney up whether she
wanted to be or not, had been as pleasant as possible, considering that her aunt treated her at all times like an
incompetent child. It had taken her mind off Spencer,
though, and that had been the point. And now it was
good to be home. She'd missed Sam terribly, and Philip.
And Papa.

They had come to the bottom of the lawn. Through the
trees that bordered their strip of beach, the setting sun
dazzled on the smooth blue of Lake Michigan, sail-dotted
and serene, a scene as old as her earliest memories. With
new eyes, she regarded the green-trimmed, white clapboard-
sided guest house on the far side of the path. "So that's
where your 'lost man' lives."

Charles said, "Yes," in a curiously hushed voice.

"My father says he'll make your fortune."

He nodded slowly, eyes slitted, gaze still focused
intently on the small, one-story bungalow. Then he came
out of his trance to chuckle self-consciously. "Not *my* fortune. I'm only your father's assistant."

Sydney knew false self-deprecation when she heard it.

"Yes, but if this man turns out to be as important as Father hopes, I should think you'd both be quite famous one day. A couple of American Darwins."

Charles turned a telltale pink, and she knew she'd struck a chord even though he made scoffing sounds. He tried to hide his secret hopes, but they were always there, guiding his life, defining him. In that way, he wasn't like Papa. For all his other flaws, her father had never been ruled by ambition; his passion for anthropology was pure and devoted, practically a religious vocation. Superfluous things—family, for instance; growing children—had never been able to compete with it.

They stepped off the path, and Sydney sat down on an iron bench under the trees, making room for Charles to sit beside her. "Sam said he saw the lost man walking along the shore yesterday with his jailer."

"His what? Oh, you mean O'Fallon. He used to be a custodian at the university; now he keeps a watch on our man."

"Does he need a keeper? Is he dangerous?" She didn't believe he could be; surely Papa wouldn't have brought him home if he were.

"He was aggressive in the beginning, at times. But he's never been physically violent toward people. Only things—his cage, his clothing."

"His *cage*?"

Charles nodded matter-of-factly. "They kept him in a sort of cage at first. Had to—he was wild; they didn't know what he might do. But he's settled down since then. In fact, if anything," he added, frowning, "it's his listlessness that's threatening our experiments now. You can't get much data from a completely passive subject. All he does that you could label aggressive nowadays is try to escape." He pointed. "Three nights ago he tried to climb out that window."

Sydney noticed the wooden bar splitting the smallish window in two, a grim addition to the pretty white house. "How old is he?" she asked faintly.

"Since he doesn't speak, we can't be sure. In his twenties, we think."

"He doesn't talk? Not at all? Even though you've had him in—in captivity for three months?" How horrid, she thought, to be speaking of this man as if he were a zoo animal.

Charles lifted a professorial index finger. "The anthropology department had him for three months," he corrected. "I—that is, your father and I—have had him to ourselves for less than a week."

"And now you've got him for the whole summer. To experiment on. Do you think you can teach him to talk?"

"Possibly. But of course, that won't be our focus."

"Oh, that's right. You're going to use him to find out if we humans are naturally good or naturally vicious."

He frowned; he preferred his anthropological jargon. "Your father and I are biological ethicists. The man in that cottage is as close to the state of raw, uncivilized nature as a human subject can get and still be scientifically useful. He's unique; there hasn't been a find like him in almost a century."

Sydney glanced past Charles's shoulder at the barred window, arrested for a second by what she had thought was a movement. But the black glass was blank; she must have seen the reflection of a tree branch bowing in the breeze.

She looked away, pensive. What would it be like to live without human society for the first twenty years or so of your life? Could you ever be a man after that, or would you be biologically predestined to live like an animal until you died, forever incapable of being "civilized"? It was an intriguing question, and one she could easily imagine obsessing her father.

"I feel sorry for him," she said quietly. "You call him a 'find'—not even a man. It might've been better if he'd never been found."

Charles only smiled.

"Philip told me he was wounded when he first came to the university, that he'd been shot."

"Yes, it was a freakish thing. A group from the Audubon Society was on expedition in Canada to photograph the winter birds. Every day they'd come back to camp to find that their food supplies had been raided. The footprints in the snow confused them—as you can imagine—so they decided it was a bear."

"Naturally."

"One night one of the birdwatchers heard something and shot at it, blind. The thing escaped, but the next day they followed its bloody trail to a cave. Imagine their surprise." Charles permitted himself a small smile. "They couldn't believe their eyes—it was a man, and he was half dead from blood loss. It took two weeks to get him to Chicago, and another two before they knew he wouldn't die."

"Welcome to the civilized world," Sydney murmured, staring again at the black window.

The sun had set, leaving behind long streamers of pinkish cloud. A gust of wind off the lake made her pull her shawl closer. "I guess we'd better go up."

"Wait." Charles touched her elbow to keep her from rising. "There's something I have to tell you." But after that, he hesitated. He looked very serious.

"What is it, Charles?"

"Your father's asked me to live with you."

She laughed. "I beg your pardon?"

"Because of the convenience. Our work with the Ontario Man will be intensive, because our time frame is so brief. We'll be—"

"The what? The Ontario Man?"

"We call him that for lack of anything better. They found him somewhere above Echo Bay."

"I thought he was called the 'lost man.' "

He sniffed. "That's what the newspapers named him— romantic drivel. The birdwatchers started it, claiming he kept saying 'lost' when he was delirious."

"But if he can't talk—"

"Exactly. Just feverish mumbling on his part, and wishful thinking on theirs." He shook his head impatiently.

"Anyway, Sydney, Dr. Winter has kindly suggested that I move into the house. Just for the summer. We'll be working very closely together," he said importantly, "so it makes sense to eliminate as much wasted time as possible. Coming out here every day on the train—it's just easier if I'm permanently on the premises, don't you see?"

She could see through his earnestness to the satisfaction underneath: he was pleased as punch about this new feather in his professional cap. Some people, especially jealous fellow professors, called her father an eccentric behind his back; but he had more supporters than detractors, and a few of them called him a genius. An ambitious young associate professor—like Charles—could do a lot worse than link his fate with the brilliant if erratic Dr. Harley Winter.

"And so." He took off his glasses and stuck them in his vest pocket; in the deepening dusk, his large brown eyes looked sober and intent. "I'm asking you again, my dear."

She didn't pretend not to know what he meant. "Oh, Charles," she sighed, feeling tired all of a sudden. He reached for her hand, and she let him keep it.

"If I'm going to live in your house, don't you think we ought to at least be engaged? For propriety's sake?"

She looked up to see if he was joking. He wasn't. "No," she said, "I think it's just the reverse. If we're engaged and you're living in my house, tongues really *will* wag."

He frowned for a second, then his face cleared. "Then we'll have a secret engagement. Sydney, haven't I waited long enough? You said you'd give me your answer when you came back from your trip."

A rash promise; she'd only given it so he would stop asking the question. She'd never known anyone as persistent as Charles. "I think it's too soon. I'm still—"

"It's been a year and a half."

"No, it's been fifteen months."

"Time enough. You were a child when you married Spencer. Now you're a woman. Marry me, Sydney."

She stood up and moved away, but he followed her,

slipping his arms around her waist from behind to keep her. "Marry me," he whispered against her hair. His breath was warm; she leaned back lightly and let him hold her. His reddish beard prickled against her temple. "I do love you, Syd. And I'll take care of you. I promise."

She closed her eyes, beguiled by a cloudy vision of Charles taking care of her. Putting her first, doting on her. Even Spencer hadn't loved her like that. "Oh, Charles," she said again. "Can't we just go on as we are? I'm so fond of you. Can't we just keep being friends?"

"You know I won't stop asking you."

Oh, yes, she knew that. "What do you see in me?" she wondered a little desperately. "Why do you even want me?"

"Why?" He laughed. "Because you're beautiful."

"That's no reason. It's not even true."

"And you make me happy."

And I'm my father's daughter? If she was wrong, that was an unkind speculation. But Charles was, first and foremost, an ambitious man.

"And you care for me a little, don't you, Sydney?"

"You know I do." But she didn't love him. She had married Spencer, for love, or at least out of friendship and deep caring; she knew what love felt like.

"Just say yes, then. It'll be easy. You'll never have to think about it again."

"Could we live here?" Immediately she regretted the question—it would give him too much hope.

"Here?"

Spencer had had to promise that, that they would live here in the house on the lake, where she'd always lived. "Because of Sam," she explained. "I can't leave him, Charles, he's too little."

He didn't hesitate. "Yes, of course. We can live anywhere you like."

That was easy. Spencer had been much harder to convince. "But your aunt can take care of Sam," he had argued, until she'd pointed out that she would die an old maid before she'd entrust the happiness and well-being of her little brother to Aunt Estelle. Spencer had given in

reluctantly—but then, Spencer Winslow Darrow, III, had
lived in a Prairie Avenue mansion. Charles West lived on
his associate's salary in two rooms of a seedy boarding-
house on Dearborn Street.

"Say yes, Sydney." He had his nose buried in her neck;
she could smell his flower-scented shaving lotion. "I've
missed you so much. God, it's good to hold you."

It felt good to be held. For a grieving widow, she certainly was free with herself, she thought hazily, at least
with Charles. He'd been courting her in earnest for
months; on virtually the one-year anniversary of Spencer's drowning, she had let him kiss her. She'd let him do
a bit more than that since then, and her only excuse was
loneliness. Oh—and fondness for him; of course she was
fond of Charles. He had any number of very nice qualities, absolutely nothing you could point to that was really
wrong with him. He wasn't particularly handsome, but he
certainly wasn't ugly. And he would not leave her
alone—honestly, she was ready to accept him out of
fatigue if nothing else. Was that a basis for a marriage?

No, of course not. But it was so hard to care. Three
months in Europe hadn't cured her of her ennui after all.

He was nibbling at her earlobe, and a wave of weakness
made her leg muscles flutter. How easy it would be to
give in. *I'll take care of you* . . . the promise whispered to
her, seducing her as cleverly as his hand sliding up from
her midriff to her breast. She watched its slow glide,
thinking he had nice hands, pale and smooth against the
white of her dress, a gentleman's hands. He started to kiss
her neck, and her head fell back on his shoulder. She let
herself drift, just for a minute. . . .

Would it be so wrong to marry him? He was murmuring that he loved her, that he would make her happy.
She couldn't quite believe it, but the idea moved her all
the same. With a lax smile and half-closed eyes, she let
him caress her, even slip his fingers inside the buttons of
her dress, to touch her through her underclothes. Part of
this illicit thrill, she knew, was Aunt Estelle's ignorant
proximity to it. Childish of her, but there it was.

"Say yes, Sydney."

"Charles . . ."

"Say yes."

This must be what the last stage of freezing to death was like. Simply giving in . . . moving toward the long, warm sleep. So much easier than continuing to fight . . .

A flicker in the barred window; a pale oval pressing close to the glass; *a face*. Frozen, Sydney saw light eyes under dark brows, a scarred cheek, a straight mouth, the lips parted in shock or astonishment. For an endless second her eyes locked with the eyes of the man in the window. The lost man. In spite of the distance, she knew when his silver stare fell to her breasts. And Charles's hands making free with them.

Muffling a yelp, she jumped away, twisting in his arms to face him. "He saw us. My God, Charles, he's watching us."

"Who?" He looked terrified.

"The man, the—Ontario Man! From the window!"

Charles's frightened expression turned to irritation, then tolerant amusement. "Sydney, for heaven's sake, what difference does it make? He doesn't know what we're doing. It's like—it's like undressing in front of your dog." He laughed at her. "He might be interested, but he doesn't have the slightest idea *why*."

He was so wrong, so completely mistaken, she gaped at him. But rather than argue, she seized his hand and tried to pull him toward the house. "Come, they'll be waiting dinner on us. Hurry, we'd—"

"Sydney, *wait*." He forced her to stop. She could see him controlling his temper, schooling his features back into affability. "I think there's a question pending here. You haven't forgotten it, have you?" His smile was false; he was genuinely angry.

But everything had changed. She barely had the patience to speak to him. "How could I forget?" she said distractedly, darting a glance behind him at the bungalow. The window was black again, but the feeling that they were being observed was even stronger. "We can't discuss this now," she all but snapped, and Charles's eyebrows shot up. "I'm sorry—it's just—it's not the time. Later, all right? We'll discuss it later."

"Sydney—"

"*Please,* Charles. Let's go up to the house."

He gave in. She tried to take his hand, but he took her arm instead—he liked to be in control. She didn't care; she just wanted to get away. Even in her haste, though, she couldn't resist a last look back, before the turn in the path hid the cottage from view. There—was that a flash of something white? Or no . . . perhaps it was her imagination.

No matter. She knew what she'd seen before, and that quick connection, that seconds-long stare between herself and the unknown, unnamed man in the window had woken her up. Her mind felt sharp and perfectly clear, as if a stiff breeze had blown through it. Poor Charles! How was she going to tell him that what had seemed so tempting a minute ago had become absolutely unthinkable?

2

18 May 1893
Notes—Ontario Man

Caucasian male. Est. between 22 and 28 years of
age. (Mental age, undetermined.) Height, 187 centi-
meters; present weight, 77.3 kilograms. (Weight at
time of capture, 72 kg.)

Distinguishing marks: broken bone in great toe of
left foot, imperfectly mended, but causes no limp or
apparent discomfort. Evidence of broken ribs, long
since healed; left collarbone, ditto. Hands and feet
thickly calloused. Numerous scars, incl. one on face,
two on throat, five on left arm, three on chest and
abdomen, one on back at base of spine, one on left
buttock, four on right leg, three on left. Twenty in all;
evidence of long and total abandonment.

General health is now excellent. All senses
extremely acute, smell and hearing keenest of all.
Physical reflexes continue normal to supernormal.

Obeys simple commands—"Stand up," "Come
here," etc. But no verbal response of any kind to date,
despite lack of evidence of injury or trauma to vocal
organs.

Accepting small pieces of cooked meat now, and
eating them without vomiting. This is progress; in
univ. lab, would eat only raw meat and fish, berries,

*chestnuts and acorns (crushed under his bare feet),
and insects.*

*Objective tests of intelligence have been difficult to
administer so far, results ambiguous at best. Subject is
in depressive state, refusing to cooperate unless bullied or bribed. Lethargy began at university; subsided
somewhat after removal here, but is recurring. O.M.
stands at window in his room and stares out for hours,
silent, morose, melancholy. Has stopped throwing off
his clothes, but still refuses to wear shoes or socks
unless coerced. Delights in outdoor walks, but must be
closely guarded. Escape attempts at univ. repeated
only once here, so far.*

22 May 1893
Personal Notes (Sydney, N.B.!)

Linnaeus's System of Nature *classifies Wild Man
(Homo ferus) as a distinct human species, noting ten
instances of these creatures, eight girls and two boys.
Also, Birch cites the case of a child taken in Lithuania
among bears in a bear-hunting. Attempts to civilize
these children all proved unsuccessful.*

*Then there was Itard's "Wild Boy of Aveyron,"
found in 1799. "When wild in woods the noble savage
ran," Rousseau rhapsodized. The truth of the Wild
Boy was that he was a dirty, frightened, inarticulate
creature of 14, with a mental age of 6. Itard, believing
that environment is everything, attributed his subnor-
mality to a lack of intercourse with other humans. But
after 2 years of ceaseless, intensive training in a most
sympathetic and humane environment, the Wild Boy
still could not speak, was barely socialized, and was
"human" only in a technical sense.*

*Slocum warns we'll have no better luck with our
Ontario Man, but I believe otherwise. Itard's boy was
a mental defective, afflicted with spasms and convul-
sions; he swayed back and forth endlessly like a zoo*

*animal, grunted and bleated, ate filth and refuse,
threw violent tantrums, scratched and bit any who
opposed his childish will. Our man, on the other hand,
has never exhibited seriously hostile behavior to
anyone (except O'Fallon). He doesn't speak, but I
think his manner indicates he could if he would.*

*And what are we to make of the claim of the
Audubon team that he did speak, repeatedly uttered
the word "lost" when ill and semiconscious? His eyes
are sharp and intelligent; when I have his attention,
they miss nothing. He comprehends my speech a great
deal better than he lets on.*

*Why won't he speak? What does he fear? No one
here has hurt him. West and I find ourselves devising
ways to catch him, trick him into revealing himself. If
he is dissembling, it's a most unwise act. Slocum
wants progress by summer's end, progress meaning
publication. But we have no starting point; without a
developmental base line, how can we measure a
man's progress? Logic is always lost on Slocum,
though. Says if we haven't gotten anywhere with O.M.
by Sept., he'll have him committed to an asylum.*

24 May 1893
Notes—O.M.

*Getting nowhere. He performs sensory perception
exercises effortlessly, impatiently, no longer hiding his
frustration. Still no violent episodes since initial capture, although he clearly detests O'Fallon. (Not surprising; O'F. guards him all day and locks him in a
small room at night.)*

*He was wearing rags and the untanned skins of ani-
mals when he was discovered above Echo Bay. His
one possession, tied around his waist with a piece of
braided willow, was a book. A book! Small (a child's
book?), torn, pages stuck together, words faded
and illegible, the title on the pulpy, mottled cover*

*completely obliterated. Even now, he keeps it in his
pocket, will not be separated from it. A talisman, a
token. Is it possible he was once able to read it?*

25 May 1893
Personal Notes

*Particularly bad day. O.M. speechless as ever, and
bored, and resentful. Ethics and altruism tests not
even begun; meeting monograph deadline is hopeless.
Is Slocum right? Perhaps the Ontario Man is not a
savage (in Itard's sense, meaning incompletely civilized). Perhaps he's really just a poor idiot.*

Sydney flipped back in her father's double casebook
to the grainy photographs at the front, tucked away inside
a black folder. She took the pictures out again self-
consciously, a trifle guiltily. There were five of them,
and two showed the Ontario Man naked from the front.
She passed over those hastily, although her interested eyes missed nothing. But really, she told herself, it
was the contrast between then and now that intrigued
her, the image of the man in these pictures compared
with the real one she'd seen twice now, from a distance,
walking beside the lake with Mr. O'Fallon. That man
was quite ordinary-looking at fifty yards, dark-haired,
tall, and very lean, dressed simply in trousers, a white
shirt, a jacket.

The man in these photographs was anything but
ordinary-looking. Nude, he crouched against the stark
white wall behind him in a defensive posture, clearly
frightened, of the camera's flash lamps if nothing else.
He was thin to the point of gauntness, with scars, punc-
tures, and abrasions checkering and scoring his body like
tattoos, like decorations. He had shoulder-length hair and
a bushy black beard that made him look like a wild
animal. But he also had a fine, two-sided blade of a nose,
the skin stretched tight across it accentuating his gaunt-

ness. She couldn't see his mouth; the bristling mustache
concealed it. But she remembered his eyes from that day
he had watched her with Charles through his window.
She'd seen pictures of wolves with eyes like that, intense
and unblinking, too light to be quite natural. Blind-
looking eyes that still seemed to see everything.

She turned back to her father's notes.

26 May 1893
Notes, O.M.

> *We are reduced to interesting but unimportant*
> *observations. West nailed a mirror on the wall in*
> *O.M.'s room. From our peephole we watched as he*
> *saw himself for the first time. His initial fear wore off*
> *in seconds (we deduced he has seen his reflection*
> *before now, imperfectly in water, ice, or the like),*
> *after which he exhibited dismay, then hilarity, then*
> *fascination. He touched and poked at his face, made*
> *grotesque expressions, walked to the far wall in order*
> *to see as much of his body as possible. After about ten*
> *minutes, however, he lost interest and returned to his*
> *usual place by the window.*

> *We observe that flowers, regardless of how showy*
> *or fragrant or beautiful, do not hold his interest even*
> *momentarily. Give him a square of bright red cloth,*
> *however, or any shiny metal object, even the lid to an*
> *old pot, and he is as absorbed as a child with a toy.*
> *Anything that glitters or gleams holds him spellbound.*
> *West gave him a new horseshoe, and now he keeps it*
> *with his other treasures, his bottlecaps and shells, his*
> *colored handkerchiefs.*

> *And, of course, his book. This object seems to serve*
> *as a totem for him, providing a zone of safety to which*
> *he retreats when upset or fearful.*

27 May 1893
Notes, O.M.

> *Introduced him to domestic animals today, with*
> *intriguing but ultimately unfortunate results. West*
> *pushed Wanda (Winter family cat) through door to*
> *O.M.'s room, then immediately retreated to join me at*
> *our peephole. No response after initial meeting; some*
> *mutual sniffing, then both ignored each other.*
>
> *Next, cat removed and Hector (family hound) put*
> *into room. Immediate fascination on both sides! After*
> *two minutes, O.M. and Hector were romping together*
> *in the manner of puppies, with much playful growling,*
> *wrestling, nipping. O.M. lay on his back and let*
> *Hector torment him, jump on his stomach, chew his*
> *hair, feet, hands, face.*
>
> *Observation: O.M. can make sounds (but not words)*
> *and can laugh.*
>
> *Experiment backfired, however. Hector (part blood-*
> *hound) accidentally sniffed out our hiding place when*
> *their horseplay dislodged the heavy chair that had*
> *partly concealed us. O.M. peered into hole and saw*
> *me. His face registered amazement, then deep embar-*
> *rassment; he actually blushed. He paced the room,*
> *highly agitated, casting angry glances at the peephole.*
> *Then he dragged over the chest of drawers to cover it.*
>
> *Evidence of problem-solving intelligence was inter-*
> *esting and noteworthy. However, the end of our secret*
> *observations is a very disappointing loss.*

"Sidney, there you are."

She almost jumped; she'd been so absorbed in his notes, she hadn't heard her father open the door and come into the study. "Papa, I was just—I was about to start tran-scribing these—I had just . . ." She trailed off, abashed. She wasn't supposed to be poring over her father's old notes, she was supposed to be typing up his new ones, and separating into two casebooks the personal from the more formal observations he would eventually submit to Chairman Slocum. But what did it matter? He hadn't noticed what she was doing anyway, and wouldn't have cared if he had.

"Here," he said briefly, dropping another looseleaf binder on the desk in front of her.

"You want me to type these?"

"Hm? Mm." He was already at the bookshelf behind her, searching for something.

Sydney stood up, frowning, full of warring emotions. "What happened to Mr. Smith?"

"Smith?"

"Your secretary. The one who typed all your notes while I was in Europe."

"Ah, Smith. Let him go."

"Why?"

"Hm?" He finally focused on her. He spread his arms, and his gentle, charming smile lit up the room. "Because now I have you again," he explained, and went back to book-rummaging.

She shook her head at him, hands on her hips. *Just say no,* Philip was always advising her. *You're not a child anymore, Syd. Why do you let him take advantage of you?* In this case, she decided she had two reasons: one, habit; two, the Ontario Man. He fascinated her.

Her father found what he was looking for and headed for his desk. Sydney got out of the way before he could bump into her—out of distraction, of course, not rudeness. His thin, white, flyaway hair was ridiculously long; obviously no one had cut it since she had, last February. He sat down in his chair, no longer aware of her presence. She watched him a moment, smiling in spite of herself, taking note of his high, intelligent forehead and the vague blue eyes behind the thick lenses of his pince-nez. He was looking all of his sixty years these days, pale and painfully thin, as if the bulk of his physical energy had been diverted to his brain. He had on one of his ancient frock coats, seriously frayed at the cuffs, and a pair of checked trousers with a shiny seat and baggy knees. At

least his shirt was clean. Aunt Estelle muttered all the
time that if he ever got lost in a bad Chicago neighborhood, he'd be arrested for vagrancy on the spot.

Sydney thought his carelessness mitigated in a way his
blindness to other people's little vanities—her new dress,
for example, or the way she was wearing her hair nowadays. You couldn't blame him for not noticing those things
about others when half the time he couldn't match his
own socks. Truly, he took the cliché of the absentminded
professor to new heights.

"Bad day," he mumbled, a quarter to her and three-
quarters to himself. "Accomplished nothing. Man's truculent. Getting nowhere. Preliminary report's late. Look
like a fool. Slocum'll gloat. See it all now."

She was used to his cryptic, staccato style of speaking,
as if he were making verbal notes instead of talking. His
students had a field day mimicking him. He had embarrassed her to death in her childhood, but thank goodness
she'd finally outgrown that. Embarrassment still plagued
Philip, though, and it was just starting to torture Sam.

"Papa?"

"Hm."

"Did they really keep the Ontario Man in a cage when
he first came to the university?"

"Hm? Yes, after his wound healed."

"Why?"

"Because he kept trying to escape."

"Yes, but—a *cage*."

"Frightened people. Didn't know what to make of
him."

"But—"

"Damn shame in retrospect. Boy had lice, fleas, what-
all, and they deloused him with lye. Had internal para-
sites—gave him emetics, diuretics. Had good, strong teeth
but a couple of rotten ones in back—gave him laughing
gas and filled 'em with gold. Traumatized him. Cut his
hair—had to hold him down. Scared hell out of him all
around. Damn shame."

"Not to mention shooting him," Sydney pointed out.

No wonder he wouldn't cooperate with them. They were lucky he hadn't eaten them.

"What are you going to do with him? What will happen to him if he never speaks?"

He sat back, folding his hands over his sunken chest. His cloudy eyes grew even vaguer. "Boy's depressed. Sighs all the time. Kicked a hole in the wall last night. Muscles weakening—needs exercise. Night vision not as keen. Smell, ditto. Used to be able to smell the paint on the wall, and newsprint, hair oil. Losing it. Retreating. Melancholia. Homesick. Doesn't care."

Amazing, thought Sydney, how sensitive he could be to the smallest details of his subjects' actions and reactions. Too bad he couldn't spare too much of that sensitivity for his family.

"Harley?" Aunt Estelle bustled into the room, pulling Philip behind her. "Harley, I would like your complete and undivided attention."

Her father looked up, pleasant-faced. "Morning, Estelle. Philip. You, too, Sam?"

Sam came in last, trying to look inconspicuous. "Hi, Daddy," he chirped, and made a beeline for Sydney. He was nervous, but he didn't want to miss anything.

"Harley, I've come to speak to you about your son."

"Hm?" He looked back and forth between Philip and Sam, smiling benignly. "Which one?"

Aunt Estelle scowled in irritation. She was four years younger than her brother, hatchet-thin and pale like him, with a graying chignon from which stray hairs never escaped. All the passionate energy Papa put into his work, Aunt Estelle put into a different kind of obsession: social climbing. The Winters weren't among the city's richest families, not by any means. And yet, due in large part to Aunt Estelle's diligence (the other part to Sydney's marriage to Spencer Winslow Darrow, III), they were beginning to join the ranks of the most influential, that privileged elite who decided who was and wasn't allowed into the highest circles of its own closed society. Her ambition was to become a human gate, in imitation of the

Armours, Pullmans, Swifts, and McCormicks, established
gatekeepers whose company she coveted. Calling Aunt
Estelle a snob was like calling her brother a little for-
getful: an understatement.

"Do you have any idea what your son was doing last
night?" She had a piece of Philip's coat sleeve pinched
between her fingers; a few years ago it would've been his
ear. "Rather than studying the mathematics and geometry
he came so close to failing last term at his expensive East
Coast college? Well, Harley? What do you think he was
up to?"

"Haven't a clue, Estie. What."

Had anyone but Papa ever called Aunt Estelle "Estie"?
It was hard to imagine. She'd never been married, never
even been rumored to have a beau. Old photographs
showed a younger version of her present self, stiff-necked
and narrow-eyed, rarely smiling. Her conversation was
either instructive or censorious—which made her the
reverse of an ideal traveling companion, Sydney had discovered. Her temperament was disapproving and unfor-
giving, and duty was her passion. Most people were afraid
of her. She was easy to respect, a lot harder to love.

She had good qualities, too, of course. She loved her
cat Wanda, *really* loved her. She did superb needlework,
and she had a spectacular green thumb; indeed, she was
the first female vice president of the Chicago Rose
Society. It was *people* she had no facility with—and if
that was a failing caused by shyness, she'd learned long
ago and very well how to disguise it as a flinty heart.

"He left the house sometime in the night and did not
return until dawn. Reeking of tobacco and—and worse,"
she finished ominously, choosing not to name, out of deference to Sam, what could possibly be worse than
tobacco.

Philip slipped out of her pincer grip and slouched over
to the window. During the second his back was turned to
her, he made a wild, moronic face at Sydney and Sam.
This, of course, caused Sam to bark out a loud guffaw. He

pressed his face into Sydney's skirts, hiding, and she automatically covered the back of his head with her hand.

Papa blinked noncommittally behind his lenses. Finally he roused himself to say, "Tsk. That won't do, I suppose."

"What do you propose for a punishment?"

"Hm?"

"You're his father. Philip is twenty years old, not a boy any longer."

"No, indeed. Not a boy any longer."

"He is heading down a path toward total self-destruction."

"Is he? Hm! Can't have that."

"After two years at Dartmouth College, his academic record is undistinguished, to say the least. His deportment is worse than Samuel's. He's insolent, lazy, and disobedient. A lax hand at this point is not a kindness to the boy, Harley: it's a dereliction of your duty as a parent."

Poor Papa. He made more humming noises, pushing the papers around on his desk, taking off his glasses and cleaning them, sticking them back on his nose and looking curiously at Philip, no doubt trying to reconcile his sister's portrait of profligacy with the handsome, mild-eyed son smiling facetiously back at him.

It was, Sydney realized, a perfect Winter family moment, everyone waiting for Papa to make up his mind, have an opinion, *do* something, while deep down each of them knew that he would never do anything. Sydney knew, too, that Philip stayed out smoking, drinking, and God knew what else for the express purpose of getting a rise out of his father, even though the impossibility of that happening ought to have been clear to him by now. She'd done something like it herself once—eloped with Spencer instead of waiting five more weeks for their elaborate formal wedding. But she had only succeeded in horrifying Aunt Estelle. Which was gratifying in its own way, but not really what she'd been looking for at the time.

"Well?" Her aunt was determined to play out this charade to the end. "What disciplinary measures do you suggest, Harley, for your son's sake?"

"Hm? Well, now. Hm. Let's see." Clueless, he tapped his pen on his ink blotter. "Disciplinary measures. Hmm." More pen tapping. "Any suggestions?"

The magic words; once spoken, the fiction that Dr. Winter was the head of his own household was allowed to die, a mercy killing, and the true commander-in-chief stepped forward.

"You should revoke his allowance for the month of June," Aunt Estelle declared without hesitation.

Sydney drew in her breath. What a harsh penalty! A glance at Philip reassured her, though. He was trying to look stricken, but she saw a twinkle in his eye and guessed the reason for it. Whatever he'd gotten up to last night, it must've included gambling. *Successful* gambling.

"Hm. Yes, that's the ticket. No money for you next month, eh? Well, Philip? Learned your lesson, have you?"

Over Aunt Estelle's scornful snort, Philip straightened from his negligent pose by the window and made his father an exaggeratedly respectful bow. "Yes, sir, I have. Thank you, sir. I'll try not to displease you again."

Even Papa smiled at that—and a warm bubble of love for him burst unexpectedly in Sydney's chest. He had a sense of humor, oh, yes, he did, drier than desert sand, lying dormant for ages, and then blowing up in your face when you least expected it.

The only person it didn't enchant was Aunt Estelle, who considered it just one more eccentricity in a man already riddled with enough of them. Duty done, she squared her shoulders, pivoted, and marched out of the room.

"Are you really flunking all your subjects, Flip?" asked Sam, patting wet sand to the ankles around his brother's bare feet.

"No, Sam, only half of 'em. Just the ones that have numbers."

"You mean like arithmetic?"

"Right. Like arithmetic."

"I can help you if you want," Sam said. "I'm really good at numbers. Want me to help you, Flip?" He still called his big brother the old nickname, the closest he'd been able to come to "Philip" when he was a baby.

Philip leaned back on his elbows and wriggled his toes, uncovering his feet. "Thanks, sport, but I think I'm past help."

Sydney brushed loose sand from the corner of the blanket, keeping quiet. Later she would ask Philip if he was failing on purpose, so that Dartmouth would throw him out and he could do what he'd always wanted to do: write novels.

Not now, though. It was a perfect afternoon, the last day of May, with cottonball clouds bouncing high over the dark blue of the lake, and puffs of bracing wind blowing in often enough to make the hot sun bearable. Sydney beamed at her brothers, content just to be with them again. Three months! It had felt like three years.

"This is the exact color my hair used to turn in the summer," she told Sam, pushing the whitish blond bangs back from his forehead. "Maybe you'll grow up to be a redhead like me. Would you like that?"

He considered it, wrinkling his freckled nose. Sydney had freckles too, but she lightened hers with powder. "I don't know," he answered thoughtfully, peering at Philip. "I think I'd rather have dark hair. Dark brown."

She couldn't blame him—Philip was gorgeous. He might hate Dartmouth, but two years there had turned him into a very distinguished-looking undergraduate. More and more, he resembled photographs of their father in the old days, when Dr. Harley Winter had been quite the gay young blade on the University of Chicago campus. Or so they had been told. It didn't seem possible, but their own mother—dead for seven years now—had said it often, so it must've been true.

"So you'd rather grow up to look like your big brother than your big sister." Sydney pouted. "I'm hurt."

Sam giggled and let her ruffle his hair again. He had changed, too, while she'd been gone. He'd gotten even skinnier, and she could swear he'd grown two inches. He was seven now, and hair-ruffling was something he tolerated only because she'd been away so long and he'd missed her. "Are you eating enough?" she fretted, squeezing the bony knee under his knickers.

"I eat all the time, I eat like a *horse*. Aunt Estelle says I eat like a swarm of locos." He scrambled to his feet. "I eat like a pack of jackals!" He trotted away, attracted to some nasty-looking thing Hector had just pulled out of the surf. Sydney hoped it was dead; changed her mind and hoped it was alive; changed her mind again.

Philip, before her very eyes, began to roll a cigarette. She made obligatory disapproving sounds, but she was spellbound. Spencer hadn't smoked. Except on trains and from a ladylike distance, she had never seen anyone make a cigarette before. She glanced back at Sam, but he and the dog were safely absorbed in their unsavory find thirty yards away. "Do you smoke all the time?"

"Sure. Passes the time." He stuck the cigarette in the side of his mouth, lit a match, and touched it to the end, somehow sucking in smoke and blowing it out through his nostrils at the same time.

She shook her head and tsked, imitating Aunt Estelle, but she was impressed. "How much did you win last night in your poker game?"

"Enough."

"Enough so you won't miss your allowance."

He just winked at her.

"You know you can always come to me if you're ever really strapped, don't you?" She still lived in her father's house, but her inheritance from Spencer's estate had left her financially independent. Rich, actually.

Philip's handsome face lost its look of sophisticated indifference; he flashed a quick grin. "You're a peach, Syd. What would I do without you?"

She watched the breeze flutter the fringe on her parasol. "Philip . . . It's not worth it, you know."

"What's not worth it?"

"Defying them."

He started to roll down the cuffs of his trousers, not looking at her. "I don't give a damn about them."

Such a guileless lie. He cared as much as she did. She longed to help him make his father's inattention and indifference not matter so much. But Philip was too much like her: exactly the same things hurt him. He was a man, though, and so the things he did to counter the hurt could have more disastrous consequences than the things a woman could do.

"It doesn't make any sense to throw away your education," she counseled softly. "You'll hurt yourself, not them."

He huffed out a laugh, as if he didn't know what she was talking about. "How do you like West living right here in the house?" he asked abruptly—changing the subject.

"I don't mind. Anyway, he's so busy, I hardly ever see him." She hesitated, then said, "He's asked me to marry him."

"What?" He stubbed his cigarette out in the sand and stared at her.

"Is it such a surprise? He's been courting me for months."

"I know, but he's—" He stopped, and she could see it dawning on him that some adult tact might be called for here.

"Why do you dislike Charles?" she challenged.

"I don't dislike him. Really. I *like* him—if you like him."

"Well, I do like him."

He was silent for a second, then squinted up at her. "I still don't like him."

They burst out laughing. She reveled in it, the closeness, the gaiety, the lovely frankness between them just for this moment. Compared to this, Charles West faded into insignificance.

She was so used to the sound of Hector's deep-throated baying when he played with Sam on the beach, she barely heard it. Now she heard it change to a higher note, excited and welcoming. She looked up. Two dark-garbed figures were walking along the water, slowly coming toward them.

"Oh, Philip, it's him," she breathed, jumping up from the sandy blanket. "The lost man."

Philip stood, too. "I've never seen him up close before."

Instinctively they both started toward Sam, who stood stock-still, staring intently, rudely, ignoring the waves breaking over his calves. The dog dashed ahead, skidded to a halt just shy of the two approaching men, and began to run around them in excited circles.

Sam was safe, Sydney knew that, but by the time she drew level with him she was out of breath from rushing, and she put both hands on his shoulders from behind, to keep him from going any closer.

"Hi," popped out of his mouth as if he were greeting a school chum. But he was nervous; she could tell by the quaver in his voice. He'd never been this close to the lost man either.

Hector jumped up on the man's legs, leaving wet sand all over his dark trousers. He was bent over, head down, gently squeezing the pup's floppy ears and letting him slobber all over his hands.

"That's Hector," Sam piped up. "He's a hound dog. He's one year old. I'm Sam Winter. What's your name?"

Hector finally backed off, and the man straightened slowly to his full height. *Why,* Sydney thought, *he's just a boy.* He was tall and too thin, and his blue-black hair had been cut very badly, as if with a dull-bladed knife. She remembered his face from the photographs, the white scar on his cheek, his strong nose, his wide, hard mouth, expressive even though he wasn't smiling. His clothes—black coat and trousers, a white shirt with a celluloid collar—looked strange, unnatural, and not just because they didn't fit him. Under the too-short cuffs of his pants, his bare white ankles showed above a pair of bulky old brogans.

"He don't understand you, son," O'Fallon explained, grinning indulgently at Sydney and Philip. He was using

Sam to make it seem as if they were all together, the
adults against the child. Sydney resented him, but not
only for that. O'Fallon had a habit of leering at her when
they passed on the grounds or in the house, where he took
his meals with the servants. His broad, hulking, prizefighter's body intimidated her. She didn't like him. Most
of all, she didn't like his treatment of the man he was only
supposed to be preventing from running away. She knew
for a fact that he kept a policeman's truncheon in his belt
and a coil of rope in his pocket.

"How do you know? Maybe he just doesn't want to talk
to you." Sam, normally polite, didn't like O'Fallon either.

The big man pretended to laugh heartily. "That's a
good one, that is! Might be yer right, but I doubt it. I'm
thinkin' 'is brain's about the size o' that dog's, there." He
laughed again, but nobody joined in. They were offended,
not only on the man's part, but also on Hector's.

The man, who had been peering at Sam with great
interest, lifted his gaze to Sydney. Immediately she saw
that she'd been wrong—he was anything but a boy. His
face had a superficial innocence, but that was only a
matter of the arrangement of his features. It was his eyes
that gave him away. She had thought they were gray or
silver from the photographs, but they were pale, pale
green, and as clear as the light on the lake in the morning.
There was a look in them, a kind of knowing . . . something old and uncanny. Not like anything she'd ever seen
before. She couldn't look away.

"That your professional opinion?" Philip asked lightly,
but Sydney heard the distaste in his casual tone. Now it
was unanimous: they *all* disliked O'Fallon.

"Here. Look." Sam pulled something out of his pocket.
"You can have it if you want." He held the object out
toward the man, who, after a startled second, bent over at
the waist to see what it was. "It's a puppet, see? You put it
on your finger like this, and then you play with it."

Sydney recognized the knitted yellow giraffe with felt
ears and a black yarn mane and eyelashes; she'd made

it for Sam years ago. Amazing that he hadn't lost it before now.

"Now, boy, you don't want to be givin' things to this
one," O'Fallon warned, still trying to sound jovial.

"Why not?" Sam asked, taking the words out of
Sydney's mouth. But she had a nervous moment when he
reached for the lost man's hand and pulled it toward him.
O'Fallon stiffened; Philip stiffened. "See, look. You just
stick it over your finger like that. Now you wriggle it"—
he twisted the man's long, strong finger back and forth—
"and make it talk. 'Hi, I'm Gerry the giraffe!' " he trilled
in falsetto. " 'Who're you?' "

The lost man blinked down at the little yellow tube
covering his first finger. He flexed his knuckle, and the
dots on the tip of the covering, meaningless to him before,
came into focus. A face—they made a face.

"See? It's a giraffe," the boy said to him, looking right
into his eyes.

Ger-af. He couldn't remember ger-af. It was a gift,
though, he knew that, and gladness filled his chest like a
sudden deep breath. He wriggled his finger into the face
of Sam, the boy, who opened his mouth and laughed, a
sound like water trickling over rocks. He laughed, too,
and then he looked up into the face of the woman.

She had hair like a fox, shiny red and gold, and she
made it stay on top of her head, not fall down. Her scent
was mixed, something sweet and something you could
eat, and over that, the smoky smell that the man had, the
man beside her with dark hair and the same blue eyes. She
had so many clothes on, and she had skin like no skin
he'd ever seen. The pink bellies of newborn racoons
looked that soft. Her lips curved up, but was she smiling?
Was she happy? Did she think he was funny?

"You should take your shoes off," the boy said,
pointing at his feet. "You can walk in the sand barefooted,
but no place else. That's what Aunt Estelle says." Sam
kept talking, too fast, the words stopped making sense. He
tried to sort them out, but he couldn't while he was

looking at the lady. Everyone had talked but her. How would her voice sound?

Soft. Not high and not fast. Like purring. "It's getting late. I think we'd better go up now." She had her hand on the shoulder of Sam, just touching, not pressing or squeezing, and Sam didn't hate it. The lost man couldn't take his eyes off the long white fingers of the lady, curving over the shoulder of Sam. The dark-haired man said something to her he couldn't understand. He looked into her eyes. Human eyes, clever and secretive, hiding things. She was hiding things. She let her eyelashes come down, so he couldn't see into her mind.

Sam put out his hand. Did he want ger-af back? No, his hand was sideways, the palm not up. Confused, he stood very still, not looking at anyone. "Shake," Sam said, and took him by his other hand, the empty one. They made their touching hands bob up and down, and while it was happening, a memory flared into his head. He had done this before. And some words in his book made sense now.

In a social gathering, do not attempt to shake hands with everyone. If your host or hostess offers a hand, take it; a bow of acknowledgment is sufficient for the rest.

"All right, then, lad." O'Fallon grabbed his arm, laughing his lying laugh. "That's enough o' that, now."

He tugged out of O'Fallon's grasp, not even looking at him. There was something he had to do.

He bowed.

O'Fallon laughed again, but the lady didn't. Neither did the boy or the dark-haired man. They all made their eyes big and round in just the same way—so he knew they belonged together. They were a pack. Then O'Fallon turned him around and made him walk away.

In the room with the bar on the window, O'Fallon said, "Oh, yer a rich one, you are, boyo. Quite the gentleman now, ain't you?" He turned away, and O'Fallon shoved him in the back, so hard he hit against the wall. He swung around, holding his cheek. O'Fallon had the black stick in his hands, and he thought how easy it would be to kill

him. Pull his throat out with his teeth and watch the warm
blood gush, slower and slower until it stopped.

"Hungry, boyo? Too damn bad. You just sit in here,
practicin' how to be a *gentleman*. Take a few more
bows." The door closed, blocking out the hate in his face.

Why were they enemies? Weren't they both men? The
fury in O'Fallon's eyes made him feel wild, mad, but not
like an animal. Like a man.

3

Sam and Sydney began to wait every day for the lost man. O'Fallon took him for a walk in the afternoons at one o'clock, while Papa and Charles ate lunch in the office and went over their notes, discussing the morning's progress. At first O'Fallon wouldn't stop, even when Sam begged him to, and a wet and sandy Hector tried his best not to let either man pass. But the guard, apparently out of nothing but meanness, wouldn't let his charge linger even for a moment. "Got no time," he'd say, one of his pawlike hands shoving at the lost man's shoulder as they hurried by. "Professor wants 'im back by two." Once he shouted out, "Have a care, lad!" when Sam came too close to suit him. "No sudden moves—no tellin' what he might do."

"He wouldn't do anything," Sam retorted furiously, and Sydney was torn between scolding him for rudeness and echoing him. She thought of talking to O'Fallon herself, trying to reason with him. She disliked him too much, though, even to speak to him—probably out of proportion to his offenses, but she couldn't help it. Instead she went to her father.

"Is that man dangerous or isn't he?" she inquired, catching his attention, so hard to get, by taking him by surprise. His study was his sanctum, and anyone who entered it during his workday had better have a good reason. Charles was with him; both men looked up from their desks and stared at her.

"The lost man, the Ontario Man—is he a threat to Sam and me, Papa?"

"Don't think so." He took off his pince-nez in surprise. "Wouldn't have him here if he were. Gentle as a lamb."

"Well, as to that," Charles began, then halted. He never liked to contradict his employer.

"Then why can't he stop with us when Mr. O'Fallon takes him for his walk on the shore?"

"He can."

"He can?"

"Certainly. Do him good, needs the company. Been thinking of suggesting it. More contact. Might help. Supervised, of course."

Thrown off her stride, she was momentarily speechless. "Tell him, then, will you?"

"Who?"

"Mr. O'Fallon. Tell him to stop acting like a prison warden." She waited, but her father already had his nose in his book. "Why does he carry a club?"

"Hm? What's that?"

"A club. He carries a billy club, Papa. Why?"

"Hm! Can't imagine."

"Well, will you please tell him not to? It scares Sam," she fabricated. He nodded vaguely. "Charles, *you* tell him not to," she tried, despairing of her father remembering to do any such thing. Charles was smiling at her, taking the opportunity to flirt. "Please, Charles, would you say something to him?"

"Of course I will," he said solicitously. "I'll do it today."

She beamed at him. "Thank you."

The next day, O'Fallon, clubless and scowling, sat on a rock thirty yards from where Sam and his new friend knelt in the surf, their pants legs rolled up to the knees, building sand castles.

Or rather, Sam built them and the lost man watched, grave and silent, shy and a little awkward, but profoundly curious. Within minutes, Sydney's nervousness changed to fascination. She sat a ways behind Sam on a blanket in the sand and stared at the man's face, the expressions ghosting across it, transfixed by his emotional transparency one minute, his intriguing opaqueness the next. Time after time she thought he would speak. His mouth, she could swear, formed a *k* whenever Sam said the word "castle," and he appeared to be spellbound by the crenelated shapes of walls and gates and towers her brother made with his inverted bucket. Sam kept up a ceaseless monologue, childish chatter that he listened to with care and politeness, and occasionally confusion.

"You should have a name," Sam told him. "What name do you want? What would be a good name for you?" The answering silence had no effect on Sam's garrulousness; he took it for granted that the lost man didn't talk. Neither did Hector; it was just one of those things.

"How about Lancelot? Do you like that? He was a knight of the Round Table in the *Morte d'Arthur*. That's my favorite book. Sydney used to read it to me when I was little, but now I can read it myself. Lancelot was Arthur's right-hand man. Lancelot," he repeated, trying it out, sizing his companion up with a long glance. "Lance," he amended doubtfully. He looked over his shoulder. "Can we call him Lance, Sydney?"

She laughed; it struck her as silly. He didn't look like a Lance to her, he looked like . . . himself. The lost man. "Lance is fine," she said—and happened to catch his eye. *He knows,* she thought suddenly. *He understands all of this.* Then he looked away, and her certainty faded.

His big hands held the tin bucket, dwarfing it, turning it slowly in his fingers. A red line marked his chin, where he must have cut himself shaving. Or—she chilled at the thought—where O'Fallen must have cut him. Yes, more likely; they wouldn't give him a razor, she was sure. O'Fallon must be the one who had cut his hair, too.

At Sam's insistence, he had taken off his coat. "Roll up your sleeves, too," he'd instructed, showing him how with the shirtsleeves of his own Russian blouse. It was charming, really, the unlikeliest friendship. And yet—it wasn't really possible to see it as cute or sentimentally touching,

or the lost man as a big, harmless, overgrown boy, the
way one might view a sweet-natured, retarded adult at
play with a child. Because whether he was walking with
his keeper or sitting in the sand or staring out the barred
window of his room, the lost man was always exactly
that, solitary and alone, and always a man.

The next day, Sam brought his rubber ball to the beach.
Bright blue, the size of a grapefruit, it was currently his
favorite toy. "Here, catch!"

The lost man—Lance—caught it somehow, purely by
reflex, then stood staring at it for a full minute. The expression on his face made Sydney press her lips together to
keep from laughing out loud. If Sam had tossed a glowing
meteorite to him, he couldn't have been more flabber-
gasted. The squishy texture bewildered, then entranced
him. "Throw it back," Sam kept saying, but he wouldn't
relinquish it. He had to smell it, squeeze it; he put his
tongue on it and bit it with his teeth. "No, don't eat it!"
Sam yelled, laughing but alarmed, and the man frowned at
him uncertainly. "Come on, throw it to me. Throw it. Like
this." He gestured, using one arm. "It's a game, see?"

Imitating Sam, the man tossed the ball in the air, high
and straight up. It landed at his feet without a bounce.

Sam ran and snatched it up again. "Good," he said
encouragingly. "Now I throw it back to you—" Again the
man snagged it with one hand. "Okay, now throw it to
me." Sam held his arms out wide. "Me, throw it to me."

Slowly, tentatively, the lost man lobbed the ball in
Sam's direction, and he caught it on the run.

"Good!" he shouted, as thrilled as if he'd taught him
how to write his name.

A game of sorts ensued, with Sydney watching from
her place nearby, trying to see what, if anything, the man
made of all this. Gradually the fierce concentration in
his face relaxed, giving way to that look of pleasant,
empty-headed absorption men wore when they engaged in
mindless sporting contests. He had much more natural
agility than Sam, of course, and it wasn't long before the
dynamics of the game reversed, with the man throwing

carefully and accurately, the little boy more often wildly. *Father should see this,* Sydney realized. Unnoticed, she scrambled up, intending to go and get him—and saw that she didn't have to. He and Charles were coming down the path from the house, and now stopping at the edge of the trees, staring in surprise. She lifted her skirts and trudged through the sand toward them.

"Great heavens." The breeze blew her father's wispy hair sideways, like a rakish white hat. "How long has this been going on?"

"Twenty minutes or so. Yesterday they built sand castles. Didn't O'Fallon tell you?"

He shook his head. "Look, Charles. Look at his face."

"Yes, sir. Very animated."

Papa could hardly contain himself. "And they said he was probably an idiot!" he gloated, rubbing his hands together. "Ha! Won't tell 'em this yet—they don't deserve to know it. Of course. Of course. Should've seen it."

"What's that, sir?"

"It's Sam—Sam's the key. We'll use him. Come on, West. You, too, Sydney. Come on, got work to do!"

When the top wolf's muzzle turned gray and his teeth yellowed, his back legs stiffened and his eyes clouded, he was finished. Unless he had a wife who stayed with him because she was old, too, he went off from the pack to die by himself. A new wolf, the strongest one, became top wolf.

With men, it was the opposite. Dr. Winter was so old, all his hair was white. He couldn't run and his eyes were watery and weak. But the professor was the top man in his pack, and nobody fought him, not even the one named West who was young and fit. Stranger still, the lowest man was O'Fallon, even though he was the strongest. But he was stupid and mean. Wolves would not have let him be the leader, either.

There was another man, Philip. He was the brother of Sam and Sydney. He was kind, not mean, but he held himself aloof; he tried to stay out of the circle of the pack.

The top woman was "Aunt Estelle." The lost man stayed away from her. They all did.

His days began to change. There was a place behind the big house with walls around it made of crumbling red stones. A garden, they called it. He could have climbed over the wall, but they didn't know it; they thought they had him, so they didn't make O'Fallon come inside the garden to watch him. The professor, West, Sam, Sydney, sometimes Philip—they all came into the garden with him, and at first he couldn't look at them. He would stand apart, listen to them speak and breathe, and think about jumping over the wall. There were woods beside the house. He could run there, and no one could catch him.

But he didn't run away. Because even the stars couldn't help him here. He was too far away to get home.

"Experiments," Dr. Winter called the things they made him do in the garden. None of it made any sense. The professor would sit in the shade on a little chair that could fold up, and make writings on paper while watching him do—nothing. Walk from here to there, or there to here; eat an apple; scratch his head or shut his eyes tight; give half of his apple to someone else. Nonsense, all of it, but after a few days he didn't care, and he lost his self-consciousness. (A new word; he had learned it from West. "He's too self-conscious, sir; he can't act naturally in this setting.") The garden was better than the lake, because he could smell the earth and the dark trees, hear the insects burrow in the grass and the birds lay eggs in their nests among the leaves, and almost believe he was home. He stopped caring that the people were watching. He began to watch them.

Sydney. Syd-ney. He could spell her name, because he'd seen Sam write it under a picture that he drew with a pencil. Sam meant for the picture to look like her, but it didn't. Not at all. She had pink and white in her face, a sort of blue in her eyes, like sky but different, darker, shinier—he wished he knew more words. He tried to catch her true scent, the one under the scent she put on herself. (Why did she do that? To hide? Was something hunting her?) But he had to be careful because if he got too close all the men, especially West, went on guard around her.

He could close his eyes and listen to the sound of her voice, not the words but just the sound, and know who she was talking to. Sam was easy; to him she talked softly while she smiled, always smiled, and when she laughed it was because of Sam. No—sometimes Philip, but then the laughter was lower, shorter, deeper in her throat, as if what was funny was also not funny. She hardly ever laughed with her father, and when she talked to him her voice got thinner, tighter; her breath stayed high in her chest and sometimes when she sighed it out he could hear sadness.

West. She called him Charles, his other name. She didn't talk to West very much, so he listened to the silence between them. It meant something. It made him wonder if they were mates. His skin got hot when he thought that. They had touched; he'd seen them. She had rested her back against West, and he had rubbed her with his hands. They had done that in secret, thinking no one saw. Then they'd stopped. If they were mates, was it for life or only for the summer?

He didn't like West. He stank of something he put on his head, and his eyes when he looked at the lost man were sharp and hungry but still cold. Sometimes he touched Sydney on her back or behind her arm, petting her when he thought no one saw. Sometimes she let him; sometimes she moved away so he had to stop.

He wanted to shoulder him away from her, bare his teeth and warn him to keep away. Animals did that in the mating season. But he wore a man's clothes now, ate cooked food, slept on a blanket. Did that make him a man? He couldn't be sure. He still wanted to fight for Sydney, though. If she wasn't West's mate, he wanted her for his.

"Sydney, close your eyes this time."

"What?"

"Stay where you are, but just close your eyes. I think he'll go closer."

Obediently, she shut her eyes and waited, leaning her head against the back of the wrought-iron loveseat. The garden door squealed on rusty hinges as her father went out. Silence for a moment, just the buzzing of a bee in the ivy. Then the door squeaked open and the lost man came in.

These studies had begun as tests of his sense of territoriality, but eventually they'd shifted—when it became clear that he either had no such sense or no intention of showing it—to observations of "aversion and attraction vis-à-vis proximity," as her father put it. While he or Charles watched through an ivy-covered chink in the brick wall fifteen feet to Sydney's left, the lost man was repeatedly sent into the empty garden—empty but for one other person. Philip, Sam, Charles, Sydney, Aunt Estelle, even Inger, the downstairs maid—they'd all had their turns at the game, and now Sydney, because she happened to be still around (everyone else, even Sam, had tired of it and gone off to take a nap), was having a second turn.

She heard a faint sound, maybe a footstep. Maybe not. How quietly he moved—she hadn't realized it before today. Seconds passed. Complete silence now; he could be sitting under the rose trellis . . . or he could be standing right next to her. Looking at her. Her eyelids began to flutter from the effort to keep them closed.

Did he think she was sleeping? She tried to moderate her breathing, slow it down and make it deep and even. Her skin tingled, and she felt a flush creeping up her neck. She became acutely aware of her whole body, everything about herself—her low-waisted yellow frock; the angle of her elbows as she clasped her hands in her lap; her knees, just touching. The dryness of her lips, which were not quite closed. Where was he? There was no sound, none at all. Was he even here?

Then it was impossible; she couldn't stand it another second. She opened her eyes.

There he was, not three steps away. Hands at his sides, body bent slightly toward her. Her sudden wakefulness didn't startle him—he had known she wasn't sleeping.

They stared and stared, and she thought, *This should be worse, this should be intolerable,* but it wasn't. The tension was gone, and there was only interest, hers the equal of his, and a new kind of acceptance. They were . . . they were *greeting* each other. Another moment passed, and Sydney said, "Hello," quite naturally. His smile came slowly, full of awareness. In one more second he would have spoken to her, there wasn't a doubt in her mind.

"Why did you open your eyes?" Her father shuffled through the gate, notebook under his arm, his querulous voice spoiling everything. "He might've gone closer, who knows? Confirms my hunch, though. Try it with Philip next. It's eyes; eyes are the thing. Go up and get West, will you? Want him to see this." He started scribbling furiously in his book, no longer aware of her.

She had stood, but when she took a step toward the lost man, he backed away from her. She couldn't read his face; the emotions passing over it moved too swiftly. She wanted to touch him, tell him—something, she didn't know what. That she wasn't in on this, it wasn't her idea. She was filled with dismay, and she thought he was, too. She reached out, but he moved then, not seeing her hand, and retreated to the low-branching willows at the end of the garden. Gone; no getting him back now.

"Excuse me," she muttered to O'Fallon, who was blocking the gate. He grinned and shifted, but not enough; she would have to brush his body to pass through. Hot anger boiled over with no warning. "Damn it, get out of my way!" she said succinctly, and he fell back, guilty, amazed, glancing toward her father to see if he'd heard. She pushed past him and sprinted for the house.

15 June 1893
Personal Notes

> *We progress. Goading O.M. to anger and testing his potential for violence do not interest me; West overruled. What I'm after is reconciling with this blank*

*slate, this tabula rasa, the contradiction between sur-
vival of the fittest and acts of apparent selflessness,
even self-sacrifice. Ants confounded Darwin; only
species that seems to thrive on altruism. Altruistic
behavior means benefiting another individual at some
cost to oneself. According to survival of fittest theory,
the bully, cheat, or cannibal ought to prosper, conquer
all. So how to account for ants? Darwin eventually
explained them away as members of one family, then
applied natural selection to the family as a unit, as if
it were an individual.*

*What about an unsocialized human being? How
much would he sacrifice for the good of the "family"?
But perhaps O.M. is no longer uncivilized; despite
precautions, perhaps our "kindnesses"—feeding,
clothing, housing him—have corrupted the essential
thing in him, his wildness, that we wanted to exploit.
Should know soon. Any rate, too late to go backward.
Unfortunate, ironic, etc. But all's not lost. Plenty to
do, and we can still get a book out of him.*

Papa made everyone sit in a circle around the little
garden pond. They were seven: Sydney, Philip, Sam,
Charles, O'Fallon, Inger—the Swedish maid, dragooned
into participating after Aunt Estelle had refused—and the
lost man.

By prearrangement, Charles opened a bag of apples,
took one, and passed the bag to his left. Sydney took an
apple, passed the bag to Sam. And so on, until Inger took
the last piece of fruit and handed the bag, empty, to the
man. He knew it was empty; he could tell by the weight.
With disbelief on his face, he reached inside anyway and
felt around the bottom of the bag. He pulled his hand out
slowly. By now they were all munching on their apples,
looking casual, making small talk—as they'd been
instructed. No one was supposed to look at him, that was
Papa's job, but Sydney couldn't stop herself. Using the
low brim of her sun hat for a shield, she glanced sideways
at him across Charles's lap.

And wished she hadn't. What was the point of this unkind experiment? To test the "innate sense of fairness and justice," her father claimed, but Sydney thought it was just mean. She wished he would get angry and snatch somebody's damned apple—preferably O'Fallon's—right out of his mouth. Instead he looked bewildered, hurt, and sullen, and he was trying to hide those feelings by staring at the ground, scratching a mark in the dirt with his finger.

In the afternoon it was oranges. Everybody got one except Inger. This time, against the rules, no one could resist sneaking peeks at the lost man's reaction. While they peeled their oranges and murmured to each other about how good they tasted, he glanced uncertainly between his orange and Inger's empty hands, her forlorn face. Copying the others, he began to rip the rind away from the fruit and separate the sections. *Maybe he doesn't even like oranges,* Sydney found herself hoping; anything to sabotage these distressing "exercises." But no luck; he put a piece of orange in his mouth and chewed it without revulsion, if no particular enjoyment.

That was Inger's cue. She was a full-figured, flaxen-haired girl of seventeen or so, a nonstop talker, if you weren't careful, in a glib mix of Swedish and English. First she heaved a loud sigh, which no one paid any attention to. Next, a soft, high whine. Beside her, the lost man stopped chewing and looked at her. "I wish *I* had an orange," she said to the group at large, who ignored her. "I'm so *hungry,*" she declared, pressing her hand to her stomach.

Philip, on Sydney's left, was having trouble keeping a straight face. She wanted to punch him—how could he think this was funny? She stole another forbidden glance, then had to look down to hide a smile of her own. Well, maybe it was funny, a little. He had such a wonderful, transparent face, and the dilemma he was wrestling with was as plain as if he'd written it on a blackboard.

In the end, he did what she had somehow known he would do: he gave Inger his orange. Not all of it; he kept a slice or two for himself. The maid didn't thank him; she looked confused, as if her instructions hadn't covered this eventuality. And everybody looked sheepish. A little embarrassed. As well they might, thought Sydney.

More tests followed. Using the lost man for a guinea pig grew more and more distasteful to her as the days passed, but she always bit her tongue and kept her opinions to herself.

Until Papa told Sam to pretend he was drowning.

Then she couldn't keep silent. How could he be so insensitive? She couldn't bring herself to say it to him straight out—"Papa, I hate this. Don't do it because it's ugly and it hurts me." Had he *forgotten* that Spencer had drowned? She tried to talk him out of it indirectly, on more general grounds, but her protests sounded confused and inarticulate. They did no good, and her father's new "scenario" proceeded as planned. Until it hit a serious snag.

In the middle of June, Aunt Estelle finally decreed that it was warm enough for Sam to swim in the lake. After that, he was allowed to paddle along the shore but never, ever, even though he was a strong swimmer for his age, to jump into the water from the end of the boat dock, a twenty-five-foot wooden pier to which the old family sailboat, *Runabout*, was tied. There was no particular reason for this rule; but then, there so often wasn't with Aunt Estelle's rules, which gathered authority more from vehemence and longevity than strict logic. Anyway, Sam knew the rule and had never broken it. Now, however, he was being instructed to do so, to further the interests of science, by his father. Needless to say, Aunt Estelle wasn't informed.

The worst was that Sydney had let herself be bullied into becoming an accomplice. No, *bullied* wasn't accurate; Papa had simply bypassed her protests by not hearing them, by making himself deaf, an old trick that rarely failed. Her role in the drama was to sit on the beach, hear Sam's phony cry for help, jump up and begin to scream that he was drowning and she couldn't swim.

"Save him, save him," she was to beg the lost man, who, through careful advance planning,would be the only other person within sight.

Words could hardly describe how repugnant she found the whole scheme. But she agreed to it anyway, because her father wanted her to. She wouldn't have done it for Charles, or indeed for anyone else; but where her father was concerned, she was helpless: she never stopped trying to please him.

It was another blindingly blue afternoon, sunny and hot, the essence of every perfect summer day of her childhood. She sat on a soft wool blanket, a copy of *The Bostonians* lying facedown at her side, shading her face from the sun with a lace parasol. O'Fallon lurked somewhere behind her, but in a few minutes he was supposed to disappear. Across the way, Sam, in his red-and-white-striped bathing costume, sat in the sand with "Lance," showing him his collection of miniature flags. "This is the Argentine," he was explaining, "and this is Rumania. This one's my favorite, Greece, but it's the Mercantile Marine, not the national flag . . ."

Cross-legged in front of him, barefooted, sleeves rolled above his elbows, the man listened as Sam rattled on, his expression patient and fond, bemused, not quite fatherly but close to it. The sun had tanned his face a golden brown, and the contrast with his light eyes was more startling than ever. His body was lithe and graceful, his movements smooth and rather slow; he had a habit of slouching when at rest that was very attractive, more a matter of folding himself up than slumping or huddling. His scarred and calloused hands were quite beautiful, Sydney thought, just the shape of them, long and bony-fingered, very dexterous and clever-looking. He was tall, lean, broad-shouldered and strong-thighed—and it was impossible not to look at him like this without thinking of the photographs. The ones in which he was naked. Thin and pale, his face disturbing because of the fear he was trying to hide, but . . . naked nevertheless. And very much a man.

Sam jumped up. He had put his flags back in their tin box. "Going swimming," he called over to Sydney, widening his eyes in conspiracy. She had thought that Sam of all people would find the trick they were about to play as distasteful as she did. But no; he thought it would be fun. "And anyway," he'd told her, "Lance won't mind, he'll know it was just a game."

Maybe. Watching Sam wet his feet at the shoreline, she could only hope so.

The lost man got up, too. He stood looking out across the lake while the wind whipped ripples across the back of his white shirt and tousled his black hair. She wondered what he was thinking while he gazed at the faraway horizon. Of his home? Just then he turned to look at her, probably drawn by her own stare. On an impulse, she scooted over on the blanket and patted it. "Will you join me?"

He lifted his gaze behind her, looking for O'Fallon. Then, carefully blank-faced, he moved in his silent-panther way toward her and sank down on the very edge of the blanket.

Except for that one brief time in the garden, she had never spoken to him directly. She sat by him now, feeling uncomfortable and unexpectedly tongue-tied. It wasn't that she was afraid of him. And yet, she wasn't completely unafraid of him. He would never hurt Sam, that she knew with total certainty—but—would he ever hurt her? Not in anger, no, and not in some sudden, uncontrollable manifestation of his so-called "animal nature." What about sexually, though? There *was* something wild about him, for all that he wore shoes and ate oranges and played games in the sand with a little boy. Despite aspects of him that were disarmingly innocent and naive, he was still a man. And he knew she was a woman.

She glanced at him then—and caught him in the act. It wasn't the first time. He jerked his gaze away, made a business of straightening the fringe on the edge of the blanket. He wasn't that innocent. How did he know—*this* was a good subject for her father to explore!—that it was a breach of human etiquette to stare (or rather, to be caught staring) at a lady's breasts?

She felt herself flushing. The silence between them was worse than before, because now it was charged with sexual awareness. "Beautiful day," she said inanely. "Don't you think?" He looked at her speculatively. She looked up. "Not a cloud in the sky. It rained every day in England. Italy was lovely, though. I went there with my aunt." She smiled, because she felt ridiculous. "We stayed for three months. I had a dreadful time. I was . . . lonely, you know. Homesick, but not really sure home would be any better. My husband . . . I was married, but he died. A sailing accident." She laughed softly, shaking her head at herself. "I'm sorry. I don't know why I'm . . ." *Talking to you,* she almost said, but that sounded rude.

"Lance," she murmured, self-conscious. "It's a silly name, isn't it?" She smoothed her thumb over the handle of her parasol and admitted, "I never know what to call you. They say you said 'lost' when they found you." She looked at him directly, smiling at her own folly. "Were you lost?"

Her smile faded slowly. She sat still, arrested by the intensity in his face, tight with an emotion she had never seen before. His eyes pleaded for, *demanded* something from her. He pressed his lips together. He said, "Michael," in the barest whisper.

She stared. The hair on her arms rose; the breath backed up in her lungs. She waited, waited, afraid she had misheard, praying he would say it again.

Then Sam screamed.

In a blur of speed, he jumped to his feet and began to run. Sydney followed, heart pounding, hating this. Sam was flapping his arms in the air about fifteen feet out from the edge of the dock, shrieking, "Help, help! I'm drowning!"

Sydney and the man—*Michael*?—pounded to a stop at the edge of the pier. "I can't swim," she cried, and her distress at least was no act. "I can't swim!"

"Help! Save me!" Sam gasped for air convincingly, pinched his nose, and went under.

The man hesitated—she hadn't expected that. His body jerky with fear, he wheeled to look behind him, searching for O'Fallon. Not there. She met his eyes, only for a second, but the cold dread in them told her the one thing she did not want to know. Before she could react, he leaped into the water.

And sank.

"Oh, my God! Sam," she screamed when her brother popped up next, "he can't swim! He can't swim!" Sam began to thrash toward her, and then she knew true panic. "No! Don't! Don't go near him!" Michael would drown Sam, too, in his terror. She whirled, scanning the line of trees. "Help," she called, again and again, but no one appeared. Father, Charles, O'Fallon—they all thought this was part of the act!

She was weighted down with clothes, she would sink like a stone like this. Tearing at skirts and petticoats, kicking off her shoes, she had no time for all the buttons down the front of her shirtwaist. In blouse, chemise, pantaloons, and whalebone corset, she dived into the lake.

Michael surfaced ten feet away, rising high—he must have sprung up from the bottom; it was only seven or eight feet deep here!—water streaming from his mouth when he gasped for air. "Stay away from him," she screamed at Sam, who was dog-paddling closer. Michael's heavy, flailing arms were going to kill them all. "Help!" she tried again, just before lunging for his hand as he went back under.

She caught it and pulled, trying to keep him at arm's length and kick them both toward the dock. But she couldn't turn; he was holding on too tight. "Sam, get out," she sputtered, "get help—" She went down with Michael, and panic engulfed her.

Her feet hit the squishy bottom, and they jumped together, breaking the surface at the same time. Her free arm struck something solid—the port quarter of the sailboat. She grappled, but there was nothing to hold onto;

the gunwale was too high. Michael's grip was like a vise, punishing and inescapable, and his heaviness was dragging her down again.

Once more her feet touched bottom, and she flexed upward, jackknifing with her legs for more power. The boat had turned; she made a grab for the painter that moored it to the dock.

"I've got it!" she yelled, clinging to the line for her life. Michael lunged at her. She thought he would swamp her, but at the last second he twisted and grabbed for the counter. The boat zigzagged crazily, almost capsized when he hurled his body halfway over the taffrail and hung there, vomiting water and gasping.

Sam swam straight to the ladder at the end of the dock and clambered up. Grabbing the painter, he hauled it in, with Sydney still clutching at it. The sailboat's stern gently bumped the dock.

Footsteps banged overhead. Papa and Charles skidded to a stop at the edge and peered down at her. "Are you all right?" they asked in unison.

"I'm fine." To prove it, she let go of the line and swam over to the ladder. She weighed a ton; Charles had to help her up and over the last two rungs. Sam pulled the line in until the boat was inches away from the ladder; her father helped him hold it steady. "Need a hand?" Charles asked, bending down toward Michael.

Michael ignored him. He climbed the ladder deliberately and walked away from all of them before he stopped, put his hands on his knees, and coughed up more water.

"Never thought of that," Dr. Winter mused, watching him. "Can't swim, eh? Hm! Who'd've expected it?" He scratched his head and blinked down at his notebook.

Disgusted, Sydney padded, dripping, over to Michael. She touched the wet coat sticking to his back. "Are you all right?" He turned, and when she saw his face she drew back in dismay. "Oh, God," she blurted, "oh, I'm sorry, I'm so sorry. It was stupid—I knew it—I did it anyway. Michael, wait—"

He wouldn't stop. Without looking back, he walked off in the direction of the guest house. After a startled second, O'Fallon followed.

Charles, solicitous as always, draped his jacket over her shoulders. "What did you call him?" he asked interestedly.

They watched the lost man plod through the sand and finally disappear into the trees at the end of the path. "Michael," she answered, miserable. "That's his name."

4

"You're saying you're going to continue with these experiments?" Sydney stopped drying her hair to stare at her father incredulously. "Even though you know he can speak? He can say his *name*, Papa, I *heard* him."

When he was feeling beleaguered, Dr. Winter's defense was to grow even more vague than usual. "Not saying any such thing," he muttered, ducking his head between his shoulders, turtle fashion, doing his best to disappear behind his desk. "Not saying anything at all. Not talking," he finished inaudibly.

Charles wasn't as reticent. "You don't know *what* you heard, Sydney. You heard him say something—"

"Michael. I heard him say Michael."

"Even so. *If* he said it, and *if* that really is his name, what does it prove? Nothing." Her father looked up at that and nodded. "It only means he remembers his name. You seem to think it means he's a Harvard graduate who happened to get lost in the woods."

Her father chuckled at that. *Chuckled.* In her anger, Sydney forgot to be tactful. "You're scientists—you're supposed to be objective. How can you ignore what's been in front of your eyes for weeks? Especially you, Papa. You knew it already, or you suspected it. You wrote it in your notes!"

"A suspicion, perhaps, the merest—"

"No, you wrote it, don't you remember? 'His manner

indicates he could speak if he would.' And you wondered why he had a book with him. Don't you see what it means? He knows everything!"

"Oh, nonsense."

"Not everything," she amended quickly. "But he's not the—the cipher you were hoping for, not by any means, so how can you experiment on him anymore as if he were a lab animal?"

Charles, who had been standing behind her father—like a son in a family photograph, nothing missing but the filial hand on the paternal shoulder—came around the desk and crossed to her. She had changed clothes, but her hair was still wet; the damp towel dangled from her fingers, forgotten. He reached for it, but she shook her head and held on. He urged her toward a chair, but she resisted. "You're upset," he said understandingly. "You've had a shock. What happened this afternoon was terrible, and you're not over it yet." Behind him, her father hemmed and hummed in agreement. "No one's going to hurt the man, Sydney. You know that, don't you? It's true we're scientists, but we're not *mad* scientists, are we?"

She hated it that he was making her smile. *Was* she hysterical? Charles's reasonable voice and his soft hand on her arm made her want to laugh one second and yell at him the next. But irritation at his condescending tone eclipsed everything else. She moved around him to confront her father again.

"Don't you at least think you should reevaluate what you can get out of him? He can't be 'Ontario Man' anymore, can he?"

"Hm, can't be sure. Too soon to say." When he reached for his pipe, she knew she'd lost him. He could easily occupy five whole minutes with finding his tobacco pouch, opening it, filling his pipe bowl, locating his matches, lighting the pipe, letting it go out, relighting it, et cetera, et cetera, all to avoid a subject he didn't feel like discussing.

"Of course we'll have to reevaluate," Charles answered for him. "It's true that he may have lost his value to pure

anthropology as a 'cipher,' as you say, someone on whom
we could've observed the layerings of civilization in a
neat, experimental environment. But his value to us as
biological ethicists is by no means at an end. We can continue to observe him as a specimen of pure man, loosely
speaking, still relatively uncorrupted by human society—
that's one way to look at it; another is that he's a savage
from whom the benefits of human society have been with-
held. It all depends on one's particular bias."

"Charles—"

"And then again, you may be right: his worth may have
passed from the realm of science to that of philosophy. Or
zoology. In which case—"

"What about his worth as a man? What about *him*?
He's not a study, Charles, he's a human being. You don't
own him, and neither does the university. Doesn't *he* have
any rights? How do you know he doesn't have parents
somewhere? The only word he ever said before today was
'lost.' Why isn't anyone trying to find out who he belongs
to? I just don't think—I don't see how you can keep him
locked up any longer, or spy on him through a hole in
the wall, or play tricks on him for the sake of some—
experiment that may not even—that doesn't even—" She
ran down, unused to speaking out like this. Her father
looked nonplussed.

"All very well, my dear," he said through a cloud of
tobacco smoke, "but it doesn't change the fact I've got a
report due by summer's end. Slocum's expecting it. Said
I'd give it to him. Can't renege."

"Yes, but if—"

"Not saying nothing's changed. Lot's changed. Have to
study, mull it over. All I'm saying." With that, he turned
around in his chair and started rooting through his bookcase.

Charles put his hand on her shoulder. "Sydney," he said
in that gentle voice that could somehow draw her in and
pull her away at the same time. "Let's go for a walk. We
need to talk this over."

"No, Charles, I can't. Not right now."

"Ah." He nodded understandingly, eyeing her damp, straggly hair. "Later, then."

Her thoughts were already elsewhere. "Later," she echoed, as vague as her father. She went out, still holding her towel.

The front door to the guest house stood ajar. She knocked once and pushed it open. A stale smell hung in the air, musty sweet and unpleasant. The source of it became clear when O'Fallon shoved up from a chair in front of the cold fireplace and took an unsteady step toward her. A bottle sat on the floor by the chair, half empty.

"You're drunk," she accused and kept walking.

"No, I ain't. Where you going? You can't go in there. Hey!" She had already unlocked the door to the inner room and opened it. O'Fallon hurried over, smelling like a barroom. "It ain't safe, miss. I can't be lettin' you go in there, not on yer own."

"I'll be perfectly safe," she snapped. "I'm going inside, Mr. O'Fallon. You can rush in and save me if you hear me scream." She sidled inside and closed the door in his face.

The small room lay in semidarkness. A movement by the window terrified her for an irrational split second—until the figure coming toward her materialized into Michael. Her heart rate slowed almost to normal. Almost. He was wearing a pair of clean, dry trousers. And nothing else.

"I, um . . . I . . ." She swallowed, feeling silly, and leaned back against the door. "I've come to apologize to you." He looked very beautiful in the half-light; if his body bore scars, she couldn't see them now. He looked perfect. "I've come to tell you I'm sorry. It was wrong of us. We—Sam and I—we pretended we couldn't swim so that . . ." Oh, how to explain this? "My father wanted to see if you would try to save Sam. He's a scientist—you know that. They've been studying you. You're the 'lost man,' and they want to find out how men are, how they act before they're civ—before they've been with other people." She rested the back of her head against the door. "Do you understand any of this?" she asked hopelessly.

Silence.

"Well. Anyway, I wanted to tell you I'm sorry. For the part I played in their little experiment. So's Sam. He feels terrible, in fact."

He had an unnerving stare, as if he saw things other people couldn't see. His nostrils flared slightly, and she knew he was scenting her. It made her blush. She didn't think he was angry or hurt any longer, though. That was something.

"Well," she said a second time. She had her hand on the doorknob when the invitation popped out of her mouth. "Would you like to go for a walk with me?"

He moved toward her, straight to her. She froze, stupidly afraid again, until she realized what he wanted. His shirt, hanging on the door behind her.

O'Fallon followed them. Michael shut him out of his mind and tried to make his steps small, like Sydney's, but it was strange to be walking beside her and he kept forgetting. Then he would have to stop, feeling stupid and awkward, and wait for her.

They came to some big rocks in the sand and she said, "Shall we sit for a while?" and they sat down on a rock, next to each other but not touching. She talked about her brothers and the summer and sailing their boat on the water, safe and calm things, but under her voice he could hear that she wasn't calm. Then she stopped talking and there was stillness between them, not easy but tight, and she turned her body toward him. Their knees bumped. She put up her hand, the way Sam had that first time on the beach.

"I'm Sydney Darrow," she said. "Are you Michael?"

He looked at her hand, small and white, and at her face, so pretty. Her smile tight and kind, full of hope. His hand swallowed hers up when he took it. He was careful with it, not squeezing too hard. He knew she was waiting for him to say words to her. He had before—one word, anyway. Why was it harder now?

But he did it. He said, "I am Michael MacNeil."

Her eyes filled up with water. She was *crying*. She took her hand out of his and turned her head so he couldn't see her face. "I'm sorry," she said with a funny laugh. "It's not sad. I'm just . . ." She put her fingers under her eyes and flicked tears away. "Michael MacNeil," she said softly and looked back into his face. He could see she wasn't sad, but she was . . . something. She said, "What happened to you, Michael?"

All he could do was look at her.

She could see the question was too big. She changed it. "Do you remember when you got lost?"

He remembered last winter when he was starving and he walked too far from home. He lost his way, and then he stole food from the humans to save himself.

But he didn't think she meant that. She meant before; the beginning.

"I remember a boat in the water." *So many words.* He hid his fear by looking at the lake and taking slow breaths through his nose.

She said, "A shipwreck?"

He nodded, although he wasn't sure. "Everyone died in the water. But not me."

"When you were a child? A little boy?"

"Yes. Like Sam."

"Sam's seven."

"I was like Sam."

When she looked away from him, he could look at her. She said very softly, "My God."

He couldn't remember exactly who God was. Did he belong to her? But O'Fallon said, *God damn you,* and the professor said, *Good God.* It was confusing.

"How did you survive? How did you live?"

Another question he couldn't answer. He thought of the dark-skinned people who had found him the first winter and had given him food. But the old woman died in the summer and the two men went away and left him. He was alone for a while, then he lived with the wolves, then a white man caught him in a trap, and then he was alone again, with no one but the old wolf.

But he couldn't say any of those things to her.

He asked her a question. "Are you with your father?"

"With him?"

"Together. You and your father and Mr. West. Are you with them?"

"Oh." That meant she understood. He could see she was thinking. "No. I'm not with them, I'm by myself. With you."

"With me." He smiled. So did she, and it was a real smile he wanted to keep or to touch. But he wasn't allowed to touch her at all, so he sat on his hands.

The sun was going down behind the water. "The sun is going down," he said. It was strange to say out loud something you could see with your eyes. But they—people—did it all the time, said things, explained in words what they already knew.

She said, "Mmm. It's a beautiful evening."

There. Could she tell what his thoughts were? "Yes, it's a beautiful evening," he repeated. He didn't understand how he could sound so calm, as if nothing new was happening to him, when inside his head everything was flying in circles.

"Michael," she said, "did you talk when you were in the wilderness?"

Wilderness. He liked that word. "Yes. No. I didn't talk with my mouth." He whispered a secret to her. "I forgot my name."

She leaned close to him. "But now you've remembered it?" He nodded. "How?"

"Once I heard Sam talking. Not to any person, to himself. Talking loud."

"Yelling."

"Yelling. His name, at the lake. For nothing—for fun."

"Yes," she said, smiling.

"Then I remembered, yelling my name over the water where I was. Michael MacNeil—I yelled it over and over.

I was little, like Sam. Scared. I didn't want to forget my name." He took a deep, slow breath. "But I did forget. I didn't call myself anything. 'I'—not even 'I.' Nothing. I just . . ."

"You just were." She sounded funny again. Was she sad? He didn't want to make her sad. Could he ask her what was in her head? He couldn't remember, but he thought there might be a rule against it in his book. They were friends now, but not like Sam was his friend. She was different. She made him feel . . . he didn't know the words. But he had to be careful with her, because so much was not allowed. One wrong thing and she might go away.

His stomach made a noise. "I'm hungry," he said.

She smiled with her whole face. "It's dinnertime." They got up and started to walk back toward her house. O'Fallon followed them. "What do they give you to eat?" she asked as they walked.

He made a funny face, like Sam. "Food."

She laughed, and it was the best sound, the happiest sound. "Don't you like it?"

He tried to explain. "It's human food."

Something happened. She kept walking, but inside she went still, and he knew he had said a bad thing. Because people hated what he ate—used to eat. He ate their food now, and it wasn't raw, not warm and bloody and pulsing. They stopped walking and he looked at his feet, wishing he could take back the last words they had said. There was a distance between them now. Even after such a short time of being with her, he didn't want to be alone again.

"Sydney! Dinner!" Sam's voice, coming from the house.

"I have to go," she said. Her face was clear again, as if nothing at all had happened. He started to leave, but she said, "Michael, I'm not sure what my father intends to do. But even if he continues his experiments, it'll be different from now on. Better. Now that they know you can speak, it won't be—"

"You'll tell them?"

"I—Don't you want me to?" Her eyes got wide. "I think it's too late! Are you afraid? They won't hurt you, I promise. It's just—it's all a nuisance for you, I know, but nothing bad will happen. Don't worry." She touched him, put her hand on his wrist for comfort, and he felt comforted. He wondered what a nuisance was.

"Okay," he said, like Sam. "Don't worry," he said back to her, so she would be comforted, too.

"Sydney!"

This time it was the voice of Aunt Estelle, and Michael backed up. They both did. Because in the Winter pack, Aunt Estelle was top wolf.

In the weeks since her return from Europe, Sydney had spoken on the telephone to Camille Darrow, her sister-in-law, but they hadn't seen each other yet. On Saturday, when Philip mentioned he was going into the city and asked Sydney if she cared to go with him to visit Cam, she immediately called her friend and made the arrangements.

They could have taken the train, but Philip told Robby, the family's elderly coachman, to drive them in the phaeton because the horses needed exercise. It was a perfect day for a drive, clear and sunny, not too hot. Sydney reveled in it, chattering with Philip all the way, until she caught her first glimpse of the Darrow house. The towered and buttressed mansion on Prairie Avenue had been like a second home for her. She had played there as a child, flirted there at parties as a debutante. Spencer had proposed to her in the billiard room, and they had danced under a striped tent to Johnny Hand's band at their wedding reception in the sprawling backyard. It was an ugly house in some ways, too big, too extravagant. But she loved it anyway, never gave its excesses a second thought, because she had always been happy there. Now just the sight of it made her want to cry. Because Spencer was gone.

Camille opened the front door herself. Embracing her Sydney did cry—this time because Cam looked so much like her brother. "Oh, I *missed* you," she exclaimed, trying to laugh, hiding the real reason for her tears. "Cam, you look *wonderful!*"

"*You* look wonderful."

They hugged in the doorway for a long time, swaying, patting each other's shoulders, while Philip looked on with amused tolerance. "Oh, hullo, Philip," Camille said when they finally broke apart. "You here, too?" They all laughed.

The women drifted into the foyer, but stopped when Philip called to them that he was leaving. "Why?" Cam wanted to know. "Come on, Philip, stay for a little while. Can't you come in and visit?" She put her hands on her hips and tilted her head in the familiar bossy manner. Short, blond, and athletic, she was the perfect feminine reverse of Spencer; they even had the same pug nose and stubborn chin, the same gestures, the same gravelly voice.

"Nope, can't. Things to do, people to see."

"What things, what people? Come in and have some tea with us."

"Manly things, important people." He slouched against the doorpost in a negligent pose, hands in his pockets, looking impossibly handsome. "I'll tell Robbie to come back for you, Syd."

"But then how will you get home? Are you coming back here?"

"Nope." He shrugged, grinned. "I'll manage." He gave them a lazy salute and started to turn away.

"Not too late, Philip," Sydney called softly.

He just smiled.

"He's changed," Camille remarked as they walked through the house to the covered veranda in back. "He doesn't even look like himself anymore. Must be the East Coast influence."

"He's not happy, Cam," Sydney confided. "I don't know exactly what he's getting up to these days, and I don't want to know. But I worry about him."

"Oh, Philip's all right."

"He never brings friends home anymore. He goes to terrible places. I think he even has a bookmaker."

"He's just growing up."

Sydney shook her head. "He needs someone strong right now, somebody to give him guidance. I can't do it, it's got to come from a man." No point in saying that it was never going to come from her father; Camille knew that as well as she did.

"Poor Philip." Camille sighed, sitting down at a glass-topped table on the veranda and signaling the maid to bring their tea. "But I'm sure he'll grow out of this. I'm sure it's just a stage."

"I hope so." Watching her, Sydney wondered if she knew—she *must* know—that Philip had always been in love with her. Even as children, they had joked and daydreamed about marrying one another when they grew up, Spencer and Sydney, Camille and Philip. Philip had never really let go of the dream, though, and it was only one more thing making him reckless and dissatisfied these days.

"So," said Cam, passing a plate of miniature iced sponge cakes, "tell me everything. How was your trip? Are you glad to be home?"

"Ecstatic. But you know about my trip, I put it all in my letters. Tell me how *you've* been."

Camille obligingly plunged into a description of her social schedule since February, the parties and dances, tennis and golf tournaments, sailing regattas, croquet matches and bicycling tours, shopping sprees and charity balls. It was all so familiar; Sydney felt a kind of evening out, a balancing inside herself as she listened. She belonged to this world, and it was comforting to be back in it. At the same time, something nagged in the back of her mind. A soft-voiced irritant that felt almost like . . . impatience.

Cam was talking about the World's Fair. "Last night Claire and Mark and I went to the Women's Building. Have you seen it yet?" Claire was Cam's sister and Mark was her brother-in-law. "It's my favorite now. You *have* to go, Sydney. There's a model kitchen, and a kindergarten, concerts every day by women composers. A woman designed the building itself, and every day there's a demonstration—"

"I haven't been to the fair at all yet."

"You *what*?"

Sydney laughed at her amazement. "Well, heavens, I've only been back in the country for three weeks."

"I know, but it's the World's Fair! It's absolutely unbelievable, a marvel, a wonder of the world."

"And I've got four more months to see it."

"Oh, but—"

"Cam, it's so good to be home, just spending the days quietly with Philip and Sam. If you knew how many museums and cathedrals and piazzas and art galleries I've been dragged to in the last three months, you wouldn't scold me."

"I suppose." She nodded skeptically. "Well, but when you do go, let's go together. I've been at least six times already, so I know where the best exhibits are. But you'll want to see everything eventually. It's—honestly, Syd, it's the most marvelous thing I've ever seen in my life, or probably ever will see."

"Philip says that, too. He's dying to take me."

"We'll all go together, then. Oh, it'll be wonderful."

Sydney set her teacup down gently. "Spencer would have loved it, wouldn't he?"

"He would have. I miss him so much."

"I miss him every day."

They both began to hunt for their handkerchiefs. "Mama's still grieving so. She simply can't be consoled. Papa's taken her to the River Forest house for the summer."

Sydney nodded. "You told me."

"I don't think she'll ever get over it. It's been awful for all of us, but worst for her, I think."

Unashamed, they both wept. But Sydney's tears came easily now, naturally. There would always be sadness, but this wasn't that hard, dry, aching pain that had plagued her for so long. She was crying now for Spencer, but also for Cam and for herself, because they had both loved him so much. It was the first time she'd been able to share her grief with anyone. Maybe she was healing.

That thought gave her the courage to say, "Charles West has asked me again to marry him."

Camille waited. Gradually the expectant look on her face faded and apprehension took its place. She had been sure Sydney would add, "But of course I've told him no," as she always had before. "Oh, no," she breathed. "Oh, Syd, you're not going to accept him, are you?"

"I've put him off again. But . . . I don't know."

"But you don't love him!" Her round face, tanned to a pretty golden from all her summer sports, darkened with emotion, and her big, blond-lashed blue eyes went wide. She looked so much like Spencer then, outraged, all bark and no bite, Sydney had to smile. "Well? Do you?"

"No. Not love, not ex—"

"Then how *could* you?"

She was truly angry, Sydney realized too late. She felt terrible, as if she had betrayed Spencer. Of course Cam would take it this way; she should have known, should never have brought up the subject.

She tried to explain. "There's nothing really wrong with Charles. He says he loves me. He's agreed to live with us, so I wouldn't have to leave Sam. He's nice enough, Cam, really he is. And I'm used to him. And—he says he'll take care of me." That sounded pathetic. "He's so *persistent*. He simply won't leave me alone."

Camille made a ball of her napkin and tossed it beside her plate. "Here's what I think. I think you were happy with Spencer and now you're lonely and miserable. Somehow you've worked it out that having a husband was what made you happy, so now you want another one, *any* husband, so you can be happy again."

"Oh," Sydney said faintly. It rang disturbingly true. "Could I really be that stupid?"

"It's not stupid, it's human. It won't be stupid until you actually do it." She pushed her plate away. "That's all I'll say." She was shutting up now so that if Sydney did marry

Charles, nothing would ever have been said, at least in words, that could put their friendship at risk. Very wise.

They got up and drifted over to the low stone balustrade that circled the veranda. Below them a fountain pool glittered in the sun, and the black and orange bodies of goldfish slid through the ripples, slow and supple, flashing beneath the lily pads.

"You haven't told me about the lost man," Camille said, deliberately changing the subject. "All the papers talked about nothing else for weeks last winter. They ran a photograph of him that looked absolutely ferocious."

"I can imagine." Sydney trailed her hand along the rough stone, absently sanding her fingertips.

"Well? What's he like? You've seen him, haven't you?"

"Oh, yes. He's . . . This is in confidence, Cam."

"Of course." She sat down on the balustrade, fascinated already.

"Because I don't know how much he's telling the university, but the last thing my father wants is newspaper reporters coming to the house, taking pictures and writing more lurid stories."

"My lips are sealed."

Sydney sat down, too. "The lost man can talk. He's always been able to talk."

"No!"

"He even has a name—Michael MacNeil. When he was about Sam's age, he was in some sort of shipwreck, we think, somewhere in Canada, and everybody drowned but him. We think he's been on his own ever since."

They had been leaning toward each other. They both sat back at that, to contemplate the enormity of it. "But how? How could a child survive, year after year? He'd freeze to death. If he didn't starve to death first!"

"I know. I know. It's incredible."

"Well, what's he like? Do you talk to him, or is it only your father?"

"No, I talk to him. Sam talks to him, Philip, Charles, all of us now. But he's . . . reticent. I think he speaks most easily to Sam. And to me." She liked to think that, anyway.

"What does he say? Can he remember his past?"

"He doesn't talk about it. I think his childhood's a blur."

"Can I meet him? Oh, I'm *dying* to get a look at him."

"Well, I'm not sure. I'll ask my father." She said it vaguely, wondering why she was uneasy at the thought of Cam meeting Michael. It wasn't Camille herself; it was the thought of *anyone* outside the tight circle of the family having contact with him. He knew and trusted them now; it would be risky for him, too scary, to introduce him this soon to someone on the outside. Sydney could see through his eyes now, feel his distress, sense his fear of the strange and the unknown, and she wanted to protect him.

Or maybe she just wanted to keep him to herself.

Later, when it was time to go, she left with a promise to invite Cam to the house soon, for a long day of tennis and swimming. But she left the date indefinite.

5

22 June 1893
Personal Notes

Ontario Man claims his name is Michael MacNeil. Specific information hard to obtain; gives one or two answers to every ten questions. Doesn't know his age. Claims he survived on a diet of mice, squirrels, fish, bugs, berries, nuts, sometimes caribou if one of his wolf friends was lucky. Food always raw. He hunted for food and furs, built fires for warmth but not to cook meat. Who taught him to make a fire? "The three dark-skinned ones." Indian stragglers, presumably, maybe Cree or Ojibwa. Then, "The old woman died in the summer," and after that he was alone, because the two men abandoned him. How old was he when that happened? Not sure; older than Sam, he thinks, but not much.

His sense of time is erratic and unreliable. Claims he lived in a cave with wolves. Even if it's true, he can't say how long this went on, other than "until the first time we were starving, then some of us went down, closer to the water." South, I suppose, maybe to Lake Huron.

Very briefly, he speaks of a time he spent with a white trapper whose name he never knew. No details, and his reluctance to talk about it leads to suspicion that he was abused. Says he "escaped," and kept clear of white people after that.

Rest of his years in the wild are a mystery. He either won't speak of them or lacks verbal skills to do so. Suspect a combination, with emphasis on former. Won't explain his book, which seems to have near-magical qualities for him. Attempts to discover what his life was like before "the boat in the water" also futile. Claims he doesn't remember.

Observation: Speaks slowly and haltingly, with limited vocabulary—all this to be expected—but interesting thing is, he seems to have an accent. Slight but definite. Not Indian; not French Canadian. Can't identify it.

All very extraordinary. I am at a loss; West ditto. What shall we do with him? Not what we thought he would be. Terrible waste if he turns out to be nothing but a man.

Michael slept like a wolf.

Not for hours, like a man, as if he were dead, but only for minutes at a time, curled up on the floor on his blankets. He would wake, rise, sniff the air to make sure he was safe. Then turn in a circle one or two times, lie down again, curl up, and sleep for a few more minutes. He preferred to sleep in the day, because hunting was better in the dark; but since he had come into the man's world he had been made to sleep at night.

But sometimes, out of habit, he fell into his little naps in the late afternoon. What woke him from this particular nap was a noise, a swish of grass. And then a soft scraping, a shoe on stone. He got up from his blankets and went to the open window, where the scent of Sydney came to him long before he saw her through the trees. The white of her dress, just that, the first thing he saw, made his heart start to pound.

She could float when she walked, glide, not bump up and down like other people. She was like a bird flying slow over water, so smooth and graceful. She had

something in her hand, but not the open-and-close thing
with the long handle; the sun was low, so she didn't need
that thing for shade. She waved when she saw him in
the window. He waved back. And then she came to him,
off the path and right through the grass, right up to his
window.

He was a little higher than her; she had to look up to see
his face. Her hat, which smelled like dried grass, fell
back, so she took it off.

"You have hair like a fox," he said. "Red and yellow
together." Then he shut his eyes and pressed his fist
against his forehead. That was wrong. He was supposed
to say something else first, *Hi,* or *How are you.* Then they
could talk.

But she just laughed, that low sound coming out of
her mouth like music. "Thank you. I'll take that as a compliment. Your hair . . ." She looked at him hard, with one
finger on her lips. "Your hair looks like a crow's wing.
After the crow flew too close to the gardener's hedge
cutters."

He touched his head, ruffled his hair, baffled. But it
must be a "compliment," because her eyes looked bright
and she was smiling. "Thank you," he said.

"You're welcome." She laughed again. "I was in Chicago yesterday, visiting a friend, and I got you these."

He reached for what she was holding up. Two things.
One was paper, white, like a book with no writing, and the
other was many pencils with a string tied around them.

"Sam said you like to draw."

He looked at her. "You are giving this to me?"

"Yes."

"It's a gift?"

"Yes."

He looked at the gift. The ends of the papers were cut
straight and perfect, and the pencils were all colors, all
sharp as teeth. He tried to make his face quiet, but he was
too happy. He smiled with his teeth showing and said,
"Thank you." Still, he was worried. *Gifts, even from close*

friends, should be acknowledged within a few days (no more than three) with a written note of appreciation.

"You're welcome."

Stillness between them. He hated the bar on the window. It made him feel ashamed.

"What did you do today?" she said.

He said, "I talked."

"To my father?"

"Yes." That's all he had done, talked, but he felt tired afterward, as if he'd been running all day. "What did you do?"

They both smiled. She thought like him sometimes, and right now he knew she was thinking it was funny to say these things to each other—*What did you do today?*—as if they were two real people. Two *regular* people—that was the word. But they both knew he wasn't a regular person.

"I played golf at the club," she said. "With Philip."

She had played a game with her brother someplace. Good, that was good. He wished he could have played it with them.

"Well, I guess I'd better go," she said. She walked backward, putting her hat back on her fox hair.

"Good-bye. Thank you for this gift."

He thought she would say, "You're welcome," but she said, "Don't mention it. I hope you like it."

"Yes, I like it," he said quickly, before she could leave, and she laughed again and said, "Good," and then she was gone.

He might have gotten gifts before, but he could only remember one, his book. He took it out of his pocket now and put it on the table, next to Sydney's gift. He felt rich.

His book didn't work anymore, it was ruined by water and time and his fingers turning the pages. That didn't matter, because he knew the words by heart.

Sydney's gift was new. The paper was too white to touch at first; he just stared at it, liking it that it almost hurt his eyes. He put his nose on the top page and inhaled the smell of wood. He untied the string around the

pencils, and before he could catch them they all scattered,
rolling across the table. He picked up the red one. It was
thin, like a twig, and harder to hold than Sam's crayons.
He put the sharp tip on the white paper, but then his hand
stopped and wouldn't move.

He didn't want to spoil the gift. Wanted to look at it
awhile longer. Maybe tomorrow he would draw a picture,
but not yet. The white paper, the sharp points on the
rainbow colors of the pencils—everything was still too
perfect.

When he heard the key in the lock, he grabbed his book
and moved away from the table. Dinnertime already? He
had forgotten to be hungry. Over the odor of cooked meat
another smell floated, familiar to him now. O'Fallon's
smell, after he'd been drinking out of the brown bottle.
The hair on the back of Michael's neck prickled.

O'Fallon wasn't walking right. The tray made a *crash*
when he set it down on the table. "This what she gave
you? I saw 'er at the window, saw 'er slip you something."
Stiff-legged, Michael went closer. "What'd you slip *her,*
eh? Tell you what *I'd* like to slip 'er, right under them lily
white skirts." He laughed loud. "Pencils, huh?" When he
picked one up, Michael bared his teeth in a warning.

"Don't you be growling at me, boyo." He swung
around, planting his feet. Did he want to fight? Michael
wanted to. "I'll make you good and sorry, you try to play
with me. Blinkin' ape. Lookit this." There was a glass of
water on the tray. O'Fallon picked it up and poured all the
water out onto the white pages of Sydney's gift.

"Back off!"

Michael kept coming, snarling with rage, curling his
fingers into claws. O'Fallon put his hand behind his back
and pulled the black stick out of nowhere.

Michael hunched his shoulders and began to circle, the
fierce warning growl still bubbling up in his throat. His
blood sang the old song he had almost forgotten, and he
could smell the fear in the sweat of his enemy.

"Back off, I said. Back up or I'll bash your brains in.
Maybe I'll do it anyway."

He waited until O'Fallon lifted the stick over his head. Then he charged.

His weight took them both down, so easy, and he was on top, the winner, fingers twisted in his enemy's hair, snapping and snarling into his face. He saw the stick coming too late.

Blinding pain—it smashed against his cheek, snapping his head sideways. He couldn't see, but he lunged anyway, and his hands curved around the stick. He jerked it away and threw it across the floor.

Now, he gloated, drooling and snapping his teeth. *Now you're beaten.* O'Fallon quivered under him, rolling the whites of his eyes, lips pale from fear. He made a squealing sound, like a mouse when you catch it in your hand. Michael lifted his head and howled.

Slowly, cautiously, he crawled off the beaten man and moved away, still on his knees. He touched the blood on his face and looked at it on his hand, smelled it. His head was hammering with pain and the excitement of victory.

"Fucking animal." O'Fallon had something shiny and pointed in his hand, something black and deadly. Michael recognized it the second before it shot fire.

"Michael and I played magic tricks today," Sam informed the family and Charles at the dinner table. "We did the scarf trick and the marble trick. He cheats at the card trick, though. He always pulls the right one out of the deck before I do."

"How does he manage that?" asked Sydney.

"He cheats!"

"How?"

"He can smell it! He says he can tell by the smell which one I touched last."

Aunt Estelle clucked her tongue in disgust.

"Tomorrow I'm going to teach him how to play Flinch. I don't see how he can cheat at that."

"I doubt he'll be able to learn it," Charles put in, using

the kindly, pedantic tone he always took with Sam. "I should think it would be a bit too complicated for him."

"No, it won't."

"Samuel," Aunt Estelle reproved.

"It *won't*. Michael can learn *anything*. You just have to tell him one time, and he knows."

"Really." Charles smiled tolerantly.

Philip glared at Charles, whom he disliked, but said nothing. He was in the doghouse again. He hadn't come home at all last night, and this time Aunt Estelle was recommending a two-week prison sentence: no leaving the house at all, and no contact with the outside world, even by telephone. Papa was taking the matter under advisement. Which meant nothing would happen until Aunt Estelle got tired of waiting, forced the issue, and won.

Papa was quiet tonight, too, Sydney noticed. That was rare. Usually he and Charles monopolized dinner table conversation with talk of the Ontario Man's progress, or lack of it. They looked confounded, she thought; a little defeated. She wanted very much to know what their plans were for Michael, if and when they decided they could no longer use him as a study subject. But now wasn't the time to ask, and she doubted if they knew the answer yet anyway.

She wondered something else. Would Charles pack up and go home if the Ontario Man experiments came to an end? And if he did, would she care? She glanced down the length of the table at her aunt. Charles sat at her left hand, deferring to her, constantly trying to win her goodwill. He didn't have a notion that it was hopeless, and Sydney didn't have the heart to tell him. Aunt Estelle was tolerating him because he was her brother's professional associate. Period. She knew he spent time alone with Sydney; she probably even knew he was courting her. Of course she disapproved, but she had never said anything about it. She didn't take it seriously. Charles West could be no conceivable threat; as a bona fide suitor, he was simply unimaginable. If she had had any inkling that he'd proposed marriage, she would faint dead away. And if she knew Sydney was actually *considering* his proposal . . . heavens, there was no telling what she would do.

But the question was, how would Sydney feel if Charles moved out of the house? She thought of Camille's theory that she just wanted a husband, any husband, and Charles was there for the taking. Was that true? And what kind of marriage would it be if the presence or absence of the husband mattered so little to the wife? She couldn't imagine—

Aunt Estelle interrupted her thoughts to say sharply, "What was that?"

They all froze, listening.

"It sounded like an animal."

"Must've been Hector."

The long glass doors to the terrace were open. The sound, a furious, low-pitched howling, had come from the direction of the lake. Sydney's eyes met Sam's. He knew what she knew: that wasn't Hector. Before either of them could move, the muffled sound of a shot shattered the listening silence.

"Good Lord! Was that a *gun*?"

Sydney jumped to her feet, but Sam was already scrambling out the door. "Stop!" she called. "Sam, you wait!"

He halted on the terrace steps, jumping up and down with impatience. She made a dash for him and caught his arm while the others spilled through the doorway and rushed toward them.

"Stay with your aunt. Stay with her!" she insisted when he tried to pull away. Aunt Estelle came out of her confusion and grabbed his hand. The men were sprinting for the guest house, and Sydney raced away to catch them, ignoring her aunt's shouted commands to come back. She was halfway to the small white bungalow when she heard another shot.

"Stay back," Philip called out over his shoulder, but she ignored him, too.

The outer room of the guest house was empty. She headed for Michael's room, where she could see Charles in the doorway. He turned when he heard her. "Syd, don't

come in—" but she shoved past him without a thought.
Her eyes were on the blood.

So much blood, everywhere. And Michael was snarling
and spitting like a dog gone mad, half sitting and half
lying on top of O'Fallon, his hands around the bigger
man's neck as if he were throttling him.

"Get him off me!" O'Fallon shrieked. "Somebody get
him!"

Michael turned his head, and Sydney shrank back,
aghast. His bared teeth horrified her. Saliva ran down his
chin; his pale eyes were narrow feral slits. Bright blood
soaked O'Fallon's shirt collar; brick-colored blood in
sprayed drops seeped into the pine floorboards all around
him. Then Sydney saw the gun beside his shoulder.

The terrible vibrating snarl in Michael's throat tapered
off and finally stopped. He took his bloody hands off
O'Fallon and rose to a crouch over him.

"I knew something like this would happen," Charles
claimed, voice quivering.

Michael straightened to his full height. With his bare
foot, he kicked the gun away; it skittered across the floor
and struck the wall.

"He tried to kill me." O'Fallon sat up and scooted away
a few feet. "He was bloody going to *eat* me."

Backing up with an unsteady gait, Michael hit the wall
with his shoulder and leaned there. He was holding his
left hand against his chest with his right. His face slowly
drained of all color, and she saw him brace his knees to
keep from sliding down the wall.

"Oh, my God," she whispered, and started toward him,
shaking off Charles's hand when he tried to stop her. "It's
not his blood. Can't you see? It's Michael's blood. It's all
Michael's."

He was panting, locked inside himself. The wildness
was gone from his eyes, but she had to touch him before
he saw her. "Let me see. Is it bad? Let me look." She took
his left wrist gently, beating back her revulsion. So much
blood. His hand was covered with it; she couldn't see the
extent of the damage.

Philip plucked the gun off the floor and examined it in wonder. "You shot him."

"I'm telling you, he attacked me. The man's a maniac."

"Sam!"

Aunt Estelle didn't grab him in time. Sam flew across the room and flung his arms around Michael's knees. Michael blinked down at him, dazed.

"Better bandage that," Sydney's father advised. "Pillow-case? Towel," he decided, pulling one off the wash-stand and handing it to her. "Tight, now, Sydney." After a startled, uncertain second, she began to wrap the towel, as gently as she could, around Michael's shaking left hand.

"Are you all daft? That bastard tried his best just now to murder me!"

Papa grunted, leaning over to snatch up the billy club from where it had rolled under the table. "Hm," he said, hefting it, smacking it lightly against his palm. "Thought we got rid of this. Let's see your injuries, Mr. O'Fallon. I observe a great deal of blood, but where are your wounds? Show us the tooth marks. Show us the savage cuts left by the beast's claws."

"I fought 'im off. I had to shoot 'im or he'd of killed me."

"You fought him off?"

O'Fallon looked around at seven pairs of disbeliev-ing eyes.

Sam still clung to Michael's knees like a barnacle. "Let him go," Sydney said softly. "Let him sit down, Sam."

Sam unwound his arms, staring up into Michael's face. "Please don't die." Michael shook his head and tried to smile.

Aunt Estelle wanted explanations. "What exactly is going on here?" she demanded, and everyone stood a little straighter, even O'Fallon.

"He tried to beat me," Michael said, speaking slowly but clearly. "For nothing. I took the stick. I made him stop."

"He was going to kill me!"

Michael turned on him so quickly, O'Fallon flinched and scuttled back against the table, almost toppling it.

"You're a man," he said, with fatigue in his voice. "I would not kill a man."

There was a pause.

"He smells like a gin mill," Philip noted, eyeing O'Fallon with distaste.

"He was drinking the other day," Sydney remembered. "I saw the bottle." She had her arm around Michael's waist. His body trembled in spasms, but she knew he wouldn't sit down. Not until O'Fallon was gone.

"Harley, did you know this man had a firearm?"

"No, Estie, I certainly did not." He turned to Philip. "Go up and call the doctor, will you?"

"Rather stay here, Dad, and throw Mr. O'Fallon out on his ass."

"Hm, yes. Don't think it'll come to that, though. Mr. O'Fallon's going to take himself off very quietly."

"You're giving me the sack?"

"Yes, very much so. Clear out now, and no trouble. Wouldn't want to have to call the police out, too."

O'Fallon swore.

For Aunt Estelle, it was the last straw. "Out!" she commanded, skinny arm and bony finger pointing to the door.

O'Fallon did what most people did with Aunt Estelle. He obeyed her.

6

O 'Fallon didn't waste any time.
   Before noon the next day, four newspaper
   reporters and three photographers swooped down
on the house. They had all taken the same Illinois Central
train from Chicago and arrived on the front doorstep in a
breathless dead heat.

"What's the story?" they clamored to know from a
bewildered and terrified Inger, who had the misfortune of
opening the front door. "Is it true the lost man went on a
rampage and tried to kill his guard? Are they going to
lock him up again?"

Then the worst happened. Sydney, who happened to be
sunning herself on the side porch, saw it all and couldn't
stop it. "Hey," cried one of the reporters, pointing down
the path to the side of the house. "Look, it's him!"

Michael and Charles halted on the path, catching sight
of the reporters at the same moment. Michael took a backward step, but Charles, out of confusion or stupidity or
who knew what, grabbed his arm and held him still. Curs-
ing out loud, Sydney bolted from her chair and started
toward them, but she was too slow—the shouting, shoving, bumping hoard of journalists got to Michael first.

Charles let himself be butted and shouldered out of the
way; good for nothing, he stood off by himself, looking
piqued rather than concerned, as if he thought the press
ought to be asking *him* questions. Over all the bobbing
heads, Sydney saw Michael's white face, stiff with alarm.
"Let me by," she kept saying, and finally the reporters let

her push her way through to his side. "Stand back, will you? Get away from him! Can't you see he's been hurt?" She made her body a shield between them and the bandaged hand he was cradling against his middle. "Get back. Please, let him alone." The reporters wouldn't budge; they kept shouting their questions and taking their photographs, relentless as dogs scuffling over a bone.

Rescue came when her father rushed around the side of the house, calling, "You there, get away from that man! For God's sake, West, make them move!" Philip ran after him, and finally the crush loosened and began to give way. The reporters recognized Papa from the interviews he'd given months ago as the university's spokesman. They veered away from Michael, aware by now that they weren't going to get a story out of him, and surrounded Dr. Winter like bees swarming a new hive. Charles asserted himself at last by sidling through the crowd to stand next to him. That gave Sydney a chance to get Michael away, with Philip's help, and the three of them made an unencumbered dash for the house.

The next day, Michael's picture was on the front pages of the *Herald Examiner*, the *Tribune*, and the *Times*, and in every one he looked wild-eyed and dangerous. In adjacent photographs, O'Fallon, in a sober suit and tie, looked grim and aggrieved. "Lost Man in Violent Melee with Guard," read one caption; "Wild Man Attacks Keeper," blared another.

Luckily the stories accompanying the photographs were much tamer. Sydney's father simply denied all of O'Fallon's lying allegations, and the tone of the articles indicated that the authors were more inclined to believe him than the ex-janitor and habitual brawler. In the process, though, Papa was forced to disclose the full extent of Michael's socialization, his *un*-wildness, so to speak—something he hadn't planned on revealing to his superiors, much less to the world at large, for a lot longer. Thanks to O'Fallon, the jig was up.

That afternoon Dr. Winter's nemesis paid a call. Chairman Slocum, according to Papa, had never liked him because he was rich and didn't have to work for a living. That made him a dilettante in Slocum's book, a reproach her father deeply resented.

The chairman stayed an hour, locked up in the study with Charles and Papa. Sydney sat in the living room and tried to read, keeping one eye on the hallway and jumping at every sound. Finally Slocum left, and a second later she went into the study.

"What happened? What did he say?"

Both men looked stricken and dazed. Her father tried to focus on the question, but the cloud of his abstraction was too thick.

Charles answered for him. "There's no more project. He's cut off our funding. We're finished."

"We get to keep him, though," Papa rallied to point out. Charles nodded glumly. "He'll be more useful to the natural historians now, but we still get to keep him. Better for him, I told Slocum. Can't keep shuffling the fellow around." He ducked his white head into his shoulders, his retreating-turtle trick.

"And we can still get an article out of him, sir. At the very least. Once they're written up, our experiments are sure to interest a few journals. Not for the nature-nurture debate anymore, maybe, but on general questions of ethology."

Sydney could barely hide her elation. "You have to stop experimenting on him, you mean? And he can stay here with us?"

Papa looked up and smiled. "He'll be a sort of country cousin come to visit. You'll like that, won't you, Sydney?"

She liked it very much. "Can he stay in the house?"

"Hm? Don't know about that."

"Sir, won't he still be needing a guard? What if he tries to escape?"

Sydney snorted. "Heavens, Charles, he's not a prisoner," she said, trying to laugh. But inside, she was torn. The idea of anyone keeping watch over Michael repelled her now—but what if he ran away? "I don't think he would try to escape," she declared with more conviction that she felt. "After all, where would he go?"

"Anywhere," Charles argued.

"*Where?* He can't go back to Ontario, and that's the only home he knows. Besides ours. Really, Papa, I think he would stay here. I think he *wants* to."

"I still say it's too risky, sir."

"And I still say he's not a prisoner." Again Sydney took the snappishness out of her voice with a laugh. "Who's guarding him right now? No one, and I'm quite sure he's sitting quietly in his room, nursing his wound and waiting for somebody to bring him his tea. Well, Papa?"

Above all things, Sydney's father hated making decisions. His hand strayed to his pipe and hovered over it on the desktop. Once he took it up, she knew any hope of a resolution would be lost.

"He could stay in the guest room on the first floor," she put in hastily. "We'd all be around, not guarding him exactly, but watching him. Looking after him."

"But that's—" Charles's mouth snapped shut, but she knew what he had been going to say: *That's my room.* She'd taken the mental leap that he would be moving out, now that his project had been canceled. She watched his face darken; his eyes glaring at her behind his bifocals contained not a hint of affection.

A lot of things became clear to her in that moment; it was as if a moving blur had suddenly been caught in a clean, sharp photograph.

"Hm. Hmm." She waited, as tense as Charles, for her father to make up his mind—or not, put off the whole bothersome subject to another time. "Suppose he could stay in the house. Sort of like having a guard. Estie's a bit of a guard, isn't she? Ha. University's done with him, Charles, on any formal basis. Means he's free. Can't hold a man against his will."

"But," Charles sputtered, "he's not a man."

"Hm! How's that? 'Course he's a man. Point is, he's only good for magazine stories now, not anthropology journals. Got to give him up, West. Writing's on the wall. Time for us to move on."

Charles had to turn away and look out the window to keep from showing what he thought of that.

Sydney ran into Inger in the hallway. "Are you taking that down to Michael?" she asked, eyeing the maid's laden tea tray.

"Ya, to Michael." Her smile faded when Sydney reached for the tray and took it from her.

"I'm going down myself. I'll take it to him, shall I?" Inger, she noticed before she turned away, looked bereft.

The front door to the guest house stood wide open. "Michael?" She crossed to the inner room; that door was open, too. "Michael?" She poked her head inside. Nobody there.

She set the tray on the neatly made bed and wheeled around. The wooden bar, still nailed over the window, blocked half the light. At first the room looked completely empty, as if he had packed up and left. But then she saw that his possessions, what there were of them, were here. He had one change of clothes in the large, black-painted wardrobe. A heap of blankets lay in a corner of the room, and something about their shape, the long, telltale curve among the folds and wrinkles, told her that that was where he slept. Not in the bed but on the floor, on those blankets. She turned away, uncomfortable with her discovery.

The paper tablet and pencils she had given him lay on top of the room's only table. Half the tablet was ruined, as if water had gotten spilled on it. There was no sign of his famous book. Perhaps he'd hidden it.

The only other object on the table was a cigar box. She opened it without thinking, and saw that his cache of treasures had grown more sophisticated since the days of bottle-caps and bright pieces of cloth. Now he had the wooden bird call Philip had whittled for him one day on the beach; a folded picture of two deer, a buck and a doe, obviously torn from a newspaper—Sydney remembered the article, something about wildlife conservation in the Sunday feature section a week ago. Had he made friends with deer when he lived in the wild? If so, these photographs must be a reminder of that, a comfort. She smiled when she saw that he'd saved one of Sam's drawings of her, one of the slightly less primitive-looking ones, with her name carefully printed at the bottom. The last object was a folded white handkerchief, and it wasn't until she turned it over and saw the monogram, SWD, that she realized it was hers.

Michael had saved her picture and her handkerchief.

The queerest feeling came over her as she quietly closed the box of treasures and put it back in the precise spot in which she'd found it. She had a sense of excitement and dread, anticipation and . . . something else, almost like fear. Not that it was any revelation that Michael thought about her. When they were together there was always awareness, and interest carefully controlled, on both sides. But these small, worthless keepsakes solidified the attraction, didn't they? Took it out of the much more comfortable realm of—at least for her—the abstract. In a way, they changed everything.

She went outside, calling his name again. No answer. *Could* he have run away? The presence of his belongings had reassured her before, but suddenly they didn't. Why would he take them? He wouldn't—he would just go, just walk away.

"Michael!"

No answer except the soft lap of waves and the chirp of crickets in the grass. *Oh, God,* she thought, *what if he's gone*? She should've listened to Charles. This was bound to happen, how stupid she had been—

"Michael!"

"Sydney?"

She saw him at the edge of the pine woods. He ran toward her at the same time she hurried down the two shallow steps to meet him. He ought not to run, she thought; he was still weak from his wound.

"What's happened?" he said in a quiet voice when he reached her, his eyes darting everywhere, searching for danger. "What's wrong?"

"Nothing, nothing. I didn't know where you were, that's all." Her heart was pounding, but not from exertion. She felt weak with relief. "What's that?" she said, so he wouldn't guess what she'd been thinking. He had something green and filthy around his bad hand. His bandage was gone! "What *is* that?"

"I think it's called moss."

She stared at him, slack-jawed. "Oh, Michael, *no*. No, you can't put that on there, you can't. It could fester, become infected. Don't you see, you could lose your hand! Come inside"—she pulled on his arm—"and let me clean it. Get rid of that." She plucked the damp, nasty clump of green stuff—it *was* moss—off his hand and threw it on the ground and pulled him the rest of the way into the house.

Luckily Dr. Cox had stitched the wound closed, so Michael's home remedy hadn't had time to do any harm. The bullet had torn through the flesh between his thumb and first finger, breaking only one small bone. Dr. Cox had wrapped a medicine plaster around his hand to keep it immobile, but somehow he had managed to unwrap it.

"What were you thinking of?" she scolded while she soaked his hand in a basin of cold water, gently spreading soap over the closed wound with her fingertips. The sharp black stitches felt strange against the smoothness of his skin; they must feel even stranger to him. "Does this hurt?"

"Yes."

Always honest. "I'm sorry. I'm almost done." She glanced at him and saw that he was watching her face instead of her ministering hands. His unblinking regard made her clumsy and oddly self-conscious.

The doctor had left bandages and a bottle of brownish swab. She blotted the wound with the medicine, which didn't seem to sting, and then set about rebandaging his hand. "Dr. Cox is going to have to come back and plaster it again," she said sternly, "and this time I want you to leave it alone. Understand?"

"Yes, ma'am." He didn't smile, but his eyes sparkled. Was he teasing her?

"Why on earth did you put moss on it?"

"Sometimes it heals."

"Maybe in the Middle Ages it healed. But medicine's come a long way since then." But she thought of all the scars on his body, and of her father's journal note that the Ontario Man's general health was "excellent." She felt less sure of herself, and not quite so smug about modern medicine.

"There, I'm finished."

He held up his bandaged hand, studying it from different angles. "I'm better with my other hand. It's good that this is this hand."

"You're right-handed," she explained. "People are either right-handed or left-handed."

"Yes, I know."

"Oh," she muttered, coloring. "Sorry."

"Why are you sorry?"

"Because I don't always know what you already know. I never mean to patronize you, Michael, but sometimes I'm sure I do."

"I don't know what 'patronize' means."

"It means . . . to condescend."

He smiled.

"To act as if I know more than you."

Now they were both smiling. "But you *do* know more than me. So you can never *patronize* me."

She laughed, embarrassment gone. How fortunate they all were that the Ontario Man was so good-natured. "I've brought you some tea. Shall we take it outside?"

They sat on the front stoop of the bungalow, she in the doorway, he on the step below her, the tray between them. The china pot contained hot chocolate, not tea, and Sydney wondered if Inger had made a mistake. "Don't you like tea?" she asked.

He made a terrible face. "Muddy water," he said, pretending to shudder.

There were two cups. That struck her as odd until she recalled the look of disappointment on the maid's face. *Hm,* she thought, pouring chocolate, no longer hot, into a cup for Michael, and watching him add one, two, *three* more teaspoonsful of sugar. Ignoring the little cheese sandwiches, he went straight for the cakes, devouring exactly half of them in short order.

She poured herself a half cup of tepid chocolate and leaned one shoulder against the doorpost. "I have some news. I think you'll like it." He looked at her expectantly. "My father's project has been canceled. Stopped. He won't be doing any more experiments on you, at least not like before. He and Charles have finished with you, Michael. It's over."

He set his cup down carefully, not returning her smile. "Then I should go?"

"No! No, not at all, I didn't mean you have to leave. Unless you . . ." She girded herself to ask the question. "Do you want to go?"

He studied her for a long time, then looked away without answering.

His black, too-long hair gleamed in the strong sunlight. She wondered how it would feel on her fingers. Sleek and soft. Warm from the sun. "You could have walked away by now," she said quietly. "Today. No one would have known."

A few seconds passed. When he still didn't speak, she put her cup down and cleared her throat, altering the odd, watchful mood between them. "If you want to, you can move into the house. Papa says that will be fine."

"Live in the house?"

"Yes, if you like."

"With you?"

"With my family, yes. Sam would love it."

He continued to ponder. "Would Aunt Estelle love it?"

"If you move in," she said, laughing, "you'll have to remember to call her Miss Winter."

"Miss Winter."

"She's *my* aunt, you see, and Sam's and Philip's. She's not your aunt." Suddenly doubtful, she asked, "Do you know what an aunt is? Aunt Estelle is my father's sister."

"Yes, I know aunts." Then he frowned, as if wondering

how he knew about aunts. "Will Miss Winter love me to move into the house?"

Sydney hesitated. He was so truthful himself, he discouraged evasion from others. "She . . . she . . . no, she probably won't like it. At first." In fact, she might even forbid it. Sydney hadn't considered that possibility until now.

"Because I'm not like others. I'm strange, the lost man. I don't . . ." He ran out of words.

"Fit in," she said faintly.

"Yes. Fit in."

"She might think that. My aunt has a different way of seeing things from most—from some people." She sighed inwardly. Explaining Aunt Estelle to Michael simply wasn't possible; he could have no reference point, absolutely nothing in his experience to compare her to. "You'll understand her better the more you see of her," she said, thinking that was a promise she could make with confidence.

There was a pause.

"I like this," Michael announced, looking around at the green lawn, the trees edging the lake, the blue of the water glittering in the distance through the fluttering leaves. It occurred to Sydney that until she had come here and called to him, today must be the first time he'd been alone, completely alone, since his capture. A man who had spent three-quarters of his life in solitude had not been allowed to be by himself in four months.

She wondered again why he hadn't run away when he'd had the chance, but she didn't ask. She didn't want the subject broached at all, she realized. She was afraid of it.

"Charles is leaving. You can have his room if you like."

He'd been leaning back against the step on his elbows, completely at ease, almost sleepy-eyed. He came to attention at that. "West is going away?"

"Going back to his own place in the city. Now that his work's finished here."

"I can have his room?"

"Yes." She didn't know why she was flushing under his intent stare. "You . . . it's bigger than the guest house bedroom. It even has a sitting room. You'll be more comfortable there, I should think. That is, if you want to move. It would be for your convenience. And the servants'. Easier for them, the cleaning and so forth." She finally stopped babbling; she smiled and shrugged.

"Sydney?"

"Yes?"

He played with the bandage on his hand, absorbed in making it lie perfectly flat across the backs of his knuckles.

"What?" she prompted.

"Are you and West still mates?"

Her mouth dropped open. He stole a glance, half smiling at her with that mix of shyness and intensity that always drew her to him. "We aren't mates, Michael. Not the way you mean." Not the way she *thought* he meant. "We never have been. We're friends."

He looked dubious. "But he . . ." Whatever he was going to say, he decided not to say it. To her relief. "Will he come back?"

"Oh, yes. Sometimes."

"Do you like him?"

"Yes, of course. We're *friends*."

"Friends," he echoed, frowning. "Like us?"

She laughed helplessly, but he just waited for the answer. "I don't know. Like us? Not exactly. I'm not sure. *Heavens*, Michael, you ask the hardest questions!"

The slow smile spread wider. Whatever he'd gleaned from that incoherent answer, he certainly looked satisfied with it.

The next day, Charles brought her orchids.

He'd finished packing; he was ready to leave. The flowers were a bribe, she knew, because he wanted back in her good graces. They hadn't argued, hadn't spoken much at all about the events of the last few days. But he knew she wasn't pleased with him on any number of scores, and he wanted to mend the rift before he left.

The orchids really were beautiful. He gave them to her

in front of Philip, Sam, and Michael, who all happened to be sitting out on the terrace with her; they'd been teaching Michael to play one of Sam's card games. She overdid her excitement with the flowers, exclaiming over them eagerly, thanking Charles profusely. She exaggerated her pleasure for two reasons: she was glad he was leaving, and she felt guilty for being glad.

He wanted to walk down to the lake with her. When he took her hand on the path, she let him keep it. It was the least she could do, and besides, he was leaving in a few minutes. Anyway, they weren't really saying good-bye; she would see him again, often—tomorrow, probably. Still, it felt as if something was ending. In spite of herself, she grew melancholy. *Any* ending was sad, even if you were halfway looking forward to it.

But she had completely misjudged him.

"Sydney, let's not put off our engagement any longer," he said out of the blue, taking both of her hands and pulling her to a stop. They were standing in exactly the same spot from which, weeks ago, she'd first seen the lost man watching from his window.

"What?" she said stupidly.

"Let's tell people we're going to be married. I don't want to wait any longer. You won't make me, will you?"

"But—but we never said we *would* marry. We're *not* engaged."

"Not formally."

"Not at *all*."

"Oh, Sydney." He put his arms around her, drawing her closer. "Are you torturing me on purpose?" In spite of herself she softened a little; the thought drifted by that she liked Charles better when she wasn't looking at him. "Please, darling. I'm so in love with you. Say you'll marry me and let me make you happy."

"Oh, Charles," was all she had time to say. He whipped off his bifocals and kissed her on the mouth, and for the first time she felt real, true passion in him. Diverted, she let him go on kissing her and sliding his hands up and down her sides, pressing her body to his most intimately.

When they finally broke apart, she felt breathless. He smiled at her, his lips moist, myopic eyes dancing. "We would be *very* happy," he promised in a suggestive whisper. "Say yes, Sydney. Put me out of my misery."

She mentally shook herself out of the momentary sensual trance. "Charles, listen. I'm afraid I've given you false hope. The truth is, I'm not ready to marry again. It's as simple as that."

"Then I'll wait."

"I can't tell you what to feel, but I can warn you that you'll be much happier if you give up the thought of marrying me. Ever marrying me. You know I'm fond of you, *very* fond, but I think we just don't suit."

"You're wrong."

"Maybe so, but this is how I feel. I'm sure of it now, and it's only fair to tell you. It doesn't have to spoil our friendship—"

"It couldn't."

"I'm so glad you feel that way." She looked down at their clasped hands, acknowledging that that was a lie. She had wanted a break between them, and he wasn't going to allow it. But at least the hardest part was over. Thank God.

They strolled back toward the house, Charles glum and silent, she trying not to let her lightheartedness show. On the terrace, Philip got up to shake hands with him. He wouldn't be sorry to see Charles go either, she knew. "Where's Michael?" she asked idly.

Sam looked up from the pyramid he was trying to build out of playing cards. "He went down to the guest house to get his stuff. Didn't you see him?"

She felt her cheeks getting hot. "No, I didn't." But there was no way he could've missed seeing *her*.

Unexpected presents, occasioned by nothing but thoughtfulness or kindness, are among life's sweetest surprises. The grateful recipient of such a gift does well to return it in kind.

What did it mean? *In kind.* That he must give *back* the paper and the pencils to Sydney? He asked Sam.

"What does it mean to return a gift in kind?"

Sam didn't know, but he asked Philip and reported back. "It means you give back a gift as good as the one you got."

As good as. Not the same as. Good, because Michael didn't know how to get more pencils and paper. So. What would he give to Sydney for a present? He thought about it for two days. He almost asked Sam, but he wanted his gift to be one of Sydney's life's sweetest surprises, and Sam would've told her.

The answer came while he was wading in the lake in the hot afternoon. Sam was trying to fly a kite on the shore. Michael didn't want him to see, so he waited until Sam got tired, waved to him, and ran up the path to the house.

He knew the colors and shapes, the speed and the get-away tricks of all the fish. He knew where their bones were and how they tasted. What he didn't know was their names. But Sydney would know, and that was what mattered. Now, what should he catch her? The long, fast, spotted fish would be best, but he hadn't seen any yet in this lake. There were plenty of the ones with little sticks on their backs; they were small and bony, but Sydney might like their red stomachs and green-blue backs. And they had no scales, which made eating them easier. Then he remembered: whatever fish he caught her, she would want to cook it before she ate it. So scales didn't matter.

He decided on one of the fat, silver-blue ones. They had firm white flesh, very good to eat, and they were easy to catch. Too bad there was not a rock here to lie down on and hunt from. Michael walked farther out into the lake and waited.

West had given his gift to Sydney outside, with people all around. Was there a rule about that? Maybe people should be around, but Michael couldn't think of a reason why it had to be outside. He didn't want to wait. He was excited, and besides, it was important for his gift to be fresh. So, just before dinner, while the family was sitting in the room they called the drawing room, he brought Sydney her present.

He put it on the little round table beside the chair she was sitting in. West's gift had had colored ribbons around it for a decoration, so Michael had tied the string from his pencils around the pretty silver fish. The bow hadn't turned out right because the string was too short, so he'd added a flower, a yellow one he'd found in the walled garden. The fish smelled good, and he thought it looked beautiful.

He wasn't sure what to say. Everybody stopped talking, and Sydney looked at Michael, then at the present. She had a glass in her hand, full of something orange that smelled terrible, not as bad as O'Fallon's bottle but almost. She had on a dress the same color as spring grass, and a filmy belt around the middle that was yellow. Sometimes she wore her hair down, not up, with pretend-flowers holding it behind her ears somehow. She had it that way now, and it was his favorite, because he could see the fox colors better, and he could almost feel how soft it would be if he touched it.

What had West said when he'd given her the flowers? *These are for you,* he thought. Something like that.

He put his hands behind his back so she wouldn't know he was nervous. "This is for you." She didn't say anything, so he added, "It's a present for you. From me." Still nothing. "Because you gave me one." He felt the first stirrings of unease. Taking one step back, he made himself say, "I am returning it in kind."

He wanted to turn around and see why Sam and Philip were coughing, but Sydney's face was too interesting. He could see the whites around her blue eyes, they were so big. Then she ducked, but he could still see her cheeks and forehead and ears all turn bright pink. She put her glass in her lap and her other hand over her mouth.

This was wrong. He remembered the things she'd said to West—"Oh, Charles, they're *beautiful,* where did you ever find them? How very thoughtful—*thank* you, Charles"—and on and on for a long time, smiling, touching West on the arm. And all for some flowers with no scent, and no use except to look at. Wasn't a fresh, fat fish a better gift than that?

Miss Winter made a noise in her throat; he looked at her, thin as a dead sapling, sitting in the big chair by the window, and saw that she looked . . . he didn't know the word. *Surprised* wasn't enough. Next to her, Dr. Winter had his hand over his mouth, the same way Sydney did.

Then he understood. They were all laughing at his fish. At him.

He could feel his face turn red, like Sydney's. *Oh, God,* he thought. He wished he could disappear, but he was afraid to move. Anything he did would be wrong now. Sydney lifted her pink face, and he saw that she was crying.

Crying. He went close again, leaned over her. "Sydney, don't cry, don't cry. I'll take it away. I'll eat it myself."

A sound exploded out of her mouth, like a captured thing suddenly bursting free. He froze, horrified—until he realized that high, liquid, trilling sound was her laughter. And he loved that sound. And her eyes, overflowing with tears, were warm and sorrowful and sweet, asking him to please, please understand.

Then it was easy. He looked at his fish, wrapped in string with a flower on top and resting on the shiny wood table. He had given Sydney a dead fish. Everybody in the drawing room was laughing or trying not to, even the dog. What could he do? He threw back his head and laughed with them.

"Michael, it was a wonderful gift."

"No, it wasn't."

"Yes, it was. It was thoughtful and practical, and you made it yourself. So to speak. And it was a nice fish, a *beautiful* fish, really. As they go."

"What kind was it? What do you call it?"

"Philip said a whitefish."

"Whitefish."

They were sitting in the garden in the twilight, watching fireflies twinkle in the treetops and listening to the birds call good nights across the paling sky. Sydney laughed softly, again, and beside her Michael chuckled. She couldn't stop thinking about the way the fish had looked, with its mouth gaping and its yellow eye staring, stretched out on the mahogany piecrust table next to the silver and cut-glass sherry decanter in Aunt Estelle's pristine drawing room. And every time she thought of it, she laughed. *Thank God* Michael had a sense of humor.

She leaned against his shoulder, sharing the joke, letting her affection for him show. Laughter made the fastest, easiest friendships, she'd always thought. At this moment she felt closer to him than she ever had, with none of the tension or strangeness that had colored their relationship in the beginning.

"Listen," she whispered. "Isn't it pretty?"

"Yes. What's it called?"

"It's a wood thrush." They listened to the rich, flutelike notes in a companionable hush, both smiling. "Thoreau wrote something about the thrush I never forgot. He wrote, 'Whenever a man hears it he is young, and nature is in her spring; whenever he hears it, it is a new world and a free country, and the gates of heaven are not shut against him.' "

Michael expelled a soft breath, his still face full of emotion. "Wait here, Sydney," he whispered. "Don't move, and be very quiet."

"Why?"

"Shh." He smiled. "Another gift." And he was gone, silent as a shadow.

She listened intently, but she couldn't hear anything except the sounds of dusk, crickets tuning, sleepy birds chirping. And the lake lapping against the shore, soft slapping sounds tonight, familiar as her own heartbeat.

What would become of Michael MacNeil? She wasn't sure if he'd had the fortune or the misfortune to end up in the custody of her scatterbrained father. She worried about him more every day; the longer she knew him, the more she wanted for him. And feared for him. He was such an innocent, in some ways a child in a man's body. How would he make his way in the wicked world? She wanted to sit her father down and make him *concentrate*, focus on this intriguing problem that had fallen into his lap, and come up with a *plan*. Michael must live from day to day, moment to moment, with no idea of a future, no shape to it in his mind. It wasn't fair, and it wasn't kind. By a trick of fate he'd become the Winter family's responsibility, and she was impatient for all of them to start shouldering it.

"Sydney."

She barely heard her name, he'd whispered it so quietly. He was behind her—how had he gotten there?—but she didn't move, didn't even turn her head, because he'd told her not to. Without a sound, he sat down on the bench, but facing the other way, so the right side of his body grazed the right side of hers. With slow and careful movements, they turned toward each other.

She wasn't surprised to see him cradling something in his hands. In her heart she even knew what it was, although her mind still told her it couldn't be. Slowly, so slowly, he opened the soft box his hands made, and inside, calm and beautiful, its little heart beating fast, sat the wood thrush.

Sydney was afraid to move, couldn't even sigh. The bird had huge black eyes and rust-colored wing feathers and a speckled breast. Michael breathed, "I took her from her nest. She has four eggs. I must let her go soon."

Sydney gave one slow, careful nod. She was still holding her breath. She wanted to stroke the sleek curve of the head, feel the flicker of the pulse in the warm throat, but she didn't dare. "She's wonderful. So lovely." And she wasn't afraid, or else Michael had put a spell on her. His hand on top was soothing, not holding her, and still the bird was motionless, the shiny eyes alert but not frightened.

He took his right hand away and held his left out and up. Sydney drew back a fraction of an inch, preparing for a wild flutter of wings and a scramble for freedom. But nothing happened. The thrush turned her head in quick jerks, surveying the lay of the land, as if intrigued by her new perspective. Michael laid the side of his index finger against her breast, and she jumped onto it, pink-legged and pointy-clawed. Another silent, breathless moment passed. Each second they kept her was like a miracle. It ended when she suddenly sprang up and flashed away into the night, with nothing but a gentle *whish*. And when she was gone, Sydney could scarcely believe they'd ever had her at all.

"Wood thrush," Michael murmured into the quiet that followed. "I like knowing the names. What things are called."

"Michael."

"Yes?"

"How on earth did you do that?"

He moved his shoulders, smiling.

"Thank you. It was a most wonderful gift."

"Did you like her?"

"Very much. She was beautiful. Thank you."

Her words made him turn to her, angle his body on the bench so that they were face-to-face. Before he lowered his long black lashes, she saw something in his eyes, a look of expectancy that had her nerves jumping, even before she knew consciously what the look meant. And she was sure of it once it hit her: he thought they might kiss now. Because she'd kissed Charles after he'd given her flowers. Michael had seen them. He thought grateful gift receivers showed their gratitude with kisses.

Well, they did, sometimes. Frequently. It was a courtesy, a social reflex . . . nothing one needed to think too hard about. . . .

She couldn't think at all. She made the mistake of glancing at him again, and caught him staring at her mouth. The stillness, the fascination, the hunger in him stopped her heart for one long, dizzy second. But afterward, he made no move toward her, didn't try to touch her. The yearning silence deepened.

Had she been wrong? After all, what did he know of

kisses? Twice he'd seen her kiss Charles; and Sam, much more often, although that was a different kind of kissing. He'd probably seen her kiss Philip and Aunt Estelle. Her father.

On second thought, he knew quite a lot.

But she was making too much of it. All this unbearable tension must be coming from her, not Michael. He was only sitting there, gazing off to the side now, his dark, clear-cut profile beautiful in the dusk. Breathless with daring, she leaned toward him and pressed her lips to his hard cheek.

He sat perfectly still, his only movement the rapid blinking of his eyelashes. The smell of him was soap and pine and man. "Thank you," she murmured, and laid her cheek lightly against his, reluctant to draw away just yet. But he never moved or spoke. She sat back, uncertain. Her heart was pounding hard and fast. He wouldn't even look at her. She touched his arm.

It was trembling, the muscles corded and rock-hard. Then she saw his fingers gripping the edge of the iron bench between them, the tough tendons flexing in the back of his hand.

She stood up quickly, awkwardly. Absurd to be afraid of Michael, and yet fear was what she felt. Sharp, panicky fear, of something wild and dark, unpredictible, and held in check by a white-knuckled control she had no idea if she could trust.

"Well, I'd better go in—it's late—my aunt—" She took a deep breath. His pale eyes pierced her, seeing through her confusion and her incoherence. He understood her fear, and he accepted it. Approved of it.

That scared her more than anything.

She lifted her hand toward him and let it fall. "Good night, Michael." She made her voice light, careless, denying that any of this was happening. But it was, and he knew it.

7

Michael's new sitting room had a clock. It sat on a shelf on the wall, wagging its wooden tail behind a glass door all day and all night. Sticks floated past numbers, telling you what time it was if you knew how to tell time. The sticks would say one thing, then you'd turn your back to put on your shirt or comb your hair, and when you looked again they'd say something else. Now he knew they moved all the time, because he'd seen them, slow, so slow, like the moon rising or the stars coming out in the night sky. You had to be patient and watchful, like when you were waiting for a rabbit to finally poke its nose out of a burrow so you could catch it.

His sitting room had furniture, too. A lot of it, all heavy and dark, made of wood but smelling like oil and wax. There was paper glued to the walls, with a picture of the same thing over and over—a bunch of blue flowers tied with white ribbons. He had a desk, two chairs, a cabinet, books he couldn't read, a bowl of dried-up flowers and reeds, and a window with no bar on it.

In his bedroom he had a box with a door for his clothes, with a mirror on the door so he could see his whole body if he wanted to. There was a chair that rocked back and forth when he sat in it. But it made too much noise; he didn't feel safe in it. He didn't use it.

His new bed had a cloth roof, and another bed under it you could pull out and have two beds. He didn't sleep in either one. Every night he took the heavy cover off the big

bed and curled up with it on the floor, and every morning
he put it back on the bed.

The house was quiet tonight. Sam had gone to sleep—
that always made it quiet—but another reason was
because Sydney and Philip had gone to the fair. No one
was here but Dr. Winter and Aunt Estelle—Miss Winter,
rather. At first Dr. Winter was going to go with Sydney
and Philip to the fair, but the aunt said, "I will not be left
alone in this house with that man." She hadn't meant for
Michael to hear that, but she had a voice like a crow, he
could be under water and still hear it. Two days ago he'd
heard her say, "His manners are atrocious," after Sydney
had invited him to eat dinner with her family. Since then,
he'd been taking his meals in his room by himself.

The stairs creaked. His room was on the ground floor,
but he always knew when someone was going up or
down. He listened; Dr. Winter was saying something to
his sister. "Well, if they are late, it's your fault," she said
back to him. "If Philip had been confined as I advised, he
wouldn't be out tonight at all." Dr. Winter said something
else. "Well, at least you've got *one* sensible child," the
aunt said before their voices got too faint to hear.

He heard a door close upstairs, then another. Under his
door came that sharp, sweet smell that meant someone
had turned off the gaslights. The house creaked and
cracked. A moth beat against his window; a mosquito bit
the back of his hand and flew away before he could slap
it. The clock clicked. The house went to sleep.

Michael got up from the chair in his sitting room. He
left his shoes where they were and went quietly down the
long corridor to the front door, where the stairs came
down and the hallway turned right. The house was shaped
like one of Professor Winter's pipes, with a long, thin
body and one fat wing stuck on behind, facing the lake.
The terrace in back was a half circle, and you could get to
it from either wing by going out through the dining room,
the drawing room, or the professor's study. Moving softly
so as not to wake up the dog, who wasn't smart like a

wolf and might bark if he saw him, Michael headed for the study.

Instead of turning on the bright light, he lit a candle he found on the desk in a shiny metal holder with a handle. Shaking out the match, he thought for the hundredth time or so about what it would have meant, how it would have changed things, if he'd had matches to light fires at home. He'd had the thought so often, he could let it go now; it no longer interested him.

He carried the candle to the wall with the books, rows and rows of books, one on top of the other, all the way to the ceiling. He knew the one he wanted; he had seen the professor put it back after looking at a picture in it. It was on a high shelf, thick, with a dark red leather cover and gold letters. He pulled it out, took it to Dr. Winter's desk, and sat down.

The beginning part, the first half at least, was all words, small, mysterious scratchings on the crisp white pages. He turned past them to the pictures, to the back where he knew *wolf* was.

There. He put his fist on his chest, pressed with his knuckles to try to stop the pain. The wolf picture didn't really look like the old wolf—this one was small and too white, probably a female. But still, it made him cry, and it made him sick for home. He wondered if his friend had lived through the bitter, hungry winter. Without Michael to help him, he didn't see how he could have lived. More likely he'd starved, or died slow in a trap, or gotten sick. Michael couldn't stand to think about it. Worst was thinking of the old wolf dying alone.

He wiped his face and turned to another page. Here were two foxes, one dark and one light. He could read the word under them, f-o-x, but not the other two words, r-e-d and g-r-a-y. He knew the letters, but he'd forgotten how to read them. He could only read "fox" because he *knew* it was a fox. But this animal on this page, he knew it so well, had played games with it, come into its burrow, eaten its food and shared his own—and he couldn't read its name. B-a-d-g-e-r. It meant nothing, just a string of

letters dancing in front of his eyes. Frustration made him
smack the book closed, almost snuffing out the candle.

He opened it again, and went back to the pictures. He
knew owl, raccoon, skunk. Bear. Because he'd always
known them. But what was m-a-r-t-e-n? And f-i-s-h-e-r?
He *knew* them, but what were their names? What were the
snakes, twelve kinds, all with different names? What were
the birds? He only knew *robin* from before, and *wood
thrush* because Sydney had told him.

To calm himself, he turned to the pages with trees and
bushes. Trees were better; some of them even grew here,
all around the house. It wasn't so bad that he couldn't
name this one, s-p-r-u-c-e, even though he'd eaten its
hard, brown flowers. He stared at the pictures and pretended he was home, looking out over a rolling green
forest from a hilltop in the summertime. Birds circling in
big loops, and the sky too blue to look at. Peace. Calm.
Safety, for a while. Nothing to hear but the plop of an
acorn, the whisper of a pod gliding to the ground. Smell
of earth. Warm skin, sun making his hair hot. Rasp of an
insect. Peace.

He heard the sound of wheels turning, the clop-clop
of a horse. He sat up straight, ears straining. He heard
a carriage door open and close, and two men's voices,
one Philip's. The carriage started, and then moved away.
Steps on the porch, and now the front door opening. Sydney said, "Shhh," and something too soft to hear, and
Philip laughed. Thud of footsteps on the staircase.

Michael turned back to his book—but straightened
again when he heard the light, quiet steps, under the
heavy ones on the stairs. Sydney's steps. She was coming
down the hall to this room.

He had remembered to close the door when he came in.
She opened it and looked inside, curious and careful.

"Michael!"

He got up and moved over to the terrace door so she
could come close to the desk if she wanted to. This was
his habit now; he'd been staying away from her since the
night in the garden, when she'd put her lips on his cheek.

Kiss. Sometimes he tried not even to look at her. He'd scared her that night—he'd wanted to take his hands all over her, keep her in his arms and press his mouth against her skin, her hair, her mouth. He wanted to do that now. So he backed away and kept his distance.

The scent of her was exciting, confusing; she smelled of people and food and horses, and a hundred other things he couldn't name. Her face was pinker than usual, and she looked tired. But happy.

"I came to get a book," she said, looking at him, looking at the burning candle, wondering about him.

"Did you like the fair?" he said. He had no idea what a fair was.

"Yes. Oh, yes. It was—well, it's too late to start to tell you about it. Because it's too big, too—too everything!"

He liked seeing her like this, glowing and excited; it made her look even more beautiful. She had on a blue jacket made of velvet, unbuttoned so he could see the shirt underneath, white, with a blue tie, like a man's tie. Her skirt came down to her toes, and all he could see of her skin was her face. Even her hair was covered up with a hat, something blue with bird feathers and ribbon. She took off her gloves, and then he could see her hands.

"What are you doing?" she said.

"Looking at that book."

She went around the desk and touched his book. He was glad when she said the name out loud. *"Hudson Bay to Tennessee: A Field Guide to Eastern Forests."* She looked at him with curious eyes.

"I wish I knew the words," he admitted to her. It shamed him, but he could say this to Sydney. "I know what the pictures are, but I can't say the names."

"Oh." She nodded. She understood. "Well, I'll teach you."

He had to go closer, just a few steps. "You would?"

"Yes, I'll teach you to read."

"To read." Like Sam, he thought—he'd be able to read like Sam. It was too good. He put his hands behind his back and held them together tight. He could feel his face getting hot. *Blushing,* Sam called it.

Sydney didn't laugh at him. She knew what it meant, what he was thinking—she always knew. "We'll start in the morning," she said. "And afterward, I'll tell you all about the fair."

After three days, it came to Sydney why teaching Michael to read was so easy. Because she wasn't teaching him, she was *reminding* him. And he wasn't learning, he was *remembering.*

"Who taught you the letters? Who gave you your book? How did you first learn to read?" When the realization struck, she had bombarded him with questions, with no idea that they were distressing him until he turned away from her, shielding his face by pushing his fingers into the hair on the side of his head. His way of hiding; not unlike her father's, but more attractive somehow. "It's all right," she had said quickly. "It doesn't matter if you can't remember. What difference does it make? Let's go on. Can you read this?"

They had begun their lessons at a table out on the terrace, which was very pleasant, but they had had to move inside when Sam wouldn't stop pestering them. His lessons at school were nowhere near as interesting as these going on between his sister and his new, special friend, and he loved to show off his own brilliance by crowing the answers to questions Sydney asked before Michael could get his mouth open. So now they sat beside each other at the big dining room table, with the door to the hall and the glass doors to the terrace firmly closed, for two hours every morning—a light schedule she had set deliberately, so that he wouldn't tire of the task too soon.

But there was no chance of that. He was a teacher's dream pupil, dedicated, attentive, eager to the point of obsession. When their time was up, he stayed put and kept on working, and nothing could budge him but the maid setting plates and silverware around him in preparation for lunch.

Needless to say, Aunt Estelle didn't approve. Her protests were vague; this tutoring business was "unsuitable," she maintained, but without explaining why. Fortunately she was preoccupied by her duties on a committee of ladies charged with protocol for the visiting dignitaries, including minor royalty, currently flocking to the World's Fair. She spent her days in meetings or on the telephone with her sister-gatekeepers, too busy for once to supervise Sydney's life, however *unsuitable* it had become.

Once he had grasped the fundamentals, Michael's reading skills progressed rapidly. Writing was harder and came much more slowly at first. He wrote in big block letters, like a child, and she knew his efforts embarrassed him. But he plodded on, dogged and determined. She taught him to write his name first, after a discussion of the various possible spellings. Was he sure it was MacNeil and not MacNeal? Or MacNeill? Or McNeal, or McNeil, or McNeill? The more options she gave him, the more confused he became, but in the end he always came back to *MacNeil*. Did he have a middle name? Michael *James* MacNeil? Robert? Edward? George? He didn't know. He thought he might have, but he couldn't be sure.

It was at this point that Sydney realized she had an opportunity to kill two very large birds with one stone. Under the guise of helping him practice his writing—which was really no guise at all, since he certainly needed the practice—she asked him to compose reports each day, short writing assignments on any subject he chose, but with a strong suggestion that he pick topics with which he was most familiar—his own past, for example. *How clever,* she thought. She could teach him composition while she discovered, without the poking and prying that made him uncomfortable, all about his fascinating history. Ingenious.

The first report wasn't quite what she'd expected.

Sydneys dress was green blue this day like her eys. She has smal feet and flotes when she walcks. She lafs like music.

After that, she suggested the topics. "Write about animals—a particular animal," she advised. "You can use the books in the library to help you with spelling and so forth."

A porcupine has quills in the tail. When you catch it wrong, it shoots the quills into your hand when you pull them out the stinger stays in and your arm sets on fire. For days you are sick and red and hot.

She was profuse in her praise of this effort, and her approval elicited more on the subject the following day.

You can clime a tree to shake a porcupine out. You can smash it on the head with a rock. You might get quills in your hand but if you are hungre you will do it. The back legs have fat wite meat that tasts like pine tree bark because thats what he eets.

Her praise was slightly less enthusiastic this time. Nevertheless, Michael's knowledge of the porcupine wasn't exhausted.

Porcupines mate only one day in the year. It is in winter. The male should be very careful. She makes her tail go over her back so he can ly on a soft place. When the baby is born it has soft quills but they get hard in a our or two.

"That's enough on that subject, I think," Sydney decided. "For your next report, tell me about foxes. Or owls."

Foxes have a smell like a skunk but not as bad. They make a sound like Gak! Gak! They mate in spring. Not for life like wolves. A gray fox can clime trees but not a red fox. I made a fox friend. I got him out of a trap a hunter set. He was friends with me a whole summer.

The next day's report read:

> Owls wings dont flap. They fly with out making any
> sound. A baby owl is beautiful. It is mostly big yellow
> eys and soft wite down. They clack there beeks and
> act fearce until they know you. They have to practis
> all summer skwawking and rasping to sound like there
> parents. By fall they can make the low hoot hoot
> sound that is so nice to heer at night.

She began showing Michael's writings to her father,
thinking they would interest him. They did, when he had
time to read them. But he was already engrossed in a new
project, with Charles acting as his assistant again, and it
was hard to capture his attention.

> Men think animals like to fight but they dont. Well
> some do but only in the rut. The time of mating. They
> compare there size to see who is stronger and then
> they dont bother to fight. They try to scare eachother
> instead of fighting.
> The meanest animal is the wolverine. Wolves and
> bears are bigger but they will let him eet a deer first so
> they dont get into a fight with a wolverine.

Every day she learned something new. Wolverines
were the surliest, but badgers were the kindest of all the
animals. They were so sociable, they didn't mind sharing
their roomy underground burrows with other species,
even foxes. They loved to dance, Michael claimed, and at
night they came out and played games that sounded
remarkably like the games children played—tag, leapfrog,
king of the mountain. In fact, he insisted that all animals
played games. Otters built mud slides in summer and
snow slides in winter, for no other purpose but to have
fun. Flying squirrels waited until the hard work of getting
ready for winter was over, then had wild moonlit parties
in the trees, gliding down from the tops to the ground over

and over again like furry umbrellas, crossing and re-crossing, in and out of the bare branches.

"What about wolves?" she asked, remembering that Michael had told her father he'd lived with wolves. "Do they play, too?"

"Yes."

"Write about that, why don't you. I'd be very interested."

Wolves play. Wolves

That was all he wrote. He didn't want to give her his paper at all, and when she insisted, she saw that he'd scribbled a little more, but blacked it out. She looked at him curiously. He met her gaze, embarrassed but defiant. "I don't want to write about that."

"All right. Don't, then. Write about something else."

He wrote about the mother bear who let her cubs torment her all summer, biting her feet, ears, tail, endlessly wrestling with her, jumping on her stomach.

The most payshent animal of all is the mother bear.

His reading improved daily, and soon Sam's school primers were too easy for him. She went to the library and found more challenging books, on subjects she thought would interest him: animals, forests, a story about a boy and his beloved dog, another about a boy and his beloved horse. Michael devoured these books; he read them again and again and didn't want to part with them, until she brought home another armload and he fell in love with those, too. Sydney began to understand what dedicated teachers were talking about when they spoke of the joys and satisfactions of their profession. It was like watching someone being born. He had a million questions, and on some days they got no reading work done at all while she tried to answer them.

She had questions, too.

She found a book about a little girl who fell off her rocking horse and lost her memory. Even though it was much too young for him by now, it was perfect for the kind of discussion she had in mind.

"What would it be like to lose your memory?" she wondered leadingly. "Memories are part of what makes us the person we are, don't you think? What are your earliest memories, Michael? Write one down. Just for fun. Your earliest memory."

He didn't have to think about it. Without a second's hesitation, he wrote, *"My father taking me on a wauk."*

She was so excited, she forgot to correct his spelling. "You remember your father?"

He nodded.

"Who was he? What was his name?"

"Father." He smiled. "He smoked a pipe, like your father. But he wasn't old. He was strong. Tall—I thought he was a giant. Black hair, like mine. He gave me candy, I remember. Made me hunt for it in his pockets."

"Do you remember your mother?"

"I remember her laughing. I thought she was beautiful. Another time, I remember her painting pictures. In a room with high windows—all I could see was the sky. After that, she was sick. I had to be quiet."

"Where did you live?" she asked, breathless.

His eyes went out of focus, not seeing her. "A big house. It had a name."

"A name?"

"Yes, a title. But I can't remember it."

"What did it look like?"

"Stone. Long halls, dark. There was a lady who took care of me who wasn't my mother."

"A nanny? A nurse?"

He nodded uncertainly.

"Where was your house? In Canada? Was it here? Do you remember what state?"

He shook his head to all of those.

"How do you think you got lost?"

He pushed his chair back from the table and put his hands on his knees, staring at the floor between his feet. A lock of his hair fell over his forehead, obscuring his face.

"I think I did something wrong. Something bad. Because I was sent away."

"Oh, no, how could that be? You were only a child."

He lifted his head. "I'm sure of it," he said, and the pain in his light green eyes shocked her. "I was sent away across the water in a ship. With two people. Aunt and uncle."

"Your aunt and uncle?"

"I can't remember their names. But I knew them." He stood up. "I don't want to talk anymore."

"All right."

"I don't want to think about this."

"It doesn't matter. We'll do something else." And she asked him to write a paragraph about the seasons.

The next day, she took the train into the city. She had been to the Maritime Museum before, years ago when she and Philip were children, and again with Sam when he was about five. It was a big, dark, depressing building with a few interesting exhibits—lifesize models of Viking ships and Chinese sampans, a diorama of Columbus landing in the New World—but for the most part it was filled with dusty, glass-covered relics, like pieces of mast and sections of sail, and lifeless charts depicting the evolution of ships from the Phoenicians to modern times.

It also had a Great Lakes Room in which, among other things, the names of everyone who had perished in disastrous shipwrecks in the five lakes were inscribed in ledgers kept in a glass bookcase. To see the names one had only to ask one of the caretakers standing around in dark uniforms, looking bored and eager for a distraction, to unlock the case. On the train, Sydney had decided that to be on the safe side she needed to look at the whole decade of the seventies; that would allow plenty of leeway on either side of Michael's present age, as well as the age, approximately six years, at which he'd gotten lost.

Details of shipwrecks in the Great Lakes in the 1870s took up two books. They weren't thick, but the print was tiny, and the desk the custodian directed her to was dim, miles from the nearest window. For an hour and a half she pored over the names of steamers, schooners, excursion vessels, cargo barges, growing more and more appalled by the lists of names, names, names of the men and women who had gone down with them in the icy, gale-swept waters of Erie and Superior and Michigan. When a ship wrecked in winter, there were never any survivors; in the warmer months, there might be a few. She found some MacNeils, but the circumstances never seemed right. What would a little boy be doing on a coal barge or a navy motor launch? Or an iceboat? Her instincts told her to look for some sort of excursion ship or pleasure vessel, but there were no MacNeils among those lists. She wrote down anything that seemed remotely relevant, though, and went home feeling discouraged.

My father gave me a book on my birthday. It is called Now I Am a Man. He said read it and learn the lessons and when I see him again I will be a man. Then he sent me away.

"What was the book about?" Sydney asked. "What sort of lessons did it have?"

Rainwater in rivulets snaked down the long glass doors that led to the terrace. The dining room was dark and dreary today, and Sydney debated lighting the lamp. But she liked the watery, greenish light, the cosy mood it imparted to their sanctum.

Michael hesitated, then reached into the pocket of his trousers and pulled out something wrapped in a handkerchief. The object, once he had unwrapped it, bore no resemblance to a book any longer; it was a blackened, mottled, shapeless lump of pulp. But his hands were gentle when he touched it, and he laid it on the table in front of her with something close to reverence.

"It tells how to be a gentleman," he said simply, and if he was aware of the irony in that, he had accepted it so long ago that it didn't need mentioning. "It tells about honor and truthfulness. And fair play. Good manners."

"Ah." That explained so many things.

"I know it by heart."

Of course he did. She nodded, taken unawares by the lump in her throat. "You were a good student. You are a gentleman, Michael."

"No."

"You don't think so?"

"I know I'm not." He scooped up his book, carefully rewrapped it in the handkerchief, and stuck it back in his pocket as if it embarrassed him.

"Why do you say that?"

He shook his head at her. She heard exasperation in his sigh. *Are you really that thick?* he could have been asking.

"Why?" she repeated. "Tell me."

"Because I'm . . ." He waved his hands, as if he didn't know where to begin. "I can't even eat in this room," he finally exploded. "I know *words* about forks and napkins and glasses, but I don't know what to do. I can't make a necktie. O'Fallon taught me shoelaces, or I couldn't do that. I have a clock, but I don't know how to tell time. What does 'How do you do' mean? It's not a real question. 'How are you?'—no one wants a real answer. What do these words mean? What is the secret? I don't know who I am, I don't understand who I could be, or what I want to be, or what you want me to be. I'm—" He put his palms on his forehead and pressed. "I only know what I'm not. A gentleman."

"No, you're wrong." She was nonplussed, but she kept talking, to minimize the momentousness of what he had just told her. It was too big to face right now, with no preparation. "Some of that is hard—I don't know who I am, either," she confessed hastily, "and some of it's easy. I can teach you the easy things. I didn't even know you *wanted* to eat with us. Stupid—I should've known—I'm sorry. Manners, that's all that is. There's nothing to it. We'll practice."

"But the aunt won't like it. She doesn't want me here."

"Then we'll change her mind. These things that baffle you, Michael, they're just tricks, things I know because I've always known them. But they're not important, they're—"

"They are if you don't know them."

"You're right. Of course they are. So we'll start right now. And I know the first thing we're going to do."

"What?"

"We're going to cut your hair."

She decided to do it in the day parlor, where Sam was playing with his toy soldiers and Philip was stretched out on the sofa with the newspaper over his head, dozing. She wanted company, witnesses, lighthearted banter going on while she performed this intimate service for Michael. There was already tension under the surface of their quiet mornings together; no need to tighten that strain, she reasoned, with unsupervised physical contact.

"I love cutting men's hair," she said, unfurling a towel around his shoulders. He sat in a straight-backed chair in the middle of the room, stiff and stoical, nervously eyeing the scissors. "I should've been a barber. I'm good at it, aren't I, Philip? I used to cut your hair all the time."

"She cuts mine," Sam chimed in. He was trying to balance two of his soldiers on Michael's thighs, to "entertain" him while he got his hair cut. "Are you going to cut Michael's hair like mine?"

"Not exactly."

"Why not?"

"Because he's older."

"So what?"

"So he gets an older haircut." She smiled at Michael, who did his best to smile back. He had thick, straight hair, soft as black satin. She watched his eyes lose that alert, worried look and turn dreamy. His shoulders began to relax as she took the comb over his scalp slowly and gently. "Tell Michael about the barbershop at the Palmer House," she said, glancing at Philip.

He sat up, stretching his arms over his head and yawning. "The Palmer House barbershop? It looks like a church. No, a Roman bath. It's got eighteen-foot ceilings, mirrors everywhere. It's got about twenty barbers, all dressed up in tailcoats and studded shirts. Marble lavatories. If you want a shave you have to lie down in a sedan chair."

"Tell him about the floor," Sam urged, then blurted out, "It's got silver dollars all over it!" before Philip could speak.

Michael frowned, perplexed. "Why?"

"Silver dollars, right inside it, so you can see them. You can walk right on top of money!"

"They're embedded in the tiles," Philip explained.

"But why?"

Nobody spoke for a moment; everybody was thinking.

"Just for . . ."

"It's to . . ."

"It makes it . . ."

Baffled silence.

Philip sat back and stuck his feet up on the ottoman, rattling his newspaper. "Hell if I know."

"Hell if I know," echoed Sam. He picked up his soldiers and carried them back to the corner, pointedly avoiding Sydney's scowl.

Michael glanced at her. "You've stumped us," she told him, shrugged, and got on with her work.

"Are you going to cut off his beard?" Sam wondered presently.

Sydney had just been asking herself that question. "What do you think?" she said to Michael. Since O'Fallon's departure, no one had shaved him, and he had a glossy black beard she found very attractive. Still, she liked him even better clean-shaven. He had such handsome cheekbones, why cover them up?

He stroked his chin doubtfully and looked at Philip— the men's fashion expert. "What do you think?"

"Shave it," Philip answered promptly.

"Not even a mustache?" asked Sydney. Philip's dark,

dashing mustache drooped down and framed his mouth on either side like two commas.

"Nope. Shave it all off."

"Sure?"

"Sure. That way nobody will ever be tempted to call him the *wild* man."

Sydney winced. Michael only looked thoughtful, though, anything but hurt by Philip's lack of tact. "Yes." He nodded positively. "Let's shave it all off. It's cooler without it. Also easier to eat."

"Philip, will you help him shave? The first time, anyway?"

"Delighted."

"Thank you," Michael said formally.

"Don't mention it."

Sydney let a little time pass before her next suggestion. Michael's haircut was proceeding beautifully, if she said so herself. A little wildness wasn't a bad thing, she considered, deciding to let the ends curl just a bit around his shirt collar. On the matter of sideburns, she struck a happy medium: mid-ear, neither too long and exuberant nor too short and skimpy. Really, she would've made an excellent barber.

Leaning over him, blowing at the stray hairs on his neck, she accidentally blew in his ear. He drew in his breath with a gasp she hoped no one else heard, and gripped the sides of his chair with both hands. A muscle in his jaw jumped. He slanted her a glance, quick and frank, and the message in his light green eyes couldn't have been clearer.

Shaken, she stepped behind him and began to slap lightly, impersonally, at his shoulders.

"Philip, do you know what I was thinking?" she said, shaking the towel out.

"What?"

"I was thinking, Michael's been cooped up for ages; in fact, he hasn't *left* here since he *got* here. It must be getting awfully dull for him. Isn't it, Michael? So I was thinking, he'd probably like to get out, see something of the world, you know, see some faces besides ours."

Philip looked dubious. "I don't know, Syd. I'm not sure that's such a—"

"The problem is, there are a few little things he doesn't know yet. Things Papa would never think of teaching him, but, um, the sorts of things only a man can tell another man about."

Now Philip looked alarmed. "Like what?"

"Oh, you know." She shrugged, pretending to think. "Tying a tie, for instance."

"Oh, *that* sort of thing."

"Or things about clothes, you know, what goes with what. How to meet people, what a gentleman says when he's introduced—just simple things you take for granted. How to order a meal in a restaurant, how to pay for it."

"I see." Philip eyed Michael thoughtfully, then interestedly. "Sure, I could do that."

Michael's face broke into a smile of pure delight. "Thank you. You'll be a good teacher."

Philip grinned back. "We'll see."

"And meanwhile," Sydney went on casually, "I'll be passing on a few things about, oh, table manners and so forth, just drawing room etiquette he probably—"

"Now that his hair looks nice, maybe Aunt Estelle won't hate it if he eats dinner with us," Sam broke in.

She sighed, almost past embarrassment on Michael's behalf by now. "Maybe," she agreed. "Anyway, before that happens, we'll need to go over a few small—"

"And *I* can teach him arithmetic. Because I'm really, really good at numbers. I can teach you how money works, what a half dollar is and a dime and everything. And games, I can teach you how to play checkers and chess, and dominoes, and card games harder than Flinch. Rummy, you could learn that. Oh, oh—and clocks! I know how to tell time and you don't! I could teach you, Michael, and someday you could get a watch, and you'd always know what time it is. And croquet, that's not numbers or anything but I could teach you . . ."

He rattled on. Philip chuckled and went back to his newspaper. With the towel tucked under her chin while she folded it, Sydney darted a glance at Michael. He caught the look and thanked her with his eyes. Smiling back, she only hoped she deserved his gratitude, and that he'd still feel grateful in a day or two. No going back now, though; the die was cast. The Winter family had just taken on Michael MacNeil as their summer project.

8

Michael's sitting room was empty. Sydney knocked softly on the open door anyway, then came inside and glanced around, curious about how he lived these days. Charles had kept this room neat as a pin, as if he hardly used it. Michael, she saw, was a different story: he had turned it into a miniature natural history museum. Every available surface was covered either with books or the objects he was looking up in them—leaves, twigs, rocks, berries, pieces of bark, cracked birds' eggs, bits of nest, innumerable dead bugs, and a lot of other things too arcane or too dessicated to identify. Naming them had become an obsession with him.

A splash of bright color drew her to the table in front of the fireplace. Amid the clutter, she found the open tablet of drawing paper she had given him to replace the one O'Fallon had ruined. There were only a few blank pages left; all the others were filled with Michael's colored drawings of . . . she turned the pages interestedly, impressed by the vividness of the images even when the subjects eluded her. Was that a tree? Was this a bird? This a human figure? Mostly what she saw was color in big, brilliant swaths and busy, repetitive scratchings, so strong that the images buried among the intense hues seemed irrelevant. She bent closer, scrutinizing the lines and strokes. How did he get so much color out of pencils? He wet them, she realized, then laid the sides, flat and thick, against the paper. Like a brush.

She would give him watercolors next. In fact, she'd get them tomorrow.

Oddly excited, she turned to go—then stopped as she heard the murmur of a woman's voice from the bedroom. Inger, she guessed, either talking to herself or to Michael. Smiling, Sydney nudged the nearly closed door open and walked in.

Michael saw her first. He shifted his look of intense concentration from Inger to her, as if both women puzzled him equally right now. Otherwise he didn't move; he remained stiffly seated on the edge of his bed, thigh to thigh with Inger, who was pressing his hands to her big, corseted bosom and smiling at him with her eyes closed.

She opened them when Sydney shoved the door against the wall, so hard the knob left a dent in the plaster.

"Oh! Ma'am!" She jumped up, flushing scarlet. "I was—I was yust making the bed, and he was helping me," she blurted, backing away, as if she expected Sydney to strike her.

She felt like it. "Oh yes, I saw how he was *helping* you," she muttered, narrow-eyed and acid-voiced.

"We wasn't really doing nothing." One of the girl's thick yellow braids had come down; it hung on her half-exposed breast, coyly hiding the nipple. She looked ready to burst into tears. "We was yust sitting, honest. Please, ma'am, please don't sack me—"

"Go make somebody else's bed," Sydney snapped, and Inger darted around her to the door. "And stay away from Michael, do you hear?"

"Yes, ma'am."

"You're teaching him bad grammar!"

"Yes, ma'am!" She fled.

The thud of her footsteps died away quickly, and then it was as if she had left all her embarrassment behind in the room. Sydney couldn't even look at Michael; she turned her back on him and fiddled with the pewter comb and brush set on his dresser. An exasperatingly long minute passed before the bed springs creaked, meaning he had finally stood up. In the mirror, though, she saw that he was looking at the floor, not at her, and his handsome face reflected more confusion than contrition.

She faced him. Why should *she* have to break this nerve-wracking silence? "Well? Don't you have anything to say for yourself?"

"I've done something wrong." He rubbed the back of his neck. "What was it?"

"*What was it?* You—you were—" She stuttered to a stop. An impulse to yell at him, shout out sarcastic questions, had to be reined in forcibly.

"You're angry because of Inger?" He pointed to the open door—as if she might've forgotten who Inger was—sounding nothing but innocent. "Because we touched?"

"I'm not angry," she denied reflexively. "But, Michael, you can't *do* things like that."

"Why?"

"*Because.*"

"You touched West," he pointed out.

"That's different."

"Why?"

"Because it is. I *know* Charles. We were practically engaged!"

Her distress finally communicated itself to him; he looked at her closely, cautiously. "But Inger said she liked it. Do you think I hurt her?"

"No, of course not."

"I didn't."

"I *know* that."

"Okay." He smiled hopefully; his expression said, *So what's the problem?*

"This is not my job," Sydney mumbled, turning around again. "Ask my brother, he'll explain it to you."

"Ask Sam?"

"No, not Sam!" Could he possibly be pulling her leg? "Michael, do you really not understand any of this?"

"Yes, I understand you're angry. You say you're not, but you are. I'm sorry I caused this. I won't touch Inger again if you don't like it."

"It's not what I like, and I tell you I'm not angry!" She

lifted her arms and let them drop to her sides in frustration. "You're not the first man to trifle with the housemaid, and I'm sure you won't be the last. Oh, this is really none of my business. You do what you like, Michael, but take my advice. Next time, don't get caught."

Even in her own ears she sounded angry. It was that look of innocent bafflement on his face that kept getting to her. She left the room in a hurry, trying not to flounce.

Aunt Estelle was closeted with Papa in his study, trying to talk to him about a charity ball she wanted to host at the end of the summer. As usual he wasn't listening. Sydney couldn't decide if it was good or bad that they were together, and that she would only have to deliver her news once.

"Oh, Sydney—good," her aunt said, breaking off in the middle of an explanation of why it was vital for Papa to personally invite Marshall Field, whom he knew through their mutual interest in natural history. "Sydney, you explain it to him. All he has to do is speak to the man, quite casually, perhaps when they're both at one of their board meetings for the new museum. What could be more natural? Of course I'll send a formal invitation to Mrs. Field, but if you would only put a word in her husband's ear, Harley, I think we might really get them. Are you listening? Sydney, tell—"

"Aunt Estelle—Papa—I have to tell you something." They both looked at her sharply, arrested by her tone. She softened it deliberately. "I'm sure it's nothing to worry about. It's just that . . . well, Sam seems to be missing."

"Missing?"

"Mrs. Harp says he went out to play after lunch, and she hasn't seen him since." Mrs. Harp was the housekeeper. "He didn't go in the water," she said quickly, and their faces relaxed. "His bathing suit is here, and Mrs. Harp said he was walking toward the road, not toward the lake. He's probably just out, playing somewhere, and he's lost track of the time."

"But it's not like him to miss his afternoon snack."

"No," she had to concede. "It isn't."

"Perhaps he's with Michael," her father suggested.

"Yes, well, actually." She dreaded this. "It looks as if he probably is. Because Michael's gone, too."

"Harley, call the police."

"Now, Estie—"

"Don't say, 'Now, Estie.' Call the police. Your son's been kidnapped by a wild man, and you say to me, 'Now, Estie'?"

"Now, Estie, don't jump to conclusions. Nothing to worry about, chances are. You've tried calling them, Sydney?"

"Yes." Until her throat hurt. "They didn't take Hector. The odd thing is, Sam's taken all the money out of his little bank."

"There! The wild man's extorted it from him!"

As worried as she was, Sydney had to laugh at that. She went toward her father, drawn by his calmness. Even if absentmindedness was behind it, it was a comfort to her right now. "Sam's not at Billy Gaylord's house, and he's not at Todd Durham's—I called on the telephone. I'm going to walk down to the village and see if he's there. It's not like him, but if he took all his money, he must be planning to buy something."

"I say call the police."

"When did you last see Michael?" asked Papa.

"This morning. We—didn't have our lesson today, and he didn't come to lunch." Presumably because he was avoiding her. Should she tell them about the incident in his room with Inger? No. No. Why should she? It couldn't have anything to do with Sam's disappearance.

"We'll give them until dinnertime," her father declared with uncharacteristic decisiveness. He gave Sydney's hand a pat. "If they're not home by then, we'll think about calling the police."

"That's a policeman. See? They always wear long blue coats and coal scuttle helmets."

And carry black sticks, like O'Fallon, Michael thought to himself. "Do they hit people?"

"Sure! But only if they're criminals, like a murderer or a robber, or somebody who's drunk and gets in a fight. Mostly they just stand in the street and direct traffic."

That was what this one was doing, on State Street and Madison, which Sam said was the world's busiest corner. Sometimes Sam said things like that and they turned out not to be true, but not this time. Michael had to back up against the brick wall of a building so nobody would step on his feet. He had never seen so many people or heard so much noise in his life. Sam told him what all the vehicles rumbling and banging down the street were: brewery truck, ash wagon, gentleman's carriage, ice cart, milk cart, grocer's sled, hansom cab, waffle wagon, ladies' phaeton. Best was the cable car, which was really four cars stuck together and moving at the same time, pulled by *nothing*. Nothing you could see, anyway; Sam claimed it was electricity, but "Sparks" was all he could say when Michael asked what that meant.

"Why are they all rushing? What's happening?"

"Nothing, it's not a fire or anything. This is how it always is."

"Why?"

Sam shrugged. "I guess they have jobs, the men do, and they're going to them. Let's go look at those guys." He pointed across Madison Street to a giant hole in the ground with metal boards sticking up and men everywhere. "They're building a new building. Come on. Maybe it'll be a skyscraper!"

"A what?"

"Like that one. See? They call them skyscrapers because they're so tall they can scrape the sky. Not really, but they just say that. That one has twenty-one stories and it's the biggest building in the world. Once I went up in it. Sydney wouldn't go, she's afraid of heights."

Michael could believe it. It felt like walking into a bobcat's den on purpose, but he made himself follow Sam out to the curb and wait until the policeman blew an

ear-piercing shriek on his whistle, stopping all the carts
and drays and people and animals going in one direction
so the ones going in the other could cross over. The stones
in the street—cobbles—felt strange on his feet through
his shoes. A man coming toward him bumped his arm
and kept going; two ladies with parasols would have
smacked right into him if he hadn't dodged out of the way
at the last second. Sam grabbed his hand and told him to
hurry up.

They watched the workmen building the building for a
long time. The noise of their hammers and riveters and
saws was deafening, but after the shock wore off he
started to like it. He and Sam had to yell at each other to
hear. They weren't the only ones who liked watching men
at work; they were part of a crowd of people, mostly men,
standing around the giant hole. The metal boards were
steel beams, Sam said, and they were so strong they could
hold up a whole building. Michael, who had always
thought the strongest things were rock and wood, didn't
know enough words to express his amazement.

"Let's get something to eat," Sam said finally.

"Good idea."

"And you pay. Still got the money?" He grinned—that
was a joke.

"Yep." He had it in his trousers, weighing him down on
the right side like a pocket full of stones. This would be
the second thing he had paid for. The first was the steam
train tickets. Their trip to the city had been Sam's idea,
and the purpose was to teach Michael about money,
adding and subtracting and how to buy things from
people.

"Let's get a drink first. This place looks okay. I can
read everything on all the signs," Sam said proudly. "Can
you?"

" 'Three cents and five cents a glass, ice cold. Sar . . .
sarsa . . .' "

"Sarsaparilla soda. We don't like it."

" 'Strawberry, lemon, vanilla, cham . . .' "

"Champagne cider. We don't like it."

" 'Birch beer, root beer, ginger ale, lemon sour. Sporting goods, fishing tackle. Pipes and smokers' art . . .' "

"Articles."

" 'Articles. Try our milkshake, five cents. One cent for *The Tribune,* Chicago's greatest daily.' "

"Very good. What kind of drink do you want?"

Michael considered. "What's vanilla soda?"

"That's what I'm getting! It's the best. Let's go in, and you order."

He did, from a jolly-looking woman in a white apron. "Ten cents," she said after drawing their drinks out of a silver tube. Michael put all Sam's money on the metal counter and found a dime. "Thank you," he said, placing it in her fleshy palm, and she said, "Enjoy 'em," with a big smile. They drank their sodas right there, standing up, because the lady wanted their glasses back.

Outside, Sam told him, "When you just give her the money, you don't have to say thank you. Because you're giving it to *her,* see? But when she gives you the soda, then you say thank you."

"What do I say after she says thank you?"

" 'You're welcome.' Or you can say, 'Thank *you*,' but I never say that. That's more of a grownup's saying."

They had conversations like this all the time, Sam explaining the simplest things that Philip and even Sydney would never think of, never realize he didn't know. "Thank *you*," he said, and Sam laughed because he thought he was practicing. But he meant it.

"Come on, I want to show you something. I want to show you *two* things, and they're both on the same street."

They walked away from the world's busiest corner, past buildings twice as tall as trees, on cement sidewalks with glass "bull's-eyes," and sometimes you could see people through the glass and know you were walking right over them. Once a man dressed in a red and white suit with yellow paint on his face and a big red nose passed by, holding a sign that said MURPHY THE TAILOR, $10 SUITS, DIVERSEY BLVD. Michael stopped in his tracks to stare. "What is it?" he whispered, shocked and embarrassed, and Sam explained that it was just a clown. You were supposed to notice him and then go buy a suit at Murphy's. It took him almost three blocks to explain what a clown was.

The first thing Sam wanted to show him was a giant set of teeth that clacked all the time. They were above the door of DR. WALLS, THE PAINLESS DENTIST, and just down the street from the second wonderful sight, a pair of enormous eyeglasses at Dr. Kramitz's, with an eye behind one that winked at you slowly and constantly. Meaningfully. "It's kind of spooky after a while, isn't it?" Sam said, and Michael agreed. He liked the teeth better.

They were starving by then, so they bought hot chestnuts and red pop from a pushcart man. After that they bought two dill pickles, a bag of peanuts, four peppermint rocks, and a yard of licorice.

Feeling better, they went into a drugstore where Sam said you could play a record on the phonograph for a penny. They played "Mother's Smile" and "The Swiss Echo Song," and then they bought Michael a fifty-cent straw hat. "Men wear hats," Sam claimed, and Michael had seen the proof of that today. He looked at himself in the mirror on the drugstore counter, trying to believe he was that beardless man in a blue suit with a bowtie, and now a hat that had a black band around it and smelled like hay. Michael MacNeil? It couldn't be. He stared and stared, until Sam pulled him by the arm and dragged him away.

They rode in an elevator; they went six blocks in a cable car, standing up and hanging on to poles; got their shoes shined; looked in store windows at wax figures of people dressed in ready-made clothes, IN THIS STYLE, CHEAP AT $8.80. But the strangest, most amazing sight of all was the Magnificent Medici's Mysterious World of Magic.

They came upon it by accident, in a little green park by the train station. They heard the music first and followed it to a clearing in the grass surrounded by people, mostly children and their mothers. In the middle of the clearing were the Magnificent Medici and his helper, a beautiful lady who could play a harmonica and an accordion at the same time. Michael had seen Sam do card tricks before, so he had thought he understood magic. Now he realized the truth. Sam was a child and the Magnificent Medici was a master. And magic was . . . unexplainable.

"I can't see," Sam complained, so Michael got behind him and lifted him up. They both gasped when the magician pulled a white dove out of his tall black hat, and then a white rabbit. Red and orange scarves kept coming out of his hand, one after another, yards of scarves that he finally tossed to the beautiful assistant while everybody clapped and whistled. He did impossible things with four big silver rings, so fast Michael's senses were no use to him. He poured milk, ink, and water out of the same bottle. Finally and most wonderfully, he put the helper in a trunk, locked it, and made her disappear!

Michael's world tipped upside down, even while something in him said, *I knew it, I knew it,* and wasn't surprised at all. Things you couldn't explain happened all the time—what was the sunrise if it wasn't magic?—and this black-caped man with a waxed mustache was a reminder of it, maybe the *proof* of it. All the way to the train station Sam tried to convince him it was just tricks, mirrors and sleeves and fake trunk bottoms. Michael got tired of arguing and pretended to believe him for the sake of peace. But he knew better. The Magnificent Medici might be a fake, *might* be, but magic existed. He had seen it. He knew.

"Pipe cleaners, flypaper! Pipe cleaners, flypaper!"

He had learned by now that it was rude to stare, so he waited until they passed the little boy, even younger than Sam, standing by the newsstand with a tray in his hands. "Is he a clown?" Michael whispered. "Why is he dressed like that?" In ragged, dirty, holey clothes and a rope for a belt, a cloth hat that looked as if he'd been gnawing on it. He had a smart, playful, baby's face, like a fox cub, and two teeth missing in front.

Sam wanted to stare at him, too. "He's poor," he whispered back.

"Doesn't he have parents?"

"I don't know. Maybe not. He could be an orphan. He's not a beggar, though, he's a peddler. He sells flypaper."

"Let's buy it."

"Okay."

They bought all of it, and all the pipe cleaners, but the price only came to seventy-four cents. They still had two quarters left, just enough to get home on the train.

"Do you want this, too?" Michael said, holding out the quarters. The little boy looked at the money, and then at him. "You can have it if you want it. Fifty cents. A gift."

He had small, grimy hands with black fingernails. One of them reached out and plucked the two quarters from Michael's palm, quick as a snake, and stuffed them in his pants pocket. Then he looked scared for some reason, like a sick animal that doesn't trust you and doesn't understand why you'd give it your food. Without saying thank you he stuck his empty tray under his arm and ran away.

"Uh oh," Sam said. "Now what'll we do? How are we going to get home?"

"Easy," said Michael. "We'll walk."

"What were you thinking of? Just tell me that. Were you thinking at all?"

"I thought we'd be back. I didn't even think you'd—I mean—"

"You didn't think we'd notice you were gone." Aunt Estelle pounced. "Isn't that right? You *sneaked away,* didn't you?"

Poor Sam hung his head. Sydney would have felt sorrier for him if she hadn't been almost as angry as her aunt. "We didn't sneak," he said to the floor, "we just walked. And you shouldn't yell at Michael because it wasn't his fault."

"Don't you tell me whom to scold, young man."

"But I told him it was going to be a lesson. On arithmetic and how to—"

"Yes, yes, we've heard that. We know how you squandered your life savings on candy and nonsense and—a *hat*."

Michael paled a little under Aunt Estelle's withering glance. He looked miserable. Sydney would have wanted to hug him if she hadn't wanted to throttle him even more.

"Harley, do you have anything to say to your son?"

"Hmm?" Papa looked up from the chicken breast he was cutting on his plate. Dinner had been delayed because of the two truants, and he was hungry. "How'd the lesson go? Did all right, did he?"

Over his aunt's loud snort, Sam said, "Oh, Daddy, he did swell! He kept all the money and paid for stuff, and he got change and counted it right and everything."

"Good, that's—"

"Harley."

"Hm? Oh." He made himself scowl. "Can't have you going off like that, you know. Worried your aunt, worried your sister. Almost called the police on you. Say you're sorry."

"I'm sorry."

"That's it. Now—"

"That's *it*?" Aunt Estelle all but screeched. Michael and Sam, who had started to relax and move toward the table to take their places—Aunt Estelle had forbidden them to sit until their case was judged—stopped short. "You," she said, pointing a finger at Michael. She never called him by his name; either she didn't believe he really had one or she thought he didn't deserve it. "Leave the room. The family would like to continue this conversation in private."

Sydney's relief that he would be spared any more awkwardness and unpleasantness changed to distress when she saw his face. Aunt Estelle couldn't have said anything worse. "Oh, let him stay," she murmured in a rush, pushing back in her chair.

Aunt Estelle prevented her from rising by getting up herself and pressing Sydney down with a firm hand on the shoulder. "You will please go," she commanded, and

Michael, his rakish new hat incongruous with the hurt in his face, did as he was told.

Sam's eventual punishment was no dinner, confinement to his room tomorrow, and a three-page composition on the wisdom and necessity of obedience in children. Sydney had no quarrel with his sentence; what he had done was wrong, and it had frightened the life out of her. Still, she could never stand to see him punished for his childish misdemeanors, however much he deserved it. Tonight, as usual, she made an illicit visit to his bedroom prison and tried to sound stern while she comforted him.

"Well, what *were* you thinking of?" She sat beside him on his rumpled bed, letting him lean on her while he snuffled and blew into a handkerchief.

"I don't know. I didn't think anybody'd care."

"Sam, how could you think that? We were all worried sick."

"Daddy wasn't."

"Yes, he was," she denied automatically. "He just doesn't show it. I'm really disappointed in you, Sam. I thought you had better judgment."

"I've taken the train before," he said defensively.

"Not by yourself."

"I *wasn't* by myself. And Michael was perfect, Syd, and we had the best time—"

"Why didn't you ask permission?" He swung his legs against the side of the bed and didn't answer. "I think it's because you knew you wouldn't get it. Am I right?"

"I guess," he mumbled.

"And you really do understand why we're upset, don't you?"

"Yeah."

"Good. Then you won't have any trouble writing a three-page paper about it."

He fell back on the bed and groaned.

She laughed. "Hungry?"

"Yes!" He sat up like a jack-in-the-box. "What did you bring me?"

"Spoiled brat."

While he ate the chicken and tomato sandwich she had smuggled out of the kitchen, he told her why he and Michael had been so late. "He gave all the money we had left to this raggedy little boy on the street. So then we couldn't take the train, so he said we should walk. So we did, but I got tired, but he carried me piggyback almost the whole way. We went along the train tracks, and he can go *really, really fast*. All I had to do was hold his shoes, because he said they hurt his feet and made him go too slow. He went over rocks and everything, and it didn't even hurt him. People saw us but they didn't think anything of it—they thought we were playing, they didn't know how far we were going. And when we got home he wasn't even tired."

"Well," was all she could say.

"I made him buy the hat. He never had a hat before."

"That was nice of you."

"And I didn't care about the money, I *wanted* to give it to the little peddler boy, but I wouldn't't've if Michael hadn't said to first. I just wouldn't't've thought of it." He lowered his voice. "I don't think he really understands about money yet," he confided. "About saving and being careful and all that."

"Probably not."

"But only because he doesn't have experience. But we're going to teach him stuff, aren't we, Sydney? You and me and Philip, we're all going to show him how things work, right? So he can be a regular person."

She nodded, sliding an arm around his narrow shoulders. "That's what we're going to do," she agreed with a little more conviction than she was feeling. She kissed him on the top of his blond head and added, "But only *after* we ask permission."

Michael wasn't in his room. On an instinct, she went outside and walked down the path toward the lake. The moon, half full, had risen above the trees, and through the leaves she could see it sparkle silver on the jet black water. At the bottom of the path, she stopped to scan the shoreline and listen to the quiet clash of waves on the invisible sand.

A movement, dark against dark. Despite the distance, she knew it was he. She slipped off her shoes and stockings and started toward him.

His senses were so acute she could never take him by surprise. This time, though, circumstances—silent sand, the whispery tide, the wind's direction—were in her favor; with only ten feet separating them she stopped, unnoticed, and took the opportunity to study him.

He faced away from her, hands at his sides, staring at the moonshine on the water. His tall, straight, lean body always pleased her, and excited her when she forgot to be on guard against her feelings. She had had all day to mull over her reaction to Inger's uninhibited interest in him, but not enough time to reconcile herself to it. Right now, such thoughts seemed inappropriate, because the droop of his shoulders gave away his mood, and told her he needed her uncomplicated friendship more than . . . more than anything else.

He pivoted and dropped into a half crouch, so suddenly she jumped.

"I'm sorry—I didn't mean to startle you!" He had startled *her;* she put her hand on her chest, feeling her heart thump. He straightened and turned back toward the water—a telling and uncharacteristic snub.

"Are you all right?" She closed the distance between them, stopping behind him. He didn't answer. When she put her hand on his back, he jerked in surprise. "Michael, are you all right?"

He said, "No," very softly, and she smiled with a strange kind of relief. Whatever was bothering him, and she could guess at most of it, at least she wouldn't have to drag it out of him. He wasn't "civilized" enough yet to lie.

"Are you upset because of the things my aunt said?"

"Yes. Not only that. Anyway, she was right."

"Why?"

"Because I was stupid. Sam said we should go to Chicago, and I never thought about why it was a terrible idea. I never thought that he was too little or that he wasn't allowed to go. I didn't think about danger, all the things the aunt said could've happened."

"Oh. That." Aunt Estelle had recited a litany of catastrophes that might have befallen Sam today in the wicked city, a horrible list that could chill anybody's blood. "Don't think about that. Anyway, why *should* you have known Sam was too little?"

"I should have."

"But why? You're being too hard on yourself. Sam's the one who knew better, not you. In a way, he took advantage of you."

"It wasn't like that. He's a little boy. I'm supposed to be a man."

"But there are things you don't know yet because you *couldn't* know them. You have to have patience. Michael, turn around and look at me." He wouldn't move. "This is silly. Are you really ashamed of yourself? There's no reason to be." She rubbed his back, where her hand lay on his shoulder blade. Just for some comfort, friend to friend. But his muscles tensed, and she was intensely aware of the tough, smooth feel of him under his cotton shirt. "Let's sit down. That's not all that's bothering you. Come and sit down with me. We'll talk." She moved away, not looking at him but hoping he would follow, and found a smooth place in the sand in the shadow line of the pine trees. She busied herself smoothing her skirts and petticoats, and presently, out of the corner of her eye, she saw him come slowly toward her and sit down cross-legged by her side.

"Tell me about your exciting day in the city. Sam says it was perfect. Did you enjoy it as much as he did?"

Finally he looked at her, his transparent face somber and serious, and full of self-doubt. "I didn't know there could be a place like that. I could never have imagined it."

"Were you afraid?"

"No."

"What, then?"

Explaining things in words was still hard for him. "All

the people. Walking fast, rushing, pushing us out of the way. Their eyes, looking in instead of out. All with somewhere to go—even the animals. A job, a reason. A place they belong. I don't belong with them, and now I don't belong where I came from."

"Oh, Michael."

"No one stared at me, so it wasn't like before. This was the opposite. But the same. Because I'm still alone. I have no place and no work, no purpose. I was the lost man before, and nothing's changed."

His halting, soft-spoken analysis, delivered without a trace of self-pity, devastated her. She couldn't tell him he was wrong; his loneliness went too deep, cut too painfully to deny. She put her hand on the back of his, where it rested on his thigh. "I hate it that you feel this way. You're *not* alone. The things my aunt said tonight weren't kind, and they weren't true. You do belong somewhere, Michael. Here, with us, for as long as you want. Sam adores you, and—and you know how I feel." Of course he didn't. How could he, when she didn't know herself? She was glad when he kept silent and didn't ask her to explain.

"You've only been in this new world for half a year, and think of all you've accomplished. You can't see how far you've come, but we can. Why, immigrants to this country don't learn to read and write as fast as you have. Of course you're impatient, but it takes time. It just takes time."

They sighed in unison, and she thought they sounded equally dissatisfied with her little speech. She hadn't gotten to the heart of things, hadn't touched the real trouble.

He turned his hand over, and she automatically linked her fingers with his. He stared at their joined hands fixedly, as if they meant something to him, as if they were a symbol. Of what? Something she wasn't ready to acknowledge.

What would it be like to live for years and years without human contact, human touch? Unimaginable.

Without thinking about it, she leaned over and laid her cheek on their clasped hands.

He went very still. And then she felt his fingers on her hair, light and diffident, infinitely tentative. When she didn't move they grew bolder, combing the hair back from her ear and stroking her there, so gently, on her temple. She had hair like a fox, he'd said. That thought made her smile, in spite of the gravity of this moment. She could try to pretend nothing important was happening between them now, that they were friends, and friends could touch each other like this—but it wasn't true. She was loath to move or speak, because this was lovely, and if she tried to define it or put it into words, to him or even just to herself, she would spoil it. So she stayed still, with her cheek on his hand, and let him stroke her hair, her face, with his slow, feather-light fingers.

"I'm sorry about this morning," he said, not stopping the gentle caress. "With Inger. I didn't understand. But I thought about it all day, and now I do."

"You didn't do anything wrong." She had thought about it all day, too.

"I did, but not on purpose. I won't do it again."

"Oh . . . it doesn't matter."

"It doesn't?"

Reluctantly, she sat up. "I shouldn't have lost my temper," she said evasively.

"But it matters, doesn't it? To you?"

The earnestness in his face was too much for her. They were on dangerous ground, but she couldn't bring herself to lie to him. "Yes, it matters."

He nodded, satisfied or relieved, almost smiling. "I only touched her because I was interested. To see what she felt like. And she didn't care—she told me to do it. But I shouldn't have, and now I know why. It's because she's only a woman. She's not you."

"You shouldn't . . ." Thoughts crowded her mind, but she couldn't focus on a single one. "You shouldn't say things like that."

"Why?" He brushed her cheek, and when she kept her

eyes down, he ran his thumb along the line of her lashes. "Is it rude?"

"No . . . You shouldn't touch me like this."

"You don't like it?"

She couldn't help smiling, and then he put his fingers on her lips, making them quiver.

"Do you like West better than me?"

"Oh, Michael," she wailed softly.

"Do you?"

The wisdom of lying crossed her mind again, but only for a second. "No," she whispered against his fingertips. "I like you much better."

He searched her face. "Is that true? But how can it be? West is a man, he's always been a man."

"Michael," she laughed, "what do you think you've always been?"

He shook his head, frustrated again because he didn't know the right words. But then he smiled; she saw the white flash of his teeth in the dimness. He slid his hand to the back of her head and bent to her, pressing his face against her neck, breathing in deeply.

Stunned, addled, she let him nuzzle her, holding on to his arms when he would have slipped them around her shoulders. *It's not kissing—we're not kissing*—she concentrated on that as he took his mouth over her throat, her jaw, the side of her face. He didn't force her, but she was in thrall to the fascinating novelty of his ardent, artless caresses. A purring noise, something between a growl and a hum, sounded deep in his throat, scaring her and thrilling her at the same time. The stars wheeled, and she found herself on her back on the soft sand, with Michael's hands pillowing her head and his face buried in her hair. His bent knee lay heavy across her legs. She let the gentle, unskilled ravishment go on, even when he started to explore her body, stroking her side, her stomach, the curve of her hip.

"Why do you always have so many clothes on?" he mumbled, rubbing his mouth against her skin above the low collar of her shirtwaist. "Can you take some off?"

"Oh, Michael. Stop." His innocent question woke her up to the danger in this too-natural passion, rising in her like a fast tide. "Don't." She pulled on his wrist, but in the next second he found her breast and gave it a soft, fervent squeeze. "Oh, God," she moaned and rolled to her side, sitting up, turning away from him. She heard the harsh pant of his breath, and wondered if he was trembling as badly as she was.

"Did I hurt you?"

She shook her head, wrapping her arms around her knees, wondering how in the world she was going to explain this to him. She heard the soft rasp of sand, and turned to see him walking away from her. "Michael?" He didn't turn. She would have scrambled up and run after him, but he only went as far as the shoreline and stopped, to stare out at the water.

This was all her fault. She had wanted to comfort him, make him feel *less* alone, and through her own weakness and thoughtlessness she'd just isolated him more. But she was out of her depth. What had just happened was as bewildering to her as it was to him. While it was going on it had seemed so natural, so . . . inevitable. Now . . .

She understood exactly how it had started. Telling Michael she liked him better than Charles had sounded like permission to him, a tacit invitation to any intimacy he could think of. He had seen with his own eyes what she had allowed a man she *didn't* like; small wonder he'd assumed she would go even farther with *him*. Oh, what a mess. If he was in pain because of her, she couldn't stand it. She stood up—at the same moment he turned around and started toward her.

"I'm sorry," they said in unison, and she put her hands on his forearms and kept talking. "Michael, it was all my fault. You don't have anything to apologize for. The best thing for us to do is forget it happened."

"Forget? Forget?"

"Put it out of our minds, go back to the way we were. Be friends again, just friends. Because we just can't—do that." She gestured behind her, embarrassed.

"Because I did it wrong and you didn't like it," he guessed, watching her again, searching her face. All his senses were focused on her, and when that happened she could never think straight.

"It's not that," she hedged, letting go of his arm.

"You did like it?"

She huffed out a nervous laugh. "Michael, this isn't something I can talk about very comfortably. Men and women—they don't usually speak of it. Not to each other."

"They don't?"

"No." She had never even spoken of it with Spencer.

"Then how do they know what to do? How do they ever become mates?"

She laughed again, a childish sound, practically a giggle. It embarrassed her so much, she whipped around and started walking. He followed, hands in his pockets, glancing at her from time to time. Waiting for his answer.

"I wish there was someone you could talk to about this. This sort of thing. Another man."

"Your father?"

"No. Ha. No. That's not a good idea." Maybe the worst idea he had ever had.

"Philip?"

"Not a good idea, either."

He sighed. "Who? I don't know any other men. Except West. I'm not going to ask him."

"Oh, no," she said faintly. "No, I wouldn't ask Charles."

"So you have to tell me." He stopped, forcing her to stop with him. "Sydney, tell me what I should do. If you don't want me, say that."

"Oh, Michael, no."

"I'll go away if you want."

"That's the *last* thing I want!"

"Are you crying? Are you laughing?"

She covered her face with her hands, mortified.

"I'm going to touch you now," he said in a warning tone, and put his arms around her.

It was exactly what she wanted. And although she knew

it would double his confusion, she hugged him back with all her strength. They stood that way, swaying, holding on to each other in blessed, merciful silence, even after the embrace stopped being for comfort and started being for pleasure. Because this was so much better than talking, she told herself. But the real reason was because she just couldn't let him go.

"Okay," he said finally, the first to draw away. She loved it when he said okay—when he sounded like Sam. "If you can't talk, it's all right, Sydney. You can tell me what to do without words." As if to test her, he put his hands on the sides of her face and slowly, hesitantly, slid his fingers into her hair. Now was the time to pull gently away, to send him the kind, wordless message that this was nice but it wasn't allowed. Instead she closed her eyes. What was it about the way Michael touched her sometimes that made it so much easier to give in than take a stand? She felt his breath, then his lips on her cheek in the slightest of kisses, and she thought, *Oh, this is allowed. This is very much allowed.* How natural it would be to turn her head now, ever so slightly, so that their mouths could kiss.

But he drew away again, and she opened her eyes to find him smiling at her. "There's a bird—I don't know its name, I haven't found it in the books yet. The male picks the female he wants to mate with, and then he courts her. At first she doesn't like it. He brings her gifts, special bugs he finds just for her, but she won't eat them."

She folded her arms. Easy to see where this story was leading.

"He has a dance he does for her, and she likes that. She lets him touch her with his beak while he does the dance, not much but a little. It's like kissing."

"Mm hm."

"It takes a long time, but he doesn't give up. Because he really wants her. He has to have her. And she's not pretending—she really doesn't want him. At first."

"What finally changes her mind? Bigger, better bugs?"

"No." His smile turned doubtful. "I don't know, I'm

not sure. I think it's that he doesn't stop. He just keeps trying. Maybe . . ." He shot her a sly glance from under his lashes. "Maybe she takes pity on him."

She laughed, and he laughed with her, his face delighted and self-conscious. "So," she said as they began to walk back toward the path and home. "The moral of the story is that persistence pays off in the end, is that it?"

It felt right when he caught her hand and swung it between them as they walked. "Persistence," he repeated, trying the word out. He sent her another sideways look, and this one was downright crafty. "Yes, that's the secret of the story. That's the moral. Persistence pays."

9

"Am I dreaming or are you still here? When the hell do you ever sleep?"

"It's morning," Michael explained, stepping back from the bed and, out of politeness, not wrinkling his nose. Philip had that nasty, sweet smell that O'Fallon used to have; it meant he'd drunk too much whiskey the night before. Michael knew this for a fact, because he'd helped put Philip to bed last night when he'd been too drunk to do it himself. "It's almost afternoon, in fact. You said to wake you up because your aunt would have your head if you missed lunch again." *Have your head* was just an expression, though; even the aunt wouldn't really cut someone's head off.

Philip pushed back the covers and sat up, groaning and running his tongue over his teeth. His legs hung over the side of the bed, bare under the long shirt he wore to sleep in. Sometimes he wore a cap, too, and when he got ready for bed he put on a soft robe over the shirt and cloth slippers on his feet. His bed had four pillows, two white sheets, blankets at the bottom, a colored quilt, a feather mattress with springs under it, and a tent thing on top called a canopy. Michael could never get over how many soft objects people needed to have on or under or over them just to go to sleep.

He stood at the foot of the bed while Philip got up and shuffled over to the washstand. He poured water from the pitcher into the bowl, stuck his hands in, bent over, and splashed the water on his face and neck and hair, making loud, pained noises the whole time. "Towel," he said with his eyes closed, searching for it with one hand. Michael spied it on the floor, where Philip had thrown it last night, picked it up, and handed it to him. "Thanks."

"Don't mention it." He sat on the edge of the bed, leaning his shoulder against the tall wooden post. Watching Philip get dressed in the morning taught him something new every day. He could tie a Windsor knot in his necktie now, and sharpen a razor on a leather strop. He knew how to part his hair neatly on the left side (where Sydney said it "parted naturally"), clean his teeth with sweet powder and a brush, and cut his fingernails with a miniature pair of scissors. Philip had given him some of his old clothes, and he was learning what went with what. You couldn't wear a frock coat in the morning, and even if it was gray you could only wear it with black trousers. You could wear a morning coat all day and even at night, but only if it was black. You could wear a lounge suit with a colored shirt and a white collar, but only a white shirt with a frock or a morning coat. If you were a "sporty fellow" you might wear a striped or a checked lounge suit, but otherwise you were better off "sticking with solids." Silk lapels were "de rigueur," which was French, and creases in your trousers were "all the go," which was slang. Philip put Ricard's Brilliantine on his hair and Merchant's Lime and Spice Cologne for Men on his face, but here Michael drew the line. They smelled wrong to him, false, more like medicine than a man.

"Do you have a hangover?" he asked, watching Philip rummage through his wardrobe for what he was going to wear today. He had a man named Martin who usually helped him get dressed, but this was Martin's day off.

"How clever of you, Michael. You've got those razor-sharp senses working this morning, I see."

Philip talked like that sometimes, grumpy as an old bear, but Michael had learned it didn't mean anything. "What does a hangover feel like?" he asked.

"Feels like almighty hell."

"Yes, but how?"

Philip threw off his nightshirt and stood there naked, staring blankly into his wardrobe. His body was perfectly white and unscarred, and Michael couldn't help envying him. "How does it feel? My head's pounding, my stomach's rolling. My mouth tastes like a privy. My brain isn't working, and I think I did something to my neck. Anything else you want to know?"

"Yes. Why do you drink when you know it makes you sick in the morning?"

Philip pretended to tear out his hair. "Will you please shut up? If you were any sort of friend you'd refrain from asking stupid questions this early in the morning. At least until I get my bearings."

Michael laughed, because it made him happy to know that Philip thought they were friends. He shut up, and just wandered around the room looking at things while Philip put his clothes on, shaved, brushed his hair, trimmed his mustache, and stared at himself in the long mirror. By the time he pinched off a flower in the vase on his mantel and stuck it in his buttonhole, Michael figured he had his bearings and it was all right to talk.

"What's it like going to college? What will you be when it's over?"

"Damned if I know."

"Don't you like it?"

"I hate it. I'm flunking out."

"Why? You mean you're failing?"

Philip wound his watch, slipped it into his waistcoat pocket, and flopped down on top of his bed. He put his hands behind his head and crossed his feet, and with his eyes closed he said, "Failing. That's it, Mike. I'm failing."

"Mick."

"What? Say again?"

A gruff voice. Wrinkled face, white whiskers. *Want to ride up here wi' me, young Mick?* Dry, scratchy hand reaching down, pulling him up into the high seat of a coach.

That was all; the memory faded, wouldn't go any farther.

"That's what somebody called me. Mick, not Mike. A nickname."

Philip sat up on his elbows. "Do you remember something?"

"Just that. A man. I think he was . . . No, I don't know." It was just out of his grasp, like smoke drifting away.

"Sydney's detective hasn't found anything yet. It's early, though. Probably can't expect anything this soon."

"What? Sydney's what?"

"Oh, hell. You didn't know." He rubbed his face with his hands. "I guess she didn't tell you so you couldn't be disappointed."

"Tell me what?"

Philip sighed. "She hired a detective. That's somebody you pay to find things out, investigate things for you. Fellow's name is Higgins. Sydney gave him your name and your history, what we know of it, and told him to find out who you are and where you came from."

Michael sat down at the foot of the bed slowly. "She did this? For me?"

Philip nodded. "You can't remember anything about the shipwreck at all?"

"Shipwreck." Something was wrong with that word, but he wasn't sure what. "No, I can't remember." Sydney had hired a detective to find out who he was. It might mean she wanted to get rid of him, but he didn't think so. He thought it meant she cared about him.

He said, "Are you going to get married soon?"

"Am I what?" Philip's eyes popped open. "What kind of a question is that?"

Michael ducked his head; he'd said something wrong. "If you want to mate with a woman, you have to marry," he explained shyly. "So . . . do you want to mate?"

Philip looked amazed, as if Michael had told him something he didn't know. But how could he not know *that*? Then he started to laugh. He put his hands on his temples and groaned. "Oh God, it hurts. Don't make me laugh."

"What's funny?"

Philip just shook his head.

"Tell me. Explain it."

"Oh, God," he said again. He sat up and put his feet on the floor. "I don't know who you've been talking to, but that's not exactly the way it works. Not for men, anyway." He rubbed his cheeks and plucked at his mustache; he looked uncomfortable and amused at the same time. "I didn't expect to have to have this conversation with anybody but Sam."

Michael turned away, embarrassed. He was still a child in the world of men, and whenever he started to feel confident about himself, something always happened to remind him of it.

"Listen," Philip said kindly, "it's really not that complicated. You understand about—mating and all that?"

Not really. "I understand what happens."

"Well, that's a start. We call it—well, we call it a lot of things, but 'making love' is one of the nicest, I always think. It's usually a euphemism, but that's what makes it acceptable in polite company. Following me?"

"No."

"Ha." He put his hands on his knees and started pinching the crease in his trousers. "The thing is, sex is different for men than it is for women. We can have it before we get married, but they can't."

"Who do we have it with?"

"Aha. Leaped right on that one, didn't you? The ostensible flaw in the system. Well, my boy, we have it with any woman who'll let us, that's who. Usually they're not so-called *respectable* girls, not our *sort,* you know. But not always. No indeed, not always. In fact, you'd be amazed."

Michael pondered that for a while. "So we do it in secret?"

"Absolutely."

"So the respectable girls won't know?"

"Now you've got it."

"Do all men do it?"

"No. Most, though. Some even do it after they're married. Which is called infidelity—not being faithful.

It's frowned upon, but done anyway. Definitely done anyway. Well!" He stood up, looking relieved. "That's over, time for lunch."

"Do women like to make love with us?"

"Hm? Some do. It depends on how good we are at it. But we *always* like making love to *them*. That's one of the fundamental distinctions between the sexes."

"Are you joking now?"

"Not a bit. Aren't you hungry? Come on, I'm starving."

"If Sydney is a respectable girl but she doesn't have a husband, how can she make love?"

Philip stopped halfway to the door and turned around. For a long time he just stared, with a look on his face that was surprised at first, then sad. "She can't," he said in a quiet voice.

Michael stared back at him, wanting the answer to be different. "She can't?"

"No. She can't." No joking, no wry tone of voice now. Just the three words, flat and heavy as stones. "Come on, Mick, let's go have lunch. Come on, there's a good lad. Afterward, I'll give you a tennis lesson."

Sydney looked beautiful. She had on a yellow dress with a white flower at the breast, and she had yellow ribbons in her hair, curling through it like vines. He smiled at her across the dining room table, and everything Philip had just told him flew out of his head as soon as she smiled back.

But she was sitting next to West. West came to the house all the time, almost every day; he might as well still be living here. *I know Charles—we were practically engaged,* she'd said that time they'd quarreled about Inger. Michael scowled at him, hating his smell, sharp and artificial, sickeningly sweet. Didn't she smell it? How could she stand it?

Dr. Winter was talking about the new project he and West were working on. Something about "the evolution of reciprocal altruism" and whether is was "in danger of being overwhelmed by the short-term advantages of selfishness." Michael couldn't follow any of it. No one but West looked interested, as usual, but they let him go on. They all liked Dr. Winter, even though he was weak, not the leader. Sydney's eyes softened when she looked at him, the way a mother wolf's softened when she played with her pups.

The maid took away the soup bowls and brought in the salad. Michael had learned to like the sour-tasting sauce they put on it. He even knew which fork to use, without having to sneak a glance at Sydney to make sure. In fact, meals were almost pleasant times these days. Not the stomach-churning trials they used to be, when he lived in fear of committing some awful mistake that would make the aunt glare at him. She'd never *said* anything when he'd eaten potatoes with his spoon or forgotten to cut his meat before he ate it, but she didn't have to. She didn't hate him as much as she used to, he thought, but it was hard to tell. She never talked to him, and hardly ever looked at him.

"Samuel, stop kicking the table."

"Yes, ma'am."

Michael used his napkin to hide behind while he smiled at Sam. Sam grinned back. He had taught Michael the most important lesson of all about dining with the family: how to sneak food you didn't want to Hector. Hector would eat anything, even vegetables, and he was good about not gobbling it under the table and making a lot of noise.

The clock over the sideboard chimed two times.

Sam said, "What time is it, Michael?"

"Twelve-thirty. Half past twelve."

"What's the date?"

"Tuesday, July the fourteenth. Eighteen ninety-three," he added—showing off for Sydney.

Sam looked around at the family proudly. "He can do the times tables up to twelve times twelve. He can do long division."

"He can beat you at chess," Philip threw in.

"He can beat you, too!"

"Samuel, don't shout at the table." The aunt rang a little bell, and the maid came back in to collect the plates.

Next came some kind of meat, hot and smoking and swimming in a brownish broth. The vegetable was peas—the worst kind, almost impossible to sneak to the dog. Michael ate some of the meat and pushed the peas around, hiding them in the gravy. He wondered what was for dessert.

The aunt said, "Reverend Graves sent a note, Harley, thanking us for our generous contribution to the church restoration fund."

"Hmm? That's nice, Estie."

Philip laughed. "You didn't tell him Papa's an atheist, did you, Aunt E?"

"I certainly did not." She looked down her long nose at Philip, giving him the look that always made Michael feel like sliding under the table.

"Know what an atheist is?" Sam asked him.

"No."

"It's somebody who doesn't believe in God."

Sydney said, "Papa believes in evolution instead of God."

The aunt made a disgusted sound.

Michael, who had been wondering about God lately, looked at Dr. Winter with interest. The family went to church every Sunday, to "worship" God—all except Dr. Winter, who stayed home. "Who is God, exactly?" he got up the courage to ask.

Everybody stared at him. It was almost like the time he gave Sydney the fish.

"God," the aunt said firmly, "is the Father of us all and the Creator of the universe."

Dr. Winter cleared his throat. "God," he said less firmly, "is a mental construct, the natural product of the collective yearning for meaning and immortality."

Across the table, Sydney snickered. "Aren't you glad you asked?"

Dessert was a cooked apple with a sweet sauce and

whipped cream. Michael cleaned his plate and hoped for seconds, but the maid never came back.

"May I please be excused?" asked Sam. The aunt said yes, and he scrambled out of his chair and ran off to play.

Soon after that everybody got up. Michael wanted to talk to Sydney, but West got to her first. He pretended to listen to what Philip was saying to him, something about changing into white trousers for their tennis lesson, while he watched West put his hand on Sydney's back and make her walk out to the terrace. Were they arguing? Sydney was smiling with her mouth but not her eyes; when she turned toward the door, West moved to block the way and wrapped his hand around her arm.

Philip was still talking, but Michael walked away, not even saying excuse me, and went to Sydney.

"I can't, Charles. It's just not possible."

"Why not? You could if you—" West saw Michael and frowned. "Did you want something?"

"I want to talk to Sydney."

"Well, *I'm* talking to her."

"I don't think she wants to talk to you. I don't think she wants you to touch her."

West had a wet, pink mouth behind his reddish beard. It made an O shape, and his small black eyes went big with surprise, then narrow with anger. Nobody moved or said anything. Michael glanced at Sydney. He thought she looked embarrassed, but also alert and interested, not mad. He wanted West to do something, hit him or shove him, so they could fight.

"Sydney?" It was the aunt, calling from the dining room. "Come inside, please, I need to speak with you."

"Will you excuse me?" Sydney was trying to sound natural. Michael said nothing; West said nothing. She moved away carefully, watching them until the last second, and then she disappeared through the door.

West was weak, white, puny; there was no point in fighting him—he would lose. But he didn't seem to *know* he would lose. So Michael told him with words, "Don't touch her again or I'll fight you."

A vein in West's forehead began to throb. He moved two steps back and hunched his shoulders, trying to make himself taller. The dislike that had always been between them finally showed its face. "Lay a finger on me, and I'll have you put right back in a cage."

"I'll kill you first," Michael said calmly, and it was the truth, not a threat. He'd been in a cage. Metal bars and a wire mesh, a box too small to stand up straight in. They hadn't kept him there long, only about two weeks. Any longer and he would have died.

The longest minute passed.

"Tennis, anyone?"

West jumped and then turned pale from relief. Philip was leaning in the doorway with his ankles crossed and his arms crossed. His face looked like Sydney's—very interested.

Michael backed up, not taking his eyes off West until Philip threw an arm over his shoulders and gave him a little shake. That broke the tension. "Let's play," Michael said. He turned his back on his enemy and went off with his friend.

Aunt Estelle preceded Sydney into her sitting room and sat down in her favorite chair, a padded rocker conveniently stationed between the window and the fireplace. It was a lovely room, maybe the house's prettiest, beautifully proportioned and charmingly furnished; it even had a view of the lake through a distant break in the trees. The thought had crossed Sydney's mind a subversive time or two that it would make a far better drawing room for guests than the larger, darker, colder "blue room" they had always used. But it was an idle notion. This was Aunt Estelle's room—they even called it that—and it would be forever. She met with Mrs. Harp here every morning on housekeeping matters; she spoke on the telephone to her acquaintances, staging her social sallies and coups; she kept up her prodigious correspondence. And she sewed.

Beautifully, exquisitely. Of late Sydney thought Aunt Estelle had grown slightly ashamed of the occupation, uncomfortably aware that it smacked just a bit too much of the *middle class*. Real ladies, meaning the idle rich, didn't sew because, of course, they didn't have to. But she couldn't give it up; she loved it too much. She got too much satisfaction from the precision and discipline fine needlework demanded.

She patted her lap, and Wanda the cat instantly jumped up onto it. Wanda lived in Aunt Estelle's sitting room, having yielded the rest of the house to Hector in a not entirely bloodless coup. She was a skinny, nervous, high-strung animal, all white, very proud, and stingy with her favors. She liked Aunt Estelle, who doted on her, but barely tolerated anyone else.

Aunt Estelle's sewing basket sat on the table at her right hand, but she didn't reach for it. She had that look about her, her stiff posture more correct than ever, lips pursed, brows raised: it meant she was preparing to do her duty. Sydney had an inkling of what their little chat was going to be about. She'd been half expecting it. The only reason it hadn't happened sooner was because she'd been avoiding her.

"Mr. West seems very attentive," the older woman opened mildly. "I believe he's quite taken with you."

Sydney drifted away from the window and sat down on the violet plush loveseat opposite her aunt's chair. This wasn't at all the subject she'd been girding herself for. "Charles? Oh, I don't know. He's fond of me, I suppose. Nothing stronger than that, though, I don't think." She fingered the grosgrain ribbon trim on her skirt casually, keeping her eyes down.

"Are you sure? I had an idea his regard might go a little deeper than fondness."

"Oh, no. Oh, I should be very surprised if that were the case."

"Well, I daresay you know best. At any rate, I hope it goes without saying that an attachment of *that* sort would be completely out of the question. I'm sure Mr. West is a fine young man, and your father seems fond of him—for what that's worth. But a relationship with a gentleman of his class that went beyond the most casual friendship would, of course, be quite unsuitable. I'm sure you agree."

She did, in this case, although for different reasons. "There's no need to concern yourself about Mr. West, Aunt. Really, I don't think of him at all."

"I'm glad." She sat back, unbending a little.

Sydney couldn't help wondering what her aunt's reaction would be if she were to say right now, "Actually, I'm involved with someone else these days—it's Mr. Mac-Neil. When he looks at me in a certain way I can't breathe, and when he touches me I'm completely lost." She lowered her head and went back to worrying the ribbons on her skirt, half afraid the flush on her cheeks would give her away. "Is that what you wanted to speak to me about?" she asked hopefully.

"No, something else. Something I expect you won't care to hear."

Immediately Sydney felt sixteen years old again—the age she had been when her mother died and Aunt Estelle had taken responsibility for her and her brothers. When would she outgrow this childishness? When she was forty? Fifty? "What have I done this time?" she muttered, trying not to sound truculent.

Aunt Estelle clicked her tongue. "Nothing, of course, don't be silly. I'm concerned about you, that's all. We've been home for nearly two months, but the changes I'd hoped for haven't occurred. In fact, as far as I can see, we might as well have stayed here."

"I have no idea what you mean."

"Europe was supposed to be a turning point for you, Sydney. A new start. I thought you understood this; I thought we'd agreed on it."

"But it *was*. I *have* changed."

Aunt Estelle had a way of narrowing her eyes into slits when anyone said something she regarded as nonsense. Words weren't necessary; the look itself could reduce the nonsense-speaker to squirming embarrassment. "Come now. If anything, you've declined more invitations since you've been home than before you left." Methodically, she ticked examples off on her fingers. "The Renfrews' house party. Margaret Ellen Wilkes's birthday tea. The Fourth of July weekend at the Swazeys'. Edward Bertrams's perfectly nice invitation to the theater. Even Camille Darrow complains that you're neglecting her."

Sydney couldn't deny any of it, so she decided to defend herself with the truth, although not all of it. "Yes, but it's been wonderful spending time with Philip and Sam. I'd missed them so much. And now that Papa's had to abandon his lost man project, the responsibility for Mr. MacNeil has fallen, naturally, to—to the rest of us. I must admit, I find it all fascinating. His development, I mean, the way he's adapted to the family, his growth as a—"

"Yes, yes." She shook her head once dismissively. "Those are excuses, Sydney. Now, listen to me. Spencer has been dead for a year and a half, and the time has come for you to think about remarriage. *Think* about it," she stressed when Sydney opened her mouth to protest. "It may be unfortunate, but society has certain expectations of a woman in your position. Widowhood past a certain point in one so young is suspect."

"Suspect?"

"Like it or not, a single woman can't remain single *and* respectable indefinitely."

"But that's absurd! You've never been married, and society's certainly never questioned *your* respectability."

"Don't be obtuse. One thing has nothing to do with the other."

"Why not?"

"For heaven's sake, Sydney. Because no one questions the virtue of a plain-faced old maid, not in the way they do that of a young and attractive widow." She closed her lips and tightened the muscles of her face, tapping her toe on the carpet in a show of impatience. Or was it distress?

Sydney watched her, a little unnerved by the implication in her words, and even more in her manner, that she wasn't as satisfied with her lot in life as Sydney had always assumed she was. What if—remarkably, the thought had never occurred to her—what if Aunt Estelle had once had different hopes for her life? Girlish dreams of a lover, a husband, a home and children of her own? With any other woman, such a speculation would come naturally, automatically; with Aunt Estelle, because of her reserve and her seeming lack of sympathy for the bulk of humanity, the thought had simply never entered Sydney's head.

"You're not plain," she said tentatively. Insincerely. "You're not old, either."

It was almost a relief when Aunt Estelle slitted her eyes and thinned her lips, as if to say, *Stop wasting my time with your foolishness.* Sydney was on surer ground with *this* Aunt Estelle, the no-nonsense one, for whom sentiment was only another name for vanity. "This is all beside the point I'm trying to make," she said, picking up Wanda and gently setting her on the floor—a sure sign that she was getting down to business. "I was speaking to Mrs. Turnbull on the telephone this morning."

Sydney slumped a little in the loveseat. "Oh?"

"She mentioned how very busy you've been lately. Too busy, evidently, to accept any of her son Lincoln's three—*three*—invitations to accompany him, with his family, to the World's Fair. And so I must ask you. Do you know of some blight on the character of this young man of which every other unattached lady in the city is unaware? Some stain on the reputation of this upright, churchgoing, charming, and agreeable paragon, who will one day inherit his father's considerable banking and financial interests? Because if you do, I would be most—"

"Of course I have nothing against Lincoln," Sydney said crossly, goaded into interrupting. "How could I? He's everything you say he is. He's *perfect*."

Aunt Estelle permitted herself half a smile. "I'm so glad you think so. Then you won't mind that I've invited the Turnbulls to dinner on Friday."

Sydney sighed, feeling tired, and wavering between exasperation and amusement. "How enterprising of you," she said dryly.

"My dear, I had thought your return from Europe would mark your new coming-out. But since that hasn't happened, something new is needed now to signal your debut. I think it should be the charity supper dance we're hosting next month."

Sydney slumped a little lower.

"It's a perfect opportunity. The best people are coming—your father's gotten a yes out of the Marshall Fields, did I tell you?—and you'll be comfortable because it's here at home. It's a perfect time of the year for an outdoor party. Supper inside, I think, but dancing on the terrace afterward, with plenty of young people of the right sort for that. And since the ostensible purpose is to raise money for the historical society, you won't feel as if you're on display. Which reminds me—I was thinking you might want to wear a pastel evening gown. White is out of the question for you now at formal occasions, but something in a pale blue or even a bright yellow—heliotrope is very good this year—would send the right message. Remember, most of these people have seen you in nothing but black for the last year and a half."

She had thought it all out. The old childish passivity descended on Sydney as she listened to her aunt go on, and on. There was no point in arguing; it would only cause unpleasantness, and Aunt Estelle's will was almost always stronger than Sydney's in matters such as this. Much easier to suffer in silence for the sake of domestic peace. Anyway, it was only a party. Who knew? It might even be fun.

Tennis didn't seem to be Michael's game.

He wasn't interested in the rules, and he didn't like keeping score. What he liked was whaling at the ball as hard as he could and smacking it as far as it would go. Which usually meant out of the court and into the weeds. Then he and Hector played a game of who could find it first. Hector always lost this game, unless Michael took pity on him and let him win.

Playing with Michael required a lot of patience, Sydney

could see, watching from the bench behind the sideline. Luckily Philip was genuinely fond of him. They had a funny relationship, she reflected; they seemed to take turns being the older brother. Philip was more worldly, naturally, but Michael was wiser and infinitely steadier, even in his naiveté. Each offered something the other lacked, so the fact that they had nothing in common was no handicap at all to their unique friendship.

"I've brought ice water," she called.

Michael started toward her, but halted when Philip said grimly, "Not until we've finished this set. It's your serve, MacNeil, and if you don't put it over the net and in my court, I swear you're going to be wearing a racket necklace."

Michael made a face of mock terror at Sydney that tickled her and made her laugh. "Yes, sir," he said, saluting—a bit of nonsense Sam had taught him. Then he threw the ball over his head and slammed it out of the court.

He was better at croquet. He could swim now, too— Philip had taught him that. He no longer needed Sydney's help with reading, but she still gave him writing assignments, and still read the results with fascination.

And he painted the most incredible pictures. Giving him watercolors had been like setting him free. His pictures defied description, at least by her. They reminded her sometimes of the Impressionist painters, but they could also be earthy and grounded and wonderfully realistic. After all the years of solitude, Michael had stories to tell and things to say, and he could express himself more naturally in pictures than words. Interesting that one of his earliest memories was of his mother painting. Papa ought to be studying *that,* Sydney realized. Didn't it make a strong case for the superiority of heredity over environment?

The hot sun shifted; she moved down on the bench, angling her wide-brimmed hat to shield her face. Watching Michael, she found herself remembering again, as she did much too often, that night on the beach when he'd touched her so intimately. The incident stood out in her mind like a mountain among foothills, not a second of it lost or forgotten. It had been as thrilling as her first kiss, or even—this was disloyal—the first time she and Spencer had made love.

In truth that night, her wedding night, had been a disappointment to her, although it was only lately that she'd been able to admit it. She'd wanted *passion* from Spencer, the missing ingredient in their comfortable, lifelong friendship, and she'd had a hope that the intimacy of marriage would miraculously provide it. It hadn't, but she had never had the courage to tell him. Now she would never know if he'd felt the same, if he had also wanted more and not known how to ask for it.

But they'd both been so young, and constrained by delicacy and convention and some strange shyness, an unavoidable legacy of their upbringing, she supposed. How could it have been otherwise? They'd been more like brother and sister than lovers. And at the end she had reconciled herself to believing that comfort and companionship were more important than the quick and unreliable heat of physical desire. Perhaps they were, but it was clear to her now that she'd compromised her hopes, and hidden the truth even from herself that she needed more.

Aunt Estelle wanted her to settle again, this time with Lincoln Turnbull. Sydney had nothing against Lincoln— how could she? There was nothing wrong with him. Like Spencer, she had known him forever; he'd even been in their wedding party. He was strong and athletic, good-looking in an earthy, bullish, thick-necked way. She could imagine him touching her easily, imagine there would be *passion* with Lincoln. But she didn't want his big, blunt hands on her. She only wanted Michael's.

Could he read her mind? Their long set wasn't over yet, but at that moment he abandoned Philip in mid-serve and jogged across the court to her. Philip called out some humorous insult she barely heard. Sweaty, panting, lean and graceful, impossibly beautiful in his hand-me-down tennis whites, Michael smiled down at her, not saying a word. He didn't have to say anything—it was all there in his eyes, alert and hot, sweeping her with a glance that left her light-headed, her fingertips tingling.

"I brought some water. I put it in the shade. There." She pointed, looking away.

"Thank you." He found the wicker-wrapped bottle beneath the bench and uncorked it. She feasted her eyes on him while he tilted his head back and took a long, serious drink, the cords in his neck stretching tight, his strong Adam's apple rising with every swallow. Perspiration dampened his collarless white shirt, making it stick to his back. He'd unbuttoned it halfway, and she could see his dark chest hair, shiny and alive, soft-looking. His tanned forearms rippled with wiry muscles, and Philip's old trousers hung on his hips just right. Her leisurely, spellbound survey came to a startled halt when she realized for the first time that he was barefooted.

"Doesn't that hurt your feet?"

"Doesn't what hurt my feet?"

What was that slight, barely discernible *something* in his speech? Too faint to call an accent, and yet . . .

"What?"

"The ground, the court. I should think it would be rough on your feet."

"No," he said, smiling as if she'd said something funny. "*Shoes* hurt my feet."

"Oh."

They continued to beam at each other.

"I made a painting of you this morning. I did it from my memory, not from looking at you."

"Not from life, we say."

"Not from life. Sometimes I start to paint a picture of something, but it turns into you. The clouds on the lake or the trees at night—they turn into you. It happens all the time."

Persistence pays. So did sweet words and heartbreakingly earnest flattery. Sydney shook her head slowly, tongue-tied.

"This morning I tried to paint you with the sun on your

face, but I got it wrong. I didn't have the colors right for your hair. Or your lips. Maybe those colors don't exist except in you. Perfect."

"Oh, Michael." It came out a whispery sigh. "Michael, you're trying to seduce me."

"Seduce?" He drew the word out; it sounded juicy and delectable on his lips. "Seduce." He smiled, and she knew he'd grasped the meaning from the context. *Bigger, better* bugs, she thought disconnectedly. Oh, this bird was weakening.

Over Michael's shoulder, she saw Philip hit one last practice serve against the backboard and then trot over toward them. She cleared her throat, to warn Michael he was coming.

"You lost," he grumbled, snatching the water bottle out of Michael's hand. "Six-oh, six-oh, forfeit."

Michael grinned. "I can hit higher than you, though. And farther, too."

"A useful skill if you're a discus thrower." Philip shook his hair back and wiped sweat from his forehead. How handsome they both were, Sydney marveled to herself. Could she say that out loud? She wouldn't have hesitated if her feelings for Michael had been less personal. As it was, silence was probably the better part of discretion.

"You and Sam still going to the fair tomorrow, Syd?" Philip pulled the ends of a towel back and forth behind his neck.

"Yes, in the afternoon." His eyes lit up when she added, "Camille wants to go, too. Her parents are still away, and she says she's tired of going with Claire and Mark. Do you want to come with us?"

He tried to look nonchalant. "Maybe. Yeah, if I'm not doing anything. Sounds all right."

Michael, she saw, was edging away from them, his face expressionless. Excluding himself from the conversation. Or were they excluding him?

"Michael, you can come, too." It popped out without premeditation.

Philip stopped in the act of tying his shoelaces. "Say,

that's an idea. Talk about a fast education, eh, Syd? Why didn't we think of it before?"

Michael turned around slowly. "Come with you? To the World's Fair?" He glanced between them, almost as if he expected a trick. A slow smile, tentative at first, bloomed on his face.

He looked so thrilled, Sydney felt ashamed. Why *hadn't* they thought of it sooner? She'd wanted to protect him for a little longer—that was part of it. She'd also been fearful, not quite sure of him, and not ready to take the chance of something awkward or embarrassing happening to him out in the real world. But whom had she really been protecting?

Thoughtless, she chided herself. Blind. She was as bad as her father—worse, because she'd been selfish, too. Michael deserved better.

But he wasn't going to punish her for it, that was certain. "Tomorrow, in the afternoon," he said eagerly. "If we stay until night, we can see the lagoon and all the lights." He pulled himself up, and his eyes went wide. "My God," he breathed.

"What?" said Sydney.

"What?" said Philip.

He looked like Sam on Christmas morning. "I'll get to ride on the Ferris wheel."

IO

"Why didn't you tell me he was gorgeous?"

There was no place left to sit in the Palace of Fine Arts, so Sydney and Camille were leaning against a bare patch of wall in the French Room, drooping with fatigue, while Michael reexamined every painting from close up and afar. If he'd had a magnifying glass, Sydney was sure he'd be using it.

"Gorgeous?" She laughed, as if the word surprised her, as if she hadn't thought the same thing herself more than once. "Do you think so?"

"Oh, my, yes. And he's not at all what I expected. He's so . . . *civilized*."

"Heavens, Camille. Did you think he'd wear a loincloth and swing from vines?"

"Well, yes," she admitted, giggling, and Sydney rolled her eyes. "No, but really, Syd, *look* at him. He looks like someone you'd love to meet. Not quite respectable, you know. Someone my parents would disapprove of. Just the way he *stands*."

Philip, whose idol these days was Oscar Wilde, had taught him to stand like that, with his hands in his pockets and his hip cocked at an angle, shoulders slightly hunched. It made him look careless and worldly, two things he definitely was not. But Sydney loved the combination of outward sophistication and inner simplicity. They made for a unique persona, funny and touching, and to her, unbearably sweet.

"And I *love* his hair. Did you really cut it for him? I

think he looks like a poet. But a dangerous one. Because of the scar."

Camille giggled some more, and Sydney couldn't help laughing with her. But it was more out of habit, a lifetime of giggling with Cam, than true amusement. The way she spoke of Michael, as if he were an object instead of a man, albeit a "gorgeous" one, didn't sit quite right with Sydney. And when Cam talked *to* Michael, she raised her voice and spoke in slow, simple sentences, as if he were deaf as well as dim-witted.

It was exactly the sort of thing Sydney had been afraid would happen, the sort of thing from which she'd wanted to protect him. He took it well, she had to admit, waiting through Cam's ponderous sentences with a courtly, puzzled politeness, letting her patronize him outrageously. He was much more gracious about it than Sydney—but she was overly sensitive where he was concerned. She'd have to work on that; it implied a lack of confidence.

On the other hand, he still had a few quirks that might reasonably shake a less protective person's confidence in him. Right now, for instance, he was carrying his shoes while he padded, in a pair of Philip's argyle socks, between paintings by Rousseau and Daumier and Renoir. But the World's Fair stretched over five hundred acres, so he wasn't the only tired sightseer who had chosen stock-inged feet over blisters. He blended pretty well with the crowd, in other words; he looked a little eccentric, but his public identity as the "lost man," that wild-looking fellow whose picture the papers had stopped running only recently, was still a secret.

Camille and Sydney were in his path; otherwise Sydney doubted he would have noticed them. Dazed-looking, he stopped in front of them, blinking them into focus. "I'm taking too long," he said. "You're tired of waiting."

"It doesn't matter." Sydney smiled her forgiveness. "We've missed our meeting time with Philip and Sam, but they know where we are. They'll come and find us."

"I'm sorry."

"Never mind, you were enjoying yourself."

"I got lost."

"Lost?"

"Inside the paintings." He glanced at Camille self-consciously, as if he knew she wouldn't understand, then back at Sydney, as if he knew she would. "When I try to see how they do it, when I get close up to the brush strokes and the shapes, I lose myself. I fall into the picture." He smiled, shrugged his shoulders. "I'm not saying it right."

"Sydney tells me you're quite the painter yourself," Cam raised her voice to say. "Were you a frustrated artist when you lived in the wild?"

He regarded her steadily. "I was," he answered, straight-faced. "After food, the thing I wanted most was a nice set of watercolors."

Philip and Sam arrived just then, and Sydney couldn't decide if she was glad or not. Michael's sense of humor was growing along with his appreciation of human absurdity, and each day it came out in a new way. It would've been fun to see how much longer he could tease Cam, who was famous for her habit of blurting out absurd things in moments of social stress.

"You're still here? You've been here the *whole time*?" Philip looked amazed. The plan had been to meet under the Columbus statue at two-thirty. The fallback plan, the one they had quizzed Sam on at least twice a day to drive the point home, was to wait twenty minutes and then return to the place where they had all been together last.

"It's because of me." Michael spoke up quickly. "I forgot about time. They waited for me."

Sam grabbed Sydney's hand and shook it to get her attention. "We heard a concert on the telephone!"

"No."

"Yes! It came all the way from New York City, and you could hear it as plain as day. Couldn't you, Flip?"

"Yep. In the Industrial Building. They hooked up loudspeakers to a telephone and broadcast a concert going on in Madison Square Garden."

They all shook their heads in wonder.

"How come you stayed here so long?" Sam dropped Sydney's hand and took Michael's. "You could've come with us and heard the concert. What were you doing?" He searched the room, looking around for something more interesting than framed pictures.

"Looking at the paintings."

"Just looking at them?"

Michael nodded, shrugged. "I like them."

"Is anybody else starving?" asked Philip.

"I am," they all answered at once, and they left the Fine Arts Palace and headed for the Midway.

Deciding where to eat at the fair was never easy. The Chinese market, the Japanese bazaar? The Irish village? The Moorish palace? Old Vienna? This time, after the requisite bickering, they decided on the Tunisian café, on the grounds that the service was fast and it had the shortest line. A waiter in a yellow robe and a turban took their order. "Try the coffee, Michael," Philip advised, and of course he did. When it arrived, he took one sip of the thick, treacly brew and went into a coughing fit.

"Aagh," he sputtered, eyes watering, blinking at Philip in disbelief and suspicion. "Bleck. It's awful."

"It's an acquired taste," Philip said blandly, taking a small swallow from his own cup. He crossed his legs and sat back, throwing his arm across the back of the empty chair beside him. Striking a pose, Sydney suspected, for Camille's benefit. It did him no good; Cam was too intent on smacking Michael between the shoulder blades while he choked on his coffee.

The bickering started again as soon as they finished their Tunisian tea. *We're tired,* thought Sydney as she listened to Sam whine that he wanted to go see the ten-ton Canadian cheese and then the Wild West show, Philip insist he wanted to stand outside the Columbia Theater and wait for a glimpse of Lillian Russell, and Cam counter that she and Sydney were dying to hear the all-female orchestra at the Women's Building.

Into the sullen silence that followed, Michael said, "I want to see everything." Of them all, he was the only one

who didn't look exhausted. "The whole world is here, all
the things I've never seen. Everything's beautiful."

That stopped the quarrel more efficiently than a fierce
look from Aunt Estelle. They all felt chastised, then gal-
vanized. With new energy, they went off to look at the
Yerkes telescope and the model apartments where a family could live on five hundred dollars a year.

There is always a long line of men who want to see
the guns in the War Department exhibit. Today Philip
and Sam wanted to go, so I went too. There were
canons, rifles, pistols, knives, bayonets, and sords, and
everybody stared and stared at them as if they were
great works of art. I thought of the hunters who came
to the woods in every season, even when the snow was
high, to shoot guns at bears and beavers, otters, deer.
They shot at me, thinking I was an animal. They
caught the wolves in metal traps, and murdered fox
mothers in their dens for their skins, leaving the cubs
to die. They made rope traps that choke to death rab-
bits and squirrels and even birds. Every season they
came, and they killed to slaughter, not to survive. The
smell of guns, which is oil and cold metal and smoke,
makes me feel sick and scared. It means death is
coming.

Tonight was an illumination night, when they turn
on electrical lights all over the Fair. If you stand on a
bridge and look down at the black water of the
Lagoon, you can see the lights twinkling like a hundred moons. It's magic. I never thought anything
could be prettier than the stars coming out one by one
when night fell on the woods where I lived. But this is
even more beautiful. There are people to see it with. I
stood next to you, Sydney, on a bridge and looked at
your face while you looked at the lights and the foun-
tains and the real stars over our heads. Just in that
time, that minute, I never was so happy.

Later, when we were walking beside the water, I

thought about the word "lagoon" and the word "lake."
They made me remember something. I used to live
near a lake when I was little, before I was sent away.
But we called it a lock. There were no buildings, only
trees around our lock. My father took me there to fish.
And we lived in a stone house that I think is called a
castle. Or maybe my mind is mixing this up with one
of Sam's fairy tales?

Today West came to the fair with us. We saw a rose
plantation, an electrical train, and also the kineto-
scope, which is a camera and a phonograph working at
exactly the same time. We played a trick on West by
taking him to the nudist colony. This is an exhibit on
the Midway that you go to with high hopes of seeing
naked people but it is a joke. You look through a hole
and see your own head in a mirror, and under it is a
painting of a naked body that doesn't show anything
interesting. West pretended to laugh, but we knew he
was really disappointed.

He reminds me of a wolf I knew a long time ago.
Wolves don't have names, but to myself I called him
Sneaky. He wasn't good for anything much except
eating meat some other wolf caught. He wanted a mate
but none of the females would have him. He especially
liked a young gray wolf with black ears and paws and
a white tail tip. She was beautiful and gentle and
playful, and she tried to be nice to Sneaky even though
he was a pest. But she never mated with him. She was
strong and he was weak.

I always thought she shouldn't have been so kind to
him. Then he'd have stopped bothering her and found
a mate who deserved him. Some scrawny, lazy she-
wolf as ugly as Sneaky.

Michael hated the Hamburg parrots.
"I'd set them all free if I could," he swore, striding
away from the exhibit.
Sydney had to hurry to keep up with him. "But they

couldn't survive here on their own," she pointed out reasonably. "They'd die."

He came to a sudden halt. "A *thousand*, Sydney. Why so many? It's crazy. I could look at one parrot and understand all parrots."

"I agree with you." She'd rarely seen him so worked up.

"They should be where they came from," he insisted, starting to walk again. "Not in cages."

"They didn't look unhappy," she ventured.

"They looked bored."

For the sake of peace, she didn't ask how an *interested* parrot would look. She changed the subject. "Tell me what else you remember about Scotland."

It worked. He said, "Scotland," reverently, and stopped scowling. "I wish I could remember something more. Anyway, we don't know for sure that I come from there."

"*I'm* sure of it. Where else do they have lochs? But the real proof is your accent. My father noticed it, too—I read it in his notes."

"I don't hear any accent," he said slowly, listening to himself.

"It's faint, but it's there. A wee bit of a brogue," she said humorously. "It means you came from Scotland, I'm sure of it. This gives us something else to tell Mr. Higgins, the detective." When he didn't answer, she said, "Michael, don't be afraid to hope. You might have a family—think of that."

"But what if I never find them?"

"What if you do?"

He shook his head; he wouldn't smile. "Maybe they don't want me. If they sent me away—"

"They didn't."

"I think they did."

"I had no idea you were so stubborn." He looked at her, alarmed. "Or such a pessimist," she threw in.

"What's a pessimist?"

They had arrived at their destination, the spectacular McMonnies fountain. They were supposed to wait here for Philip and Sam, who had gone to look at the battleship

Illinois. "A pessimist is someone who always expects the worst."

"I don't do that."

"He can't look on the bright side, because he's afraid of being disappointed."

He looked down at the ground. "I do that. I'm afraid. I don't want to find out that they threw me away."

"Oh, Michael." She had the strongest urge to touch him, push the black hair back from his forehead. "They *couldn't* have done that, I know it. I wish you'd believe me."

She saw the hope and fear in his eyes, and the gratitude when he smiled at her. The tenderness. Her heart caught. "Let's sit down here, Sydney." He took her hand. "Are you tired?"

There was room for them at the end of a long bench full of exhausted sightseers. The lagoon sparkled at their backs, and the fountain splashed in front of them. Clouds were bunching overhead; it was starting to look like rain. "Not too tired," she answered. "But you are, I think."

He always told the truth. "I feel like my head is blowing up."

And he was nervous these days, restless and distracted, sometimes even irritable, although not with her—not yet. "You need a break from all this. It's too much. You're overstimulated, you need a rest."

"No, I can't stop. I have to see it all."

"But you have time. The fair will be here for months."

"I'm not like you—I can't see things just once and know them. It's all new, so I have to go back again and again."

She sighed. It was true; he really couldn't stop. He wanted to come every day, and when that wasn't feasible, he found books in her father's library about the things he'd seen at the fair the day before. He knew more about classical architecture now than she did, which wasn't saying that much, and a great deal more about electricity, agriculture, and mining. He still dutifully completed the reports she assigned—"Write a paper on what we saw at the fair today, Michael"—and she read them with fascina-

tion, especially when they revealed more about his earliest memories or the details of his life in the wilderness.
Or when they sounded more like veiled love letters than
"reports" . . .

A drop of water fell on her wrist. "Uh-oh. It's raining."
More drops spattered on the warm concrete walkway. The
crowd filing past them began to hurry, and the bench on
which they were sitting started to empty. "We can't
leave—they'll never find us if we move." She glanced at
Michael. He had turned his face up to the sky; he was letting the rain fall on his fluttering eyelashes while he
smiled gently, blandly, drawing in deep breaths of the
wet, fresh air.

"We're going to get soaked," she said practically.

"Open your umbrella. This won't last."

"It won't?" He was never wrong about the weather.

"Let's just sit and look at the people."

It was his favorite thing to do. He was still too shy to
enjoy speaking to strangers, but he never got tired of
staring at them. He was entertaining while he did it, too.
"I knew a badger who looked just like him," he would
say, gesturing toward a kindly-looking, pointy-faced old
gentleman with round spectacles. Or, "Look how sleek
and satisfied she looks, like an otter with a bellyful of
fish," about a particularly well-turned-out matron.

Sydney unfurled her umbrella and held it between
them. Michael moved closer so that they were hip to hip
and took hold of the umbrella, too. They sat without
speaking, both absorbed in watching the parade of
passersby, hurrying for the exits or for shelter.

"I dreamed about home last night."

"Home?"

"I dreamed I was lying on the side of a hill with the old
wolf. I told you about him, remember? My friend."

"I remember."

"It was summer. Hot. No clouds. We weren't hungry,
and there was no danger. All we could smell was the
earth and the air. There was nothing but peace. And there
was nothing—between me and the earth and the sky." He

frowned, choosing his words carefully. "I mean there were no borders between me and everything around me. It was as if I had no skin. I was free."

She looked at his clean profile, the intensity in his face that mirrored his struggle to tell her the truth. "It's not like that now," she murmured, guessing at the point of his dream, even though she didn't particularly want to know it. "You're not free here."

"No, I'm not free anymore. Life is complicated. Choices I don't understand. So many possibilities. Like a chess match—I have to think about what will happen three or four moves in the future."

She gave his fingers a squeeze around the handle of the umbrella. "I never thought of it that way." She waited a moment, then said casually, "Do you think about going back?"

"Yes, I think of it. When my brain is full, when it feels like it'll explode if I put one more fact in. Then I think of going away." She felt chilled until he added, "But I can't now. I've changed too much. I think I would die if I went back. Not of cold or hunger. Of loneliness."

She didn't know what to say. There was a sadness in him she wished she could ease, but alongside her own melancholy was a ferocious relief, because he couldn't leave. She had him for good.

"Most of the time I can't believe I'm here. Now, for instance—sitting with you on a bench in this place. In this city. With shoes on my feet."

They laughed. "Very nice shoes, too," she noted. Philip had taken him to Field's and had bought him the best they had, sturdy English walking balmorals in fawn-colored leather. He wore them every day, and claimed they didn't hurt his feet a bit.

"It's because of you that I am here."

"What do you mean?"

"For me, you're like . . . a light when it's dark. You make me feel strong even when everything is changing and going too fast."

"Michael."

"I think it would scare you if you knew what I feel," he said softly. "It's as if there's a storm inside me. There's no peace, but it doesn't matter so much. I'm not just surviving, I'm alive. And I know what I want."

He spoke with his eyes lowered, as if to spare her the intensity that he had correctly guessed would frighten her. Once again she couldn't think of the right thing to say. Their pattern was for her to discourage him now, turn him away from these thoughts, these dangerous words. That would be rational and safe.

But what if she took the next step? What if she threw away caution and sense and went forward, *toward* him instead of away from him?

"Your brothers."

"What?" She didn't want this spell to break.

"They're here. Someone's with them."

She looked up with a pasted-on smile, which faltered slightly when she saw who Philip and Sam's companion was.

"It stopped raining," Sam greeted her. "Why do you still have your umbrella up?"

She closed it without answering, and turned her smile on Lincoln Turnbull. "Why, what a nice surprise. Twice in one week—what a coincidence." She had seen him at a party last Saturday, where, with Aunt Estelle's guidance ringing in her ears, she had made an unusually strong effort to be cordial to him. "How are you, Lincoln? Where did you find these two?"

"On board the *Illinois*," he told her, holding her gloved hand for rather a long minute. "You look wonderful, Sydney. Did I tell you that the other night? Either way, it bears repeating."

"He's been on the battleship *five times*," Sam marveled. "He showed us stuff even the guide didn't know about. Special guns and stuff, and where they keep the ammo."

Lincoln smiled, ruffling Sam's hair. "Ships interest me."

"Especially *battleships*," Sam specified, and Lincoln nodded, grinning.

There was a pause. With odd reluctance, Sydney turned

toward Michael, who had taken a step back from the group, and lightly touched his arm. "Lincoln, you haven't met Michael MacNeil, our—house guest. Michael, this is an old friend, Mr. Lincoln Turnbull."

"How do you do?" Michael said courteously and held out his hand.

Lincoln said "MacNeil" in a loud voice and gave his hand a powerful shake. In her charity work, Sydney had seen visitors to institutions for the mentally retarded greet residents like that, casually and too heartily, the roughness hiding either embarrassment or fascination.

"Sorry to tell you this, Syd," Philip drawled.

"What?"

"We made the mistake of telling Lincoln you've never been up in the Ferris wheel."

"Uh-oh." She smiled—then started in surprise when Lincoln slid his hand inside her elbow and began to lead her away.

"Come on, Sydney, no time like the present."

Laughing, she cried, "Wait!" He stopped when she resisted in earnest. "Why do I have to go? You all go, and I'll wave to you from the bottom."

"No, no, you said you'd go," Sam cried, trying to grab her other hand. "Come on, you promised you would someday!"

"Yes, but I didn't say today."

"The rain's made everybody go home early," Philip pointed out, "so there won't be much of a line."

Michael was watching her interestedly. "Why don't you want to go?"

"Why don't *you*?" she countered.

"Because I'm afraid."

They all laughed, even Lincoln, amused by his candor.

"Well," said Sydney, "the thing is, I'm not very fond of heights. I avoid them whenever possible."

"But this is history," Lincoln wheedled, pulling on her arm again. "Something to tell your grandchildren you did, way back in ninety-three."

"Come on, don't be a chicken," Sam taunted. "I've been on it, and I'm just a kid. I wasn't scared at all."

She groaned, vacillating between excitement and curiosity on one hand and real fear on the other.

"If you like, I'll go with you," Michael said in a low voice.

"Ha! There!" Sam started jumping up and down. "Now you *have* to go!"

It seemed that she did. Resigning herself to her fate, she let them tow her away to the Ferris wheel.

The crowds really had thinned, warned away by heavy clouds that hinted at a downpour and by a cold, gusty wind blowing in off the lake. The Midway was as close to deserted as it ever got. "Have you really been on the *Illinois* five times?" she asked Lincoln as they strode along. He had maneuvered her ahead of the others, taking it for granted that they were a couple.

"Six, counting today. I've always been a bit of a naval artillery buff, you know. Say, Sydney."

"Hm?"

He leaned close to speak in her ear. "Is it all right for you to be alone with him?" He jerked his chin sideways, over his shoulder.

"With Michael? Yes, of course, why wouldn't it be?"

"Well, I mean . . ." He smiled, showing his teeth. "You know."

"No."

"Well, it's just that some might say he's not quite . . ."

"Civilized?"

He laughed easily. "Well, that's what I've heard."

"Have you? Well, as you can see, it's not true. Does he look uncivilized to you? Does he look like a wild man?" Her tone was too harsh; she softened it with a laugh. "Really, I think Michael's one of the most civilized people I've ever known." Dangerous, maybe, but that was a different matter.

"Well, if you say so." He laughed again, and the surface tension he had created between them faded. She wondered why in Cam this sort of talk was mildly amusing, but when it came from Lincoln she found it offensive. He wasn't a bad sort—her aunt hadn't exaggerated any of his sterling qualities. He really was good-looking, with sun-streaked brown hair and a healthy complexion, an athlete's muscular body, a strong-featured, intelligent face.

She was being too protective, she supposed, too sensitive on Michael's behalf. And he was strong, he could look after himself; he didn't need her to defend him. Still, Lincoln's attitude stirred up an emotion in her that actually came close to rage. Where did *that* come from? She didn't know, but she was helpless to control it.

She glanced back to see Michael striding along behind her, with Sam sitting proudly on his shoulders. She smiled, delighted—but at that second Lincoln slid his hand inside her arm again in a firm, proprietary way. She turned back to stare straight ahead, her smile fading.

The Ferris wheel, as Michael had noted in one of his reports, was two hundred and sixty-five feet high. It might as well have been two thousand and sixty-five for all Sydney cared, because anything over two or three stories—thirty feet, say—she avoided like the plague. She had always been that way, although she couldn't have said why; she couldn't remember anything, no height-related trauma in her past to account for it.

Waiting in the sparse line for tickets, she craned her neck with the others to see to the top of the gigantic contraption, and peered through the long glass windows of the cars as they swept past to examine the expressions of the thrill-seekers inside. Were they white-faced and screaming? Frozen silent with terror? No; they looked excited but perfectly composed, and there were as many children in the spacious cars as adults. What was there to fear? The wheel must be safe or they wouldn't let people on it. She told herself that over and over while the endless, deafening clatter of the motor, housed in a ridiculously small building at the base of the behemoth, shredded and clawed at her nerves.

"You're not really scared, are you, Syd?"

"No, of course not," she lied, giving Sam a big smile. "Especially if you'll hold my hand."

"I will. I won't let go."

"Then I'm all right."

Michael looked a little white around the lips. "Hold mine, too," he said, and she didn't think he was joking. "What holds it up?"

Lincoln started to explain it to him, but Sydney shut her ears. She didn't want to know what held it up, what made it go, what kind of engine ran it. All that information would just give her more to worry about. Better to plunge to her death in ignorance, she reasoned, than add the excruciating ingredient of understanding to her last few seconds on earth.

Then it was time to get on the damn thing. Because of the rain, their roomy car wasn't even half full when the attendant closed the door on them. And locked it, she couldn't help noticing. Was the lighter load good or bad? Maybe forty people evenly spaced around all four sides gave the wheel stability. Maybe fifteen people walking around anywhere they liked created a hazard. What if everybody on all thirty-six cars suddenly walked over to one end? Wouldn't that tip the whole thing over?

She yelped when the car suddenly jerked backward and glided up into thin air, then abruptly stopped. Philip and Lincoln laughed at her, and so did a few of the other passengers. She laughed with them, to show what a good sport she was, and to mask her hysteria. "Ow," said Sam, and when she let go of his hand he shook it, to ease the pain in his fingers. "You okay, Syd?"

"Fine."

"Because it hasn't even started yet. They're just letting the people off two cars below us."

"Right."

Sam deserted her to join the others, including Michael, who had moved to the windows to look out and see the sights. She wrapped her arms around one of the upright poles running the length of the car and tried to decide where to look. Closing her eyes or staring at the floor made her nauseated, but the view through the windows, even when the car wasn't moving, made her light-headed. The car jerked again. She managed not to scream by biting her knuckles and pressing her damp forehead to the cold metal pole.

It kept happening and it wouldn't stop. Each time the wheel jolted to put off and take on new passengers, her stomach plummeted. The stationary periods were worse, because then the hovering car rocked in the wind, slowly and gently. Sickeningly. Those were the times her life flashed before her eyes.

Conversation drifted to her in random patches, interspersed with a dull roaring. "That's the new university, see? It'll be huge when they finish it." "Oh, look, see the skyscrapers? There's the Masonic Temple, and there's the Home Insurance Building on LaSalle." "Sydney, come look at the lake, it's really beautiful. You've never seen it like this."

But she couldn't move. Then the worst happened: the last car disgorged and refilled, and the giant wheel, which she loathed now with every cell in her body, began to turn in earnest.

Nightmare. Which would be worse, to disgrace herself by vomiting, or to have a heart attack from terror and die? Somebody was patting her shoulder, and somebody else—Philip—was chuckling and saying comforting things at the same time. So: she was a joke. Vomiting *on* Philip began to appeal to her. But so did dying, because then he'd be sorry.

She still didn't know where to look. The ceaseless, kaleidoscopic swirl of buildings and sky, buildings and sky, brought her as close to fainting as she had ever been, but closing her eyes made icy sweat pop out all over and pushed the nausea so high in her throat she had to keep swallowing to force it back down.

Michael's ashen face loomed in front of her. He mouthed her name; her teeth were clenched; she couldn't reply. He tried to take her hands, but she was incapable of letting go of the pole—her lifeline. Finally his voice penetrated the roaring in her ears.

He said, "I'll make it stop."

Or maybe she only thought he said that. An aural hallucination.

She locked her gaze on him, and his body became her visual lifeline, a black-coated sliver of solidity in a slipping, sliding ocean of panic. He squeezed her shoulder hard, right through the padding of her jacket. Then he turned away, and she watched him clutch at one pole, pause, lunge for the next. He made his way across the car like that, and the significance of his jerky, stiff-legged gait slowly sifted through the fog of fear around her brain: he was almost as scared as she was.

At last he reached the door, the locked door, the one facing the guts of the infernal machine. As the car swooped downward toward the bottom of its hellish cycle, he began to pound on the glass and shout out at the top of his lungs, "Stop! Stop! Stop!" But no miracle occurred, and with a sick lurch in her stomach Sydney felt the dizzying ascent begin again.

The window opened with a crank. Michael found it and tried to wind the glass pane down, but it was stuck. No one helped him; no one went near him. In her peripheral vision she saw a dozen people, including her brothers and Lincoln Turnbull, staring at him in motionless disbelief. Finally the window dropped down, and when the wheel neared its next nadir, Michael stuck his head and shoulders out and screamed, *"Stop!"*

Nothing happened.

He began to pound at something on the outside of the door—the metal dowel between the two brackets that kept it closed. "Hey," somebody in the car said, and someone else said, "What are you doing?"

Unlocking the door and opening it—in midair, while the Ferris wheel glided to the top of its circuit, hovered for that horrible, unvarying instant, and then started its ghastly downward pitch.

"Michael!" She shrieked it, in pure, absolute terror. No

one moved—no one tried to grab him! And her own hands were glued to the pole, frozen stiff. She watched him lean far, far out into nothing, hanging on with one hand to the slippery edge of the door frame, waving his other hand in the air, and now standing on only one foot so he could lean out even farther. *"Michael!"*

"Stop it!" he yelled. "Stop it! Stop this goddamn machine! *Stop it!"*

They stopped it.

It took two more revolutions, the last one agonizingly slow. When the car finally touched firm, unmoving ground, Sydney's knees buckled under her, and only her white-knuckled hands, still wrapped around the pole like twin vises, kept her from sliding to the floor.

"My God, Syd," Philip said wonderingly, prying her fingers off the pole. At his elbow, Sam stared up at her with the same stunned and sheepish expression. Behind him, Lincoln shook his head over and over, dumbfounded.

Outside on the platform, Michael was having an altercation with two uniformed engineers, one of them the man who had put them in this car a few minutes ago. *A few minutes ago?* It felt like hours, days, a lifetime in hell. "Go fix it," Sydney uttered with a strangely thick tongue. She had to repeat it, but once he understood, Philip went outside to help straighten out the mess. A little later, with Sam holding one of her arms and Lincoln the other, she managed to exit the car with a particle of dignity. It felt as if the whole world was staring at her, but she had no emotional energy left to care. She would take intense embarrassment over heart-stopping panic any day.

The farther they walked from the Ferris wheel, the better she felt. Some of the jokes at her expense that Philip and Lincoln traded even began to draw a wan smile out of her. What she still wanted badly to do, though, was throw her arms around Michael and burst into tears and kiss him all over his face.

They said good-bye to Lincoln at the train station. He told her he was looking forward to her party, and she just stared at him, blank-faced. "Your aunt's dinner dance. In three weeks. For the historical society?"

"Of course. Yes, I'm looking forward to it, too." Almost as much as she was looking forward to his train coming, so he would go away.

It finally did, and they waved him out of sight. Her shoulders slumped with relief. Philip hadn't stopped teasing her yet, but thank God it was just the family again.

On the ride home, Sam fell asleep against her shoulder. In the opposite seat, Philip found a newspaper and buried his head in it. Sydney stared across the short space between the seats at Michael, who stared back at her. "Thank you," she mouthed, and he silently mimed, "You're welcome."

How inadequate. She very much wanted to sit on his lap and hug his neck and tell him he was her hero.

"What made you do it?" she murmured to herself, too softly for him to hear.

But he did hear. Leaning toward her, he touched the hand she was resting on her knee. "You were afraid," he breathed, his grayish green eyes warm and caressing.

"So were you."

"Not as much."

She turned her fingers over, to clasp his hand. "Michael." She sighed, not wanting to let go. What was happening to them?

Philip rattled his newspaper. They dropped hands hastily and sat back. Sam yawned, rubbing his eyes. Presently the conductor called out their stop, and they filed off the train tiredly. Nobody said much as they tramped home in the gray, windy twilight. At dinner that night, the story was told and retold, with much laughter and amusement and relief and astonishment. Sydney waited, but nobody said the main thing, the truest thing, the *moral* of the story: that Michael MacNeil was the most extraordinary man any of them had ever known.

II

Little Egypt wasn't really naked.

Still, even though Philip had played a joke on him, Michael couldn't say he was disappointed. While she did a dance called the hootchy-kootchy, Little Egypt wore a filmy skirt he could see her legs through, including the tops of her thighs above her garters and black stockings. All she wore on top was a gold blouse cut off above her stomach, with a little fringe hanging down that looked like it would tickle her skin.

"Is that how all ladies look?" Sam wanted to know. "Is it, Papa? Under their clothes, is that how they really *look*?"

Philip snickered, but Michael wanted to hear the answer, too. Dr. Winter pulled on his ear and made a humming noise. Finally he said, "Well, I expect some of them do, yes."

"The lucky ones," Philip said out of the side of his mouth.

Sam stood on his toes, trying to see around the man in front of him. "But they don't look like that in their clothes. We look like ourselves in our clothes, but ladies don't."

Michael had noticed the same thing. He had seen paintings of naked women, but until now he had never known for sure which was accurate, the shapes of the women in the pictures or the shapes of the clothed women he knew—Sydney, for instance, in her S-shaped dresses with the little hump in the back. Interesting.

Little Egypt didn't move like any other women he'd ever seen, either. While a man sitting with his legs crossed played a thin, sad song on a flute, she held her bare arms over her head and swayed her hips in a slow circle, showing off the muscles in her stomach and the fat curves of her breasts. She had dark hair and white skin, and she smiled while she danced, flashing her black eyes at the people in the audience.

"As far as we know, women didn't begin wearing corsets or stays until the close of the Middle Ages, a time coinciding with the end of the War of the Roses," said Dr. Winter, without taking his eyes off Little Egypt. "Before that they wore smocks—that's the Saxon name; the Norman word is chemise."

"What do they wear now?" Philip asked, looking sly.

"Nowadays they wear—" He started to cough, glancing down at Sam. "Never mind about that. Mind your manners, Philip."

Philip grinned and gave Michael a wink.

Little Egypt's dance ended. She disappeared behind a silver beaded curtain while the people standing below the stage on the Midway clapped and whistled and yelled, "More!" But she didn't come back, and the crowd started to break up and move away.

"Time to go home." Dr. Winter took Sam's hand. "No need to, ah, hm." He coughed again and straightened his spectacles. "No need to mention to your aunt that we saw this, hm, dancer, Sam."

"You mean it's a secret?"

"Ha! No, no, just no need to mention it, that's all."

Sam looked puzzled. "Can I tell Sydney?"

"Hm? Oh, well. I suppose so. Suppose that's all right. Now, you, Philip."

"Sir."

"Don't want you staying out till all hours of the night, hear me?"

"Yes, sir. I won't."

"Hm." He leaned closer. "Wish I were going with you. Madhouse at home. Women've lost their minds."

Michael laughed when Philip did, realizing it was a joke. Sydney and the aunt and all the maids were getting the house ready for the big party they were having in two weeks. Everything was a mess. "Chaos," Dr. Winter called it, and locked himself in his study.

"Could we, Papa? Why can't we go with Philip and Michael? Why do we have to go home now? Can't we go with them?"

"No, we can't."

"Why not?"

Dr. Winter gave his older son a funny, knowing look, then leaned over and whispered to Sam, "Because I'm too old and you're too young." He winked at Philip, and for the first time Michael saw the resemblance between them. It was in their lips when they smiled, a way they both had of twitching their mouths sideways when they were making a joke but pretending they weren't. Being "dry," he'd heard it called.

After Sam and Dr. Winter left, Michael said, "Where are we going now?" They were having dinner together, at Philip's invitation, and afterward they might even go to a show. Michael had been looking forward to it all day.

"Downtown, so we need the northside station." He pointed across the lights of the Midway. "It's right over there, you can even see it. But it's a twenty-minute walk because the lagoon winds around in the way. Too bad we can't portage over to it with a gondola—we'd be there in no time."

Michael stopped in his tracks. "Portage," he said softly. "Portage."

Philip went a few steps before he noticed Michael wasn't with him. "What's wrong?" he said, coming back.

Michael stared at him. "Portage—what does it mean? What does that word mean?"

"Portage? It's when you carry your boat overland from one body of water to another. Small lakes, say."

"A small boat? A light boat. A—"

"A canoe, usually. Why?"

He put his fingers in his hair and pulled on it. "That was it. It wasn't a shipwreck. That's what happened."

"What are you talking about? You mean when you were a child?"

He could *see* it. "White water, not blue."

"Rapids!"

"The canoe went under. White foam. Ice cold. That's all I remember. I woke up on the land, the bank, and they were all gone." A picture flashed in front of his eyes: fear on the faces of his uncle and his aunt, and another man he didn't know—the guide, it must have been. "Everyone drowned but me." He had known it before, buried down deep in his mind, but now he could see their faces. It made him want to cry.

Philip squeezed his arm. "That's good, Michael. It is, because it'll help Sydney's detective. He's been searching through lists of shipwrecks in the Great Lakes, but now he can look for *inland* drownings. And he can probably narrow it to southern Ontario."

"Why didn't I remember before? It's so clear now. Why did I have to hear that word?" *Portage.*

"I don't know. Are you all right?"

"Yes." But he felt queer.

"Come on, let's get out of here. What we need is a drink."

They got lots of drinks. In places Philip called "sporting saloons," here the patrons were all men with names like Slick and Dink and Fast Paddy. They all knew Philip, and they all wanted to buy him glasses of beer.

"I didn't know there were places like this," Michael said, blinking at Philip through the cigar smoke at Burke's Ten Dollar Saloon. He was sipping his first beer and finding that it tasted a little better than it smelled, but not much.

"City's lousy with 'em."

"Men just come here to talk to each other? Is that it?"

"Talk and drink. And do a little business."

Philip had done business in the last two saloons, paying

money to a man in one, getting money from a man in the second. Since he'd brought it up, Michael felt all right about asking, "What is your business?"

"Horses."

"You bought one?"

"Ha! Almost. No, I play the horses. Bet on the races at Washington Park. If my horse wins, I win. Yesterday I won; tomorrow, who knows?" He grinned, biting down on the fat, smelly cigar between his teeth. He didn't look like the others, though, the Slicks and Lefties in this saloon. It was as if he was playing a game, Michael thought. A joke on everybody, even himself.

They ate bloody steaks for dinner at a restaurant on Clark Street. The wine Philip ordered tasted better than beer, but after half a glass Michael started to feel dizzy.

"This is different from the time Sam took me to Chicago," he noted, thinking of the darker, narrower streets outside, where there were almost as many people crowding the sidewalks as there were in the city. They weren't businessmen, though. He couldn't make out what they were, except loud and reckless.

"I should hope so," Philip said, pouring more wine into their glasses. "What do you think of that girl over there? The one with the old guy."

Michael craned his neck. "The lady with black hair? She looks nice," he said doubtfully. "But her husband looks tired."

Philip stopped with his fork halfway to his mouth and started to laugh. Pretty soon he was roaring. Michael didn't know what was funny, but he laughed, too.

From then on, everything was funny. They went to a theater on Fourteenth Street and saw a play called *The Bohemian Girl,* in which men on real horses galloped onto the stage, kidnapped the heroine, and rode off into the wings! Afterward, Michael couldn't stop talking about it, couldn't get over the wonder of it. It was getting late, but instead of going home they went to another saloon, in a different neighborhood. This saloon had ladies in it. They were called waiter girls, and they served drinks and entertained people by singing and dancing on a stage. They showed their legs, like Little Egypt, but they danced to a fast piano instead of a mournful flute, so the feeling he got from watching it was completely different. Not exotic. More like what he was learning to think of as Chicago: fast and rough and full of energy. He tried to imagine Sydney singing and dancing on a stage while men watched her, but he couldn't.

"It's true what Sam said," he confided to Philip in a low voice while two of the waiter girls sang a song called "Under My Lemon Tree." "Their bodies really are different from the way they look in their clothes."

Philip was drinking glasses of whiskey with his beer now. "You've never had a woman, have you? Never had sex with one."

The way he said it, just casually, not laughing at him, made telling the truth easy. "I've never made love," he said, using the term Philip had taught him. "What kind of girls are they? Why do they do this?"

Philip laughed and didn't answer.

"Do they like it?"

"Sure, why wouldn't they?" He drank all the whiskey in another little glass with one swallow. Afterward he made a face, as if he was in pain.

"Are they rich?" They all wore flashy clothes and a lot of sparkling jewelry.

Philip slid down low in his chair. "No, they're not rich. They do it to make a living. I don't know if they like it or not." He watched the two ladies on the stage for a minute, smiling a tight, hard smile. "Probably not."

Michael could see him slipping into one of his gray, quiet moods. "Let's go someplace else," he said quickly. "Someplace where there's a show." He thought of *The Bohemian Girl* and how much it had lifted Philip's spirits.

"A show?" He threw down some money on the table and stood up, stumbling slightly; Michael had to reach for his arm to steady him. "Now, that's a hell of an idea. I know just the place."

* * *

Mrs. Birch lived in the Levee. When Michael asked what that meant, Philip said, "It means you never want to come here by yourself. 'Specially at night."

Mrs. Birch's house, at the bottom of a dead-end street, looked dark and deserted, but a man opened the door as soon as Philip knocked. "Who's your friend?" he asked, standing back to let them in.

Philip threw his heavy arm around Michael's shoulders. "This is Mick. He's visiting from Canada."

The man led them through a narrow hallway ending at a long, heavy curtain that smelled like leather. He pushed the curtain open.

Bright light—music—people laughing and talking. Michael blinked in surprise. Was it a show?

The first thing his eyes focused on was a lady in her nightgown, sitting on the lap of a fully clothed man. The second thing was another lady, also in her nightgown, dancing by herself to a song with violins coming from a phonograph. She had her eyes closed, and she was really stretching more than dancing. Maybe she was asleep. He had heard of people who could walk and even talk when they were sleeping.

"What is this place?" he whispered to Philip. The room, which looked sort of like the Winters' living room only with much more furniture, was full of people. The men were all dressed and the women were all undressed, and nobody seemed to think a thing of it. So many candles were burning, it was almost as bright as day. There was food on a low table, fruit and bread and little cakes, but what the room smelled like was a mixture of perfume, cigarettes, and sweat. And one more thing.

"What is it?" he said again, but before Philip could answer, a woman glided up to them.

"As you can see, we're crowded tonight," she said in a low voice that didn't go up or down. She had clothes on, a shiny red dress that covered all of her skin, and she had dark brown hair, as curly as Sam's. Her face was very white, and when she talked it didn't move at all.

"Not too crowded for an old friend, I hope," Philip said in a too-loud voice. "How are you, Mrs. B?"

She flicked her heavy eyelids over him coldly. Michael stood straighter, feeling stiff and uncomfortable. Philip was drunk and saying the wrong things, and this had never happened before. Mrs. Birch didn't answer his question; she said, "What are you gentlemen in the mood for this evening?"

"A drink, to start."

"Wine?"

"No, champagne."

That made her smile a little. "Are you celebrating?"

"I'm not—he is." He smacked Michael on the shoulder with his fist.

"How nice. And then?"

"And then . . . I think my friend and I are just in the mood to watch tonight. At first, anyway. Afterward, who knows?"

Mrs. Birch nodded her head, still without any expression. She looked more like a doll than a person. "Will you have your wine here or upstairs?"

"Mmm," Philip hummed, swaying slightly as he looked around the room. "Upstairs."

She lifted her hand, and a girl who had been leaning against the shadowy wall came toward them. "This is Lily. She'll take care of you this evening. Enjoy yourselves, and let me know if there's anything else you require." Mrs. Birch glided off through a dark archway into another room.

"Lily," said Philip, and to Michael's amazement he took the girl's hand and kissed it. "Didn't you used to be Stella?"

She laughed, showing yellow teeth; Michael could smell tobacco on her breath. She had thin, straight, orange hair, pulled back behind her ears with pins. Her face was white, like Mrs. Birch's, but she looked younger. She looked like a child.

"That was last month. This month I'm Lily. Don't I

look it?" She laughed again. "Hello," she said to Michael, blinking her eyes at him.

"Hello." He held out his hand to shake.

She laughed some more—she thought everything was funny. "I've never seen you before."

"I've never seen you before, either."

"Are you going to be my friend?"

"Yes," he said politely.

She rolled her eyes at Philip. "He's a *darling*. Where have you been keeping him?" She hooked her hands through their arms, making them turn around. "Shall we go upstairs, gentlemen?"

She took them up a wide staircase lit by more candles, and then down a hall to a closed door on the left. When they went in, Michael thought they were in a bedroom at first, until he noticed all the couches and chairs scattered around. No, it must be a sitting room. But why would you put a bed in a sitting room?

"You gents make yourselves comfortable, now. I'll be right back with your refreshments."

After she left, Philip flopped down on the biggest sofa and stretched out with his head on a pillow.

"Do you know these people, Philip?"

"Some of them." He closed his eyes, as if he was going to take a nap.

Michael started to prowl the room. "Is there going to be a show?" Philip didn't answer. There were some paintings on the walls, but nothing on the tables, no pictures or flower vases or anything. Half of one whole wall was covered by a green velvet curtain. Maybe there was a stage behind it. No; when he pushed against the curtain, he touched something hard—the wall, he assumed. He turned back to Philip. "Is there?"

"Hm?" He sounded like his father. "Yeah, sort of a show."

"Where's the audience?"

He wore a funny smile. "We're the audience."

He was keeping a secret, Michael could tell. He didn't

like it. It made him think of the experiments Professor Winter used to perform on him.

Lily came back, carrying a tray. "Here we go." She put the tray on the bed and started to open a bottle. Bang! Michael jumped up in the air when the cork flew up and hit the ceiling. Lily laughed as if it was the funniest thing she'd ever seen. "Haven't you ever had bubbly before, honey?" He shook his head, standing back. "What's your name?"

"Michael MacNeil."

Even that made her laugh. "Just say 'Michael,' honey. We don't use last names here."

"Don't you want any?" he asked when she gave a glass to him and one to Philip.

"No, I got my own special brew." She picked up a glass of something clear—water, he thought. "Well, boys, bottoms up, so we can get this show on the road."

Bubbles popped under his nose and tingled on the surface of his tongue. The champagne tasted cold and sweet; he liked it better than the sour red wine they had drunk at dinner. But after only two swallows, it made him belch. He put his hand over his mouth and said, "Excuse me," while Lily laughed and laughed.

" 'Scuse *me* for one sec." She went outside, but came right back in. "Okay, it's all set, so whenever you're ready." She went around the room, blowing out all the candles but one. Philip moved his legs when she started to sit down beside him. Their couch faced the curtained wall. "You wanna sit down here with us, Michael MacNeil, and get real, real comfortable?" When she crossed her legs, her nightgown fell open, showing her knees and part of her thigh. Michael choked on a sip of champagne, and Lily let out a real laugh this time.

"Y'know, I don't think we're quite ready." Philip made an effort to speak slowly and clearly. "Lily, sweetheart, would you mind going out again, just for a minute or two, while Mick and I have a word in private?"

"Well, sure, honey, but you might miss the beginning. I can't hold back progress, y'know."

"That's all right. We'll use our imaginations." They both laughed while Michael looked on, mystified. Lily got up and left the room.

Philip started to stand, but his legs gave out and he fell back onto the couch. "Whoa, Nellie." He patted the place beside him, where Lily had been, and Michael sat down.

"Are you all right?"

"Sure, sure. I'm just thinking this shouldn't be susha big surprise. Don't want you having a heart attack at Mrs. Birch's, do we? Papers'd have a field day."

Why would he have a heart attack? What was a field day? Michael's head was starting to hurt. "Philip, where are we?"

"Mick, my boy, we're in a whorehouse."

"What's a whorehouse?"

Philip peered at him, bleary-eyed, as if to make sure he was serious. He set his drink down, cleared his throat, and sat up, putting his hands on his knees. "It's a place where men come to have sex with women. Usually. There're variations, but that's the kind of house this is. You with me? We pay money to girls like Lily—she's a whore and that's her job. Everybody's happy."

"We pay them money?" He laughed, waiting for Philip to join him. "Tell me the truth. Really, what's going to happen?"

"I just told you."

"No. No. For *money*?" He laughed again, but not with as much certainty. Philip just stared at him, not even smiling. "You're saying people have sex with each other because they *pay*?"

"Yeah. Helluva thing, isn't it?" He looked at Michael strangely. "God damn. That is a helluva thing." He picked up his drink and took a big swallow. "So anyway. Here's the thing. Since you've never done it before, I was thinking Mrs. Birch's would be a good place to start, because it's got a, um, special feature you don't find in too many houses."

"What?" His mind was still racing.

Philip pointed to the green curtain. "See that? That

covers a big window. And behind it there's a room jus'
like this. And right now there're two people in there. One
of 'em's a whore, and the other's a man who doesn't care
if people watch while he's doing it with her."

"Having sex?"

"Right."

No, it couldn't be. Couldn't be.

Philip scratched his head. "'Course, we don't have to
do this if you don't want to. We can just go home, I don't
care. But this's how it's done. If you want a girl and
you're not married, this's about the only way you're gonna get one. Because most of the other ones won't do it."

"Why?"

"Because. It's not respectable. They think. Not moral."

"It's wrong for them, but not for us?"

"Right." He sat back, sloshing champagne on his
trousers. "Wrong for them, not wrong for us. That's it
exactly." He blinked at the wet stain spreading over his
knee. "So what's it gonna be? Stay or go?"

The door opened and Lily came in, carrying a bottle of
champagne in each hand. Michael stood up. "Well?" she
said. She stood in front of the only candle she'd left
burning, and he could see the shape of her hips through
her nightgown.

"Have you done this before?" he asked Philip.
"Watched people?"

He looked away; Michael thought he wasn't going to
answer. For the first time since they'd come here, he
looked embarrassed. "Yeah, I've done it. There's nothing
wrong with it." He almost sounded angry.

Lily bent her knees and sagged her shoulders, pretending the bottles were getting heavy.

Michael said, "Okay, then."

"Okay, then." Lily set the bottles on the table by the
couch and sat down again next to Philip. "Honey, you pull
that string next to the curtain, and then you come on over
here and sit beside Lily."

Michael pulled the string next to the curtain, but he
didn't sit down beside Lily. Even though she laughed at

him, he went around the couch and stood behind her. He didn't want her to see his face.

Even now, up until the very last second, he didn't really believe it. *Philip's joking,* he thought in the back of his mind; *it's going to be a trick.* But his body jerked backward as if he'd been shoved in the chest when he saw what was on the other side of the window.

A woman. And a man. He had his trousers and his shirt on, but she—she was completely, completely naked.

But she was taking his clothes off. They stood at the foot of a bed in a room like this one, exactly like it except theirs was bright from a lot of candles. She took his shirt off for him while he petted the white skin on her ribs and her breasts. Michael couldn't get enough of the sight of her body, he wanted to see more, he wanted to *devour* her with his eyes. She unbuttoned the man's pants and pulled them down his bare legs, and while she did that the man looked straight into the window, smiling a small, tight-eyed smile. Michael wanted to turn, hide, cover up. But he couldn't move and he couldn't look away.

Hands, mouths, breasts, legs. The woman had yellow hair on her head and black hair between her legs. The man stood behind her in front of the glass, touching her all over, resting his chin on her shoulder. Did she like it? Her face was a mystery. He squeezed her heavy bosom with one hand and put the other in the patch of hair between her legs, pulling her up close. She bent her knees, and his hand slid in lower. Michael's body felt too tight. He was going to break soon, burst right out of his skin.

They moved to the bed. The woman fell back, and the man covered her. He kept his feet on the floor and she wrapped her legs around him. Now they were doing it, having sex. Their bodies strained, curved, pushing and pushing, but their faces stayed empty, their eyes open. The man grabbed her hands and held them while he pushed into her fast, fast, fast. She opened her mouth wide and put her head back.

Then it was over. The man rolled off, onto his back beside her. She got up. She said something; he didn't answer. She came toward the window, swaying, hands on her hips, pushing her stomach out. When she got to the glass she pressed her whole body against it, flattening her breasts, thighs, her palms, even her lips to the window. Lily laughed at that, as if it was a joke, but it was ugly. Michael was glad when Philip didn't laugh with her.

Lily stood up and went to close the curtain. "All right, gents. Who wants to go first?"

Chilly wind blew wet paper and pieces of trash across the alley, sweeping them into the gurgling, dammed-up gutter. The smell of dank water and rotting garbage rose from a black grate in the cobblestones. Michael huddled inside his coat and thought about how soft he'd grown. This was nothing, this cold rain blowing in his face and down his collar, and yet here he was, shivering like a cornered rabbit and wishing he had a thicker jacket.

Across the dirty street, the door to Mrs. Birch's house opened, but two men came out and neither of them was Philip. It would be dawn soon. The blurry moon had already sunk below the jagged line of rooftops across the way. Now the street was deserted, but an hour ago rough-looking men, some of them staggering from drink, had prowled past him on the muddy sidewalk. Only once had anyone tried to bother him, a big, stringy-haired man who stank of beer and reminded him of O'Fallon. Michael had straightened up from his crouch in the alleyway, ready to fight, *happy* to, clenching his hands in his eagerness to hit something. So much bad energy was swirling inside him, he was almost sick from it. The man got close enough to see into his eyes, and then the meanness in his face turned to fear. He cursed him and shuffled away.

Michael rubbed his cold arms and shifted from foot to foot. Only half a year ago he could have lain in icy snow without moving for an hour or more while he waited for his prey, a rabbit, a mouse, to poke its head out of its burrow. Now he was somebody called "Michael MacNeil," and his life had turned into a struggle not to survive but to understand what that meant. Tonight he had found out something important about what men did. But instead of making him more comfortable inside his new self, his new skin, the thing he had learned only made him feel stranger. Because he couldn't do what men did.

His body had wanted to, though. It still did. Pictures of the naked girl in the window kept coming back into his head, making him hard, making him ache. He kept seeing that moment when she had fallen back on the bed and opened her legs, and the man had used his hand to steer his penis into her. He couldn't make that scene go away. He wanted to touch himself to relieve the ache, but he was afraid someone might see. That was one human lesson he was learning fast—that sex was a secret thing. You weren't even allowed to talk about it. Men wanted it so much they even paid for it, but they couldn't admit it in public. It was a big, sneaky secret.

"Who wants to go first?" His cheeks burned when he remembered Lily's laughter following him down the hall, down the stairs, after he had told her he didn't want to do it with her. "Why not, honey? You scared? Oh, c'mon, you'll love it." She'd rubbed her hands on him, inside his jacket, and every time she had taken a step toward him he'd taken one back. Finally he'd smacked up against the door with his back—even Philip had laughed at that. "What's the matter, honey? Don't you like Lily?" He hadn't wanted to hurt her feelings, so he had blurted out, "I don't have any money," fumbling behind him for the doorknob. But that hadn't stopped her. "Well, you are such a big, handsome thing, I think I'll give you a *dis-count*." He could only imagine what a discount was—a strange position? some different way of doing it? "No, thank you. I—I'm—" What was that excuse Sydney used to get off the telephone? "Well, I know you're busy, so I'll let you go." Even as the words were coming out of his mouth, he had known they sounded idiotic.

But he couldn't help it. Lily had laughed and laughed, but still he could never have told her the truth: that every-thing about her was wrong. Her smell, her voice, her pretend-friendliness. The emptiness behind the made-up interest in her eyes. She was *other*. She was *off*. The main thing was, she wasn't Sydney. Mate with Lily? No, he couldn't. It would be like . . . a wolf mating with a bear. Upside down. Not natural.

Across the street the door opened again, and this time the man who came out was Philip. He looked around, but he didn't notice Michael until he walked out of the stinking alley and came toward him. The rain had turned into a fine mist. Philip turned his collar up, hunching his shoulders, and met him in the middle of the street.

He looked pale and sick. "Jesus," he said, "look at you. You're soaked through." He shuddered inside his jacket; his teeth chattered.

"Are you all right?"

"No. Christ, Michael, I'm sorry. I'm really sorry."

"It's okay. Let's go home now." He took Philip's arm.

At the station, they bought coffee and carried it in paper cups on board the train. Michael couldn't help remembering the day he gave all Sam's money away and they had to walk home. That had been an interesting day. Last night with Philip had been interesting, too, but in a different way.

Too bad Philip was sick. He took one sip of his coffee, turned green, jumped up, and stumbled out of the car. When he came back a few minutes later, he looked white and sweaty, but at least he wasn't shaking anymore.

It was so early there were only two other people in the car, and they were at the other end. All the same, Michael kept his voice low, and leaned across the space between their seats to ask Philip, "How was it? With Lily? Did she keep laughing at me?" He smiled, pretending he didn't care.

Philip lifted his head out of his hand. The whites of his eyes were pink and watery. Instead of answering, he asked, "Why did you leave? Not because you were scared."

"I was a little scared." But Philip was right, that wasn't the real reason. "It didn't feel right," he said slowly. "It's hard to explain. Being with her—it's all right for you, but not for me."

Philip groaned, and went back to pressing the heels of his hands against his eye sockets. "Why?"

"Because . . ." He shifted, not knowing how to say it. "It's personal. I don't think I should tell you. I don't think you would like it."

"That you're in love with my sister?" He didn't even lift his head.

Michael put both hands on the edge of his seat and sat back.

"That's it, isn't it? If so, I already knew it."

He felt hot and cold at the same time, and his skin prickled with anxiety. "How do you know?"

"Ha. You're not exactly a Sphinx when it comes to your emotions."

"A what?"

"You're no good at hiding what you feel. That's not an insult, by the way."

He stared at Philip's bent head, watched his fingers press hard against his temples. "What do you think about it?" he got up the courage to say. "Are you angry with me? Because of Sydney?"

"No." Finally he looked up. "Want the truth?"

"Yes."

"I'm afraid it might not work out."

Michael had to look away from the sympathy in his eyes. He was afraid to ask why. Besides, he already knew the answer.

"So. Is that why you didn't stay? Because you were being true to Sydney?"

He shrugged. It sounded foolish when Philip said it. "Aren't you in love with Camille?"

He sat up straight. A little bit of color came into his gray cheeks. "What?" he said softly, narrowing his eyes to warn him, looking as if he wanted to fight.

Michael smiled, and then shrugged. "You aren't a Sphinx, either." Whatever a Sphinx was.

The fight went out of Philip; he sagged against the

window, pressing his forehead to the glass. Michael thought the conversation was over until he said "I wish I were like you."

"What?"

"I used to be."

He tried to laugh. "When you were seven years old."

"No." Philip wrapped his arms around himself, shuddering again. "I used to be able to see things the way you do. Everything fresh and new. I wasn't like this. Sydney says . . ."

"What?"

"She says I'm *not* like this." He shook his head. "I don't know what the hell I am." He hunched his shoulders and turned his face back to the window.

"I wish I were like *you*."

He gave a bitter laugh. "Why?"

He thought. Not because of Philip's looks or his clothes, his gestures, not even his cleverness or the easy way he had with people—all the surface things Michael admired about him and tried to copy.

"Why?"

"Because Sydney and Sam and your father love you. Three people love you."

Philip looked at him strangely, and after a moment Michael turned away, afraid he might see pity in his friend's long, thoughtful stare.

12

"This is sissy. I don't see why I have to learn this."

Sydney got a better grip on Sam's stiff, stubborn little body and maneuvered him into another box step, roughly in time with the waltz tune playing on the gramophone. "You have to learn this because you're a gentleman. Gentlemen dance."

"I'm not dancing with anybody. Ick, I hate girls."

"Even me? Who's going to rescue me from all those buffalo-footed men Saturday night? You're the *only* one I want to dance with." She smiled over his shoulder at Michael, who was lounging against the terrace wall, watching them.

"Hmpf," said Sam. He didn't really believe her, but he liked the idea.

"Besides," she added, playing her ace, "isn't this better than lessons at Mrs. Waring's?" Mrs Waring taught cotillion dancing for the children of Chicago's rich and privileged. Sam had gone to her class one time, and vowed afterward never to return.

"Yeah, I guess," he grumbled with a little inward shudder.

"Then pay attention. The sooner you learn this, the sooner you can go out and play."

If only he *would* go out and play. In truth, she was taking time out of an incredibly busy day to teach Sam the waltz for the express purpose of keeping him out of everybody else's hair. "I can't even turn around because he's always underfoot," the cook complained, and the maids said the same thing more politely. The house was in chaos. Hired caterers had taken over the kitchen; maids were attacking the house as if it had never been cleaned before; extra gardeners were at work on last-minute land-scaping to accommodate an orchestra platform in the yard. All the confusion had disrupted Sam's routine; he had grown overexcited and hard to control. Or . . . not quite as sweet-natured and easygoing as usual, Sydney amended fondly.

"Now here's a wholesome family scene."

Sam tried to pull out of her arms, embarrassed for Philip to see him in such a "sissy" attitude, but Sydney held on tight. "Michael's next," he said defensively. "He can't dance, either."

"No? I'd better teach him, then." Laughing, Philip pulled Michael to his feet. "I'll be the lady," he declared, and to Sam's delight, the two of them began to box-step around the terrace in ungainly circles.

Sydney laughed with them—Philip's example was good for Sam. But even more, she was happy to see him so lighthearted, not quite the same cynical, morose loner he had been all summer—sarcastic observations about wholesome family scenes notwithstanding. She wasn't sure when his foul mood had begun to lift, but she was glad for it.

The music stopped; Sam slipped out of her grasp like a wet fish. "I learned it. I can do it, Syd. I was doing it perfect, wasn't I?"

"Perfectly. You were better, but—"

"Perfectly! You said so! Now I can go help the work-men put up the tent."

"Sam—" Too late; he had already skipped off down the path toward the lake. "Oh, Philip," she wailed. "He'll drive them crazy."

"I'll get him," he said, chuckling. "I'll take him for a walk."

"Bless you. Philip?" He stopped and looked back.

"Could you do something with him tomorrow, too? Take him to the zoo or something?"

He shrugged. "All right. Michael, you want to come with us?"

"Sure." He looked thrilled. "What's a zoo?"

Philip gaped, then laughed. Sydney sympathized: staying on top of what Michael knew and what he didn't know was getting more and more complicated. Sometimes it was the simple things—zoos, for instance—that eluded him nowadays, while bigger, more complex phenomena—God, Republican politics—held no mystery at all.

"We'll surprise you," Philip told him, winking at Sydney before he trotted off to find Sam.

Michael leaned against the wall with his hands in his pockets, watching her. She had almost grown used to the silent, alert, penetrating way he looked at her. Almost. She found it disconcerting but not frightening; she never felt like a predator's prey, in other words, or a hunter's target. She did feel studied, though. Brooded on. Fathomed.

Would she have known there was something special about him if they had met for the first time last night, say, at someone's dinner party? She thought so. Even if they only shook hands and said, "How do you do?" she thought she would know. "Gorgeous," Camille called him. A slight exaggeration. Anyway, he was better than gorgeous with his pale green, intelligent eyes, his aristocratic nose. The long, thin scar on his cheek added mystery to his face, a suggestion of wildness. And his hair . . .

"Hmm," she said critically. "Your hair could use a trim before the party. I'll do it for you if you like."

"All right," he said agreeably. "But don't think you can get out of teaching me how to dance."

Laughing, she gave the phonograph a few fresh cranks, put on a new disk, and held out her arms.

Her smile faltered when she saw the undisguised wanting in his face as he came slowly toward her. She almost dropped her arms. This invitation was suddenly too intimate; she hadn't been offering what it was so clear he wanted to take. Had she?

But they came together, and it was like coming home. The momentary tension evaporated, and all she could think was how perfectly they fit together, and how much she had been wanting to touch him. The downward glide of his lashes hid his expression, but a faint flush on his cheek gave him away. "The waltz . . ." she murmured, distracted by the hardness of his shoulder, the neat way his hair grew behind his ear. When he blushed, the scar on his cheek stayed white, accentuating the pinkness around it. He might be perceptive, his senses keen as an animal's, but there wasn't much he could hide from her, either. "The waltz is a very simple dance. It's in three-quarter time, with the accent on the first step."

His arm around her waist flexed, bringing her closer. "I like this dance." His low voice thrilled her. But they really weren't dancing at all, and the music had become a barely heard accompaniment to this embrace. "Last night, Sydney, when you lit the candles in the paper lanterns . . ."

"Japanese lanterns," she murmured. "They're pretty, aren't they? They'll be nice for the party."

"That's how your skin looks. Soft light shining through thin white paper. Ivory and gold. I wish I could paint that color."

She closed her eyes briefly. "You're dangerous."

He smiled, complimented, and drew her closer.

"Michael . . . I'm afraid someone will see us."

"What do you want to do?"

"Dance? Remember, it's—"

"*One*, two three."

They didn't move, though, except to sway lightly against each other. He dipped his head and kissed her hand clasped in his, and a fresh wave of ineffectual anxiety swept over her.

"We can't stand here doing this," she told him, whispering for some reason. "Somebody will see."

"The dining room?" They were standing in front of the open glass doors. It would be so easy. Michael's mouth moved against her forehead, kissing her between her eye-brows. He whispered, "*One*, two, three," and they waltzed in graceful, perfectly executed circles, off the terrace and into the dining room.

"You've been practicing," she accused, breathless, just before he backed her up against the oak sideboard and kissed her on the mouth.

He hadn't been practicing kissing. He did it too hard, with his lips closed tight and his eyes open. She liked it anyway, because of the newness, and his intense, single-minded focus on her alone. And because it was Michael.

"Like this," she told him, stroking her fingertips across the firm, elegant line of his lips. "Softly." She leaned in and pressed a soft, soft kiss to his mouth.

His eyes closed; he sighed. "That's better," he agreed, nuzzling her. He brought his hands to her face and caressed her while they gave each other slow, sweet, experimental kisses. "Sydney, you are . . ." He never fin-ished, because she diverted him by giving his bottom lip a little tug with her teeth. His eyes flew open. "It's playing," he realized. He looked delighted. "I thought it was . . . it looked so . . ."

"What? What did?"

Before he lowered his lashes again, something flashed in his eyes; she would have said it was guilt, but that couldn't be. They kissed again, and cutlery rattled when her elbow struck something on the sideboard; she was dimly aware of the smell of silver polish and furniture wax, but every other sense was concentrated on Michael. He stopped kissing her to look into her eyes while his hand slipped from her shoulder to her throat and then lower, inside the demure neckline of her blouse. *May I?* he was asking without words. He took her trancelike silence for permission, which it was, and touched her.

She wore no corset today, only an old cotton shift under her shirtwaist. His fingers fumbled, and she helped him—*helped* him—unfasten the first few buttons of her blouse. *What are we doing?* she thought hazily, but she didn't stop him. She loved the intense concentration in his face.

The whole world shut down, and there was only Michael, caressing her in this unbearably sweet, breath-stealing way. "Kiss me again," she whispered, and he did, in the new way she had taught him while his careful hands teased and fondled her.

"You like it," he noticed, murmuring the words against her mouth.

She hummed in agreement and slipped her tongue between his teeth. He drew in his breath; his hand on her bare breast went still. "This is playing, too," she whispered, tasting him. "Like it?"

Surprised laughter, low in his throat, vibrated under her caressing fingers. He began to stroke her, long, hard, lustful sweeps of his hands over her hips, down her buttocks, even her thighs. This was a different kind of playing, much more serious, and she knew better than he did where it might lead. But she couldn't stop, not yet. With her arms wound tight around his neck, she kissed him freely, passionately, not holding back, and they turned in slow, lazy loops, until the wall was a steadying surprise at her back. He pressed his hard thigh between her legs, and her knees buckled.

What might have happened next never happened. Instead, the bottom dropped out of her life.

"Sydney?"

She jumped—Michael whirled. Aunt Estelle stood in the doorway to the hall, a drift of yellow dahlias clutched in her hands so hard, the stems shook. Her face—she had lost all color; she looked like a wide-eyed corpse, gaunt cheeks sucked in, absolutely motionless.

Michael's broad shoulders weren't a big enough shield—her aunt saw Sydney's frantic fumblings at the buttons on her blouse. She went even whiter, more rigid, and her black eyes burned with fresh outrage. "You. Get out." She pointed at Michael, then at the terrace door behind him.

He didn't move. Sydney touched his shoulder. "Go," she whispered.

His expression heartened her; there was no shame in it,

not even embarrassment. Only surprise, and that sharp, animal alertness he never lost. And a hint of defiance. He shook his head.

"It's all right," she assured him. But her aunt's fury was almost palpable, filling the room like a bad smell, and Sydney understood why he didn't want to leave her alone. "Go," she said again. "I'll find you." She nodded, telling him she was all right.

Still, he hesitated. To Aunt Estelle he said politely but firmly, "Don't you hurt her." If the situation hadn't been so awful, so unrelievedly horrible, Sydney would have giggled. He meant it, though; the stare he leveled at her aunt, whom he had effectively silenced, held a very definite warning. With a last glance at Sydney, he walked out through the terrace doors and disappeared.

As soon as he was gone, she wanted him back.

He waited for her in his room, thinking she would look for him there first when she finished with the aunt. He could tell time now, and he sat on his bed and looked at the hands on his clock, trying to catch them moving.

He wished Sydney had let him stay. It hardly ever happened that there was something he could do for *her*, but this was one time, finally, when he thought he could have. Maybe. She was gentle and soft, and the aunt was hard. For once she needed him to stand with her, to make the aunt understand that what they had done was right, not wrong.

Very right. He couldn't stop thinking about what it had felt like, kissing Sydney, touching her. Kissing: what a wonderful invention. Animals did it, sort of, but it was more like nuzzling; they didn't really *connect* the way people did. He wanted more of it. The hands on his clock wouldn't move. It must be broken.

He understood everything about sex now. All the things that had been vague and scary and mysterious made sense to him. He wanted Sydney to be his mate for life. He wanted to lie down with her and make love. Not like the man and woman in the whorehouse—that was rutting, not loving. Wolves made love. In the early spring, when the snows began to melt. The she-wolf grew more and more playful, like a puppy, her voice high and silly, beautiful, and her mate turned passionate and tender, yearning for her. And after they made love, they sang.

"Michael?"

He sprang up. How quietly she had come. He went toward her and reached out to touch her, just his hand on her arm, but she shied away. He jerked his hand back in surprise. "Sydney, what's wrong? Did she hurt you?"

"No, of course not, don't be silly. I'm fine." She gave a false laugh and moved away from him, out of reach. At the window, she took hold of the ring on the end of the string that pulled his shade up and down and started to fiddle with it. Where the sun lit up her hair, he could see each strand, glowing reddish gold. He wanted her so much. But something had happened. She was untouchable now; she didn't want him to come near her.

He could guess what was wrong. "She told you we can't do what we did. We can't be together anymore. That's it, isn't it?"

She tossed her head. "She's my aunt, not my mother. She doesn't run my life. I respect her, but I'm a grown woman; I make my own decisions."

He listened to that again, weighing the message and Sydney's voice. It was just words, with nothing behind them. No truth. "What did she say, then?" he asked her. But they were just playing a game now.

Her eyes turned dark, so he knew that whatever the aunt had said, it had hurt her. "What does it matter? Nothing you can't guess. Michael . . ." She dropped the string, but she kept clutching at her hands, squeezing and bending her fingers. "In some ways, she's right. What happened this morning—it probably shouldn't have happened. I wasn't thinking. I lost my head, and I'm sorry. It's my fault."

So, he thought, but his mind stopped and wouldn't go any further. To keep the conversation going, he said, "What is your fault?"

"Everything. I shouldn't have let it happen. It . . ." She couldn't look at him; she looked out the window. "I'm afraid it mustn't happen again."

He leaned against the doorpost, watching her, thinking how words could hurt worse than any physical pain. And wondering how he could ever have thought he could have her. She looked so beautiful in the sunlight in her sky-colored dress, so beautiful that what they had done together began to seem like a dream. She couldn't belong to him. She was Sydney Darrow. She had a pack. Friends. Everybody loved her, and she could go anywhere and do anything because she was free. What was he? Lost. The last man in the world she would choose for a mate.

"Oh, God, Michael, don't look like that." He turned his head so she couldn't see. "I'm sorry. I'm so sorry." She started to cry. "I don't know what to do. Look at me, tell me what you're thinking." Her hand on his back was light and shy, like a stranger's hand. "Please don't be sad. Oh, Michael, please."

She wanted him to smile and say he was fine, the way Sam did when she kissed him after he fell and scraped his knee. "But I am sad," Michael said, turning around to look at her. "I love you. We didn't do anything wrong, Sydney. You know that. If you loved me, it wouldn't matter what the aunt said." He stepped away from the door, so she could leave. "Don't tell me not to be sad," he said for the last time. "It doesn't do any good."

She just kept crying. She didn't move.

"Don't you want to go? Or do you want me to go?"

She put her hand on her throat. She tried to speak, but she couldn't, so she shook her head.

"I'll go, then." He made her a little bow—he had seen Lincoln Turnbull do that once—and left her in his room by herself.

All the way to the zoo on the train, Sam drew pictures to try to cheer him up. "This is the lake, and this is our house, and this is my window. This is my face in it. This is your window, and here's you. See?"

Michael smiled and said he liked it. He said he liked the picture of the horse, too, and the train, and he kept smiling the whole time. But he didn't think he was fooling Sam, or Philip either. How did they know? Since he couldn't tell them what had happened, he was trying to pretend that nothing had. But he was pretty sure they knew.

"Look, Michael, it's you. You're laughing."

He looked down at the drawing Sam had laid on his lap, of a round face with black eyes and a big, grinning mouth. The head had black hair and a neck with a spotted tie, like the one he was wearing today. MICHAEL MACNEIL BY SAMUEL ADAIR WINTER, Sam had printed at the bottom.

"Thank you."

"Keep it in your pocket. Fold it up, and when you get sad you can look at it and feel happy."

"Okay." His throat felt tight and thick. He wanted to hug Sam, but he didn't. He had been forgetting that he didn't really belong to this family, but yesterday Sydney and the aunt had reminded him. He wasn't going to forget again.

The zoo was in Lincoln Park. By now he knew what a zoo was, because Sam couldn't keep the secret and told him. At first he had thought it was a joke. "It's a big place where they keep animals so people can come and look at them," Sam said, which didn't sound likely. How could you keep animals? How could they belong to anybody? But as soon as he walked through the high stone and iron gates of the park, he knew from the strong smell of captivity that it was true.

"Let's see the elephants first. Over there, next to the giraffes. Know what a giraffe is, Michael?"

Not really, and when he saw one he couldn't believe his eyes. "Look at its neck," he marveled, letting himself be pulled over to a low metal railing in front of another fence, much higher. What sort of creature was this? "Look at its *eyelashes*."

Sam laughed gleefully, leaning against him and clapping

his hands. "Look at his neck! It's so he can eat the leaves on trees. Dad says it's evolution."

Elephants were even stranger than giraffes. They were *huge*. And slow and plodding and kind-eyed, with ivory tusks and hides like rubber. They seemed like fairy-tale characters out of one of Sam's books, not real animals. "Where do they come from?" he asked, watching Philip toss a peanut into their enormous cage.

"These are from Africa," Sam answered, pointing to a sign nailed to the railing. "There's Indian ones over there. Look, it can eat out of my hand." He stretched his arm toward the cage as far as he could, and the long, wrinkled trunk uncurled over his open hand. But at the last second he gave a shriek and jumped back, dropping the peanut on the ground. "Rats." The elephant picked up the peanut with his trunk and stuck it in his small, dainty mouth.

Amazing—Michael couldn't get over it. "How do they get here? Why don't they let them go?"

"They're captured by game hunters and sold to zoos. Why don't they let them go?" Philip laughed. "Because they'd trample things. This one weighs about three tons, and God knows what it eats. Anyway, they couldn't survive on their own. This is Chicago, not the veld."

"Then why don't they leave them alone?"

"Because then we couldn't look at them."

"We could look at pictures," Sam said uncertainly.

"They don't mind being here," Philip told him. "They like it."

"How do you know?" Michael peered at the gigantic animals, trying to read happiness in their gray, unknowable faces.

"Why wouldn't they? All they have to do is eat and sleep."

"Yeah," said Sam, brightening. "They like it here. Come on, let's look at the hippopotamuses."

Hippopotamuses had frog eyes and tiny ears, huge jaws and big flabby tongues, and they were the ugliest creatures Michael had ever seen. One was a baby, only seventy pounds, the sign said. It looked like an enormous puppy, and never left its mother's bristly, thick-skinned side.

Rhinoceroses were just as peculiar, interesting but not quite real. They looked like scaly, overweight unicorns, but beyond that he couldn't make much of a connection with them. Maybe Philip was right and these animals, captured on the other side of the world and put into fenced paddocks and concrete pens so humans could look at them, really did like it here. Who could say? They looked peaceful.

The lions were beautiful, but they wouldn't wake up. "Hey!" yelled Sam, clapping his hands. "You! Hey!" Nothing; the four gorgeous animals lay on their sides, flicking their tails and panting from the heat, too hot to open their eyes.

"Do they like it here, too?" Michael asked Philip, and he shrugged and said, "Sure." But he didn't seem as positive as he had been about the elephants.

The tigers looked bored. Sam couldn't get their attention, either; they wouldn't even glance at him. "They'll eat you if you go near them," he warned, and then told a horrible story about a little girl who had gone too close to the cage and got eaten alive.

"Is that true?"

"It's really true," Sam assured him, and even Philip nodded without smiling. Still, it was hard to believe. They looked like big, lazy cats. Then he saw the leopards.

There were two of them, and after watching them for a few seconds he realized what was wrong. "They've gone insane." Sam and Philip laughed uneasily. "No, look. Because of the cage. They've gone mad." They had worn a deep path in the dirt around all the sides, and they never stopped pacing around and around the small square, with their jaws slack and their whitish eyes crazy. Plod, plod, heads swinging, tails flicking.

"Animals don't go insane." Sam waved his arms. "Hey! Are you crazy?" Without even looking at him, one of the leopards slashed at the bars with its clawed paw and roared.

Sam screamed; everybody around the cage jumped back in shock. Then they felt silly and tried to laugh, and a man next to Philip taunted the leopard in a nervous, nasty voice. The animals ignored him and kept pacing, pacing, staring and pacing.

Michael's heart slowed down gradually; he could feel his rational mind returning, pure instinct starting to recede. This animal wanted his blood. Nothing had stopped it from killing him but the bars on its cage.

"They were probably captured as adults," Philip said as they walked away. "They do better if they're born in captivity."

"Yeah," said Sam. "Then they don't know what they're missing, right, Flip?"

"Right."

Bears next. Michael didn't know the fierce grizzlies, or the blinding white polars, or the small brown Europeans. But he knew the black bears. They hadn't been his friends, exactly, but they hadn't been enemies, either. They were . . . neighbors. He had respected them and had kept out of their way, and they had done the same for him. So it was strange to look at them through metal bars and watch them sitting and leaning, lounging and lolling, tame as children, playing begging tricks on the people around their cage. One mother bear sat down and held her feet with her front paws so people would throw peanuts into her lap, like a lady's apron. Another one sucked on his paws while he made a loud humming noise. Sam said he wished he could play with them, and Philip told another horrible story, this one about a lady who had been pulled by her clothes against a bear cage and slowly eaten.

Michael didn't doubt it. They might look it, but he was sure these bears weren't tame. And their clumsy, lumbering walk was deceptive. He had seen them at night, chasing their next meal at that bounding trot that was twice as fast as he could run.

Then again, maybe these dopey, wheedling animals were tame. They embarrassed him. Doing nothing night and day had turned them into fools. People were laughing at them, and they deserved it. They had lost all their dignity.

They saw kangaroos, then anteaters and East African warthogs. Mongooses, wallabies, musk oxen. Then monkeys—what a revelation they were. They looked like animal-men, and Philip said his father called them the link in the evolutionary chain between humans and beasts. They made Sam laugh and laugh with their silly play and their amazing agility.

Michael felt glad for the silliness and the laughter, because inside something was happening to him. Or something was going to happen. He was waiting for it, not doing anything to stop it, while a sickly dread filled up in him like fear, like slow, killing hunger. He smiled, spoke to Philip and Sam when they spoke to him, but he thought they knew. They knew something, not everything. When they bought food from a vendor and carried it to a table to eat under some trees, he couldn't get it down. It stuck in his throat and almost made him gag.

"What'll we see next? We could go to the reptile house."

Philip made a face. "You go, I'll wait outside."

"Philip's scared of snakes. *I'm* not, and I'm only seven. But he is, and he's a man."

" 'Scared' isn't the word I'd use. I'm averse. I have an aversion to slimy things. Which seems eminently sensible to me."

Michael didn't say anything, didn't give an opinion. Whatever they would see next, they would see. If it was the thing he was most afraid of, that's what it would be.

It was.

SMALLER CARNIVORA, the sign said. "Meat eaters," Philip explained as they walked down a path toward a group of low buildings and small, fenced pens. Sam remembered the foxes from another visit. "Let's go in here," he said, and even though Michael's blood had begun to throb in his throat, he let Sam pull him through the open door of a squat stone building, where the heavy smell of dumb, blind confinement hung like smoke.

There wasn't even a cage, not one with bars. The foxes lived behind a glass wall in a bright square box, with a log and some dead moss for cover. A long window ran along the length of the back wall.

"There's one, I think." Sam pointed to a ball of dirty gray fur, curled up and partly hidden behind the log. "Is that one? Last time you could see it. It came to the glass and looked at me." He tapped on the glass with his knuckles.

"Don't do that," Michael said, and Sam looked at him with curious eyes.

If he stared hard at the fox, he could just make out a movement, a tiny rise and fall of the animal's hide above the shoulders; otherwise he would have said it was dead. Dead for a long time; its dingy fur had no color, no shine. Was it alone in the glass cage? Nothing else stirred. Maybe they hibernated here the year round. What else could they do? Foxes lived for two things: running and burrowing. Behind the glass wall of this little case, this box where it was always daylight, they might as well be dead.

MARTEN, said the sign on the next cage—MARTES AMERICANA.

"Is that one?" Sam pressed his face to the steamy glass. "I think it moved. See it? That brown thing?"

"Marten," Michael mouthed.

"They eat squirrels," Sam read from the sign, "and mice."

And birds. They traveled from tree to tree in the early morning or the late afternoon, miles and miles through the trees, playing, looking for food. For some reason they liked cloudy days best.

"They're boring," Sam decided and moved on.

Fisher and weasel, ermine and skunk. Raccoon. Badger.

Michael couldn't look at the badgers, couldn't bear to peer through the smudged window at their shabby cage. At home, they had been his good friends. They came out of their dens to play games before they went foraging.

They would go to a stump or a fallen tree along one of their familiar trails; one would climb to the top of the stump, and the others would try to pull him down. They played that game over and over, taking turns being on top. And sometimes, on moonlit nights, they danced.

"Let's go, this is dull. Let's go outside and look at the wolves."

Canis lupus. Gray wolf.

Six of them. In a square paddock, maybe fifteen feet on a side, with wire between the bars of the high fence around it. No trees, no shade. Odor of urine and feces. The wolves lay in the sun on the hard, grassless dirt, raggedy-looking, like pieces of a dirty rug flung around. Some kind of food, lumps of something, lay on the ground beside bowls of water, overturned or empty or fouled. The wolves' faces were empty, their eyes blank. He couldn't tell who their leader was. Maybe they had no leader. Their stillness wasn't peaceful, it was numb. Dead.

A wolf came out of a wooden shed at the back of the pen. He had a thick coat of silver-gray, with a black ruff around his shoulders. He was taller than the others, and older, maybe ten or eleven. He stood still, blinking at nothing, his hot tongue lolling. For the space of one second his yellow eyes met Michael's. And then they slid past him, indifferent. Blank.

" 'Solitary and nomadic, the North American gray wolf is a vicious and dangerous predator.' " Sam read. " 'Unchecked, his relentless hunting has decimated the Canadian and Alaskan caribou herds, and his attacks on men have made him one of the most feared of all the carnivores.' "

"That's a lie."

"What is?"

Michael didn't answer.

"What is?" Sam repeated.

"All of it."

"Why? Why, Michael?"

The big wolf came forward a few steps, circled twice,

and lowered himself to the dirt, chest first. He put his head on his forepaws and closed his eyes.

Michael thought of the old wolf. He was bigger than this one, and his coat was brownish gold; he had a white tail and white paws, and his eyes were the color of amber. Now that he knew his own age, Michael could reckon the number of years they had known each other: about fourteen. If he was still alive, the old wolf, his brother, would be seventeen or eighteen now. But last winter had probably killed him.

"Michael?"

There were no pups, at least not outside. They didn't breed here, he was sure of it. They lived and died here, and when the zoo wanted more, they set traps and captured them.

"Michael?" Sam was leaning against his thigh, looking up into his face with wide, searching eyes. "Let's go, okay?" He slipped his hand into Michael's and squeezed it.

They walked away. Philip didn't say anything, but Michael could feel his glance, as worried as Sam's. "Shall we go look at the seals?" Philip said, trying to make his voice sound happy.

"Oh, yes, the seals!" Sam tugged on Michael's hand, smiling up at him, trying to make him smile back. "You'll like them, they're so funny."

He went with them for a little ways, but then he stopped. "No, I can't."

They didn't ask why. "Shall we just go home, then?" Philip said.

He nodded, because that was easier. He didn't say the true thing, that he had no home.

Sam finally stopped talking and fell asleep on his shoulder, lulled by the rocking of the train. Across the aisle, Philip looked up from the puzzle he was working on in the newspaper and smiled. Michael smiled back.

For a while he had tried to pretend that they were his brothers. Sometimes it had seemed that way. His little brother and his big brother, and him safe in the middle; a family. But it was like the dream he had had over and over when he first got lost, that his mother and father found him in the forest and took him home, holding his hands on either side, and him safe in the middle.

A dream. Not real.

Outside the window, he could see the blue of the lake through patches of trees in Jackson Park. Close up, little houses flew by, shabby houses where Sam had told him poor people lived. The train was crowded; people had to stand in the aisle, hanging on to leather straps, swaying and bouncing. They smelled like sweat and frankfurters and newsprint. When their dark, human eyes slipped over him, sometimes resting for a second, they didn't think anything of it. They were sure he was one of them.

"South Shore. Next stop, South Shore."

Michael put his hands on Sam's shoulders and carefully leaned him in the other direction, against the window. He didn't even stir.

Philip looked surprised when he stood up. "Lavatory," Michael mouthed. Philip nodded and went back to his puzzle.

Outside on the platform, he moved with the crowd toward the exit, but stopped just short of the stairway. The train jerked once and began to slide away. He saw Sam's bright blond hair in the window, the tip of his ear flattened against the glass. And behind him, the white edge of Philip's newspaper. Then they were gone, and the train was just a blur.

He went down the steps and started to walk the other way, back toward the city.

13

"What do you mean, he didn't get off the train?"

Philip pulled his chair out and sat down at the dining room table. "Just what I said. He got up to go to the lavatory, and that's the last we saw of him."

Sydney stared. "Did you look for him? Why did you get off without him?"

Sam came to stand beside her chair. She took one look at his face and put her arm around him, drawing him up close. "Flip says he probably got off," he said in a wobbly voice. "He thinks he ran away."

"Ran away!"

"But this is dreadful." Aunt Estelle squeezed her napkin into a ball and dropped it on the table. "The poor man! We must find him. Should we call the police? No—no. Harley, what do you think?"

Sydney's father pulled off his eyeglasses and examined the lenses by candlelight. "Hmm," he said. "Hmm."

Across the table, Philip put up a hand to shield his face from Aunt Estelle and sent Sydney a look of wild inquiry—*What the hell is the matter with her?*—that under any other circumstances would've made her laugh. As it was, she sat back in her chair, still holding on to Sam, and told Philip the news without a smile. "Mr. Higgins phoned this afternoon. He's found out who Michael's parents are. They're—"

"Who's Mr. Higgins?" Sam cut in.

"A detective who's been looking for Michael's family."

"And?" said Philip, goggle-eyed.

"They're—"

"It seems we've underestimated our Mr. MacNeil," Aunt Estelle interrupted with a simpering smile that set Sydney's teeth on edge. All day she'd been battling a hot rage against her aunt, even knowing it was irrational. "It seems he's—"

"He's the son of an earl," Sydney blurted out, purely to deny Aunt Estelle the satisfaction of saying it first. "His father is the Laird of Auldearn. Michael's called 'the Younger of Auldearn.' He's Scottish royalty."

Everything was ready for the party. The workmen and gardeners and landscapers had gone away late in the afternoon, their jobs finally finished. Flowers in borders, flowers in clumps, flowers in great pots littered the lawn, scenting the still night air. The tasseled sides of the yellow-and-white striped awning winked in the first light of the moon rising over the lake. The lanterns, the ones Michael had said looked like Sydney's skin, were dark now, but they waved gaily when the whisper of a breeze caught at their papery sides. Sydney had seen weddings less elaborate than this supper dance her aunt would host tomorrow afternoon. Now everything was just right, down to the last linen napkin, bleached snowy white and ironed by the maids with military exactness.

How ironic that Sydney's personal life had never been in a bigger mess.

"Where is he, Philip?" she asked, hugging her knees, peering into the darkening yard as if she could see him, as if her hard stare could conjure up his lean, lanky form on the path, sauntering toward her, smiling his shy smile.

"He'll come back."

"Will he?"

"Sure. I think he just wanted some time to be by himself."

She put her chin on her knees, wishing he was right, wanting him to convince her. But the memory of the last things Michael had said to her, and the awful things she'd said to him, stole away her complacence.

"He was sad today," Philip said thoughtfully. "Not himself at all. He hated the zoo. We shouldn't have taken him—it was stupid. I never even thought."

"What?"

"The animals, the cages. Everything. He hated it," he said again. "But he wouldn't talk about it, so we didn't, either. Maybe we should have. He's not happy, Syd. Something's wrong."

Yes, and she knew what it was. "Oh, God," she mumbled into her hands, wretched. Philip began a soft massage on the back of her neck, and in spite of everything it comforted her a little.

"He'll come back. Don't worry. This is his home, we're his family."

She put her hand on her throat, trying not to cry. "I hurt him," she confessed, and immediately the tears overflowed, stinging the backs of her eyes. "This is all my doing."

"Come on, Syd. What are you talking about?"

The need to tell somebody and the need to keep her awful cowardice a secret battled and clashed inside, increasing her misery.

"I know he's in love with you."

She straightened slowly. "You—he—" Philip's hand fell away as she turned her head to stare at him. "How?" she finally managed.

He smiled. "I've got eyes."

"Did he tell you?"

"He didn't have to. What happened, Syd?"

She took a deep breath. "Aunt Estelle caught us together. In the dining room," she added hastily.

"Aha." Philip looked relieved, but kept his voice carefully toneless.

"She was—not pleased. Ha. We had a terrible quarrel." She hugged herself, shuddering, remembering it. *Do you intend to marry this person? Or are you only going to have a sexual affair with him?* Hearing her aunt say the word *sexual* had absolutely appalled her. It had sounded so dirty on her lips, and in that one moment Sydney had felt real shame.

Philip started to laugh. "I can imagine."

"It's not funny. I told Michael we couldn't be together anymore, that what we'd done was a mistake. And then— he left me. He said he loved me, and he left me. He knew it was over."

Philip gave her his handkerchief and she buried her face in it. She could have sobbed all night, but she didn't want him to see her like this.

"What's this?" he said softly, rubbing her back. "Is this guilt, Syd, or something else?"

She blew her nose and didn't answer.

"Hm? What's going on? You didn't go and fall in love with Michael, did you?"

She felt her heart break, right in two. "I did," she choked and covered her face again. "I did, I did, I did." The confession cheered her up a little.

"Well," he said, his glibness deserting him for once. "Well, well. This is a bit of a sticky wicket. As they no doubt say in Scotland. He's the son of an *earl*?"

Some kind of hysteria bubbled up, making a giggle and then a sob catch in her throat. "And Aunt Estelle wants to claim him! All's forgiven—she wants me to dance with him tomorrow night at the party!"

Philip laughed, and this time she didn't scold him. She couldn't join in, but the sour humor of the situation wasn't lost on her.

"It'll work out," he said consolingly, still chuckling. "And just think: if you marry him, you'll end up a countess or something. Lady Sydney of Auldearn."

"I don't care about any of that. Oh, Philip, I can't stand this. I have to see him, talk to him." The night had turned black while they spoke. She couldn't make out the path to the lake anymore. "Where is he, Philip? What do you think he's doing right now?"

First he set the wolves free.

He found the key to their pen in the keeper's shed,

neatly labeled, hanging from a hook next to the keys to the cages of the other "carnivores." It was easy. The shed wasn't locked; all he had to do was wait until the keeper fed the animals and went away, then wait a little longer for the moon to rise, while he crouched in the cover of low bushes beside the path. So easy. Humans were the simplest to fool; he had done it all his life. And he had no fear of them, not now, not here, with the ground hard and sure again under his bare feet, the rich, complicated scent of the night in his nostrils. He'd shed his coat, but his dark shirt and trousers would hide him well, better than his white skin. He would be invisible to these whistling, mumbling, slow-moving zookeepers in their green uniforms and flat-topped caps.

There were eight wolves in the pen, lying on the ground under the stars, scattered around, no two together. They jumped up, first one and then all of them, and when he unlocked the paddock and pushed open the gate they backed up with their ears pricked, smelling him, eyes intent.

He made a mistake then. He said a human word, "Come."

They darted away, bunching together, fear making them a pack. Two ran through the low door to the enclosure at the back, snarling as they went, their tails tucked. The others retreated to the fence, keeping him in sight, never turning their backs. He went three slow paces toward them and dropped to his haunches.

Time passed while they watched each other, and it was the old time, the kind he had never thought to measure in minutes or seconds. He could feel himself slipping back, and everything falling away, memory, time, wanting, fear, until there wasn't anything except this now, this here. The wolves were part of him and he was one of them, and there was nothing between all of them and the night, the sky, the smell of dry earth and the touch of sharp, dark air.

The big wolf, the leader, moved out of the middle of the pack and came forward on stiff legs, the black ruff on his shoulders standing straight and prickly. Michael held out his hand, palm up to show it was empty, fingers spread. The wolf showed his teeth but didn't move. Behind him the others stirred, whining uneasily, asking a question.

In their own language, Michael told them why he'd come. They froze.

He stood up slowly and began to back through the gate. Outside on the path again, he stopped and spread his arms wide. The big wolf sat down to stare at him some more, breathing through his mouth, his tongue lolling. He looked over his shoulder at the others. They had a silent debate. When it was over, the wolf got to his feet and led the way out of the pen while the rest followed, slowly, carefully, shivering with excitement, and Michael backed up in time to their steps, keeping the same distance away.

A low cry rose from the back of the pen. Through the gloom he saw the two wolves who had run into the shed before. They were cowering against it, one a female, young, gray with a white face, the other a male, all gray. The female was afraid, and the male wouldn't leave her.

So, he'd been wrong. They did mate in captivity.

He moved into the shadow of the trees to watch while the big wolf trotted back inside the pen and the other wolves milled in the open, sniffing at the ground they had never walked on before.

Twice the big wolf went close to the other two and told them something, turned, and trotted out of the pen. But they wouldn't move. The third time, the gray male followed him halfway to the gate, but when the female called him, he went back to her and sat down. Whimpering, she laid her chin on the back of his neck, holding him still. The big wolf turned his back on them in disgust.

Outside the pen, the other wolves prowled and snuffled in confusion, and Michael realized they didn't know what to do. How could they? But he wasn't their leader, and he had no idea if they would go with him.

He started to run, crouching low and keeping close to the trees, away from the lamps that burned on poles along the path sides. A scent, a noise—he stopped short, and a man walked out of the shadow of a building. A guard, not a keeper; he wore a different kind of hat, and he twirled a black stick in his hand. The kind of stick O'Fallon had kept in his belt.

Michael turned his head slowly, slowly, and peered into the blackness behind him. There wasn't a sound, not a stir or a breath, but six pairs of yellow eyes glittered back at him in the moonlight.

The man heard nothing, saw nothing. He strolled on out of sight, and when his scent faded Michael ran again.

The place wasn't far. Part of the zoo was fenced, but not all. He knew the boundaries because he had searched them out an hour ago while he waited for dark. Half of the back of the zoo ran into a wood, thin and scraggly at first but thickening as it climbed up a steep, stony slope. He didn't know how far the wood went or what came after it. But when the wind was right he could smell the lake. That had to be a good sign.

The wolves had run past him, but they stopped when he did, turning to watch him in a tense silence. The leader took a few uncertain steps toward him. *There.* Michael looked behind him toward the hill and pointed to it. The big wolf licked his lips to show he wasn't afraid. Michael returned his keen, thoughtful gaze for a whole minute. Then, with a shake of his head that made his ears flap, the wolf wheeled around and ran with his pack up hill and out of sight. The thud of a stone falling behind them, loosened by a hurrying, scrambling paw, was the last sound they made.

He could have run then, with them or away from them. He could have found safety, at least for a while, if he'd started to run, anywhere, and not stopped until morning. But the moon was high and the thrill of the hunt was in his blood. *What the hell?* as Philip said—that was how he felt. Reckless, wild. *What the hell.* He would let them all go.

Getting the keys was easy again. Not so easy was getting the weasels and ermines to leave their cramped cages and scamper off into the trees of the park. He ended up herding them out, using his feet to nudge them through the fake moss and dead, dry stumps. The half-grown babies could run now; in fact, freedom looked better to them than it did to their parents. When they jumped and darted away, the older ones took off after them.

The skunks he left alone; opened the door to their cage and left in a hurry. They could do what they liked.

The racoons wouldn't go; they were too tame—they liked it here. He said, "Stay, then," and moved on.

Martens and fishers were smart; they knew what he was about even before he could show them. He had hardly gotten their wire gate open before they spilled out and tumbled away, black and brown balls of scrambling fur, gone in seconds.

But the foxes didn't trust him. They were beaten down, they couldn't believe anything would change. He had to run with them at first to wake them up, make them believe. He stopped at the foot of the hill, and the foxes who hadn't scattered already ran past him, sprinting flat out, racing to freedom.

The beavers had an enclosure, but inside it they had dammed up a stream that ran through the middle of the park. So he left them alone. They were already free—their life's work was right here. Same with the otters; all they needed to be happy was a mud slide, and they had one inside their roomy outdoor cage.

Badgers next. They were his favorite. The smartest, too—they knew exactly why he'd come. But they were so kindhearted, they wouldn't go. "Go," he told them. "Run!" It wasn't in them to hate anything, he realized, not even the zoo. It was a bitter disappointment.

He had to get different keys for the deer. They were the *artiodactyla,* and they lived in small, dusty, trampled paddocks at the front of the zoo. Good: he would herd them right out the main gate.

He didn't know there were so many different kinds, maybe ten, twenty, maybe more. But once he started he couldn't stop. He released the caribou and the white-tails first because he knew them, had lived through the

thick and thin of their yearly migrations for as long as he
could remember. The others he set free at random—
Kashmir deer, European red deer, fallow deer, sambar,
chamois, water buck, Alpine ibex, Virginia deer, American moose, eland, elk, big-horn sheep, Canadian goat,
barasingha, axis, gemsbok, pronghorn antelope, mule
deer, roe, Sika, Indian hog deer, white-bearded gnu—

What in the world had made him think he could herd
them anywhere, much less through a twelve-foot gate
fifty yards away? But he kept on, doing the best he could,
and about a third of them went where he drove them. The
rest scattered in fright and confusion, and it wasn't long
before the sound of their hooves and the smell of their
fear woke up the whole zoo. And brought all the guards
running.

He wasn't afraid—they would never catch him. But he
hadn't finished yet, and he wished he had let the deer go
last. Moving fast in the dark, skirting the main building,
easily eluding the men running here and there with
lanterns and torches, shouting questions and curses at
each other, Michael headed for the bear house.

In the caretaker's building, a choice slowed him down.
Beside the key to the black bears' cage he saw the key to
the wolverines'. He despised wolverines. Small, powerful,
ugly, mean, they ate everything, even moose, even deer,
porcupines, birds, bait, animals struggling in traps, and
what they couldn't eat they spoiled with musk and urine
and droppings. His hand hovered over the key too long—
he couldn't decide! Outside, a man shouted. The nearness
of the danger made his mind up for him. "Sorry," he muttered, although he wasn't sorry at all. Grabbing the keys to
the bears' cage, he slipped back outside.

He let the black bears go, but not the others. He didn't
know them, the hulking grizzlies, the enormous polars;
they were like lions or elephants to him, strangers he
couldn't trust. But black bears never hurt anyone: all they
wanted to do with humans was stay out of their way.

Everything was chaos, caged animals screeching and
bellowing, guards yelling, running in circles. Michael had

hidden his shoes and his jacket under some shrubbery near the main building. He'd need them, once he got out of here, to look normal on the streets and not attract attention. Circling around, avoiding the lighted paths, he heard the rasp of a shoe on stone, just before a man walked out of a copse and straight toward him. Too late to hide—he had seen him. Michael ran right at him.

"Hey! Stop, you—" The man jumped out of the way at the last second, his moonlit face round with surprise. He started after him, shouting for him to stop, and then he yelled, "Get him—right there, he's the one! Stop that guy!"

Another guard appeared on the path, holding a lantern. He set it on the ground when he saw Michael and lifted his fists, preparing to fight. Michael changed direction and ran around him.

Too late to get his clothes now—too many people that way. He'd go the other way, back way, and disappear in the woods.

Deer everywhere. He could hardly run in a straight line. But he could hide sometimes, crouching down among them, running alongside them in their panic. So many deer. It was funny, really. Maybe someday he would laugh.

He lost his cover when a loud *crack* scattered the deer. He knew that sound. Every animal knew what it was. Gunshot.

Crack, again—from the direction of the wolf pen. Everything in him said *escape,* run as fast as he could from the sound. He started to—then swerved back onto the concrete walk, his feet slapping loud on the hard pavement, and pounded down a long, shallow slope toward the shots.

Two men, one with a lantern, one with a gun. They had backed the wolves, the two who wouldn't run, against the outside front of the fence to their pen. The female had lost her mind. Frenzied by fear, she made short, snarling dashes at the men, then hurled herself back against the fence, slamming her body against it, mad to escape. The open gate to the pen was eight feet away—all she had to do was run through it to be safe. Caught, but safe. The male, snarling and whimpering in his confusion, darted to the opening and almost went through it, but then shied away and ran back to his mate.

The man with the gun raised it to his shoulder. Michael was too far away to stop him. He screamed, *"No,"* a second before the rifle spat fire. The she-wolf gave a high cry as her body hurtled back against the fence, hung for a second, and dropped. Blood spattered the white of her ruff. She twitched and went still. The man made the *click* sound with his gun that meant he would shoot again.

Michael smacked into him at a full run. The gun fired and the man said, "Hunh," at the same time. The rifle flew out of his hands and they went sprawling on the ground, turning and turning, trying to grab each other's hands. Michael saw the gray wolf standing frozen, stiff-legged, eyes crazed with grief. *Run.* Sounds of men running, men shouting. *Run.* The man he was fighting struck him in the face with his fist, and he tasted blood. When he looked again, the wolf was gone.

Someone yanked his head back by the hair. He growled out his rage, snapping his teeth at the air, trying to twist away. Shouting, wild-eyed men surrounded him, jumping back when he lunged at them. He heard the *click* sound of a gun, and his blood turned sluggish, froze in his veins. A black stick saved him. Before the gun could shoot, it came slashing down, first on his shoulder, then his cheek. He slumped over his enemy and let the blackness take him.

Aunt Estelle wasn't enjoying her party. She had wanted the theme of the evening, the primary topic of conversation on the lips of her important guests, to be Sydney's second coming out. Instead, what everyone was talking about was what sort of madman would break into the zoo and set all the animals free.

"I heard the elephants stampeded," Lincoln Turnbull pulled Sydney closer to say, raising his voice over the waltz music Reggie Arrow's orchestra was playing at the rear of the terrace. "Randy Collier said he heard the lions ate the leopards, the tigers ate the lions, and the bears ate everybody."

Sydney turned her face away.

"The *Tribune* said only a few species were released, but the *Morning Herald* said it was all of them. They're still rounding deer up from as far away as Oak Park."

"I'm sure that's an exaggeration. The papers never get anything right." The sharpness in her tone silenced him. She thought of apologizing—he was her guest, after all—but she wasn't sorry. If she had to smile through one more outrageous zoo story tonight, she was going to fly to pieces. The afternoon paper said the animal-freeing madman had been "subdued by clubbing" before he'd managed to shake off his captors and escape. The phrase chilled her. She imagined him hurt, wounded, alone and frightened and unable to come home.

She stole a glance at her watch, pinned to the wrist that lay across Lincoln's broad, sturdy shoulder. Seven-forty. He had been missing for over twenty-four hours. By now at least a dozen people had asked her where he was. "I hear he's quite civilized now," Marjorie Clemens, whom Sydney had never liked, had been silly enough to add. "I'm just *dying* to meet him. Where is he?" "Oh, somewhere," she had answered vaguely, glancing around, as if he might be out on the lawn, or eating shrimp toasts with Sam under the striped canopy. She had answered everyone that way, when she had answered them at all—sometimes she pretended not to hear. The family ought to have come up with a story, she realized too late. Who knew what Philip was saying, or Papa, or Sam?

Oh, Michael. She scoured the edges of the trees when Lincoln twirled her around the terrace in time to the music. Could he be out there somewhere, watching and hiding? What in the world had he been thinking of? How could he have done such a mad thing? Oh, if only he would come home!

Lincoln said something, and she nodded, smiled, pretended to listen. Would it have been better if they had caught him? At least then he'd be safe. Men with guns were looking for him now. So far, thank God, they didn't know *who* they were looking for. If they found him—

"Music's stopped."

"What? Oh." She dropped her arms, laughing to cover her awkwardness.

Lincoln frowned at her with real concern. "Sydney, what's the matter? Are you all right?"

"Yes, fine, just, you know, in a dither. Parties do that to me. My own, I mean. Oh—my aunt's giving me one of those looks; it means she wants me." Her aunt wasn't even looking at her. "Excuse me, will you?"

"Sydney—"

"I'll come back. I will, I promise." She twinkled her eyes at him until he finally smiled. Then she escaped.

The orchestra began a new song. She put on a purposeful face so that no one would ask her to dance, moving smoothly through the crowd toward the lawn. Air, she just needed some air. And if she could be by herself for five minutes—

"Sydney?"

Camille, blond and beautiful in a gown of shimmering white organza, put a hand on her arm to make her stop. Her blue eyes, so much like Spencer's in the way they crinkled at the corners, narrowed on her with worry. "Are you all right?"

Why did people keep asking her that? "Yes, I'm fine. Don't I look all right?"

"You look lovely," Cam said quickly. "I love your hair that way. You have to show me how to do that. Is it a French roll?"

"What? Yes." She patted the back of her head distractedly. "Cam, go and dance with Lincoln, will you?"

"Lincoln?"

"You don't mind, do you?"

"No, but why? Is he being a pest?"

"No, no, he's just . . . oh, you know."

Cam looked at her strangely. "All right, if you want me to."

"Thanks." It would keep him occupied for a while, out of her way. She left Cam, forgetting to say good-bye.

The night turned into a blur. She greeted, smiled, danced, talked, laughed, her secret goal always to get away from where she was without being rude or too obviously distracted. Time crawled. An hour went by, but when she looked at her watch she saw it had only been ten minutes. How could she stand this? If it didn't end soon, she was sure she would lose her mind.

". . . such a nice idea, having it outside. And aren't we lucky the weather cooperated? What would you have done if it rained?"

She answered something, but her restless gaze traveled past her friend Helen Ivy's head, always searching the dancing, milling crowd. A scowling face startled her out of her abstraction. Charles West, standing by himself at the edge of the terrace, stared straight back at her, not returning her tentative smile. Her briskness to him lately had finally gotten through, to the point that he had not only stopped asking her to marry him, he had stopped talking to her at all. His anger seemed unjustified to her— she had treated him, under the circumstances, as gently as she could—but she supposed it was understandable. Ought she to go over to him, speak to him, try to pretend nothing had happened? He looked uncomfortable and out of place in his borrowed evening clothes, one hand nervously stroking his gingery beard. She sighed. What good would it do? It might even give him false hope. Besides, her mind was too fragmented; she had too much on it right now to try to deal tactfully with Charles.

Mrs. Prettiman, a friend of her aunt's whom Sydney had known all her life, approached her between dances and spoke to her so kindly she was afraid she might weep. How close to the surface her emotions were tonight! "I won't keep you standing here talking to *me*," Mrs. Prettiman said, with an old lady's self-deprecation to the young, "but I had to tell you how very glad I am to see you again, Sydney. Out and about," she added meaningfully. "Spencer was a dear man; I always liked him, always thought you and he made a perfect couple." She took Sydney's hand and pressed it gently. "I'm happy for you, my dear. Because the time has come. You're young and beautiful, and you've done enough grieving."

Philip saved her from embarrassing herself. "Evening, Mrs. P," he said breezily, coming up behind Sydney and putting his hands on her shoulders. "Mind if I borrow my sister for a minute? Urgent hostess duties, you know."

The two women gave each other quick, intense hugs, then Sydney let Philip lead her way.

He took her to a dim, deserted place on the lawn. With his back to the dancers, his face changed; all the gaiety left it. "What is it?" She clutched at his arm, sudden dread making her whisper. "What's wrong?"

"They're here. They've found out."

"Who? Oh, God! The police?"

He nodded grimly. "They're with Dad in his study. They're asking him questions."

Detective Lieutenant Moon stuck his thick, bluish chin out and barked like a bulldog. "You sure he's not here? How long has he been gone? How come you didn't report him missing?"

Sydney's father took cover by pulling drawers out of his desk and peering into them, pretending to look for his tobacco. "Have a seat, Lieutenant?" he asked pleasantly, his head half hidden by his desk. "You and your associate?"

Moon only rolled his shoulders and took a more bullish stance. Sydney recognized his type with a sinking heart: rich people scared him, and he covered his intimidation with aggression. "We know he's the one, we got him dead to rights. Now, who saw him last?" He glared at Sydney, at her father, at Philip, not because he suspected them of anything, but because he had decided that was the safest, most dignified way to deal with them.

"How do you know it was Michael?" Sydney ventured, trying to look simultaneously unconcerned and slightly insulted. "What proof do you have?"

Lieutenant Moon's face was pear-shaped, all the fat

and flesh at the bottom; he looked particularly ugly, like a spoiled pumpkin, when he smiled. He drew a piece of paper out of his pocket. "Here's proof. Got it in black and white."

She went closer. Philip groaned under his breath, but she didn't recognize Sam's primitive artistic style until she read the neat caption in his handwriting at the bottom of the sketch: MICHAEL MACNEIL BY SAMUEL ADAIR WINTER.

"Where did you find that?" Papa asked interestedly.

"In the pocket of a jacket we found under some bushes. In the zoo," he added. "Along with a pair of shoes. The guy who let the animals out of their cages didn't have a coat on, plus he was barefoot."

"Still," Philip said weakly. "They could be anybody's clothes."

The lieutenant turned to his assistant, Sergeant Somebody. "Show 'em," he said, and the other man opened a cloth bag and pulled out a wrinkled gray jacket and a pair of fawn-colored balmorals. "Recognize these?"

Nobody answered.

"Well?"

Philip opened his mouth, but Sydney said, "They're Michael's," before he could speak. He'd been going to lie, she was sure, and that would only have made things worse. "They're Michael's clothes. My brother gave them to him."

Moon gave a sour nod, satisfied, and took a notebook out of his pocket. "Okay, now. He's not here, you say, hasn't been here since yesterday morning. Who saw him last?"

"Is he hurt?" Sydney went closer, ignoring the question, disregarding the policeman's belligerent scowl. "How did he get away? The paper said they hit him with clubs."

"Yeah," Moon growled, "but not hard enough. Guards thought he was out, didn't cuff him. Turned their backs on him for a minute, and next thing they know he's running for the hills. Now, who saw him last?"

While Philip kept his answers short and as uninforma-
tive as possible, Papa lit his pipe and blew clouds of
smoke around his head to hide behind. Sydney wandered
to the curtained terrace doors. Pulling the cloth aside an
inch, she stared out at the dancing lanterns strung out
across the yard, the guests milling about, happy and oblivious, on the lawn. Anxiety was like a loud buzzing in
her ears, drowning out the strains of the music, making it
impossible to think. "What will you do with him if you
find him?" she heard Philip ask. "Anyway, what are the
charges?"

"Assault and battery, trespassing, criminal mischief.
Grand theft. Breaking and entering. Reckless endanger-
ment, vandalism. That'll do for a start."

Her heart sank. The newspapers had treated the incident as a sensation, a prank, elaborate and expensive but
not very serious in the long run. Obviously the law didn't
see it that way at all.

"We're putting a patrol around the house in case he
tries to come back," Moon continued. "Meanwhile, I'd
advise you people to be careful."

"Why?"

Moon frowned at her. "Because the man's dangerous.
He's desperate, too; no telling what he'll try next."

"He's not dangerous," she scoffed—then froze. "He's
not dangerous," she repeated, in a different voice, beating
down panic. She moved toward her father's desk,
imploring him with her eyes. "Papa, tell him—tell him
Michael's not dangerous."

"Hm? 'Course he's not." The vagueness in his eyes
cleared; he understood what frightened her. "Daughter's
right—no need to pursue MacNeil as if he's a criminal.
Man's not violent, never has been."

"In other words," Philip put in tensely, "guns aren't
necessary."

Lieutenant Moon misunderstood. "If you're worried
about your party," he said with a sneer, "don't be. My
men'll be discreet. None o' your important guests will
even know they're here."

On cue, the door to the hall flew open and Aunt Estelle burst into the room. "Harley—police everywhere—we're ruined—"

To Sydney's knowledge her aunt had never swooned before. She did it well. She even made it to the couch first and crumpled onto it gracefully before she fainted dead away.

A day passed. At four o'clock on Monday morning, Sydney got out of bed, threw on her robe, and crept downstairs. Hector greeted her in her father's study, where he'd been sleeping since Michael disappeared, by rolling over on his back and thunking his tail on the floor. "Shhh," she told him, kneeling down to scratch his chest. "You miss him, too, don't you?" Hector had been behaving badly, upset by the excitement and disruption of Aunt Estelle's party, and then the strange men, newspaper reporters, and policemen loitering outside the house at all hours of the day and night.

But things were settling down now. A day after what surely must have been the longest party in history—it had been for Sydney—journalists had finally stopped knocking at the door and calling on the telephone, and the police patrol had diminished to only two men, who took turns circling the grounds at thirty-minute intevals. More men on the job than that was excessive, Lieutenant Moon had decided, especially after Papa made him a solemn promise to call the station if Michael did come home. He had had no choice. Sydney saw that now, but at the time she had felt betrayed.

Now she was only distraught. The whole family was distraught. As soon as the last shocked, fascinated guest went home on Saturday night, Aunt Estelle had taken to her bed, and she hadn't been seen since. Papa was taking it hard, too, and not only because what Michael had done would have repercussions for him, political and professional, at the university. He was genuinely concerned for Michael himself—Michael the man, not the scientific subject.

Philip blamed himself, for reasons that made no sense. "I should've known better than to take him there in the first place," he kept saying, when he wasn't saying, "I should never have let him get off the train." Sam went on searches for him, taking Hector for long walks in the neighborhood and along the lake. Michael's zoo escapade had fired his imagination and increased his hero worship; he wanted to hear over and over about the animals Michael had freed, which ones had been recaptured and which ones had escaped. At the same time, it was just beginning to dawn on him that he might never see his friend again.

Tonight he had cried when Sydney tucked him into bed. "What if he doesn't come back? What if he tries to come back and they hurt him? What if they catch him and put him in jail?" She had dried his tears and reassured him as best she could, but inside she was weeping with him.

Hector stopped grinning up at her, rolled over, and ran to the closed terrace doors, whining. "Hush," she ordered at the same time she followed him, pulling back the curtain over the window to look out. Nothing. Black night. Still, something made her unlock the door and open it a crack. The better to see, she thought—but the next thing she knew she was whispering to Hector, *"Stay,"* putting her bare foot across his chest to hold him, and slipping outside.

The half-moon shone directly overhead in a cloudless sky; she felt vulnerable and exposed in her thin white night robe. But she tiptoed to the edge of the terrace anyway, drawn by something strong, a feeling she *knew* was more than hope. *"Michael?"* she whispered, straining to see through the darkness. Was that a movement, there in the trees, beside the walled garden? She stared until her eyes watered, stopped breathing in case there was something to hear.

Nothing.

Her shoulders sagged. He wasn't there. The police were wrong: this was the *last* place he would come. Michael knew everything about how to hide and how to run. He would be a fool to come home.

She turned. And there he was, standing in a moon shadow at the side of the house. She felt no fear and she knew it was he, even though all she could see was the dim outline of his body. Her heart contracted painfully. She ran toward him and saw amazement in his weary face just before she flung herself into his arms. "Michael." It came out a stifled sob, muffled against his hair. His arms tightened around her, lifted her off her feet while he pressed his mouth to her cheek, her jaw, and finally her lips. Relief made her weak; when he set her down, her knees wobbled. "Hurry," she said, "come inside."

"No."

She halted and looked at him sharply. "But there are policemen—"

"They're in front."

"All right, but come in, you—"

"No, Sydney."

"*Why?*" They were both whispering.

"I just wanted to see you. To say good-bye."

"Damn it. Damn it, Michael. If you don't come inside—" She started to cry.

"All right." She was squeezing his hand so hard he winced. "Just for a second," he said and followed her into the house.

Hector went berserk. She had to close the hall door so the noise of his joyful whimpering wouldn't wake the whole house. Michael sat on the floor with him to calm him down. Sydney lit a candle. She watched them, grinning, wiping her face with her handkerchief, and finally sat down, too. With Hector between them they petted the dog, petted each other's hands, leaned over and kissed again. "You look awful," she said tenderly. The sight of his bare feet brought her to the brink of more tears. "Are you all right?"

"Yes. I'm tired."

He looked exhausted. And dirty, and hungry. He had a bruise on his cheek. "Where have you been?"

"Here."

"Here! The whole time?"

He nodded. He bent his head to the dog, but glanced up at her through the lock of unkempt hair that fell across his forehead. "I thought you'd be angry."

"Why?"

"Because of what I did."

"Oh, no, Michael. Worried sick, but not angry." But she had to ask. "Why did you do it?"

He looked at her, and she thought he might be judging her, deciding if he could trust her with the answer. But his eyes were gentle and loving, and in the end all he said was, "I had to. And now I don't have time to tell you why. I have to go away for good."

"You can't," she said flatly.

He shook his head and stood up.

"They'll find you!"

"No, they won't." He started to back away from her.

"Michael!" Through the beginnings of panic, the answer came to her. *"Michael Terence James Brodie MacNeil."*

That stopped him. His expression almost made her laugh. "What?"

"That's you!"

He was having trouble making his mouth work. "That's me," he finally agreed, his eyes wide with wonder.

She went to him, her heart so full it hurt. "Your father is Terence MacNeil. He's the Laird of Auldearn. Your mother is Elizabeth. Your house is a castle in the Highlands of Scotland. You're Michael, the Younger of Auldearn."

"Auldearn." He said it strangely, not the way she said it at all. *All-dern.* His gray eyes had a faraway look, as if he were remembering.

"So you see? You can't go," she said softly, stroking the rough stubble of beard on his cheek. "The detective is sending cables to Scotland, and when he finds your parents they'll come for you. They'll help you."

"But I don't have the time. If I stay, the police will lock me up in jail."

"But if they catch you—"

"They won't catch me."

"They might. This isn't the Canadian wilderness, Michael, it's the real world. You're vulnerable here. Defenseless," she explained when he shook his head impatiently. "Open—unprotected. This isn't your world, it's theirs, and they'll find you here."

"No, they won't."

She wanted to stamp her foot and shake him by the shoulders. "They *will*. Don't you see, you have to *hide*, not run. Then, once we find your parents, everything will be different."

"Why?"

"Because—that's just the way it works. You're nobody now, but when you have people behind you, important people, everything will change."

He looked skeptical, but he said, "Then I'll hide."

"Yes." She hugged him, exultant. "But not out there." She pointed toward the door. "That's where they're looking for you, out there. It's too dangerous."

"Where, then?"

"In my world. It's the last place they'll look. Stay right here, Michael, and promise you won't leave. Stay here and play with Hector. I won't be long."

"Sydney—"

"Promise." With her pleading eyes and her clutching hands, she begged him to trust her.

"All right. I promise." He blinked when she kissed him on the lips. "What are you going to do?"

"I'm going to get dressed and pack a bag."

"Where are we going?"

The idea must have been there all along, growing in her mind without her conscious knowledge, because suddenly it was a full-blown scheme. "We're going to the Palmer House Hotel."

14

"Mr. and Mrs. Vernon Tuttle, Topeka, Kansas.'
Michael printed the letters as fast as he
could, trying to ignore the sharp-eyed man
behind the marble counter watching every stroke of the
pen. When he finished, he looked at what he'd written and
wished he could do it over. It looked false; the man was
going to know it was a lie.

"Welcome to the Palmer House, Mr. and Mrs.—" The
register book sat on a big revolving plate. The clerk spun
it around and read, "Tuttle. From Kansas. How are you
folks this morning? Just get in?"

His mind went blank. All he could think of to say was,
"Fine. Yes."

Sydney slid her arm through his and leaned against
him. "Tell him about the room, Vern," she said in a soft
voice, but loud enough for the desk clerk to hear. "Tell
him what we'd like."

Michael cleared his throat. "We just got married," he
recited. "We would like—"

"Well, congratulations! Isn't that nice."

"Yes. Thank you," he said, thrown off his stride. He
had to start over. "We just got married, and we would like
the honeymoon suite, but we don't have reservations." He
let his breath out slowly, listening to the echo of the
words while he watched the clerk's face for signs of disbelief. He hadn't been this nervous when he let the zoo
animals go.

"Ah. Well, now, that might be a bit of a problem." The

clerk looked sad and started leafing through the pages of the book.

Sydney gave Michael a nudge with her elbow. He looked at her blankly for a second, then remembered. "We'll pay cash, and we'll stay for a whole week."

The clerk gave him a quick, very polite up-and-down look. Michael was glad he was wearing Philip's black coat, waistcoat, high-collared shirt, and paisley necktie. Sydney had parted his hair in the middle and made him put on a pair of Dr. Winter's silver spectacles. If anybody asked him what he did for a living, he was supposed to say, "Cattle."

"I do hope you can accommodate us," Sydney said in a sort of purring voice, nothing at all like her real voice. She looked so strange in her aunt's ugly veiled hat, Michael was afraid to look at her, afraid he might laugh. "I've *always* wanted to stay here. I just know we'll love it—and then you can start having your meetings here, Vern. Of the Topeka Cattlemen's Association," she explained to the clerk. "They've been having them at the Richelieu, but I just think that hotel is too hoity-toity for its own good. Now, *this*—" She gazed around at the huge, echoing lobby, with white marble columns holding up the ceiling and plants everywhere, and a fountain in the middle splashing as loud as a waterfall. "*This* is real class."

That did it, although Michael wasn't exactly sure why. Before he knew it, a boy in a purple uniform was taking their two suitcases—"We're having the rest sent," Sydney smiled at the desk clerk—and leading them across the carpeted lobby to a gold-colored cage Michael didn't realize was an elevator until it started going up. Luckily he had been in one before, with Sam, or he might have done something stupid. Sydney grabbed his hand, and he remembered she hated heights. Her fear made him forget all about his. He put his arm around her, not caring if the bellboy saw, and she gave him a shaky smile.

Their room was gorgeous. *Rooms;* there were two—no, three if you counted the bathroom. Sydney told the bellboy what they wanted to have for breakfast, and she told him they wanted it here, not in the dining room. Then Michael gave him a quarter and he went away.

As soon as he was gone they both burst out laughing. It was the tension, he knew, not because anything was really funny. They looked at all the rooms, Sydney turning around with her arms out, pretending she was dancing, touching things and saying, "Oh, look at this—oh, and this—" They had a living room full of heavy, velvet-covered furniture and pictures on the walls of flowers and fruit. The bathroom had a bathtub as big as a bed, and white tile everywhere, a marble sink with gold handles, towels thick as pillows, and mirrors on all the walls. The bedroom was almost as big as the living room, and with a bed in it the size of . . . he didn't know what. "The size of Kansas," Sydney said, and they burst out laughing again.

She sobered first. "I've got to go call Philip," she said, picking up the purse she had just thrown on the bed.

"You left him a note."

"Yes, but I want to tell him we got here, let him know we're safe."

"Are you going to tell him where we are?"

"I don't know yet. Maybe."

"Should I come with you?"

"No, you stay here. You can't come out at *all*, Michael. Nobody can see you."

"Okay," he said quickly, so she would stop frowning at him like that.

"Okay." She took the key to the room and went out.

When she came back, she pretended she wasn't upset until he pried out of her what was wrong. "He wasn't very understanding," she finally admitted. "He said I've gone out of my mind." She looked small and disappointed as she dropped down on one of the fat, velvet-covered chairs in the living room. "So I didn't tell him where we are. 'Someplace safe,' I said, but that's all, even when he yelled at me."

"Are you afraid he would tell the police?"

"No, but he might tell my aunt."

Michael nodded; telling the aunt would be worse than telling the police.

"And he'd definitely come here and try to make me go home."

"Sydney." He sat down on the edge of the low table in front of her. "Is this the right thing to do?"

"Yes," she said, and she made her hand a fist and banged it on the sofa arm of the chair. "This is the last place in the world they'll think to look for that wild man who set all the animals free. All we have to do is stay here and wait until Mr. Higgins finds your parents. I know it doesn't sound like much of a plan, but if we stick to it we'll be safe. And you have to admit, Michael, it's better than you being in jail."

"But now you'll be in trouble, too. For being with me."

"No, I won't. Because I'm not here, I'm in Joliet. I left this morning for a visit with my old school chum, Mary Kay Blayney. She got married last year, and I've never met her new husband."

He laughed—she looked so pleased with herself. "Is there really such a person?"

"Yes, and she'll tell that story if I ask her to. But it won't come to that, I know it won't."

They both jumped when two loud knocks sounded at the door. But it was only the man with their breakfast. They had ordered so much food, it came on a rolling cart with a long white tablecloth. "I'll do this, Vern," Sydney said, taking a coin out of her pocketbook. She had coached him on the train about how much to tip the boy with their suitcases, but not the man with their food. If they were really going to be here a week, he would probably need another lesson in tipping.

Eggs, bacon, porridge, and toast had never tasted so delicious. "When did you eat last?" Sydney wondered, staring at him.

He remembered to swallow before answering. "Can't remember."

"Two days? Three? You look as if you're starving."

"I'm not starving." There had been long winters when

he had starved. This wasn't anywhere near that bad. He hoped she wouldn't ask *what* he'd eaten last; the answer would spoil her appetite.

She didn't have much of one anyway; either that or she was pretending so he could have almost all the food. She poured herself another cup of coffee and sat back in her chair and watched him while he ate. When there was nothing left on his plate or hers, she poured him more hot chocolate from a heavy silver pitcher, and he drank it while he looked at her.

"What day is this?" he asked.

"Monday."

"I lost track. What day was the zoo?"

"Friday."

So. He had stayed hidden for three nights. "I thought of you on Saturday. How was your party?"

She sent him a soft, slow smile over the top of her cup. She had the prettiest eyes, and when she smiled they got narrow and twinkly. "Awful."

"It was?"

"I wanted to dance with you, and you weren't there."

He wanted to get up and kiss her, but his arms and legs felt pleasantly heavy; he didn't have the strength. The morning sun shone on the side of her face, lighting up the green in her eyes and the red in her hair. "You look beautiful, Sydney."

She didn't blush or look away. She said, "So do you."

That made him laugh. He set the cup on his thigh and rested his head against the back of his chair. The sun felt warm on his right arm and right knee. Through the open window, the noise of horses and people and vehicles was all mixed together into a faraway blur. Sydney was talking about going shopping. "You'll be needing some things," she said, and started mentioning what they were. He listened to her soft voice rise and fall, rise and fall. He used to fall asleep in the summer listening to the hum of crickets in the trees. Sydney's voice was like a waterfall. Music. Water splashing on rocks, playing different notes. . . .

"Michael. Wake up." She took the cup out of his hand and put it on the table. "All right, now. *Up* we go."

"I'm not Sam," he protested, but he let her pull him to his feet. They went into the bedroom, she holding his hand. "I can do this." But she just kept doing what she was doing, pulling the covers back and plumping the pillow, lightly pressing him down on the bed, making him stretch out. She even took his shoes off.

"Close your eyes," she said, and he did, but when she tried to move away he kept her hand. "What? A good night kiss?" Smiling, she bent over and put her lips on his forehead.

"I'm not Sam," he said again. She lifted one eyebrow. Then she kissed him on the mouth.

"What will you do while I'm sleeping?" he asked with his eyes closed.

She started to tell him in her waterfall voice.

When he woke up, the shadows on the blank white ceiling overhead bewildered him; he had no idea where he was. But a second later it all came back—he was in the Palmer House Hotel. The clue was the pillow under his head and the soft mattress under his body. Sydney had put him here, and he had pretended this was normal, nothing out of the ordinary. But as far as he could remember, it was the first time he'd ever slept in a bed.

It wasn't too bad.

How long had he been sleeping? He got up and padded over to the window and drew back the curtain. From the light he judged it was either late in the afternoon or early in the morning; in the city, with no dew or crickets and no birds to speak of, he couldn't tell.

He combed his hair with his fingers and tried to smooth out the wrinkles in his clothes before he opened the door to the living room. He opened it quietly, in case Sydney was sleeping.

She wasn't there.

"Sydney?" No answer. Through the open door to the bathroom, he saw that that room was empty, too.

He turned on the gaslight and went in. His face looked the same in all the mirrors: terrible. No wonder she hadn't much wanted to kiss him. At least his beard didn't look too bad—he had shaved before they left her house, so he wouldn't look like a wild man when they registered at the Palmer House. But his skin was pasty, his bones stuck out, and his eyes had blue circles under them. However much sleep he'd gotten today, it hadn't been enough.

A bath, that's what he needed. He began to fill the tub with hot water, expecting it to run out and turn to cold after a few minutes, like the Winters' tub did. This one didn't, though; the water stayed boiling hot until he turned it off, and then he had to add cold to it before he could get in.

"Ahhh." He lowered his backside into the tub slowly, an inch at a time. "Ahhh." The hot water made his sore shoulder ache at first, but it was a pleasant, numbing ache. When he was all the way in, nothing showing but his head and the tops of his knees, a simple, humbling truth came to him: he liked living in civilization better than the wilderness. Because this bath had a cold stream, as Philip would say, beat all to hell.

He had almost fallen asleep again when he heard the door in the living room open and close. He sat up straight, tense and quiet, then relaxed when Sydney called softly, "Michael?"

"I'm in here."

He had left the door open. She poked her head in, saw him, and jumped back, smacking her hip on the doorknob. "Oops, sorry." He saw her face turn pink before she ducked it and disappeared.

He didn't know why that made him want to laugh. Made him feel happy, in fact. Sydney had looked a little silly, but that wasn't it. It must be because he was usually the one doing the silly things and making a fool of himself. It was nice, once in a while, having it the other way around.

"I've brought you some clothes," she called through the door in a very casual voice. "I'll leave them on the bed."

"Thank you. I'll be right out."

"Oh, take your time."

But he washed his hair and scrubbed himself clean in a hurry, because now that she was here, soaking by himself in a tub of hot water wasn't nearly as much fun.

In the bedroom, he stripped off his wet towel and put on the clothes she had brought him: dark trousers made out of some soft material; a silky white shirt; a loose, knitted jacket he thought was called a sweater. She had bought pajamas, too, and slippers, the soft leather kind Philip wore. In the long mirror on the wardrobe door, he shook his head at himself, amazed. He really looked normal. Like a regular person.

"You look wonderful" was the first thing Sydney said. She was sitting on the sofa with her legs folded under her skirt, the newspaper in her lap. She was still beautiful, but now she was the one who looked tired. "Did you sleep well?"

"Yes. What day is it?"

"It's still Monday," she said, laughing.

So it was late, not early. Now that he knew, the sky through the window looked like nothing but an evening sky, pale as a pearl overhead, fading to pink on the edges.

"I've called down for dinner."

"How?" He imagined her standing at the top of a flight of stairs, shouting out what she wanted to eat.

"There's a house telephone on every floor, by the elevator. It rings at the desk, and you just tell them what you want."

"Gosh," he said. She laughed again, and he knew it was because he was talking like Sam. "That's damned amazing," he added, but now he only sounded like Philip. He looked forward to the day when he knew enough to sound like himself.

"I bought the afternoon paper." She moved it to her side and gestured at the sofa, wanting him to sit next to her. He did. "You smell good." She looked away after she said that, turning pink again. He ran his hand over his slicked-back hair, feeling shy, too. "How did you get this?" She lifted her hand and almost but not quite touched the bruise on his cheek. His bath had turned it darker and even more colorful.

"It doesn't hurt."

"How did it happen?"

"At the zoo. A man hit me with a stick."

She stared at him. She started to say something, but changed her mind and sighed.

He looked down—and saw a picture of himself on the front page of the newspaper. "Oh, God," he whispered. "Oh, no."

"No, this is good, Michael. Really, it's *better* that they printed this photo."

He didn't agree. It was the one they had taken the day after O'Fallon shot him. He looked crazy, really dangerous, and the wildness in his eyes he knew was fear, but to anyone else it would look like cruelty. He turned his head away, not wanting to see it any longer. "What do they say about me?" he asked, although he didn't want to know that, either.

"Nothing they didn't say yesterday or the day before."

"Where I've been, there weren't any newspapers," he reminded her. "You might as well tell me."

"They just talk about how much it'll cost to replace the animals that were lost or destroyed, what animals they recaptured. Security measures they plan to take in the future. That sort of thing. And how the search for you has been unsuccessful so far. Michael . . ."

"Yes?"

"Do you want to talk about this? About what happened?"

"Did they get the wolves back?"

"What?"

"You said they recaptured some of the animals. Did they get the wolves?"

She looked down at the paper, then back at him. "I don't think so. It doesn't say anything about wolves."

Then he had done one thing right, he thought, staring straight ahead, rubbing his hands over the knees of his new pants. Out of all the trouble he had brought down on the people he loved, that was the one good thing.

"Do you . . ."

"No. I don't think I want to talk about it right now."

She nodded, and they fell silent. He was glad when, a few minutes later, a waiter came in with their dinner.

They ate it while they watched the sun go down outside their living room window. Neither one of them said much. He wanted to ask her why she was quiet, and if she was sorry she had come here with him. But he was still so tired, and he didn't think he was ready to hear the answer.

"Come and look out," he invited her when dinner was over, opening the window wider. "It's nice when the people go home. Quiet." Sydney came and stood beside him, but she didn't lean against the sill and look down with him. "This is not the world's busiest corner," he said, remembering what Sam had told him. "The world's busiest corner is State Street and Madison. This is State and Monroe."

"Very good." She laughed. "But you can see Madison from here."

"Where?"

"Over there." She pointed without moving. "One block north."

"You don't like heights," he said, remembering.

"Not much. I don't know why—no one else in the family is like this."

"I don't mind heights like this," he said, gesturing to the window. "What I don't like is when they're *moving*." She gave a pretend shudder, and he knew she was thinking of the Ferris wheel.

They were silent again until she said, "Summer's almost over. It's still hot, but you can tell. It's something in the air."

"It's because the days are getting shorter. The birds don't even sing the same songs."

She sighed.

"Sydney . . ."

"Mm?"

"Are you sorry we came here?"

"No."

"Are you afraid?"

"A little. Not right now."

The red sky warmed the pale skin of her cheek and made it look soft as a flower petal. He wanted to touch her, but he didn't dare. Things weren't quite the same between them in this place. She was nervous—so was he. He couldn't be sure what she wanted. If there was going to be touching, she would have to be the one who started it.

"I'm tired again," he said truthfully. "Every time I eat, I get tired. I think I'd like to go to sleep again. If you don't mind."

"No, I don't mind."

"Excuse me," he said formally.

" 'Night, Michael."

"Good night."

In the bedroom, he put on the blue striped pajamas she had bought him. He wouldn't have done it for anyone else—they looked ridiculous, they served no purpose he could see, and he was pretty sure he wasn't going to be able to sleep in them—but Sydney had given them to him, so he wanted to wear them.

Lying in bed, half asleep, it occurred to him to wonder where she would sleep. Right here, with him? He hoped so. He would love to lie beside Sydney in this big soft bed. But there was a couch in the living room; maybe she would sleep there. Maybe *he* should sleep there. Should he get up and ask? She was more likely to sleep here, though, if he didn't say anything. He would just pretend he had never thought about it. See what happened. Anything might happen.

He drifted off, hoping it would happen soon.

While she ran water in the tub, while she bathed, while she dried herself and put on her nightgown, Sydney thought about where she ought to sleep. It was no trivial decision; in a way, everything depended on it.

This intimacy they were sharing—taking baths in the same tub, for instance—excited and scared her at the same time, because she knew where it was leading. Probably leading. The question was, did Michael? Five days ago she had told him it was wrong, that they could not be together. Being a man without guile, he had taken her at her word. But things had changed since then—*she* had changed—although he didn't know it. How could he? She hadn't gotten up the courage to tell him. So far, she hadn't even been brave enough to show him.

She finished cleaning her teeth and brushing her hair and wandered into the bedroom. He had left the light on. For her? She crept closer, so she could look at him. He slept curled up on his side, his arms and legs folded in as if to protect his body; and even though he was deeply asleep, there was still a kind of vigilance in his posture, an alertness, as if the line for him between sleep and wakefulness was razor-thin.

Slowly, carefully, she sank down onto the edge of the mattress. Sleep had sculpted his dark hair into a comical-looking crest, like a cardinal's. She smoothed it with her fingertips, watching his eyelids flicker as if he were dreaming. How beautiful he was. Everything about him pleased her.

She yawned. She was tired, too. She hadn't slept a wink last night, and not much the night before. Silly to sleep on the sofa when there was this nice bed. They were both exhausted, and they were just going to sleep here, after all.

Michael shifted then, slowly uncurling from the tight ball and straightening out onto his back. Leaving plenty of room for her. If that wasn't an invitation, she didn't know what was.

She put out the light and lay down beside him, drawing the covers up over both of them and wriggling pleasurably in the warm place he had just left. This was so nice. She moved over a couple of inches so their arms could touch. She could smell his pajamas, that cottony, store-bought smell of brand-new clothes. She thought of

Spencer, his solid, reassuring presence beside her every night in their bed. She had had that for only a year—long enough to be sure that nobody should have to go without it.

It was wrong to sleep alone, she decided, her mind beginning to drift. Aunt Estelle slept alone every night. No wonder she was miserable most of the time. People were supposed to find each other. It was nature's way . . . and she was where she was supposed to be, where she belonged. . . .

Hugging herself, she rolled toward Michael. She fell asleep with her knees touching his thigh and her forehead pressing against his shoulder, breathing in the fresh, linty smell of his new pajamas.

"As soon as you remembered it wasn't a shipwreck, Michael, Mr. Higgins stopped looking among the lists of drownings in the Great Lakes." Sydney leaned forward over the breakfast table, so the morning sun wouldn't shine in her eyes. "He started concentrating on hunting, trapping, and fishing expeditions, limiting the area to southern Ontario. He did find a MacNeil, who accidentally shot himself to death on a camping trip near Rainy Lake in 1876, but the other circumstances didn't fit— there were no drownings, and no little boy in his party."

Michael nodded, listening intently, letting the forgotten cup of chocolate in his hand turn cold.

"So then Higgins started looking into pleasure excursions, vacation tours of the area around Echo Bay—where they found you. Nothing. But when he widened the search to the east, toward Sudbury and Georgian Bay, his luck turned." She crossed her arms on the table and leaned closer, feeling his excitement and letting it fuel hers. "Do you recognize the name MacDurmott?"

His eyes, burning on hers, dimmed for only a second, then snapped back into focus. He whispered, "My uncle."

"Yes. Duncan MacDurmott—"

"And Aunt Kate."

"Yes. They were lost, and so was their guide, a man named Hastee."

He squeezed his eyes shut, then shook his head. He couldn't remember the guide.

"Everyone thought you drowned, too. In the record, it lists 'Duncan MacDurmott, his wife Katherine, and their nephew, Michael MacNeil, younger of Auldearn.' "

He pushed back his chair and walked to the window, his body blocking out the yellow light.

"He's cabled your parents in Invergordon, and now we're just waiting for them to respond. Maybe they already have. I'll call Philip in a little while and find out. Michael? What are you thinking?" He didn't answer. She stood up. He had put on his clothes, but she was still in her nightgown and robe—a bold move, she had thought this morning, occasioned by the waiter arriving with their breakfast much sooner than she'd expected. "Surely you don't still think they sent you away. This proves they didn't. You were on a trip with your uncle and aunt."

When he kept silent, she sidled around the table and went to him. "When they find out you're alive, they'll be so happy. A miracle, they'll think." She put her hand on his shoulder and made him turn so she could see his face. "What is it?"

"There was something they said that I heard, Sydney. I wasn't supposed to hear it. I don't remember all the words, but I think . . . I think they were glad I was going away."

"Oh, no."

He shut his eyes tight, trying to remember. " 'Peace and quiet'—my father said that, and then my mother laughed. They wanted me gone. But I can't remember . . ." He opened his eyes, and they were full of sorrow and confusion. "I can't remember what I did wrong." She put her arms around him. "It's all right. It was so long ago. But I wanted you to know—that they might not think it's a miracle."

"Then they don't deserve you," she whispered fiercely. She drew his head down and kissed him. And then again.

The first kiss was for comfort, because he was her dear friend and he hurt. The second was for pleasure. She took her time, softening his mouth with hers, listening to his breathing change. She didn't think he was thinking about his parents anymore. Now that the time had finally come, she couldn't get over how calm she was. Calm and sure.

Looking into his eyes, she pulled his shirt out of the back of his trousers, slowly, deliberately, so she could slide her hands up and touch his bare skin—and so there could be no doubt in his mind about her intentions. Ah, smooth. Soft and sun-warmed; thin, delicate skin over the small bumps of his spine, the subtle quiver of rock-hard muscles. "Michael," she whispered. "The last time we did this I spoiled it. I said it was wrong, but I was the one who was wrong."

The cords in his neck were stretched tight from tension. She had taken him off guard; he hadn't been expecting this. "Because of the aunt," he guessed.

The memory of her spinelessness that day could still make her blush. "Yes. Because of my aunt."

"She's not here now."

"She certainly isn't." His skin where she stroked him felt like hot satin. "I was so stupid. It took almost losing you to realize how big an idiot I was."

He made soft circles on her cheek with the side of his thumb. "It's okay. The aunt scares me, too."

She captured his hand and pressed kisses into the center of his palm. "I'd like to make love with you. Right now. Do you know what making love is?"

Michael closed his eyes, trying to contain himself, trying to believe what he was hearing. "It's a euphemism."

"What?"

He opened his eyes. He could see he had broken the mood. "Philip said that." It was embarrassing to confess. "I don't really know what it means."

Her smile came back. "It's only a euphemism if the two people making love don't love each other."

"I love you, Sydney."

She touched the sides of his face with her hands so gently. "That's good. Because I love you, too."

He kissed her the way she had taught him, softly, slowly, while inside, his heart filled and grew until it felt too big for his chest. She loved him. Sydney never lied. She loved him. He whispered her name, holding her in his arms, pulling her close so he could feel her, all of her, the whole front of her pressed up hard against him. She had on hardly any clothes, and when he took his hands over the soft material of her night robe, he could feel everything, her round bottom, her shoulder blades, the way her hips curved into her little waist. "Will we really make love?" he whispered, still hardly able to believe it. It was too much like a dream.

"I want to." Sydney was trembling when she drew back from his kisses and his hot, seeking hands. "Michael," she said, surprised when it came out an unsteady croak. "Have you, um . . ." She laughed weakly. "Have you ever done this before?"

"No. But I've seen it."

She blinked at him, watching his ears turn red. "You've *seen* it?"

He cleared his throat. "Philip and I," he muttered, then trailed off, keeping his eyes down.

Philip again. She decided to think about that later. "Just tell me one thing. Do I need to show you what to do?"

"Yes," he decided after thinking it over a few seconds. "I think you'd better."

She pulled away to see if he was joking. There was a light in his eyes, and the longer she stared at him the more his lips twitched. She couldn't really be certain what that meant, though. All at once she smiled full in his face. "Oh, I'm so happy. I've never been so happy as I am right this minute."

"Good. I'm happy, too. All my life I've been waiting for you, Sydney, and now . . ."

"Now you've got me."

They drifted into the bedroom and sat down on the bed, side by side. When he didn't touch her, she put her mouth in the warm hollow of his throat and kissed him. "First," she breathed, tasting him with her tongue. "First we take off our clothes. But you probably knew that." He kept his eyes down and didn't acknowledge that one way or the other. Except by slowly letting out his breath. When he reached for the top button of his shirt, she took his hand and redirected it. "And sometimes it's nice if we . . . do this for each other."

Michael smiled, thinking of the girl in the window at Mrs. Birch's house, how she had taken the man's clothes off for him. What those two had done was a *euphemism*, though. This wasn't going to be anything like that. He watched Sydney's face while he untied the bow at the collar of her robe and started to undo the buttons. He had never seen her eyes like this, heavy-lidded and dark, sexy, and loving. He liked undressing her. But how was he going to stand it if they kept doing everything this slowly?

Her nightgown had buttons down the front, a hundred of them, all the way to the hem. When he got them undone to her waist, though, she slipped her arms out of the sleeves and let the gown fall down around her hips. Oh, God, she was beautiful. He had known she would be. But seeing her like this, a naked lady . . . *his* naked lady . . . he couldn't breathe right anymore.

"You can touch me," she whispered.

He wasn't sure he could. His hands cupped the air, copying the perfect shape of her breasts without quite touching them. And then one pink tip grazed the center of his palm, and he had to hold her.

The way she sighed surprised him. She let her head fall to the side and let her eyes close; she looked as though she was dreaming some slow, sweet dream. He put his lips on the silky skin of her neck, breathing in her smell, keeping his hands full of the soft weight of her breasts. "You're so beautiful," he told her, wishing he knew better words.

The caress of his hair on her throat tickled. Sydney slid her fingers into it, behind his ears, rubbing him softly.

Raw need slammed into her, making her grit her teeth and press her knees together hard. She pulled him up and found his mouth, gave him deep, hungry kisses, nothing like the soft kisses she had taught him before. She was starving for him. He took his hands off her.

Cloth ripped; buttons popped. He tore at his shirt and pushed her down, and she couldn't wait for the hard, heavy press of his weight on her body. He lay between her legs, and what shocked her was how natural it felt. She broke away from one of his ravenous kisses to hold him, just hold him, because she was afraid it was happening too fast. "Michael," she panted, "wait, wait. Let's wait."

"Why?"

"Because. It's better that way." She blew a strand of hair out of her eye. "Besides, we still have our clothes on."

He rolled to his side, unbuttoned his trousers, stripped them off, and kicked them on the floor.

"Ha," she said, breathless. "That was quick." Leaning over her, braced on his elbow, he hooked his fingers around a fold of her bunched-up nightgown and tugged, uncovering her stomach. "Sure you haven't done this before?" she asked with a shaky laugh.

"Take off everything, Sydney. I want to see all of you. I can't wait any longer."

"Oh, Michael." What a time to feel shy. But she couldn't help it, and she wished it was night, not broad, bright daylight for their first time. Feeling brave, she slithered out of her nightgown and threw it in the direction of his pants.

They came up on their knees, pressing together, holding tight. He couldn't get enough of the feel of her bare bottom; he took his hands over and over the warm, sleek skin, squeezing her tight flesh, kneading her. She rested her head on his shoulder, making soft sounds, tickling his neck with her tongue.

He sat back on his haunches so he could look at her. They both had navels and nipples and hair between their legs, but after that the resemblance ended. Where he was hard, Sydney was soft; where he was straight, she curved. And she had skin like flowers, like warm water. He put his hands on her thighs, stroking his thumbs along the soft, soft insides, just brushing the red-gold hair at the top. He wanted to touch her there, bury his face there, taste there, but he was afraid to do anything until she told him, afraid of making a mistake.

He lifted his head, catching a look in her eyes he wasn't expecting. She tried to smile, but it wasn't real. "What's the matter, Sydney?"

"Nothing."

"No, something. Did I touch you the wrong way?" She shook her head, but now he couldn't believe her. "I'm sorry. I was too quick."

"It's not that." She sat back on her heels, and when he started to take his hands off she held them still. "It's this," she said. "And this. And this." Light as a feather, she ran the tips of her fingers over the scar on his chest, the long one across his stomach, the scar between his ribs. He had more—he was covered with them—but she didn't touch the others.

He turned his head away. "It's ugly."

"*No. No.* Oh, Michael, don't look like that." Sydney wrapped her arms around him and held him, kissing his cheeks, desperate to explain. "It's just that I think of what happened to you, how hard it was, how lonely, the things you must have suffered—and I can hardly bear it. It hurts me. It just *hurts.*" Her emotions were too ragged, too open; she hated herself for crying now, *now,* of all times.

"It wasn't so bad." He smiled at her, trying to make her smile back. "Shh, Sydney, don't cry. Don't be sad, not right now. Let's do this now."

His singleminded tenderness brought her around. She laughed, a thick, teary sound, and dashed the moisture from her eyes. "You're right. Let's do this now."

They lay down, facing each other in the center of the bed. At first they were content with just touching each other, playing and fondling, exploring and inspecting. Michael was fascinated by her breasts, but Sydney grew restless as one of the finer points of erotic stimulation kept eluding him. "These are the most sensitive places," she finally revealed to him, "here, and here"—a sentence she could not have uttered to another human being, not even Spencer, had he needed such a lesson. But to Michael she could say it, albeit with a blush, because . . . well, because he liked all of this so much.

"Here," he murmured, brow furrowed, watching her nipple crinkle and curl under his curious fingers.

"Right . . . there." He made her toes curl.

"Animals don't do this," he noted. "As far as I know."

"They don't know what they're missing."

"The mother's breasts are just for feeding milk to the babies. *After* the lovemaking."

"Ha," she said with her eyes closed. "Well, humans are different."

"Is it the same with men? I have breasts," he said, looking down at his chest.

"Let's see." She tickled his left nipple with her fingernail.

"Hunh." His eyes lit up in surprise.

"Aha. Interesting. But . . . it's more so for women, I don't know why. And . . ." Oh, this was excruciating. Could she really say this? "You know the way baby animals suckle their mothers for milk?"

"Suckle," he repeated—a new word. He went back to playing with her nipple.

"Well," she said to the air over his shoulder, "when a man puts his mouth on a woman's breast that way . . . as if he were suckling her . . . it gives her a great deal of pleasure. When they're making love. As . . . we are."

He looked into her eyes, amazed, and it was all she could do not to hide her face, or kiss him to distract him, pretend she'd just been kidding. Frowning with concentration, he bent his head, and at the first soft tug of his lips on her bosom, she gasped. "Like that?"

"Yes—" He did it again, and she moaned.

"This is good, Sydney."

"Isn't it, though."

He pushed her onto her back and moved to her other

breast, nuzzling and nipping and tonguing her—the cleverest pupil, so quick—drawing strongly on her hardening nipple and making her groan. It was a relief to stop directing and just let it happen. Nothing she could have told him now anyway, nothing he needed to know. He was like a storm, lashing and battering at her senses. She gave herself up gladly to the force of his passion, because she had no choice.

But he was holding himself back. And she wanted more, she wanted everything, and he *must* know what came next. But he wouldn't proceed until she told him to. And even though it frustrated her to madness now, it was what she loved about him the most—that animal wildness in him that he controlled with his absolute humanity. O'Fallon's brutality, her father's tests, his own desire for her—in every case he had checked his impulses by an act of will. In truth, Michael was the most civilized man she had ever known.

She couldn't stand not touching him, even though it might shorten this act of love and end it too soon for her. But she needed that deeper intimacy with him now. Murmuring his name, she fumbled her hand between them until her palm brushed the satiny tip of his penis. His whole body jerked; he sucked in air through his teeth. She squeezed him lightly, playfully, but he didn't relax. "You can touch me, too," she invited in a tense whisper, hoping she wouldn't have to say where.

She didn't. But she had to say, "Soft—soft," and he gentled his hand instantly, opening her as if she were a delicate shell, a flower. "Oh, Michael, Michael, Michael."

"You like it," he noticed, pleased with himself.

Two could play that game. "You like this." She stroked the velvety underside of his cock until he gasped. She stopped at once, afraid she had gone too far, succeeded too well. "Not yet," she whispered. "Not until you're inside me."

"I want to be inside you."

"I know. But not yet."

"Why?"

"Shh."

She tortured them both a little longer, teasing him with her slow fingers, which had never felt so clever, so flawlessly inventive. Each time she paused, he explored her very gently while she held her breath and watched his face, his eyes downcast, a fixed, concentrating half smile on his lips. Knowing that he had never touched a woman this way gave her the tenderest feeling, of power and good fortune, and nearly unbearable excitement.

"Sydney." A muscle in his jaw spasmed rhythmically. He had reached his limit, and so had she. But she felt a little wistful as she kissed his mouth and took his full weight on her, because she had come so close just now, so very close.

With no preliminaries, he widened her legs with his knees and guided himself into her, releasing his breath in a long sigh as he sank deeper, deeper. To her surprise, he stopped then, holding still inside her. There was no need for words, no reason to say out loud *I love you*. And certainly no reason to cry. And yet soft, stingless tears welled in her eyes. For as long as she lived, no matter what happened, she would always remember this moment.

In the end she was the one who moved first, stirring him with her stroking hands and the slow, rolling motion of her hips. The feel of him inside . . . indescribable; a glorious, sexy miracle. It wouldn't last; she knew the signs, and Michael was at the breaking point. But she wanted to give him the gift of herself, and for now nothing else mattered. She would find her own pleasure later.

Or so she thought. Until it changed, slowly, imperceptibly at first, then unmistakably, and something else began to matter very much. She couldn't fight it, this new urgency, and she couldn't pretend it wasn't there. It had her in a fearful grip, stripping away her hold on the known and familiar. She flew. She clutched at him, begging him with her body not to stop, and finally with her mouth—*"Oh, God, don't stop"*—whispering it against his damp throat, because if he stopped she would die.

Passion made him speechless, but not silent. The grinding sound of his guttural, uninhibited groans took her even higher. He tightened his arms around her, his face buried in her hair, his breath coming in the same ragged pants as hers. The rough rhythm of sex beat in her blood; her body ached for release. "Don't stop, don't stop, don't stop—"

Pure, gasping pleasure took her by surprise. She cried out some garbled exultation, heady with triumph at the top of her spiraling climax. Through the pummeling waves of sensation she heard Michael's answer, a rising roar of deep animal satisfaction. The sound entered her, went straight to her heart and the marrow of her bones, and became part of the pleasure.

Afterward, she couldn't move. He had *more* energy—"I feel like shouting out the window," he declared, "or lifting something heavy over my head"—but she could barely talk. And he wanted to know if it was always like that. "Absolutely not," she told him, and she was sure, because it never had been before.

"Why not?" He traced the bumpy line of her collarbone with one finger, a speculative light in his eye. "It ought to be."

She agreed. "But it isn't."

He leaned over and kissed the mole on the side of her left breast. He smiled. "We'll see."

15

At least Philip had stopped yelling. At least Sydney didn't have to pull the telephone away from her ear every few seconds during their brief conversations. After three days, he had finally figured out that outrage wasn't going to get him anywhere.

"Just tell me you're still in the state of Illinois."

"Of course I am."

"Tell me you're still in Chicago."

"Yes."

"You are?"

"Yes."

She heard him sigh. "Well, I guess that's something."

"Philip, I'll tell you where I am if you'll promise to keep it to yourself and not do anything about it."

"Sorry."

They'd been through this before, but she had hoped his answer would be different this time. "Then I'm not telling."

Silence, tense on her side, angry on his.

"What's it like at home?"

"What do you think it's like?"

The elevator doors rattled open; an elderly couple got off. Sydney kept her back to them as they strolled down the left-hand corridor and out of sight.

"Have the reporters stopped calling?" she asked in a subdued voice.

"Pretty much. So far your alibi's holding up. Aunt

Estelle told everybody you wanted to get away from all the 'unpleasantness,' and nobody doubts it."

"Good."

"You'd just better hope no enterprising cop decides to look you up at your good friend Mary Kay's."

"That's not likely," she scoffed, although the possibility had occurred to her, too. "Philip . . ."

"What."

"I guess you'd have told me by now if Mr. Higgins called."

"That's right, I would've." A pause. In a softer voice he said, "No word since yesterday, Syd. I guess he hasn't gotten an answer to his cables."

"Will you do something for me?"

Silence; then two impatient breaths; then, "What?"

"Call and ask him to send another wire. Maybe the others didn't get through." That sounded pathetic. "There must be *some* reason they're not responding." She caught herself and lowered her voice. "Will you just tell him to try again? And—ask him if he's got any connections in Scotland."

"Any connections?" Philip sounded amused.

"Anyone he knows who might help us get in contact with the MacNeils."

"If they exist."

"Of course they exist."

"Sydney—Oh, never mind."

"What?"

"Nothing."

"You don't think they exist?"

"Skip it. I'll call Higgins and tell him to send another telegram. What's his number?"

"In the little book in my desk, in my room."

"Okay."

She rested her forehead on the cold black metal plate above the mouthpiece. "How's Sam?"

"Sam misses you."

She shut her eyes. "Is he all right?"

"Yeah. Sydney, come home."

"I can't."

She heard a rhythmic clicking: Philip drumming his fingernails on the edge of the telephone table in the front hall. It was a habit of his. "Are you in love with him?" he asked after a long pause.

"Very much."

Another heavy sigh. "All right, listen. Your secret's safe. Just tell me where you are so I can stop worrying. Slightly."

"Really? You won't tell Papa? You won't tell anybody?"

"Not a living soul."

"Swear?"

"I swear."

"We're in the honeymoon suite at the Palmer House Hotel."

"Damn it, Sydney—"

"We are."

"If you're lying—"

"I swear it." He muttered wondering curses under his breath, which she heard perfectly. "Language," she admonished, smiling.

"That's—brilliant. I have to admit it."

"I thought so." She wished she could see his face.

"Sydney, you amaze me." He laughed softly. "You know, this isn't like you at all. I'm impressed."

"Thank you."

"I never thought you'd get out of it. The rut—Aunt Estelle, the country club, being the proper young widow. All of that."

"No," she said faintly. "Neither did I."

"I've got to hand it to you. When you decide to break out, you sure as hell do it in style."

Michael never knew that someone was at the door until they knocked or a key scraped in the lock. It bothered him; his senses usually warned him of things like that much earlier. But the carpets at the Palmer House were like a thick blanket of snow, and the doors were solid as trees—"soundproof," Sydney had called them. He heard a key in the lock now; it startled him, and his pencil bore down too hard on the paper. He made a black scratch on the wolf's haunch. The door opened and Sydney walked in.

She smiled at him but didn't say anything. He knew what that meant. "How is Philip?" he asked, standing up.

She had put on her hat to make the call, even though the telephone was only down the corridor. "A disguise," she called it, with the brim down low over her left eyebrow. Now she took it off and threw it on the table another hint that the news was bad. Usually she was neat and tidy, and wouldn't think of throwing her hat. "I told him where we are," she said.

He studied her face. "He's not angry anymore?"

"Oh . . ." She gave a thin smile. "I wouldn't say that." She walked around the room, picking things up and setting them down. "Everything's quiet, he says. No more reporters. Aunt Estelle has put out the Mary Kay story, and nobody doubts it."

"And Sam?"

"He's fine."

"Really?"

"Yes."

"That's good." She wasn't going to, so he finally said it. "No word has come from Scotland."

"I'm sure it won't be much longer, though." She came toward him, squeezing her hands together. She had on a white dress with yellow and pink flowers across the front. It made her look like a young girl. He had asked her not to put her hair up this once, and it fell loose around her shoulders, tied back with only a thin white ribbon. "I've asked Philip to tell Mr. Higgins to send another cable. Then I'm sure we'll hear something."

He smiled so that she would smile. "Yes, I'm sure we will." He sat down, pleased with the way he was learning to play this game people played: saying the opposite of what they knew was the truth. It wasn't lying, because everybody was in on it.

She came to him, sat down on the small stool in front of his chair. "What are you doing?"

"Nothing. Drawing a picture."

"May I see?"

"This isn't supposed to be here," he explained, handing the paper to her, pointing to the black mark. "My pencil slipped."

"Oh, Michael." Her long black eyelashes swept up and down, up and down. "Oh, this is wonderful." A lock of her shiny hair had slipped out of the ribbon. He rubbed it between his fingers before tucking it gently behind her ear. "This is really extraordinary."

He didn't see anything extraordinary about it. He had drawn the old wolf the way he remembered him best toward the end, lying down but alert, his ears cocked, a thoughtful look in his slanted, wide-spaced eyes. "This was my friend," he said carefully, watching Sydney's face. "I knew him for a long time."

She bent her arm over his knee and rested her chin on her wrist. "What happened after you got lost?"

The question was so big, he had to sit back in his chair to think about it. "I don't remember that time very clearly."

"What do you remember?"

"Nothing. Until some people found me. They took care of me, gave me food."

"Who were they?"

"Now I know they were Indians. It was a woman and two men. The woman was old. After the first winter, she died."

"Were you sad?"

"Yes." He thought of the toothless old woman in her huddle of blankets and furs, of how she never smiled and never talked to him, how she would hit him with the palm of her dark, knotty hand when he did something wrong. One morning she didn't wake up. The two men took her body away and left him by himself.

"What happened to you?"

"The others went away and I was alone."

"But how did you live? You were a *baby*."

"I was eight, I think. It was spring, the snows had melted. I knew how to make fires." He didn't think she would like to hear of the things he had eaten to stay alive. "I learned how to live during that summer with the Indians. How to find food, how to keep warm. When winter came, I followed the wolves to the place where it was warmer. Closer to the water."

"Georgian Bay?"

"No, I don't think so. Smaller." He had studied a map in Dr. Winter's office once, looking for the landmarks of his life. "There's a lake called Nipissing. I think I lived there for a while."

Her clear green eyes were wide on his face. "But weren't there any people? Didn't you ever see anyone who could help you?"

"No one who could help me. I saw men who killed the animals who were my companions, my family—wolves and foxes, bears. Badgers. Men set traps that they died in slowly, in great pain. Or they poisoned them. Or shot them. Maybe it was wrong, but I learned to stay away from men."

Sydney took his hand and pressed his knuckles to the soft skin of her cheek, not saying anything.

"I think about that now," he admitted. "What would have happened if I'd come out of hiding. Gone to one of the hunters and spoken to him."

"You'd have been saved."

"I didn't think of it that way, though. I didn't think I needed 'saving.' Men killed for nothing, and I had the same fear of them that my friends had. I had taken sides," he tried to explain. "Humans were the enemy." She nodded, but he didn't see how she could understand. He was telling her that he had become an animal.

"And so you lived by yourself," she said, her voice solemn and quiet. "Were you very lonely?"

"I honestly don't know. Now I can say that I was, I must have been, but then . . . it's hard to describe. How my life was, my thoughts. Completely different from now. Everything—flowed. Day into night, season into season. The book my father gave me—I read it until I knew it by heart, so I couldn't forget that I was a man. But time kept moving, year after year, until everything except the moment I was in began to seem like a dream."

"You lost yourself," she said.

He hadn't meant for the story to make her sad, but she looked ready to cry. "I'll tell you about the old wolf," he said, reaching for the drawing she had let fall to the floor. "We were best friends. We did everything together."

She sat back and put her hands on her hips. "How in the world could you be friends with a wolf? Why didn't he eat you?"

"Oh, Sydney." He laughed at her. "Wolves only eat people in Sam's fairy tales."

"Is that true?"

He sighed. "At the zoo, there's a sign in front of the wolves' enclosure. It says they travel alone, they're vicious and dangerous, they attack people and slaughter the caribou. That's all lies, every word. Wolves never hurt men. Never. They run for their lives from men, even when they're starving. What they eat—usually they eat mice. That's a wolf's main diet. They can't run as fast as a deer, so when they chase the caribou they look for the old ones, or the sick or wounded ones. It's true that they thin the herd, but the deer they kill are going to die anyway."

"And they don't travel alone?"

"That's the stupidest lie of all." He stood up, agitated. "Wolves have families, just like people. They live together, just like you live with your family. They have aunts and uncles, cousins, sisters, brothers—mothers-in-law. They stay together and take care of each other. And when they mate, it's for life. *They fall in love.* They're as passionate as you and I are, Sydney. As tender. As— devoted." He looked away, embarrassed by the nakedness of these words. He had never heard anyone say them before. But he knew what they meant, and he'd been glad when he'd learned them, so he could give names to his feelings.

"There aren't any wolf orphans," he continued when he saw that Sydney was smiling at him. "If the mother dies, someone else will take the pups, maybe a female from another den. And the father goes with them and becomes part of the new pack."

"They're not enemies? The two packs, I mean. Not even rivals? For food?"

"No. In fact"—she probably wouldn't believe this— "they pay visits to each other. Two sisters, or a mother and a son, for instance. Their packs live far apart, so they go see each other sometimes."

"Why do they live far apart?"

"For food. Each pack has its own territory, and they never cross each other's boundaries, not for food."

"Only for visits." She stood up. "They sound as if they're more civilized than we are."

"They are."

She crossed the room to where he was standing and put her arms around him. These were the times, when Sydney held him, or touched him with great tenderness, or said in words that she loved him, that he knew he must have been lonely when he had lived alone. Since then he'd changed, and she was a part of the new man he'd become. To lose her now, to go back to the old life—that was unthinkable.

"Tell me about your wolf friend. How did you meet him?"

It was hard to concentrate when she kept playing with his hair behind his ears, trying to make it curl by winding it around her fingers. "He was caught in a trap and I set him free."

"Ah," she murmured. "Your specialty."

"He was young, only about a year old. I knew where his den was. I took him there, gave him back to his parents. And then I just . . . stayed."

"The houseguest who never left."

"What?"

"Nothing." She kissed his ear. "And you knew him all his life?"

"Yes."

"Did he ever have a family?"

"He had a mate who was very beautiful, almost pure white."

"And . . . children?"

"Yes. Three cubs, born in the spring. In the summer, she ate poisoned meat a bounty hunter left, and she died."

"Oh, Michael. What happened to the babies?"

"His sister took them. He stayed with her pack until they were grown, and then he left. I went with him." Without realizing it, he had untied the ribbon in her hair. He used his fingers for a comb, lifting it from the back of her neck. As always, she smelled like flowers. "It wasn't like Sam and Hector—I mean, the wolf was never mine, like a boy and his dog. We were just together. Friends."

"What happened to him? Is he still alive?"

"He was very old. Last winter was a bad winter. I was stealing food for him when they caught me."

Sydney took his face between her hands and began to kiss him. He closed his eyes, letting the warmth of her lips on his cheek, his eyebrow, the side of his nose, soothe away—as he knew she intended—hard memories of the old wolf last winter. "We don't kiss enough," she murmured, and since she was smoothing her fingertips over his eyelids at that moment, he couldn't tell if she was teasing. It seemed to him they did a lot of kissing. But she was right. Not enough.

Backing up, he sat down on the side of the desk, and she stepped between his legs. She smiled, her head a little higher than his, so pleased with herself because she'd changed his mood. He had an urge to pull her close and put his mouth in that sweet place, that valley between her breasts, and kiss her there through her clothes until she sighed. "Mouth kissing," she whispered—she'd been reading his mind. "That's what we don't do enough of."

She threaded her hands through his hair and tipped his head back. Their lips touched. She had the softest lips.

She wet them with her tongue and kissed him with her eyes wide open, watching him. Then she wet his lips with her tongue. Stirred, he slid his fingers from her waist to her breast, but she pulled them away, very gently. "Just kissing," she instructed, dreamy-eyed.

"Just kissing." He sighed, pretending it was a sacrifice.

Resting her forearms on his shoulders, she clasped her hands behind his neck and leaned in close. She gave him soft kisses, starting at one side of his mouth and going to the other, making that little sound, that *kiss* sound that was never exactly the same twice. When he smiled, she gave him a stern look, as if she were warning him, saying, "This isn't funny." He stopped smiling when she slipped her tongue inside his mouth and nudged his tongue with it. He loved this game. Animals did this, something like this, but never, never would he have believed that people did it until Sydney showed him.

He felt her softening. She tilted her head, as if it were getting heavy, and her breathing slowed down. "Michael," she said against his mouth, and this time when he put his hands on her bottom and pulled her close to him, she didn't correct him. Kissing was fine, but they could never do it and nothing else for very long.

He stood up.

"Wait." She was remembering the rule. "No, now, we're just—"

"Kissing." Picking her up, he turned, set her on the desk where he had been, then leaned over her until she was lying on her back. He moved *The Palmer House Guide to Chicago* under her head for a pillow. Settling himself between her thighs, he went back to kissing.

Now it really was a sacrifice. Sydney's soft mouth was delicious, but he wanted more of her. Knowing he could have it any time just made the torture worse. But she had made a rule, so he held her hands and didn't touch her while he kissed her and kissed her, falling in deeper, losing himself in love with her.

Somebody knocked at the door. It happened just when

Sydney was starting to break the rule, by squeezing her legs around his hips and squirming.

"Maid!"

They scrambled off the desk. Sydney smoothed her skirts and tried to tidy her hair while Michael grabbed up the pens and pencils and pieces of hotel stationery that had fallen off the desk. A key turned in the lock. By the time the door opened they were on opposite sides of the room, Sydney looking out the window, he reading the *Palmer House Guide to Chicago* upside down.

The maid came every morning, and every morning they moved from room to room to room to stay out of her way as she changed sheets, dusted and tidied, scrubbed the bathroom, put fresh flowers in vases, ran a carpet sweeper over the floors. They knew she must wonder why they didn't just leave, go out and look at the sights like any other visitors to the city did, even honeymooners, *eventually*. It was a little embarrassing, but funny, too; by the time the maid left they were usually holding back laughter while they thanked her and said they would see her tomorrow.

Of course they couldn't go out, for fear of being recognized; even Sydney limited her outings to absolute necessities—buying Michael drawing paper and watercolors, for example. How amazing, they began to marvel to each other, that day after day of enforced confinement in two smallish rooms and a bath didn't drive them batty. They weren't even restless. There was plenty to occupy them. They had books to read—Sydney borrowed almost daily from the small library of novels in the hotel's reading room—and cards, and a chess set she appropriated from the men's smoking room late one night. "Are you bored?" one would ask the other at least once a day. "No, are you?" "No." It was true. They could live together at the Palmer House Hotel for the rest of their lives, they decided, and be perfectly content.

Sometimes they daydreamed, though. Spun fantasies of eating a meal in a restaurant together, just the two of them, sitting at a window table. Or going to Field's to shop for clothes, a hat for her, new shoes for him. Seeing a play together at the Royal Theater. Taking a walk along Michigan Avenue on Sunday morning, or going to Washington Park on Derby Day. Riding the cable car.

They would fall silent after these flights of fancy, both wondering, but never voicing the question, if any of them would ever come true. This idyll they were sharing couldn't last; knowing that only made it sweeter and more precious. They wouldn't spoil it by allowing too much of the real world into their two smallish rooms and bath.

"The staff looks at me very strangely these days," Sydney announced on Friday afternoon, stripping off her gloves and setting them, along with the newspaper, her pocketbook, and her hat, on the back of the sofa. "I know they're talking about us."

"They're jealous of me." Michael looked up at her over the watercolor he was working on at the desk, beaming at her, as if she'd been gone for days instead of twenty minutes. "If they were married to you, they'd never come out of this room, either."

She snorted, but she had to go over and kiss him. "How's the painting coming?" She leaned against him, smoothing the hair back from his forehead and gazing down at the small picture among the paints and jars and brushes on top of the desk. "You haven't gotten very far since I left," she noted. In fact, it looked as if he hadn't done anything.

Still, the half-finished painting was impressive. She didn't understand how he could get such fine detail out of something as coarse as a paintbrush.

"I need my model. I can't get the colors right when you're not here."

"Hmm," she said. He looked up innocently. "I think you just want to get me naked again."

He opened his mouth, widened his eyes—then spoiled it by laughing. Blushing, too; he ducked his head, but she saw the tips of his ears turn pink. He tried to pull her against him, but she swiveled out of reach, laughing, and went to retrieve the newspaper.

Each day they put the "lost man" story farther back. Today it was on page nine. Sydney read in silence for a few minutes, then smacked the paper down on the sofa beside her. "Oh, for God's sake."

Michael looked up from his painting. "What's wrong?"

"Oh, this is the best yet. Listen to this." She picked up the paper again. " 'Authorities continue to search for the fugitive,' blah blah, 'who has evaded capture for seven days,' so on and so on, the usual. 'Meanwhile, sightings of the lost man continue to be reported. Mrs. William Skaggs of Evanston told police yesterday that a man wearing an animal skin loincloth appeared at her back door, brandishing a club. In LaGrange, Mr. Abel Whacker claimed a naked man entered his barn sometime Wednesday night and set free a mare and her foal, two holsteins, twelve chickens, and a rooster.' " She threw the paper on the floor and glared at it. "How can people be so stupid? It's mass hysteria. I'm surprised Mr. Whacker didn't see the naked man *eating* his chickens."

Michael stuck his brushes in the water jar and came over to sit beside her. "It doesn't matter, though, does it? What do you care what they say?"

"I know. I don't. It just makes me mad."

He retrieved the paper and smoothed it over his thigh. "You called Philip, I guess?" he said in a careless voice, not looking at her.

"Yes."

"No word yet?"

"Not yet."

He folded the newspaper in half, in half again, then again, lining it up on his knee each time until it was a bulky, four-inch square. "Sydney," he said at the same time she said "Michael." They both smiled, but his smile didn't reach his eyes. "Sydney. Listen."

"No." He had tried to have this conversation with her yesterday.

"No, just listen. This must be bad for your family, you being here with me."

"They don't know I'm here with you."

"Philip knows. Anyway, they know you're somewhere with me. What must your aunt be thinking?"

"I don't care what she's thinking."

He sighed. "What about Sam?"

"Sam's a child. He misses me, but he'll be all right." But in her private heart she ached for Sam, and every day she longed to see him.

Michael picked up her hand. "We can't stay here forever."

"Why not?" She avoided his patient eyes. She knew she sounded childish, but she hated this discussion and she wasn't going to help him out by being reasonable.

"What I did was wrong."

"What do you mean?"

"I've read the papers, the parts you don't read out loud. I know how much damage I caused."

"That's just money."

"No. They shot all but three of the bears."

She bowed her head. "But that wasn't your fault. They panicked, they didn't have to shoot them."

"The deer—so many deer died, and they're still dying. And property, people's stores and houses and yards—it was a crazy thing, and it was against the law. I shouldn't have done it. The wolves I'm not sorry for, I'd do it again, but the rest—"

"I can't believe you're saying this!"

"I just think—"

"Michael, are you sorry we came here? Do you want to leave me?" He shook his head; he started to speak, but she cut him off. "If you run away, they'll catch you. And even if they don't catch you, where would you go? You're not the 'lost man' anymore, you can't—slip back into that life like an old glove. You're Michael MacNeil. Your parents—"

He stood up abruptly. "My parents have nothing to do with this. You talk about them as if they're magicians, as if they could change everything that's happened if they would just send us back a telegram. But that's not going to happen."

"How do you know?"

"Sydney—" He lifted his hands and dropped them to his sides, finally exasperated with her. "Let's not talk about this anymore."

"Fine. I never wanted to talk about it in the first place."

So they didn't talk about anything for five whole minutes. Such a thing had never happened before. Michael went into the bedroom and closed the door while Sydney unwrapped the little square he had folded the newspaper into and pretended to read it.

Not a sound came from the other room. An awful thought struck her. What if he was packing? She dropped the paper and bolted for the bedroom.

He was lying on the bed with his hands behind his head, staring up at the ceiling. He looked miserable. He started to get up when he saw her, but she took four long strides to the bed and pressed him back down. "Oh, forgive me," she pleaded, holding his shoulders, threading her hands through his hair.

"For what?"

"I don't know. Weren't we fighting?"

"Were we?"

"Let's make love."

He was already unfastening the snaps at the back of her blouse. She got the buttons of his shirt undone, and then, in the interest of speed, they took the rest of their own clothes off. "What if the maid comes?" Sydney fretted, pushing down her stockings, shimmying out of her skirt.

"We'll tell her to leave."

As usual, he was faster. She was still fumbling with chemise ribbons when he tumbled her onto her back and threw a bare leg over her knees. "But she'll see us."

He had made a knot in the ties. Growling, using his teeth, he tore a rip in the thin cotton, peeled her out of it, and hurled it to the floor like an old dust rag. She gaped at him, astounded, excitement beginning to hum in her veins. "She won't see you," he assured her, grinning like a wolf. "She'll just see me." His long, hard body covered her, and she forgot about the maid and everything else in the world except Michael.

I'm possessed, she thought, giving herself to him. *I sur-render.* The words fit, but no sneaking shame accompa-nied them, no secret resentment. *I'm helpless,* she thought, and reveled in it. Everything they did, everything they wanted, every act of love that crossed their minds was absolutely right. She belonged to him completely, but she had never felt so free.

His mouth was a hot, hungry caress on her body, driving her higher with every sensuous, slow-burning kiss. She could feel herself unraveling, stretching and unwinding beneath him, coming undone. He could make her bones melt. One minute she could hardly lift her weak woman's hand to touch him, and the next she felt like an Amazon, muscular and athletic, his perfect match. His mate.

At the moment he came into her she said, "Don't leave me."

"Sydney," he whispered, but he was lost, she could see it in his eyes, too deep in passion to heed her.

"Michael, don't leave me."

He took her mouth in a rough, ravishing kiss that blurred the edges of her mind and gradually extinguished every conscious thought. Nothing but sensation now, the deep heated beat of desire. It pulsed through her, she could feel it pulse through him, burning them together, binding them even closer. Sweat made their bodies slick. They rolled, and in their eagerness they lost their intimate joining. The world rushed back—they were in a bed, in a room, in a city—and when they came together again the world vanished. Her name—he breathed it in her ear like a sigh, again and again, until the syllables blended and merged and all she heard was *I love you.* Everything came together, body and soul, all together. She flew with him up and over the rushing edge, into a pleasure so intense she lost him, lost herself. Oblivion. She found him again, and held on for her life.

When it was over, she tried to explain it to him. "With you, Michael—I don't know—I feel free. Anything I want, I know it's all right." She struggled for words, unwilling to talk about Spencer with him—that would be a betrayal. But in private, she couldn't help remembering that sometimes, with Spencer, she had had the feeling that they were . . . getting away with something. Not that it was dirty or shameful—well, a little, though. Yes, a little. Sex was something they ought to have been *above*. But they weren't, and so they had had to hide their enjoyment of it. Which made the enjoyment less.

"You're good for me," she tried again, lying on her side, holding his hand between her damp breasts and kissing it. "Nothing embarrasses you. And so, since you don't have any inhibitions, you sweep away mine."

He was absorbed in the smooth skim of his hand from the swell of her hip to the crevice of her waist, to the curve of her rib cage, back and forth, back and forth. "What are inhibitions?"

She laughed gaily. "Never mind," she said after thinking it over. "They're something you'll never have to know about."

The curtain at the window billowed in the breeze. She snuggled closer, and he pulled the sheet up to cover her. A delicious lassitude crept over her. "Shall we sleep?" She closed her eyes, smiling, knowing he was still watching her. She loved to fall asleep with him. So *sweet*. Such a tender intimacy. "Love you," she whispered, and drifted away.

Love you, Michael echoed in his heart. He wanted to kiss that small, pinkish place on her cheek, where she had rubbed too hard against his stubbly jaw. Or he had rubbed her. His fingertip hovered over it, but didn't touch; he didn't want to wake her.

How beautiful she always looked in sleep, after they made love. Her red hair was a mess, scattered across the pillow like a flag, her face still pink and damp. She slipped so easily into sleep, smiling at him one minute, breathing deeply the next, her lips parted as if for one last kiss.

He slipped out of bed. His clothes were all over; he gathered them up quietly and carried them into the other room to dress. Sydney's pocketbook had fallen into a corner of the sofa. He was glad when he found the room key on top; he didn't want to snoop through her belongings.

When he opened the door, the maid was two steps away with her hand up, ready to knock. They both jumped. He smiled politely and moved forward, so she had to move back. Closing the door quietly behind him, he said, "My wife is sleeping. Could you come later?"

"Yes, sir, of course."

"Thank you."

She did that bobbing thing maids did, and he stayed where he was until she went down the hall and around the corner. Then he went the other way, toward the elevator.

He knew the number; Sam had taught it to him. He sat down at the little table that the telephone sat on and picked up the earpiece. There was a hollow crackling sound; after a few seconds a woman's voice came through it and said, "May I help you?"

"Yes. I would like to call someone."

"Speak up, please."

"I would—" He had forgotten to talk into the mouthpiece. He leaned closer. "I want to call someone."

"Number, please."

"Four-nine-oh-one."

"Hold, please, I'll ring."

"Thank you."

"You're welcome."

Clicking and crackling. Ringing.

"Hello?"

He gripped the earpiece tighter, pressed it closer to his ear until it hurt. The voice had come over too faintly. Whose was it? Philip's?

"Hello? Anybody there?"

"Philip!" He almost shouted, he felt so relieved.

"Hang on." A muffled squeaking, then a sharp sound, like a door closing. Then Philip's voice again, tense and clipped. "What's wrong?"

"Nothing—"

"Where are you?"

"The same place. I—"

"Where is my sister?"

"Here. She's fine. She doesn't know I'm calling you."

"Why are you calling?"

He's furious, Michael realized. Sydney hadn't told him that. "I'm calling to ask you how things are. How things are at the house."

"Oh, really? Well, I'll tell you. My father doesn't know if he's still got a job at the university, my aunt won't come out of her room, and my brother cries all the time. Anything else you'd like to know?"

Michael curled his shoulders inward, feeling as if he'd been punched.

"Well?"

"Yes," he finally managed to say. "There's something else."

He heard Philip sigh before he said in a voice that wasn't so angry, "What?"

"Tell me what would happen if we got caught. To Sydney, I mean, not me."

"Why don't you ask her?"

"I have asked. She said, 'Nothing.' "

"She's lying."

He pressed the heel of his hand against his eye socket. The elevator doors opened; somebody got off, but he didn't look up to see who. "You tell me," he said into the telephone.

"Well, two things. One's for certain, the other's probable. First, she'd be ruined."

"Ruined. How—"

"Banished. From everything. She travels in high circles and she plays by the rules. Or at least she used to. If her society friends found out where she's been and who she's been with, it wouldn't matter if you two have been reading the Old Testament to each other for the last five days. She would be finished. Understand? With the possible exception of Camille Darrow, she wouldn't have a friend in the world."

Michael tried to say something, but he couldn't.

"You still there?"

"The second thing."

"The second thing. She could be arrested. Aiding and abetting a fugitive is a crime. I don't know what a good lawyer could do for her—maybe she'd get off. Are you hearing this?"

"Yes."

"And you understand what I'm saying?"

"Yes."

Neither of them said anything for a long time. Finally Michael said, "Don't worry."

"What does that mean?"

"She'll be all right. It's over now."

"What are you going to do?"

"I have to hang up."

"Wait. What are you going to do?"

"Thank you for telling me this."

"Listen, Michael. Don't do anything fast. Let me—"

He hung up. He had to do everything fast now; there was no time to lose.

The living room was empty, the bedroom silent. She was still sleeping. Leaning over the desk, he scratched out a note, writing it so fast the words were barely readable. He left it there, and then, even though everything in him said to *go now,* he moved quietly across the room, stopping at the open door to the bedroom.

He wanted to go closer, but he was afraid she would wake up. Would she think he was a coward to sneak away like this? Would she hate him for it? He couldn't help it. He was doing the right thing, finally. Regret was like a sour taste on his tongue when he thought of how long he'd kept her in danger, how stupid and blind and unthinking he'd been. But maybe he could fix it. If he went right now, maybe no harm would come to her.

She moved—he froze. She muttered something, but it was thick, garbled; she wasn't awake. He'd heard her talk in her sleep before; once she'd said clearly, "But that's not how it is," and another time, "Oh, you." She was smiling now, a small, patient smile, tolerant-looking. If only he knew what she was dreaming. If only he'd heard those last words.

He was afraid even to whisper. *I love you,* he told her, just mouthing it. *Good-bye.* He went back to the living room, making no noise on the thick, muffling carpet. At the desk, he scrawled a P.S. to his note, and moved it closer to the edge, so she couldn't miss it.

"Michael?"

His heart stopped.

Racing to the hall door, he opened it carefully and slipped through. Her soft, sleepy voice came again. He closed the door on it, and walked out of her life in a hurry.

Sydney found his note half a minute later.

"SYDNEY," he wrote in block letters, the rest in his big, childish scrawl. "I know where the police station is, Sam showed me a long time ago. I am going there to give up. I'll say I have been hiding in Lincoln Park. It isn't a lie because I did hide there for a while. You are in danger and must go home right now. We should not have done this, even though it was the best time in my life. I love you. I wish I had time to say it all. Things I should have said before. I don't know what will happen now, but I have to go. Michael.

"P.S. Don't be angry. This really is the best thing to do."

16

The police almost arrested Charles West for harboring a fugitive.

Sydney was horrified when she heard the news from John Osgood, the criminal attorney her father had hired to defend Michael. She scolded Philip severely when he laughed, but the irony was too much for him, and he'd never liked Charles anyway. Still, Sydney knew that if God was kind and by some miracle this nightmare of Michael's went away, one day she, too, would look back and find Charles's predicament very, very funny.

The problem for Charles was that when Michael walked into the Clark Street police station to give himself up, he didn't look like a man who had been hiding in a public park for eight days. Where had his clean clothes come from? Who gave him a razor? Why wasn't he hungry? He wouldn't answer. That someone in the Winter family might have been "harboring" him never seriously figured in the police's suspicions—and needless to say, that Sydney herself had been hiding with him in the honeymoon suite of the Palmer House Hotel never entered a single detective's head. Unluckily for Charles, Michael's circle of acquaintance was small; when the police thought about who might have helped him during the week he was on the run, West's name was on top of the list.

But not for long. They couldn't find any proof, not a shred of evidence, and Charles's vehement denials were very convincing. So the matter was dropped. Since they were probably never going to find out where Michael had been hiding, the police simply decided it wasn't important and stopped thinking about it.

The Winter family breathed a sigh of relief.

But that was the only good news. "There's no bail," Philip reported, bursting into Sam's room on Monday afternoon. Sydney and Sam were sitting on the floor, putting finishing touches on Sam's "nature album," a messy collection of leaves, twigs, grasses, and stones that kept eluding their best efforts to paste them into the book. Since her return, Sam had hardly left Sydney's side. He thought it was "dumb" of her to go visit a friend in Joliet at the very time Michael was in trouble. But, true to his sweet nature, he'd forgiven her for it.

"No bail!"

"They're moving him to the county jail until the trial. Osgood says he can get the trial date expedited, but Judge Tallman won't allow bond. He claims Michael's a bad risk."

"But he gave himself up!"

Philip squatted down beside them on the rug, and Sydney made an effort to calm down, aware of Sam's anxious eyes searching her face. "The judge is a FOZ," Philip explained, and her spirits sank even lower.

"A what?"

She ruffled Sam's hair. "A FOZ is a Friend of the Zoo—somebody who gives money to support it." She looked at Philip. "Shouldn't he disqualify himself, then?"

"Osgood says that's not enough to constitute bias. And if he moves for it and the judge refuses, we'll make an enemy of him."

Sydney swore softly, without thinking, and Sam's eyes nearly popped out of his head. "Sorry," she muttered.

To Philip she said, "How was it? How did he look? Did you talk to him?" Michael's arraignment was this morning. She'd been advised by everybody not to attend on the grounds that it would only upset her. There was nothing she could do; newspaper reporters would hound and harrass her; she or Michael might do or say something to give themselves away. None of that swayed her, and she would have gone anyway except for one thing: Aunt Estelle was having a nervous breakdown.

"If you go to this court proceeding, Sydney," she had declared, white-lipped with rage and in complete earnest, "I swear I will never, ever speak to you again." She meant it. Sydney's own anger had tempted her to accept the ultimatum and make a break with her once and for all. But she hadn't. She'd given in.

It wasn't like the other times she'd bitten her tongue and yielded to her aunt's stronger will, though. This time she had made a free choice, based on prudence and logic. She wouldn't go to Michael's arraignment because it would hurt the family—Sam, she was thinking of—by exposing them to sensational publicity. Her aunt's threat didn't even figure in the decision. Thank God, the days of slavishly obeying Aunt Estelle because she was inflexible and intimidating were finally over.

Philip leafed through Sam's nature album, avoiding her eyes. "He looked all right. I didn't speak to him. The judge asked him how he pled, and he said, 'Not guilty.' That's all he said. The whole thing was over in five minutes."

She would find out later, she decided, how Michael had really looked, when Sam wasn't around. Until then, Philip's evasiveness made her uneasy.

"Osgood cabled some lawyer colleague of his in London," Philip went on, looking up. "To try to find out what's going on in Scotland."

"Good."

"He thinks finding Michael's family is vital. He also wants to play up the earl business to the press more. He says it's one of the few things in Michael's favor."

"But it doesn't have anything to do with the case. Does it?"

"No, but he says it's the sort of thing that could sway a jury anyway. A man who comes from Scottish royalty, whose father's an earl—how could he be dangerous? You wouldn't argue it in words, you'd just let the jury figure it out for themselves."

"I see." But if Michael's family couldn't be found, they wouldn't even be able to do that. "Does Mr. Osgood know about Michael and—" She stopped, glancing at Sam, and changed the question to, "Does he know where Michael was last week?"

"Not unless Michael told him. Which isn't likely."

Sam leaned against her thigh, his blond-lashed blue eyes mournful. "I want to go see him, Syd. Can't I visit him?" She shook her head. "But why? He's my friend, too."

"I know, sweetie."

"And I made a picture for him. Look."

"Oh, it's nice. Look, Philip."

"It's all of us, see? This is the lake and this is Michael, this is me, here's you, and this is Flip."

"We're playing ball," Sydney said tentatively.

"No, that's Hector. Come on, Syd, I want to give it to him. You're going to visit him, so why can't I come with you?"

"What?" Philip turned on her. "You're going to visit Michael?"

"I have to. There won't be any photographers," she added, already feeling defensive.

"Does Aunt Estelle know?"

"Not yet."

"Why can't I?" Sam persisted. "Why can't I come with you when you go?"

"Because children don't belong in jails, that's why."

"But—"

"Sorry, but the subject's closed." She gave him a hug to forestall more argument. "I'll take him your drawing. You can write him a letter, too, if you like. And I'll tell him how much you miss him."

"When were you planning on dropping this little bomb on Aunt E?" Philip asked.

She closed her eyes, already dreading that encounter. Putting it off would only make it worse, though. "Now," she answered tiredly after a glance at her watch. "She'll be in her garden."

"Yeah," agreed Sam, "talk to her when she's in the garden. That's when she's in the best mood."

"Oh, hello, Papa." She was surprised to see him outside in the middle of the afternoon, not cooped up in his study. "Is everything all right?"

"Hm? Oh, sure. Just telling your aunt about her phone call." He sat down on the ledge of the terrace and took off his pince-nez, patting his pockets for a handkerchief. After an unsuccessful search, he pulled his shirt out of the front of his trousers and used it to polish his lenses.

"Her phone call?"

"Hm? Yes, from that rose fellow."

That rose fellow. "Mr. Wilkerson?"

"Wilkerson. Says he's abdicating."

Wilkerson was the president of the Rose Society; Aunt Estelle was the vice president. "He's abdicating?"

"Resigning, quitting, forget the word he used. Ill health. Wants Estie to take over." He looked at Sydney, focused on her. "She won't even take the call. She's wanted that man's job for as long as I can remember, and now she won't even come to the phone." He shook his head, sticking his glasses back on his nose. Behind them, his sad eyes looked bewildered.

"Oh, God." Sydney sighed, dropping down on the ledge beside him. "This is all my fault."

He didn't contradict her. To her amazement, though, he put his arm around her shoulders. "Well, you couldn't help it."

"Oh, Papa, I couldn't," she said in a rush, touched by his unexpected sympathy. "I just couldn't let him go. And if he'd gone off by himself, they'd have caught him. I *had* to go with him."

"You love him."

"I do."

"And he loves you?"

"Yes."

"Nothing more to be said, then." He looked up at the sky, his craggy face wrinkling in a hundred lines and creases. The breeze lifted his sparse white hair straight up, like a fuzzy halo. She kissed his cheek. He glanced at her, pinkening a little, smiling sweetly. "You look more like your mother every day."

"Do I?" What a lovely compliment; she had thought her mother was beautiful.

"Nobody ever knew what she saw in me, you know. Least of all her parents. She wasn't a bit stubborn, but that one time she didn't listen to anybody. She went ahead and married me, and it was the right thing to do. We made each other happy."

"I know you did." She took his bony hand between hers. Her father was a dear, kind, gentle man, and yet she never had conversations like this with him. She wanted it to go on and on. "Do you still miss her?"

"Every day."

"Me, too."

He nodded, falling silent. She was afraid he was slipping away from her, sliding into one of his daydreams, but a moment later he shook himself and focused on her again. "Blame myself for this business with Michael. Partly, anyway."

"Oh, Papa, why?"

"Abandoned him. Couldn't use him anymore, West and I, so we dropped him. Wrong of us. Wrong of me. Boy needed guidance, and I forgot all about him. Handed him over to you and Philip and Sam, never gave him another thought."

"If it's anybody's fault . . ." She shook her head decisively "It's *not* anybody's fault. You're not to blame, Papa, and neither are we, and neither is Michael."

"Hmm."

"It just happened."

"Well, you may be right. Thing is, I can see exactly why he did it. If you put yourself in his place, it makes perfect sense."

"I know. I think of that all the time." They shared a soft laugh that comforted her. "I'm going to see him, Papa. I've made up my mind. Aunt Estelle . . ." She trailed off;

no need to finish that thought. He patted her hand and stood up. Sydney sighed—their tête-à-tête was over.

He pulled his pipe from his vest pocket and stuck it between his teeth. "Shouldn't go alone." He started searching in his other pockets for his tobacco pouch.

"Philip will go with me if I ask him to."

"Good, good. I'll come, too."

"You—you'll what?"

"Not as grim if we all go. He'll be glad to see us, won't he?"

"Y-es, he'll love it. Oh, Papa, thank you."

"Estie won't like it. You going to tell her?"

She nodded, nonplussed.

"Good. Leave me out of it. Don't even mention my name." He winked at her and headed for his study, still slapping his pockets.

Aunt Estelle was killing aphids. A seasonal occupation, it gave her an enormous amount of satisfaction. She enjoyed mixing her tubs of water, soap, and quassia chips, and spraying the resulting goo on the tiny white pests that would otherwise have sucked the life out of her precious roses.

"What actually is an aphid?" Sydney opened brilliantly, standing, hands behind her back, a respectful six feet from her aunt while she aimed a hose at a rosebush with one hand and pumped a plunger in a bucket up and down with the other. "I mean, it never moves. Is it a plant or an animal? Or an insect? Or . . . an organism, a sort of . . . amoebalike thing," she floundered, vaguely recalling the word from a long-ago biology class.

To all of these queries Aunt Estelle said nothing, merely went on with her spraying and pumping as if she were alone. She had on her garden getup, which consisted of her oldest dress and a full-length apron, cloth gloves to the elbows, and a wide, low-crowned straw hat.

"Papa says Mr. Wilkerson is retiring," Sydney tried next. "Nothing seriously wrong with him, I hope—but won't that be nice, if you succeed him. You'd do a wonderful job. Better than he did, I'm sure. And you'd be the first woman. That would . . . really . . ." She bowed her head, coloring. "That would really be something," she finished softly. To herself.

"What do you want?"

The harsh words startled her; she jerked her head up. Aunt Estelle still had her back to her, spraying and pumping, spraying and pumping. The rigid set of her shoulders, the angry line of her neck, everything about her told Sydney she had come on a fool's errand. She had to try, though. Wanted to try. Maybe it was those sweet, surprising moments with her father that made her feel bold with Aunt Estelle for once, even daring. Or maybe it was just time she grew up.

"I want to apologize to you. What I did . . . I know it's hurt you very much, Aunt. I'm truly sorry."

Nothing. She picked up her bucket and moved to the next rosebush.

"I didn't do it to hurt you—although I won't lie and say I didn't know it would."

Was that breathy sound an indignant puff, a stifled snort of derision? If so, Sydney probably deserved it. Running off with Michael had shocked Aunt Estelle to her moral core. Social ruin had yawned like a monster's jaws for five days and nights, and she was still trembling, figuratively, in reaction. Sydney had given her the scare of her life, and forgiveness was not going to come easily.

"I didn't go to the arraignment today because you asked me not to," she said, deciding to get the worst over with at once. "I respected your reasons for opposing it—the reporters and photographers would have exploited the situation, and even though it would have helped Michael, it might have hurt the family. But . . ." She girded herself and said it. "Tomorrow I'm going to see him. In the Cook County jail. Philip's coming with me. And so is Papa." When there was no reaction, she hurried on. "There won't be any press there, no one to hound us. No one will even know we're there except Mr. Osgood and a few policemen. So." Her shoulders drooped. "I'm going," she finished dispiritedly.

Aunt Estelle kept her back turned; when she moved her head, the floppy hat hid her profile. A bee landed on her right shoulder blade. Sydney flicked it off unthinkingly. Her aunt whirled at the touch. Anger and hurt blazed in her eyes—Sydney expected that. What she wasn't prepared for was tears.

"Oh, Aunt—"

She twisted around and went back to her spraying, attacking the pump with a jerky vigor that gave away her agitation as surely as sobs would have. Sydney watched in helpless misery for as long as she could stand it. Then, taking a chance she would never have dared before now, she went close, closer, so close Aunt Estelle had to stop pumping or risk spraying her with insecticide, and put her hand on her arm. For an awkward second, neither of them moved. "I love you, Aunt Estelle," Sydney said in a whisper. It was the first time she had ever said it—maybe the first time she had ever realized it. "I'm sorry for what I did because it hurt you. I've fallen in love with Michael. It's not infatuation, or—lust, and it's not some kind of rebellion. I love him. I couldn't let him go, and I couldn't let the police take him. I'm not ashamed of what I've done. I'm only sorry it's given you such pain."

Her aunt murmured, "Sydney," and looked away, using the back of her heavy glove to wipe her eyes.

"It looks like no one's going to find out," Sydney went on, striving for a lighter tone. "That should please you. It's hard for me, too—I've had to lie to Cam, my best friend, and that was awful." She took the older woman's hand and tried to turn her; but Aunt Estelle planted her feet and wouldn't move.

"Can't you forgive me? You and I are so unlike, but I always thought we'd be friends. I would hate to lose you." Now they were both weeping. Sydney took another chance. She leaned over and kissed her aunt's flushed cheek.

Aunt Estelle mumbled, "Oh, now," her face still turned

away, and she gave Sydney a clumsy, one-armed hug. And then, with a loud sniff, she went back to spraying her roses.

Sydney's heart beat fast. Her emotions were raw; she wanted to cry, she wanted to dance with Aunt Estelle around the garden. Fumbling for her handkerchief, she blew her nose. "Well," she said, backing up a step, then another. Clearly she wasn't going to get anything more than "Oh, now" out of her aunt today. But what a wonderful start.

"Don't forget," she couldn't resist, though, from halfway across the yard. "He is an earl's son."

Aunt Estelle kept spraying and didn't turn. But Sydney caught a glimpse of her profile when she leaned down to add more poison to her bucket. She thought—she wasn't sure—that minuscule curve at the corner of her mouth was a smile.

John Osgood was short, broad-faced, stoop-shouldered, and balding; he smoked cigars and he smelled like it. He was more of a family acquaintance than a family friend. Dr. Winter had known him for years, from some university board or committee they had both served on, and Sydney occasionally said, "Hello, how are you?" to him at social functions. The family had never had a need for the services of a criminal attorney before, and Mr. Osgood was the only one they knew. Sydney hoped he was both smoother and shrewder than he looked.

"Philip, nice to see you again. Harley, hello, didn't expect to see you! How've you been? And Sydney—well, well, it's been a long time. Awfully sorry about your husband, just awfully sorry. I didn't know him, but I heard only good things about him, nothing but good things."

"Thank you."

"Well! Are there enough chairs? Sorry the room's so small. This is all they'd give me, and frankly, I was only expecting Philip."

They took seats around a table that took up most of the space in the tiny, depressing room. Did the police do interrogations here, Sydney wondered, eyeing the dark-painted walls and the one small, streaky window with distaste. Had they questioned Michael in a room like this? Unbearable thought; she set it aside and asked Mr. Osgood the most important question.

"Is he all right?"

"He's fine. I've just come from a little chat with him myself, and he's just fine. Looking forward to your visit," he added, glancing at Philip. "It's all set for one o'clock."

Sydney sank back in her chair, shaky with relief. Now she could acknowledge how real her fear had been that something awful had happened, that they'd hurt him somehow, or decided he couldn't have visitors, or—this was the worst—that he had decided it was better not to see her.

"Good news," Mr. Osgood was saying. "They've dropped the grand theft charge, which never held water anyway. I thought they'd drop it eventually, and it's good that they've done it early; now we won't have to prepare for it."

The lawyer glanced occasionally at Sydney, occasionally at her father, but for the most part he directed his remarks to Philip. He had kind eyes, she noticed, light brown and fatherly, and a beautiful voice. Would they be enough to convince a jury Michael was innocent?

"I've convinced him, fortunately, that it's better if he doesn't testify. With luck, we'll have enough—"

"What?" She cut him off, too startled for courtesy. "Michael's not testifying? But why?"

Osgood looked down at his hands folded on top of the table and widened his lips in a sort of grimacing smile. "Two reasons," he said slowly and thoughtfully. "One, he's too inarticulate. Two, he's too honest."

"I beg your pardon," Sydney began, hoping she could hold on to her temper. "Mr. Osgood, Michael is *not* inarticulate. And how is it possible to be too—"

He held up one short, chubby finger. "Let me explain. I should have said he's too *direct* instead of inarticulate. If he took the stand, the prosecuting attorney would draw a full confession out of him in two minutes. No—less than two minutes. 'Mr. MacNeil, did you willfully and unlawfully break into four separate outbuildings on the grounds of the Lincoln Park Zoo, steal the keys to the cages of the deer, the wolves, the foxes,'—so on, I've forgotten the rest—'and set these animals free?' 'Yes, sir, I did.' 'And did you assault a zoo official in the process of this illegal activity, lunging at him and sending him to the ground, thereupon wrestling and grappling with him until you were forcibly subdued?' 'Yes, sir, I did.' "

"Yes, but Michael wouldn't—"

" 'And what was your motive, sir? Tell us why you committed these illegal acts.' 'Because I had to.' 'Thank you, Mr. MacNeil, you may step down.' "

Sydney closed her eyes and pressed her fingers hard against the beginnings of a headache.

"For better or worse," Osgood went on gently, "Michael doesn't even know how to shade the truth, Mrs. Darrow, much less lie. And if he were coached before he testified it would only be worse, because he would sound coached. He committed these acts, and yet his plea is not guilty. He isn't sophisticated enough to understand the difference between technical guilt and legal innocence. Which is a quality we may secretly admire, but for now it's also a vulnerability he needs to be protected from. Am I making myself clear?"

She nodded unhappily.

The lawyer reached across the table and patted her hand. "It's not as bad as it sounds, trust me. If we have some luck, I think there's an excellent chance we can get him off."

"What sort of luck?" Philip asked.

"Well, we've already had some. As I told you, the prosecutor didn't oppose my motion to move the trial date up, and the judge has agreed to it."

"Thank God," said Sydney. That meant Michael would spend less time in a prison cell. *If* he won the case.

"Yes, well." Mr. Osgood pulled a cigar halfway out of

his pocket, remembered himself, and pushed it back in. "That's good news and bad news combined, actually."

"How can it be bad?"

"The later the trial, the better our chances of locating the MacNeils."

"Does that really matter so much?"

"It might. A well-connected defendant always has a better chance than a loner or an indigent. Not fair, but there is it."

"But Michael's not—"

"Plus his story's romantic, just the sort of thing to capture a jury's imagination. But only if it's true, and only if they can *see* that it's true."

"In other words," said Philip, "only if they *see* Michael's rich, aristocratic family."

"See them, or even just hear about them in some reliable, unimpeachable way."

"But we don't even know if they are rich," Sydney pointed out. "We're not even absolutely certain, not really, that they're aristocrats."

"True, but at this point we don't have much else to use. If the case comes down to character, finding the MacNeils is probably the best we can hope for." He slipped his watch out of his pocket and flipped it open. "Almost one. You don't want to be late; they don't let visitors stay long." Everybody stood up. "Unfortunately, only one of you can see him," he said apologetically.

"Only *one*?"

"I'm afraid so. Since you're not family. Which, by the way, is a lucky thing in another way. If you *were* family, the zoo would undoubtedly be suing you for monetary damages in a civil case. So—who's Michael's visitor to be? You, Harley?"

Sydney's father scraped his thumbnail across the tooth marks on the empty pipe he'd been holding for the last ten minutes. "Hm," he said decisively. "Hmm."

"You, Philip?" Osgood guessed next.

Philip rubbed the back of his neck and squinted into space.

Sydney cleared her throat. "I'd like to see him."

"Oh." Osgood rounded his eyes at her and rocked back on his heels. "Oh, I see."

She wasn't sure if he did or not. Sometime during the course of this meeting, though, she had decided to trust him. If he really *did* see, she no longer feared the consequences.

"We'll wait for you outside," Philip told her. He and her father shook hands with Mr. Osgood, who said he would be in touch.

The lawyer took her arm in a kindly grasp and escorted her down the dingy hallway, up a flight of steps, and then down another narrow corridor, and into a large, crowded, poorly lit waiting area. A uniformed policeman sat behind a desk at the front of the room. "Take a seat," Mr. Osgood suggested, motioning. "I'll get you set up with the sergeant here, and then I'll be on my way. Shouldn't be long."

She thanked him for his kindness. She found an empty chair in a corner of the room, and sat down to wait for Michael.

Ten minutes later the policeman at the desk read out a list of names, hers among them. She stood up. As she was ushered with the others through a doorway, a policeman asked for her pocketbook, her shawl, and her hat. For an awful moment she thought he might search her, but he didn't. "Through here," he directed. "The visitors' room," he added when she hesitated.

"But I thought . . ."

"Move along, lady, you're holding up the line."

Sydney sat down in the chair she was directed to, mentally reeling from the contrast between this meeting and the one she had constructed in her mind. They would have a small room to themselves, she had thought, or at worst, she would hold his hand through the bars of his private cell while a guard tactfully looked the other way.

This was dreadful. A double row of long, back-to-back tables divided the room approximately in half, and between the two rows stretched a floor-to-ceiling screen,

a dense metal grid resembling a one-sided cage. Behind
the tables, families huddled around the one chair allotted
to them, parents and three children on Sydney's left, four
adults on her right, and beyond them more people, in
pairs, threes, fives—six seemed to be the allowable limit.
Everybody was talking at once, so that the noise in the
room was almost intolerable. The tables were three feet
deep; doubled, that made six feet—so leaning across to
touch the hand of a loved one through the wire barricade
was impossible. Even *seeing* through the mesh wasn't
easy. Sydney had to squint to make out which man in the
group of shuffling, identically dressed prisoners being
ushered through the door in the back wall was Michael.

There. In the second before he saw her, she blanched
from the shock of his pallor, the beard-stubbled gauntness
of his beautiful face, and the shadows around his haunted
eyes. Like the others, he wore a striped smock over
striped, ill-fitting trousers, so loose on his lean frame that
they hung on his hips and bunched at the ankles, above
shoes from which the laces had been removed. When he
saw her he stopped in his tracks, just for a second, before
the guard urged him forward with a hand on his shoulder.
His face had been set before in a grim smile, expressing
polite, stoic anticipation. But when he saw her it collapsed in pain and gladness, and what was left of her heart
broke in half.

She had risen when she saw him. They sat down at the
same time, eyes locked, and she knew she was smiling the
same joyful, anguished smile that he was. His mouth
moved. She leaned forward, cupping her ear, unable to
hear him over the din. "I thought Philip would come," he
repeated.

"He's here. My father, too." She almost had to shout to
be heard.

She thought he mouthed, "Your father?" He shook his
head to show his wonderment. "Sydney, you shouldn't
have come."

"I had to." He couldn't hear. "I had to!"

The people to her right were fighting. The prisoner they

had come to see yelled an obscenity at them, and the two adults shouted back. The guards looked on, bored.

"How are you?" Sydney asked, trying to smile, trying to beat back her despair.

"All right." But he looked ill and exhausted. "How are you?"

She smiled and nodded to reassure him. "I miss you!"

"I miss you."

She didn't know what was worse, shouting intimacies to him through a wire screen, or the pained silences that fell between the shouts.

"I like Mr. Osgood," she told him. "He's a good lawyer."

He nodded and said something she couldn't catch. "I'm sorry I left you," he repeated in a low, strained voice, leaning toward her. "That day. Just a note." He made a futile gesture with his hands.

He'd been suffering over this, she could see it in his face, hear it in his voice. "It's all right," she assured him fervently. "I understood—I knew why you did it. I wasn't angry!"

He put his fist on his chest and smiled with relief. In that moment, Sydney realized she wasn't going to be able to get through this without crying.

"Michael, you're going to get out of here. You are, I know it."

His mouth tightened in a parody of a smile as he looked down at his hands, gripping the edge of the table like twin vises. He couldn't lie, so he didn't say anything.

Another awful silence.

He spoke. She said, "What?"

"How is Sam?"

"He misses you."

"And Philip?"

"Fine, he's fine."

"He must hate me."

"No. Oh, no, he doesn't, he couldn't—"

"All right, folks, it's time. Everybody stand up, please.

Now, please. All visitors, up and out. Prisoners, on your feet."

She couldn't believe it. So soon! They hadn't said *anything* yet. The noise of scraping chairs and shouted good-byes was deafening. Michael pushed back his chair and stood, and at once hot tears overflowed. She swiped at her cheeks, dismayed and embarrassed. Damn, damn, she hadn't wanted him to see her like this!

"Good-bye, Sydney."

"Oh, Michael." She hadn't even told him she loved him.

"Please," he said, backing up obediently. "Please, Sydney—"

"What, Michael? I can't hear you!"

"Don't come here again. Sydney, don't come back." The guard stepped between them, blocking him from view.

Someone jostled her. Through the screen she saw a dark-haired man in striped clothes disappear through the door at the back, then another, then another. She couldn't even tell which one of them was Michael.

"All right, miss." The impassive policeman herded her expertly toward the other door without touching her. Outside, another policeman gave her back her belongings. She would have to lie, she realized as she walked blind-eyed with the others toward the stairs. She would have to tell Sam that Michael had loved his drawing.

17

In the middle of Mr. Warren T. Diffenbaucher's testimony, somebody came into the courtroom and handed Michael's lawyer a yellow envelope. Mr. Osgood read a little yellow letter that was inside the envelope, and afterward, for the first time since the trial began, he smiled.

Michael wondered what could make him look so happy A second before, he had looked miserable. Mr. Diffenbaucher, who was an accountant and also a trustee of the Lincoln Park Zoo, had just been explaining how many animals had been lost, injured, or destroyed during the incident. "The incident" was what the lawyers had finally agreed, after an unbelievably long argument, to call the thing Michael had done. The figures had been printed in the newspapers, but something in the way Mr. Diffenbaucher's voice sounded when he said the names and numbers of the lost and dead animals made it worse. And when he answered a question about how much money "the incident" had ended up costing altogether, some people in the courtroom gasped.

But Mr. Osgood was smiling. He looked up from the letter and grinned. He leaned toward Michael to whisper something, but just then Judge Tallman said, "Cross-examine?"

"Yes, Your Honor," Mr. Osgood said quickly. Before he stood up, he passed the yellow letter over to Michael.

"Mr. Diffenbaucher, how long have you been a trustee of the zoo?"

At first Michael couldn't read the letter. The small print was faint in some places and smudged in others, and the top was rows of numbers and letters that made no sense.

"About four years now, sir."

Reginald Cawes, Esq., Q.C., Dillard & Cawes, 10 Ryder St., London SW1.

"And you are also a member of the board of directors, is that right?"

John Osgood, Esq., Osgood, Thurber, Weyland, & Tews, 400 Dearborn St., Chicago, Ill.

"Yes, that's right. I serve as treasurer."

John: MacNeils located in Florence, Italy stop Touring Continent since mid-July stop Family embarked for U.S. from Genoa on S.S. Firenzi, arrive New York 17 or 18 September stop All's well that ends well stop. Reggie.

Michael read the message again, then a third time, a fourth. By the fifth reading, he was almost sure it meant what he had thought it meant the first time. Against the rules, he twisted around in his seat to look at Sydney. She wore a different dress from yesterday, and a hat with a veil, because of the photographers. But she had pulled the veil back, and when she saw him looking at her she started to get up. Philip put his hand on her arm. Mr. Osgood, who had eyes in the back of his head, asked Mr. Diffenbaucher a question about his education while he backed up, getting between Michael and Sydney, and without even looking he gave him a slow, firm squeeze on the shoulder.

It steadied him. Whatever would happen would happen. His family was coming, and Mr. Osgood thought that was a good thing. Michael had a different opinion, but he might be wrong. Mr. Osgood was smart, he was a lawyer,

people trusted him—Michael trusted him. But he had kept
from him one important secret: his parents had sent
him away.

Too late to tell him now. They were coming. Whatever
would happen would happen. He pressed his fingers over
and over the creases in the letter, ran them across the
words "MacNeil" and "family" and "arrive," as if by
touching them he could make himself believe and not be
so afraid. The need to talk to Sydney felt like a hunger.
She'd always said he had a family, and even though he'd
pretended to believe her he never had. But she was right,
and whoever they were, they'd been "traveling on Continent since mid-July." He tried to make that a picture in his
mind, but he couldn't.

"Pay attention," Mr. Osgood whispered in his ear, and
when he looked up he saw that there was a brand-new
man on the witness stand. Michael had never seen him
before. His name was Brady and he said he was a
patrolman. He started talking about the night of the incident and how he'd been called to the zoo because of a disturbance. He didn't have much to say, because by the time
he got there "the defendant had already escaped."

There was a man in the jury box that Michael liked to
watch. He sat in the second row, two seats from the end.
Michael couldn't tell his age—he could never tell
people's ages—but he wasn't young, like Philip. He had
neat, thin brown hair and soft-looking skin, and a chin
that went from his lips right down into his collar, a plump,
pink slope of flesh. His eyes were soft and he was always
smiling, just a little, no matter what was going on in the
courtroom. He looked like a nice man. Michael would
look at him to see what he thought about what one witness
said or another witness didn't say. His face didn't change
much, but Michael thought he could tell what he was
thinking. Sometimes, as the trial went on, he even looked
at him to find out what *he* was thinking.

The patrolman finished testifying, and then the prosecuting attorney, Mr. Merck, called a witness Michael recognized. His name was Anthony Cabrini, and he was the

man who had shot the wolf. The man Michael had knocked down and wrestled with on the ground. Because of that fight, Michael had been accused of assault, which Mr. Osgood said was the most serious charge against him. For that, if the jury said he was guilty, he would have to go to jail.

"Mr. Cabrini," the prosecutor said, "tell the jury what happened after you and Mr. Slatsky arrived at the wolf pen. What did you see?"

"I saw two wolves, a male and a bitch, running back and forth beside the gate. They were the only ones left; he'd let all the rest go."

"Objection," said Mr. Osgood. "Assumes a fact not in evidence."

"Sustained," said the judge.

"Just tell us what you saw," said Mr. Merck.

"Yes, sir. Well, these two wolves was going crazy, banging into the fence and howling like banshees. The bitch started to come at me, and I shot her with my thirty-eight. Next thing I know, this crazy man's on top of me, trying to kill me. Slatsky smacked him with his stick, and that was the end of it. Till he come to. We thought he was hurt, but he got away when we wasn't looking. Slatsky had the gun then, but he wouldn't shoot, and the fellow could run like a damn gazelle. So that was it."

The judge told Mr. Cabrini to watch his language, and he frowned and said he would.

"And do you see in the courtroom today, sir, the man who attacked you that night in the zoo?"

"Sure. It was him, fellow right there."

"Thank you. Your witness."

Mr. Osgood stood up. "You say the female wolf tried to attack you?"

"Yeah, come at me, growling and slavering."

"Were you actually in fear for your life?"

"Hell, yes. I mean yes. A wolf'll kill you as soon as look at you."

"I see. How long have you been a night guard at the Lincoln Zoo, Mr. Cabrini?"

"Me? Couple, three years, I guess."

"Before that night, had you ever been attacked by a wolf?"

"Attacked? No."

"Have you ever worked with anybody at the zoo who was attacked by a wolf?"

"No."

"Ever *heard* of anyone at the zoo who was attacked by a wolf?"

"No. But I've—"

"Thank you. Now, you say that after you shot and killed the female wolf, Mr. MacNeil was suddenly 'on top' of you."

"Yeah."

"In fact, you say he tried to kill you."

"Right."

"Tell me, did you sustain any physical injuries during this altercation you claim to have had with the defendant?"

"Like what?"

"Answer the question, sir. Any physical injuries?"

"Yeah, I think I hurt my elbow. Mighta bruised my knee, too."

"Did you require medical assistance?"

"Like a doctor? No, I didn't need no doctor."

"And yet you still maintain under oath, sir, that Mr. MacNeil was trying to kill you?"

"Yeah. Yeah, that's how I saw it."

The next witness was Mr. Slatsky. Michael didn't recognize him, but he testified he was the one who had held the lantern and hit him twice with a nightstick.

"Would you say," Mr. Osgood asked him on cross-examination, "from your experience as a zookeeper, Mr. Slatsky, that the female wolf was a threat to your life that night?"

"Objection."

"Overruled."

Mr. Slatsky rubbed his chin. "Well, a wolf can be unpredictable when it's scared, and this wolf was pretty scared. She might've tried to hurt somebody, especially since we had her cornered."

"You mean she might have attacked you?"

"Not attacked. A wolf isn't going to attack a full-grown man, not unless it's rabid. But if we'd tried to catch her, I'm saying she'd've probably bitten us."

"What if you'd left her alone?"

"Objection."

"Overruled."

"Well, if we'd left her alone, I'd say she'd probably have gone back in her cage eventually. Or run off. Like I say, she was scared."

"And the other wolf?"

"I guess he'd've gone with her. They were mates."

"Thank you. Now, sir"—Mr. Osgood went over to look at the jury while he talked—"you heard Mr. Cabrini testify that he believed the defendant was trying to kill him when he knocked him to the ground, didn't you?"

"Yes, sir."

"Do you agree with that opinion?"

Mr. Slatsky shifted in his seat, looking uncomfortable. "Well, it's kind of hard to say. They were wrestling, that's for sure."

"Well, let me ask you this. Did you ever see Mr. MacNeil strike Mr. Cabrini?"

"No, sir."

"Did you ever see him put his hands around Mr. Cabrini's neck?"

"No, sir."

"Did you see Mr. Cabrini strike Mr. MacNeil?"

"Yes."

"And when you struck Mr. MacNeil with your stick, were you trying to kill him?"

"*No.* No, I just wanted to stop the fight. Tell you the truth, I didn't mean to hit him on the head at all. I just wanted to stun him. Get his attention, like."

"So in your opinion, the defendant was never a threat to the life of Mr. Cabrini or, indeed, of anyone else? Is that right?"

"Your Honor, I object."

"I'll sustain that. You've made your point, Mr. Osgood."

"Thank you, Your Honor. No further questions."

The prosecution called Philip as a witness. "State of mind," Mr. Osgood whispered to Michael while they swore him in. "That's what he'll testify to."

"Whose?"

"Yours."

Philip looked nervous. He gave Mr. Merck short, unfriendly answers. He was a "hostile witness," Mr. Osgood had explained, and Michael could see that that was true.

Mr. Osgood had also explained what perjury was. Lying. Michael sat on the edge of his seat waiting for Merck to ask Philip a question about the five days after the incident. If he did, Michael knew Philip would lie, to protect Sydney.

He had everything planned. Before Philip could answer, he was going to stand up and say to the jury, "I'm guilty of these crimes, and you don't have to have this trial anymore. I did it, I'm confessing."

Fortunately, Mr. Merck never asked the question.

"So you would say Mr. MacNeil was 'upset' that day at the zoo, is that your testimony?"

Philip mumbled, "Yes."

"And on the train home, he said nothing at all? Nothing, that is, until he excused himself to go to the lavatory? After which, you never saw him again until after his arrest?"

"Compound question, Your Honor."

Before the judge could rule, Philip answered coldly, "Yes, yes, and yes."

"Thank you—"

"But I was upset, too. So was Sam. We—"

"*Thank you.* No further questions."

"Your witness?" said Judge Tallman.

"What were you upset about?" asked Mr. Osgood.

Philip's face changed; his anger fell away. He looked

straight at Michael while he answered, "The same thing he was. Seeing wild animals penned in cages. The thing about Mi—Mr. MacNeil is that, after you've been with him for a while, you start seeing things through his eyes. And you learn a lot. After a while, things that you've always taken for granted begin to seem strange. And in this case, barbaric."

"Your Honor, I object."

"I'll allow it. Go on, Mr. Winter."

Philip looked down, a little embarrassed. "I could give you a hundred examples."

"Stick with the zoo," Mr. Osgood said gently.

"All right. I've been to the zoo I don't know how many times in my life, at least a dozen, but that day with Michael was the first time—even though he didn't say anything, it was the first time it ever occurred to me that capturing animals in the wild and putting them in cages so we can gawk at them may not be the—the highest expression of our humanity. In fact, it might be unforgivably cruel."

"Your Honor, I object and move to strike all of that as unresponsive and irrelevant."

"All right, sustained. The jury will disregard that last answer. Anything else, counsel?"

"No, Your Honor, I think that'll be it." Mr. Osgood walked back to the table smiling.

West testified that Michael had threatened him.

" 'I'll kill you.' That's what he said; those were his exact words."

Michael glanced away from West's squirrely, red-bearded face to look at the kind-faced man on the jury. Did he believe West? He had one finger on his cheek, his mouth puckered up in a circle, and his eyes looked troubled.

Mr. Merck sat down and Mr. Osgood stood up.

"What do you think provoked Mr. MacNeil to make such a threat, Mr. West?"

"Absolutely nothing. It came right out of the blue."

"Right out of the blue. You hadn't done anything that might have goaded him to say such a thing?"

"I certainly had not."

"I see. Let me ask you, what was your relationship with Professor Winter's daughter?"

"Objection. Where could we possibly be going with this, Your Honor?"

Judge Tallman put his hands together and looked over the top of them to say, "I was about to ask the same question."

"Your Honor, if you'll bear with me, I think the relevance will become clear very shortly."

The judge thought for a minute. "All right, I'll allow it. Answer the question, Mr. West."

He didn't want to answer. He squirmed in his seat and scowled at the floor. "She was a friend," he muttered finally.

"A friend." Mr. Osgood went closer. "Did you ever propose marriage to Mrs. Darrow?" he asked pleasantly. "Please answer the question. Did you ever ask Sydney Darrow, your employer's daughter, to marry you?"

West glared at him with loathing. "Yes."

"And was your proposal accepted?"

"No," he said through his teeth.

"Thank you. Now, sir, did there ever come a time when you said to Mr. MacNeil words to this effect: 'If you lay a finger on me, I'll have you put back in a cage'?"

After a pause, West said sullenly, "Maybe."

"And what might have occasioned that remark?"

"I don't remember."

"Do you recall an occasion when, during a conversation, you detained Mrs. Darrow against her will by putting your hand on her arm?"

"No, that never happened."

"And when Mr. MacNeil interrupted you, you threatened him?"

"No."

"And that's when he said he'd 'kill you first'—if you tried to put him back in a cage?"

"I don't remember anything like that."

"No? Mr. Philip Winter observed such an incident. Shall we recall him to the stand?"

Mr. Merck objected. The lawyers argued; the judge ruled.

"Something like that might've happened," West said in the end. "But it was a long time ago, and I can't remember the details."

The judge excused him, and Mr. Osgood came back to the table smiling again.

O'Fallon was the prosecution's next-to-last witness.

"He was like an animal. They had to keep him in a cage at first because he was always trying to bite people. When I was with him, I always made sure I had my billy with me, for self-defense. And I never turned my back on him if I could help it."

"Why was that?" asked Mr. Merck.

"Because he gave me the creeps. He never said a word, and he had a way of staring at me, like he was a bear and I was his next meal. They had to starve him half to death before he'd eat his meat cooked—he liked it raw better. I seen him eat bugs. They had to teach him how to use the toilet. He slept on the floor even after they gave him a bed, just curled up on a bunch of blankets like a dog. He was worse than an animal."

The man on the jury had his whole mouth covered with his hand; his shoulders were stiff and his eyes sparkled with alarm. Michael wanted to turn around and see what Sydney's face looked like. But he sat still, afraid of what he might see.

He felt hatred for O'Fallon rise up in his throat like vomit. He remembered every blow, every drunken shove and filthy curse as if they'd happened yesterday. Maybe O'Fallon was right, maybe he was wild. But he wasn't an animal. Animals didn't kill their own kind, and right now he had a fierce and bloody urge to kill O'Fallon.

"Now, sir, you've testified that you didn't trust the

defendant, that you were afraid of him. Did there ever come a time when your fears were realized?"

"Huh?"

"Did he ever attack you?"

"Yeah. Same night Dr. Winter fired me. It was in all the papers."

"Tell us in your own words what happened that night."

"Sure. I brought him his dinner, he didn't like it, and he tried to kill me. Come at me like a maniac, spit coming out of his mouth, growling and snarling. I was sure I'd bought it. He wrestled the stick right outa my hand, so I went for my gun. Lucky I had it or I'd be a dead man today."

"You shot the defendant during this altercation?"

"Yes, sir. I only meant to wound 'im, so I aimed for his hand. After that all hell broke loose. The professor said *I* attacked *him,* if you can believe that, and gave me the sack on the spot."

When it was time for Mr. Osgood to ask questions, the courtroom went very still. If Michael hadn't known already, that nervous, waiting hush would have told him that what was coming was going to be important. O'Fallon's lies had hurt him, and this was his last and only chance to fight back.

"What do you do for a living these days, Mr. O'Fallon?" the lawyer started off. Mr. Osgood was a little, stoop-shouldered man; when he went to stand close to the witness box, it made O'Fallon look huge. Michael wondered if that was why he did it.

"I work at an eating establishment on Twentieth Street."

"Ah, an eating establishment. Would that by any chance be the Dirtwater Saloon in the Levee?"

"Yeah, so?"

"I'll ask the questions, if you don't mind. What do you do at this *eating* establishment, sir?"

"I make sure everything's nice and quiet."

"You're the bouncer."

O'Fallon glared, then nodded.

"Is that a yes?"

"Yes."

"Thank you. You've had experience at that kind of job before, haven't you?"

"I don't remember. Yeah, maybe."

"In fact, you've had a variety of colorful positions in the past, wouldn't you say? You were a prizefighter, were you not, until a few years ago."

"Yeah, so?"

"Until that unfortunate incident in the ring with Mr. Murphy."

O'Fallon's face turned bright red. Michael thought he was going to jump out of his chair and go for Mr. Osgood's throat. "Hey, nobody ever proved *nothing* on me, see? That chump had a glass *brain,* it wasn't my fault he checked out!"

Mr. Merck jumped up and started shouting objections. The judge sustained them and told the jury not to regard the witness's last answer. He gave a warning to Mr. Osgood, who hung his head and looked sorry—but when he came over to the table to get a paper, he slipped Michael a wink.

"Now, Mr. O'Fallon, before you worked for Professor Winter, you worked for the University of Chicago, is that correct?"

"Yeah."

"In a custodial or janitorial capacity, I believe."

"Yeah."

"Tell us what you did immediately before that job."

O'Fallon narrowed his eyes suspiciously. "I tended bar in a tavern."

"What was the name of it?"

"I don't remember."

"Where was it?"

"Over on the West Side."

"What street?"

"I don't remember."

"No? Well, let me see if I can help you out. I have a copy of the employment application you filled out when you first applied for your janitor's job at the university. You wrote down that you'd last worked at McNulty's Tavern on Van Buren Street. Does that ring a bell?"

"Yeah, that's it. McNulty's, right, on Van Buren. Now I remember."

"That's the job you had *immediately* before your university job?"

"Right."

"And you're sure of that?"

"Yeah, I'm sure."

"What if I told you I have information suggesting your last job was as an orderly at St. Catherine's Asylum for the Insane? Would your answer be the same?"

O'Fallon squirmed and didn't answer. At the table to Michael's right, Mr. Merck put his head in his hand.

"And what if I told you I have a sworn affidavit from Dr. James Coleman, the superintendent at St. Catherine's, in which he asserts that you were discharged from that job for—and I quote—'a history of neglect, mistreatment, and brutality to the inmate patients'? Would you say Dr. Coleman is—Well, what would you say, sir? Mistaken? Lying?"

"Objection," Mr. Merck said weakly.

"Overruled."

"Well, Mr. O'Fallon?"

"I don't remember."

"What don't you remember?"

"Nothing about St. Catherine's."

"You don't remember working there?"

"I don't remember nothing."

"What about serving six months for assault and battery in the Chicago House of Corrections two years ago? Remember that?"

"No." He glanced at Mr. Merck in desperation, but the lawyer kept quiet.

"Do you have any kind of brain injury that might account for these memory lapses, Mr. O'Fallon? Maybe from your boxing career?"

Before Mr. Merck could object, the judge said, "All

right, now," very gently, and when some people in the
courtroom laughed, he didn't scold them.

"I'll withdraw that, Your Honor. And I think that'll be
all. No more questions for this witness."

Mr. Merck didn't have any questions for him either.

On the morning of the last day of the prosecution's
case, Mr. Osgood told Sydney to go home. "Better yet, go
shopping," he said. "Go someplace where you can't be
reached." Why? she asked, bewildered. "Just in case
Merck takes it into his head to call you as a last-minute
witness. I don't know why he would, but anything's possible when a lawyer starts to get desperate. I doubt he'd
subpoena you, but if you're sitting twenty feet away, the
temptation might be too much for him. So make yourself
scarce. Because I think the last thing you want, Mrs.
Darrow, is to take the stand."

She hadn't confirmed or denied that. But Osgood was a
smart man, and his timely warning confirmed the suspicion she'd had all along—that he knew about her and
Michael. Oh, not the particulars, but enough to realize
that the outcome of her being called to testify would be
one of two things: social disgrace or perjury.

So she went home, reluctantly; as hard as it was to sit
through the ups and downs of Michael's trial, it was ten
times harder to stay away and imagine them. But Pshe
didn't miss much, they told her in the afternoon. Merck
called one more witness, a zoo employee who only repeated what the others had said before, stressing the chaos
and destruction Michael's "criminal and irresponsible
act" had provoked.

The prosecution rested.

Mr. Osgood asked for a two-day recess, but the judge
denied the request even before Merck could object to it.
Sydney knew why Osgood was stalling—he wanted
Michael's parents to arrive, maybe even testify, before the
trial concluded. He was a good lawyer and he probably
knew what he was doing, but the importance he attached

to the presence of the MacNeils puzzled her. She couldn't believe it would make that much difference.

In any case, at ten o'clock the next morning, he opened the case for the defense, and his first witness was Sam.

Sydney had known about it, and she had finally agreed to it. But she didn't like it. Neither did Aunt Estelle, neither did Papa. They would have forbidden it except for one thing: Sam was dying to testify. In fact, he had put his seven-year-old foot down and insisted on it. He talked of nothing else, and he wasn't the least bit nervous; excited, but not nervous. For him the trial was like a school play in which he was one of the leads; without him, he really believed, the show couldn't go on.

"I do," he piped enthusiastically to the clerk who administered the oath. Around her, Sydney could feel a softening in the courtroom, almost a silent *Awww*. Sam had on his new argyle stockings and navy blue kneepants, a jacket, shirt, waistcoat, and bow tie—too many clothes for the warm September morning, but there had been no talking him out of any of them. In the high witness chair his feet didn't quite touch the floor. He folded his hands in his lap and stared around the room with huge eyes, clearly intrigued by his new, superior perspective. From the knees up he looked like a little grownup, sober and serious, ready to do his civic duty. From the knees down he looked like a child, unconsciously banging his heels against the bottom of his chair.

"Tell us about the first time you met the defendant," Mr. Osgood said after Sam gave his name and age. "Where were you, and when did this meeting occur?"

"I was playing in the sand and I saw him coming along with Mr. O'Fallon."

"You were at your house, and you were playing by the lake, is that it?"

"Yes, sir. And Hector saw him, too, and jumped up on him, so then Sydney and I went to talk to him, and I shook his hand."

"And Hector is—?"

"Our dog."

"And Sydney's your sister?"

"Yes, sir."

"You say you shook hands with Mr. MacNeil. Weren't you afraid of him?"

"No."

"Why not?"

Sam just stared at him.

"Hadn't you heard that he was a 'wild man,' and that he'd once been kept in a cage?"

"Yes, sir, but I wasn't scared of him."

"Why?"

He shifted a little, not prepared for this question. "Because I could just tell."

"Tell what?"

"That he was a regular man. He wasn't wild—he even had his shoes on." Gentle laughter. "I gave him my giraffe puppet to play with, and then after that we played ball. And we've been friends from then on. He didn't talk at first, so I called him Lancelot before I knew his name was Michael. We did everything together, and it was like having another big brother."

With a bemused expression, Mr. Osgood turned over several pages of his notes. Sam was getting ahead of his orderly plan of questioning, but Sydney doubted if he minded it. "Now, Sam," he resumed gravely, "did there come a time when your father asked you to help him with an experiment on Mr. MacNeil? An experiment," he went on when Sam looked blank, "that involved you and an apparent swimming accident?"

"Oh, yes, sir. Dad told me to pretend like I was drowning so he could see what Michael would do. See, he was doing these experiments to see if people are really good or really bad, and since nothing had ever happened to Michael in his life before, nothing in the world or in the city or anything, he was a perfect person to experiment on."

"Aha. Well, just tell us about this incident when you pretended you were drowning."

"Okay. Well, I jumped in off the dock and started yelling, 'Help, help, save me, I'm drowning,' and holding my nose and going under and everything, and Michael came running over and jumped in after me, but then he *sank*. So then—"

"He sank?"

"Yes, he *sank,* because he couldn't swim! Everybody was so surprised, and Dad said afterward, 'Hm, never thought of that.' But he jumped in anyway to save me, so then Sydney had to jump in and save *him,* and he almost drowned but she pulled him over to the sailboat, and then I pulled the boat to the dock and he was okay. But it hurt his feelings, and afterward I told him I was sorry. Right after that we found out he could talk, and he told me he wasn't mad at me. And we're still best friends."

Mr. Osgood took a moment to leaf through his notes before looking up and saying kindly, his satisfaction poorly hidden, "Well, I think that covers it. Thank you, Sam. No further questions."

Mr. Merck declined to cross-examine.

Dr. Slocum, Papa's boss and the chairman of the anthropology department, testified next. Sydney thought he would have made about as good a witness for the prosecution as the defense. He gave an unsympathetic account of Michael's arrival at the university, his silence and hostility, examples of his "violence"—which Mr. Osgood was quick to argue were really attempts to escape, not hurt anyone. Without badgering him, Osgood made Dr. Slocum appear at least remiss, possibly even negligent, for hiring a man like O'Fallon in any capacity, much less one of trust and responsibility. When the chairman stepped down, he left an impression behind that maybe Michael MacNeil had been treated badly by the University of Chicago.

Next witness: Dr. Harley Winter.

"All anthropologists are interested in the question of heredity versus environment in determining human nature. After fertilization of the ovum, the female egg, we can say that every particle of matter in the human organism is contributed by the environment; and it is the interaction of specific environmental conditions with a fertilized ovum of a definite character—*of a definite character;* that's important—that determines the nature of the resulting structure. Trouble is, we can't prove that hypothesis because we can't study it."

"Why not?" asked Mr. Osgood, looking wary; he knew by now that when Papa got going on anthropology, nothing could stop him.

"No human model. You'd need an experimental model for the lack of human intercourse during the young, impressionable years, when the ordinary child is learning to be a human being."

"*Learning* to be a human being. So you're saying—"

"What you'd really need is a pair of identical twins. Rear one in an ordinary environment and the other in a vacuum. Now *that* would be interesting."

"Hm, yes." Scratching his head, Mr. Osgood scanned his notes. "So you and Mr. West were going to use Mr. MacNeil to study the question of heredity versus environment? Because as far as you knew at that stage, he *was* an experimental model for the lack of human intercourse during the impressionable years?"

"No, no. No, that's what Slocum and the others wanted to use him for. When he wouldn't cooperate, they gave him to me. West and I, we had a different theory to test."

"And what was that?"

"Altruism, the origins of."

"Could you explain that? In layman's terms, if possible."

Mr. Merck stood up to say that this whole line of questioning was irrelevant, but the judge overruled him.

"Well, from a biologist's perspective, the difference between altruism and selfishness—"

"First of all, what is altruism?"

Papa blinked in surprise behind his lenses, opening and closing his mouth a few times, having trouble adjusting to the level of simplicity to which Mr. Osgood wanted his answers to descend. "Altruism. Altruism is an unselfish regard for the welfare of others. In animals, it's behavior that's not good for the individual, may even harm it, but benefits the survival of the species. Take ants, for example. Ants provide a fascinating parody of human social life in—"

"I see, thank you. Just, ah, could you tell us very briefly, sir, and very simply, what exactly you and your colleague, Mr. West, hoped to learn from the defendant in the early days of your experiments?"

"Well, in human beings, the difference between altruism and selfishness, biologically speaking, is the difference between right and wrong, you might say. As an anthropological ethicist, I'm interested in the *origins*. Why would an organism—in this case, a man—risk his life for another organism? Why? Did he learn it in school? Is it an instinct he was born with? Where does this habit, this propensity, which seems to fly in the theoretical face of Darwin's natural selection, come from? Why—"

"And were you and Mr. West able to come up with an answer to this question, using Mr. MacNeil as your guinea pig?"

"No, of course not."

"Why not?"

"Because he turned out to be no model at all. He could talk, he was already socialized, he had a conscience, he could even *read*. I might as well have taken *you* for a model, or anyone else in this room. No, Mr. MacNeil was a miserable failure as a study subject, I'm sorry to say. He was entirely too civilized."

"Thank you," Mr. Osgood said with feeling. "And so your studies of him ceased, then, sometime in late June or early July, is that correct?"

"Correct. After that I didn't see much of him. Just at meals, you know."

"At meals?"

"He moved into the house, became one of the family."

"Nobody supervised him?"

"Oh, no. After I fired O'Fallon, Michael was on his own. Well, except for the children—they took him under their wing. Sydney taught him to write, Sam taught him arithmetic, Philip taught him . . . how to play tennis. They took him to the city, to the fair. Trying to bring him up to

speed, you know." He looked over Osgood's shoulder at
Michael and sent him one of his soft, sweet smiles. "Succeeded, too. Boy's a credit to them. Not to me—I did him
more harm than good."

"How's that?"

The smile turned wistful. "I forgot I was dealing with a
man, not just a research subject. I used Michael. Simple
as that. Not very altruistic of me, was it? And when I
couldn't use him anymore, I let him go, forgot all about
him. Lucky for him, I've got three wonderful children,
and not one of 'em takes after me in the least."

Sydney's hand crept over to Philip's, and they both
squeezed. Through an embarrassing blur, she saw her
father's smile come again. *I love you,* she told him with
her eyes, and he said it back to her with his.

"Did you ever try to find out who Mr. MacNeil's parents were, Dr. Winter?"

"I didn't, but Sydney did. She engaged a detective to
look for them. Last I heard he'd found them."

"Would that be the Earl and Countess of Auldearn—"

"Your Honor, I object to any testimony regarding this
defendant's alleged parents, who may or may not even
exist. It's hearsay, it's prejudicial, and at this point it's
completely speculative."

"Sustained."

"But Your Honor—"

"Counsel, approach the bench."

The courtroom buzzed while the judge and the two
lawyers had a whispered conference. Sydney could only
speculate on what they were discussing, but when it was
over she knew from Mr. Osgood's face that the argument
hadn't gone his way. Back at his own table, he said
brusquely, "Nothing further," and sat down.

After lunch, Judge Tallman asked if the defense had
any more witnesses to present.

"May I have a moment to confer with my client?"

"A moment," the judge said severely. He was tired,
Sydney could tell, of Mr. Osgood's requests for delays,

recesses, conferences. He was stalling. Even the jury must know it by now, although they probably didn't know why.

Michael and the lawyer put their heads together. Osgood murmured; Michael listened. Sydney couldn't decide what she wanted the outcome of their conference to be. If Michael testified, Mr. Merck would surely get him to admit he was guilty, and then what could the jury use to acquit him? But if he didn't testify, what would they think of *that*? Not to take the stand in your own defense—didn't that imply you were guilty?

"I said a moment, Mr. Osgood. You're trying my patience, sir."

The lawyer mumbled an apology and stood up. "Your Honor, the defense rests."

She couldn't interpret the meaning behind the soft rumbling in the courtroom in the wake of Osgood's decision. But Mr. Merck smiled, and that couldn't be good. And Michael looked grim.

Her shoulders sagged. Philip gave her a bracing pat on the knee, but he must realize, too, that the only weapon they had left now was Mr. Osgood's closing argument.

Mr. Merck's summation was simplicity itself. Michael's clothes and his name on a "document"—Sam's drawing—had been found at the scene; two witnesses identified him as the perpetrator, and the defense had never challenged their testimony. He was guilty; nothing could be clearer. The defense's "case"—Merck's cynical tone put the word in quotes—amounted to nothing but a pathetic attempt to obfuscate the real issue: crimes had been committed and this defendant had committed them.

"You may feel sorry for Mr. MacNeil. You may understand why he did what he did. A few of you may even appreciate why he did it. But you can't in good conscience find him innocent on any of those grounds. In your hearts you know there's only one choice. It's your duty, gentlemen, however much you dislike it, to make that choice. Thank you."

Mr. Osgood stood up slowly. He spoke slowly. He

summed up his case slowly, and then he repeated himself. Slowly.

When he started to summarize a third time, the judge interrupted to snap, "This case is going to the jury this afternoon, counsel, whether you're through arguing it or not. Do I make myself clear?"

Osgood nodded dispiritedly. "Yes, Your Honor."

He faced the jury. Straightening his shoulders, he took a deep breath. "Gentlemen, I won't try your patience for much longer. I'll only ask you to look at this man and see him as he really is: an innocent. And I put to you that, for him, the confinement of animals in zoos is torture on a massive scale, unconscionable, inhumane, and inhuman. Michael MacNeil had not yet learned that the wholesale imprisonment of his fellow creatures on this earth, representatives of virtually every species human science has so far been able to identify—is perfectly acceptable, no crime whatsoever. Indeed, we think of it as one of our God-given human rights to while away a summer afternoon, wandering from cage to cage, looking at wild animals behind bars. If there's cruelty in that, we're blind to it. It's harmless, we say; it's natural in this human world—no law is broken.

"But Michael MacNeil is new to the human world. New and innocent. He did a bold and daring deed that happens to be against our human law, but for him it was no crime. It was a necessity. He acted on pure, selfless impulse, as irresistible to him as a mother's impulse to run into a burning building and save her child. Or his own impulse, when he risked his life to save the little boy he thought was drowning.

"He must have known he couldn't get away with it. He probably even knew the futility of it. Those considerations didn't stop him. I would ask you to put yourself in his place, but I know you can't do that. Neither can I. None of us can. Michael's life has been unique, too far beyond the realm of our experience even to imagine.

"And that is the reason you must let him go, find him innocent. Because he *is* innocent, in the profoundest sense of the word. There's no violence in this man, no cruelty. What you have in Michael MacNeil is a human being at his most natural. Uncorrupted. Fine. Flawed in small ways, like any man—he leaves wet towels on the bathroom floor, they tell me, and sometimes he doesn't hear what people say to him because he's daydreaming—but not yet flawed by the daily depredations of society. Michael is what God made him, and what men haven't had a chance yet to spoil. He's innocent.

"And so I ask that you let him go. Not because you condone what he did. But because you respect what he is. Thank you."

Sydney swallowed down a lump in her throat. Michael had looked modest, tortured, and uncomfortable during his lawyer's speech, hands clamped together, his gaze locked on the edge of the table. How awful it would be to listen to yourself being vilified in front of strangers one minute, glorified the next. The jurors sat stonefaced; try as she might, she couldn't read them.

Mr. Osgood resumed his seat. Michael leaned over and said something that made a tired smile flicker in the older man's face. Judge Tallman cleared his throat. He only had a few things to say before they began their deliberations, he told the jurors in a grave voice. Sydney half expected Osgood to jump up and request another recess. But he didn't, and with no further delay, the judge began to give the jurors their instructions.

And then a sound like low, curious murmuring started at the back of the courtroom. Sydney turned her head, but the hat of the woman behind her blocked the view of the door. The muttering rose in volume until the judge noticed it and broke off. "Order in this court," he commanded, frowning down the center aisle at the source of the disturbance.

Sydney craned her neck again. She saw the head and shoulders of a tall man with black hair, bent in a solicitous posture over a woman. Her breath backed up in her lungs. Could it be? And then Sam, who had an aisle seat and a better view, suddenly jumped up from his chair and announced in clear, ringing tones, "There's Michael's father."

The courtroom erupted. Judge Tallman banged his gavel and banged it again, but no one paid any attention. Sydney's rapt gaze raced back and forth between Michael and the man who looked so much, so heartbreakingly like him. Michael pushed back in his chair slowly, as if in a dream, and rose to his feet, never taking his eyes off his father.

"This court's in recess," Judge Tallman bellowed, giving up on restoring order. "Bailiff, escort the jury to the jury room."

Sydney stood, too. Philip gave her hand a pat, and she realized she was clutching his arm with all her strength. Everybody was standing now, but instead of crowding into the aisle they stood still, all eyes riveted on the dark, imposing gentleman and the woman, pale, trembling, lovely—Michael's mother?—beside him.

"Bailiff! Take the jury out, I said."

There was a girl behind them, tall and willowy, brown-haired, with Michael's mouth and his father's proud bearing. They made their way down the aisle, all three MacNeils, pulled like magnets toward Michael, whose face was . . . indescribable. At last the swinging gate in the low railing was the only barrier between them, but for breathless seconds no one moved. Lord Auldearn's hard, smooth face was ruddy with emotion; he seemed rooted to the spot. In the end, it was his wife who broke the spell. With a little sobbing cry, she pushed open the gate and rushed to her son, arms outflung.

"Bailiff!" the judge tried again, but the jury wasn't moving.

Michael's father hesitated for one more awkward second, then embraced his son and his wife at the same time. The girl, Michael's sister—oh, how pretty she was—stood apart at first, wonder shining in her face, and then gradually crept closer. Her hand on Michael's shoulder shook slightly and touched him so lightly he didn't feel it. His eyes were shut tight. He was crying—so were his parents. Sydney's vision clouded as she watched the jury file out. Some of them were blinking hard; all of them were moved.

At the prosecutor's table, Mr. Merck slid down, lower and lower, until the back of his head touched the back of his chair. He had his eyes closed, too, but he wasn't crying. He looked like a wilted balloon.

Thirty-seven minutes later, the jurors returned with a verdict. They found Michael MacNeil not guilty of all the charges except vandalism—he had broken a lock on the zoo's front gate—a misdemeanor punishable by a fine of eight dollars, plus court costs.

18

Michael kept wondering what his family would think if they knew what he wanted to do with them: roll around on the floor. Time and again he had to stop himself from laughing out loud, imagining their faces if he told them. Kate might not mind—she might even do it!—but his mother probably wouldn't understand. And his father . . . stifled laughter overtook him again, just thinking about it. The Laird of Auldearn definitely wasn't a man to wrestle and play games on the floor with his pack. The Laird of Auldearn was top wolf; he was dignified. But he was tender inside, and kind, and full of love. Michael knew this, because he had seen him cry.

"How beautiful the lake is at night," Kate said from the balcony of their fifth-floor room in the Leland Hotel. "The moon's shining, and you can see the lights from the boats." She turned around to smile at him. "It's much bigger than our loch, Michael. Do you remember it? It's called Loch Rannoch."

"I remember watching you fish," he said to his father. "Throwing the line in. You caught a trout." He could see it perfectly, speckled brown and gray. He could see his father's hands working the hook out, and his father's black boots, the tweed trousers tucked inside.

"I remember that, too. You were too little to hold a rod, so you played with the net in the shallows. You caught a minnow. You didn't want to go home, even though it was pouring."

Michael didn't remember that, but the idea pleased him. He could add that now, the picture of gray rain pounding on the loch, the smell of wet wool and the feel of sodden clothes, to the other memories of his childhood.

They were sitting in the big room of the suite of rooms his family had taken at the hotel. They had come here after the verdict to get away from reporters, and all they'd done since they got here was talk. And look at each other. His sister couldn't stop staring at him, his mother couldn't stop touching him, and his father couldn't stop smiling. And he still wanted to roll around on the floor with them.

It was hard for him to talk; mostly he just wanted to listen. He thought of what Sydney had said this afternoon, after the foreman of the jury said not guilty and everybody had started clapping and cheering. She had held both of his hands and whispered to him, "Michael, I'm so happy." He couldn't even say it back—speech failed him; he couldn't match words to his feelings, and "happy" just wasn't enough. All the MacNeils had met all the Winters, but only for a minute. Newspapermen and photographers and strange people had gotten in the way, and before he knew it he was in a carriage with his new family, moving down Jackson Street to the Leland Hotel.

They had dinner sent up, and kept talking the whole time they ate. "We were having breakfast in the dining room of our *pensione* in Florence when the cable came," his mother said. She liked telling this story, and none of them had gotten tired of hearing it. "We didn't believe it at first—we'd had so many hopes ruined, years ago when we first employed people to look for you. I remember thinking, even here in this beautiful city, after all this time, it's followed us. The sadness. Your father didn't want to call the lawyer in England, but I told him he had to."

"I told him, too," Kate said, and his mother and father nodded that that was true.

"So I called him," his father continued, "and he said there was a boy, a man, who claimed he was. Michael

MacNeil, and that his aunt and uncle had drowned in a canoe accident in Ontario eighteen years ago."

"So we had to come," his mother said, smiling, dabbing at her eyes with a handkerchief. "I was afraid to believe it could be true."

"She kept saying, 'It's just a trip, a chance to see America,' " Kate put in. "She wouldn't even talk about it, why we were going or what might happen when we got here."

His mother laughed. "I said, 'It won't be for nothing— at least we'll see the World's Fair.' " She leaned forward and pressed her small hand over Michael's, and her eyes filled up with happy tears again. She was so beautiful, he was almost afraid of her. He loved her with his whole heart; he didn't even know her, but he would die for her, and he knew she felt the same.

I have a sister, I have a sister, he sang to himself sometimes, staring and smiling at the beautiful girl. Katherine Mary Rose MacNeil, who looked like his father and his mother together. She was almost nineteen, born the year after he got lost. They were shy of each other at first, just watching and smiling, both interested but not saying much. Her shyness wore off first, and since then she had told him about her life—the ladies' school she didn't go to anymore, the names of her friends, the books she liked to read, the jumping contests she entered with her horse, whose name was Phantom. She didn't want to marry, she wanted to go to the university and study medicine. Or architecture, she wasn't sure. Then again, she might want to be a playwright. She dazzled him.

When they finished dinner, they moved back to the sofa and easy chairs and kept talking. Sometimes Michael didn't even listen to the words, just the sounds going up and down, soft and loud, and the laughter. They were all tired, so tired, but they didn't want anything to change, couldn't bear the evening to end. But Kate fell asleep curled up in a chair, and soon after that they woke her and told her to go to bed.

She came to him and kissed him on both cheeks. Her

shyness had completely disappeared. She must have seen him blush because she said, "It's easier for me," with her hands resting on his shoulders. "I've known about you all my life. Poor you—you didn't know I existed until a few hours ago. But you'll get used to me, and then you'll be glad you have a sister. I hope."

She was laughing with her eyes, so he knew it was a joke. But he said anyway, "I'm glad now, Kate. I never could stop hoping that I had a father and mother, but I never even thought of a sister. You're a gift."

She gave him a strong hug and turned away quickly, calling good night as she sailed out of the room. He thought she might be crying. He hoped so; up to now Kate had been the only dry-eyed one in the family.

His mother and father had their arms around each other. She was so small and delicate, she barely came up to his shoulder. But she wasn't a weak woman. No—but how did he know that? He just knew. "It's late," she said. "We should all go to bed. And when we wake up, you'll still be here. I've had so many dreams . . ." She pressed her lips together and shook her head. "A miracle," she whispered. His father blinked his eyes and gave her his handkerchief—she had soaked all of hers.

"I have something to show you." Michael went closer. He took his book out of his pocket, unwrapped it, and held it on his palm. "Do you remember this?"

They shook their heads, staring at it so strangely that he saw for the first time what it really looked like. Nothing; a pulpy, black lump of nothing. He started to laugh, but it caught in his throat.

"Father," he said. That was for the first time, too. "It's a book. Was a book. You gave it to me on the day I sailed away. *Now I Am a Man*—that was the name of it."

"I remember." He put out his hand, and Michael gave him the book.

"You said, 'When I see you again, Michael, you will be a man.' And you shook my hand. I know it by heart still. I think if I hadn't kept it, I might have forgotten I was a man."

Nobody could say anything for a while, but it wasn't a bad silence. Finally his mother said, "Why did we ever let you go?" She leaned her temple against his father's arm and smiled. "I wonder how many times I've said that in the last eighteen years. You're here now, and I thank God for that, but I expect I'll still ask the question. Every day, for the rest of my life."

Michael felt as if he was standing in front of a locked door. His life on this side was perfect, except that he couldn't go forward. No matter how much it might hurt, he had to unlock the door, because it was dividing his past from his future.

"Why did you let me go?"

His mother touched his sleeve. She had such pretty green eyes. They went wide when she asked, "Don't you remember?"

He shook his head. He didn't want to say what he remembered.

"It was because I was pregnant. I kept miscarrying—I'd lost three babies after you were born, and we thought this might be our last chance. The doctors said I must have complete rest and quiet. *Complete*—I wasn't to be allowed out of bed for the whole nine months. We . . ." She looked at his father, as if she wanted him to finish it.

"My brother and his wife, your Uncle Duncan and Aunt Katherine, were going to Canada and America for two months on a holiday. They offered to take you with them, and the doctor said it would be a good idea. You were a normal six-year-old boy. Noisy and active, in other words. Rambunctious."

"Oh, but you were a lovely boy," his mother said in a rush, "the *best* boy. You were handsome and smart, you could read before you were four, and you never lost your temper, you had the *sweetest* disposition—"

"Show him the picture."

"The—oh!" She laughed at herself as she pulled on a gold chain around her neck. Out of her dress came a locket—he knew that word because Sydney had a locket. It was gold, with a design on the front, a crest or a shield.

"Look," she said, opening it. "It's you. You were just five. You wouldn't sit still for a photograph, so I did this miniature. And this—" She folded back a little hinged piece of glass behind the picture. "This is a lock of your hair. Remember how I cried when you cut it the first time?" His father nodded, smiling at her with love in his eyes. "Undo it, please, Terence." She bent her head, lifting the hair from the back of her neck, and his father unfastened the chain. She caught the locket in her palms.

"It's yours, Michael. I never took it off in twenty years, but I don't need it now. Because I have you."

It wasn't just a locket she slipped into his hand, the smooth metal still warm from her body. It was a key, too. It opened the door to the rest of his life.

Midnight. Too late to call Sydney. He would see her tomorrow—his parents were inviting the Winters to dinner—but that was such a long time from now. He wanted to see her face, hear her voice. Show her a picture of himself when he was five and had a family who thought he was a "lovely boy."

Lying in his too-soft bed in a room next door to the MacNeils' suite, he stared and stared at the locket and wondered if the painting in it really looked like him. If so, he had been an angel, not a child, with his pink cheeks and sweet, happy face; all he needed was a halo and this picture could go on a church ceiling. He loved it, though. He loved *himself,* that little boy, because his mother and father had loved him. That one fact changed everything.

He felt so happy—so sad. The baby that his mother had tried so hard to have had died after all, she had told him; she lost it the same day they told her Michael was dead, drowned. But now there was Kate, and that was a miracle. How could he wait until tomorrow to tell Sydney these things?

She would like his family, and they would love her. And he'd give her this picture of himself that his mother had painted, so she would know that he had been a real boy, a good boy, and his parents hadn't thrown him away.

They had loved him. Because of that, *she* could love him, without hiding it. He would be worthy of Sydney.

How could he wait until tomorrow to see her?

"Went to Scotland in eighty-eight, you know, Auldearn." Sydney's father raised his wineglass in a mini-salute to his host at the other end of the table. "Went to see the natural history collection at the Royal Scottish Museum. Stayed a week. Good show."

"Auldearn"—it was what they were supposed to call Michael's father. Sydney thought it sounded disrespectful, like calling her father "Winter," but Aunt Estelle insisted it was correct. She would know: she had spent all afternoon researching the subject in her collection of etiquette books. "Either 'Auldearn' or 'my lord' or 'your lordship,' " she had instructed them at length on the carriage ride into town—not the train for this grand occasion, needless to say; only the carriage would do.

"Oh, yes," his lordship returned agreeably. Everything he said was agreeable. He had a stern, even a severe version of Michael's face, but since Sydney had met him he had rarely stopped smiling. "Did you get up to St. Andrews, by any chance? The library at United College is very good in your field, you know. I've a bit of an interest there myself."

"Have you!" Papa couldn't have been more delighted. Across the table, Philip actually took time out from monopolizing Michael's sister Katherine to give Sydney a wink. She sent one back, silent acknowledgment that poor, unsuspecting Auldearn had just launched Papa into a monologue on his favorite subject.

"Your father is a genius, Michael tells us," Lady Auldearn said to Sydney in a soft voice, underneath Papa's louder one, with a humorous look that said she'd seen the wink. Sydney smiled at her, unexpectedly at ease. She had never met a countess before, much less had dinner seated next to one in a private dining room of the Leland Hotel. But it was impossible to feel intimidated by this petite, soft-spoken, serene-faced woman. "My father was a genius, too," she said, "or so I was frequently told. He was an amateur entomologist."

"Entomology," Sydney said slowly. She could never keep entomology and etymology straight. "That's . . ."

"Bugs."

"Ah." Maybe she was imagining it, seduced by her ladyship's sympathetic manner, but the look they exchanged just then suggested to Sydney that they had a *world* of things in common. "You were a painter, Michael told me."

"Did he remember that?" She lifted her gaze to Michael, sitting at his father's left hand at the other end of the table, and her green eyes went soft with fondness. "Well, I am still a painter. Not one you would have heard of, I'm certain, but I—"

"Elizabeth, don't be so modest," Auldearn put in with gruff affection, taking advantage of a lull in Papa's opinion of the relative merits of the anthropology departments at the universities of Chicago and Edinborough. "My wife has had two shows of her own in Glasgow, as well as a group show in London. She is an artist of great sensitivity and intelligence."

During the short, pleasantly embarrassed silence that followed this pronouncement, Sydney wondered what Michael had told the MacNeils about her. They were graciousness itself, they couldn't have been kinder to her— and yet they didn't exhibit that *particular* curiosity that would have meant they knew Michael was in love with her and she with him. He must not have told them, then. She didn't quite know what to think about that.

"Michael's an artist, too," Sam piped up. "Right, Michael?" They sat next to each other, between Sydney and Lord Auldearn, and from time to time they put their heads together and whispered. Sydney suspected they were confiding in each other how much they wished Hector were here, so they could feed him the flageolets and onions à la Grecque they were pushing around and trying to hide under their *pommes soufflées*. Sam looked as happy and contented as any of the MacNeils, thrilled to have his friend back; in fact, he hadn't left Michael's side all evening. Until now, Sydney hadn't quite realized how much he adored him.

She let the conversation ebb and flow gently around her, content to watch Michael, fascinated by the happiness that shone so clearly in his face. She was dying to be alone with him. She had thought he might call her last night, but he hadn't. So she had called him, a little after ten. The desk had refused to disturb him; "The MacNeils are not taking telephone calls, madam." She had understood; the press must be tormenting them horribly. But . . . he hadn't called today, either. She had hoped he would. Thought he would. She had stayed in the house all day, in fact, so she wouldn't miss his call.

Just then he laughed at something his father said, smiling broadly across the table at his sister. How selfish she was being, Sydney chided herself. Of course he would want to be with the family he'd just found. She was ashamed for wanting him to herself so soon. But she did.

"How unfortunate . . ." Aunt Estelle had to clear her throat. "How unfortunate the Osgoods couldn't join us," she ventured in a low voice, completely unlike her, as if she were speaking in church. "You said Mrs. Osgood was in ill health, my lord?" The title rolled off her tongue naturally, fluidly, as if she'd been speaking to Scottish nobility all her life. And yet of all the Winters, Aunt Estelle was the most intimidated by the grandness of Michael's family. This was no ordinary social coup she had pulled off, sitting at the right hand of an earl, dining *en famille* with a countess; this was a revolution. All her hopes and aspirations had come true tonight in spectacular fashion. So far, interestingly, the effect was to reduce her to virtual speechlessness. Sydney had faith in her, though; soon she would shake off this out-of-character bashfulness and assert herself.

The waiters collected the plates and brought a new course, braised lamb cutlets; Sydney wondered what Michael and Sam would do with the spinach-stuffed mushrooms that accompanied it. Her father was talking to

Lady Auldearn; she heard him mention that he planned to be in touch with Mr. Diffenbaucher, the trustee from the zoo, to discuss "ah, compensation for monetary damages resulting from the, ah, incident." He would have done it sooner, he explained, but Mr. Osgood advised him to make no overtures of that sort until Michael's legal case was resolved.

Lady Auldearn leaned toward him and said in a confidential tone, "Thank you, that's very kind of you. It won't be necessary, though. As it happens, my husband looked into that matter this afternoon, and now I believe everything has been taken care of. Indeed, I'm told the zoo authorities are perfectly satisfied."

Her slight emphasis on *perfectly* told Sydney as clearly as words that Lord Auldearn had been generous. Very generous. The slant of the stories in tomorrow's newspapers ought to be interesting. Really, it wouldn't surprise her if, before it was all over, the reporters turned Michael into a folk hero.

"Have you been able to see any of the city yet?" Philip inquired of Katherine, from whom he had hardly taken his eyes all night. He had asked her the question during a lull in the general conversation; everyone heard it. Self-conscious, he pretended he hadn't been speaking exclusively to Kate (Sydney had overheard an earlier exchange between them, in which she had invited him to call her Kate) but to the table at large. "It would be a shame if the newspaper reporters kept you cooped up in the hotel and you never got to see the sights."

"We did stay in our rooms all morning," Kate said with a wry smile. "But this afternoon Father and Michael gave interviews to three different papers, all at the same time. We're hoping that will make them leave us alone."

"How was it?" Sydney asked, looking at Michael. She couldn't imagine him fielding rude reporters' questions. But perhaps they hadn't been rude; perhaps the presence of the Earl of Auldearn had had a civilizing effect on the press. At least for a while.

"I didn't have to say very much. My father spoke to them."

My father. He said the words with so much pride and love, such reverence, Sydney had to look down.

Dessert came—almond tortes and *coeur à la crème,* which Sam and Michael ate with gusto. The waiters brought champagne and fruit, and Auldearn rose to make a toast.

"Ladies and gentlemen, my new friends, my dear family. I'm often called upon to give speeches. Once at a state dinner for three hundred and fifty exalted guests, the Queen of England among them, I was asked to propose a toast to Her Majesty—with no preparation whatsoever—on the occasion of the passage of the reform bill extending the household suffrage to county constituencies. This was nothing. Permit me to say, I was eloquent. I know this, because they told me so afterward."

Sydney chuckled with the others, stealing a glance at Lady Auldearn. She was smiling down the table at her husband with a look that perfectly combined tolerance, amusement, and deep fondness.

"Tonight, however, I am finding it almost impossible to match the right words to my feelings. While I'm a religious man, I confess I've always thought of miracles as historical events, wondrous events that happened long, long ago, certainly not in the last decade of the nineteenth century. But . . . I was wrong." His voice dropped, hoarsened; Sydney thought he might weep, but he didn't. But he was deeply moved and unable to hide it, and she sensed he was a man to whom his own dignity mattered enormously. "My son—has been returned to me. The little boy whom I loved more than my own life has come back to us. A fine—and a good young man. I am . . . so very happy. And proud. My dear friends—" Shiny-eyed, he raised his glass—"drink with me to this miracle."

All the women, even Aunt Estelle, had to search for their handkerchiefs.

"Did you really meet the Queen?" asked Sam when his lordship sat down. That lightened the mood. Auldearn explained to him very kindly that even though he was a Scotsman, he sat in the English House of Lords, and had occasion to see, meet, and even speak to Queen Victoria quite often. Sam was hugely impressed.

"One day Michael will sit with the Lords as well, I've no doubt." Father and son smiled at each other, and the similarity in their sharp-edged profiles was uncanny.

"Will I?" Michael said shyly.

"You will. After a wee bit of grooming, perhaps."

"Father says Michael can go to St. Andrews and study anything he likes," Kate put in, beaming at her brother. "It's the oldest university in Scotland. And it's Father's alma mater," she added, laughing, "so we know they'll take Michael." She turned to Philip. "Did you know he's a baron? Michael, I mean."

Sydney thought her aunt might cut herself with her fruit knife. The awe in her face was comical. But Sydney didn't feel like laughing.

Presently Aunt Estelle pulled herself together to say, "I hope you will be kind enough to allow me to introduce you to a small, a select number of people, in whose society I believe I can assure you you would not feel uncomfortable. I would consider it the greatest honor to host a small reception in my home. Or here in the city, for your convenience—my brother is a member of the Chicago Club, a very old and dignified institution, indeed, the most exclusive in the city. You would not—"

"Madam, you are much too kind," his lordship said smoothly—so smoothly, Sydney couldn't tell what he really thought of her aunt's effusiveness. Perhaps he was used to that sort of servility and thought it no more than his due. "On a return visit, nothing would please us more. Unfortunately, our schedule won't allow us the luxury of the sort of social occasion you suggest, delightful as it sounds."

"Auldearn has business in Edinburgh that can't be post-poned," her ladyship put in. "Indeed, we were making arrangements only this afternoon for passage on a liner home. But I know we'll return," she added warmly. "How could we not? You're our friends now, and we owe you a debt we can never repay."

Aunt Estelle replied with something; Sydney didn't hear the words, only the flattered, disappointed cadence of her voice. The conversation turned into a meaningless buzz. Without thinking, she took a tiny bite of cake. It stuck in her throat and she couldn't swallow it; it tasted like sand.

"I'd like to make a toast." Michael rose, holding his glass up and out in a perfect imitation of his father. He had even borrowed Auldearn's evening clothes, to stunning effect; they fit him almost perfectly, but more than that, they *suited* him. He was changing before her eyes, turning into an elegant, dignified stranger.

"I'd like to drink to everybody. This is the happiest night of my life. I love you." His eyes touched everyone, but they lingered on Sydney. She smiled at him with all the love in her heart, but there was a core of coldness spreading through her that even his warmth couldn't melt. They all drank. Michael sat down, and his father said something that made them both laugh. It was the same sound, deep and generous, the same angling of the head. His sister murmured to him, reaching her hand across the table toward him, love and tenderness glowing in her eyes.

Sydney was losing him. She could see it, feel it; the evidence was everywhere, but most particularly in the affection that filled this room like the scent of flowers. She had looked forward to this night with excitement and anticipation, the way a bride looks forward to her wedding day. Tonight was to be the crown of her happiness, heaven on earth, the perfect resolution to everything. Michael would get what he deserved, and she would get Michael.

Self-hate made her skin prickle. She was the traitor here, the Judas at the table, the only one who didn't wish him well in his new life. Not only did he not need her anymore, his *schedule* no longer permitted him to enjoy the sort of *social occasion* she represented. And—he was a baron!

"Now I'd like to propose a toast." Her father stood up, his face wreathed in smiles. He cleared his throat—

Sydney pushed back her chair and got to her feet. "Excuse me." Horrified, she realized she couldn't control her voice. Her smile felt stiff and false; humiliating tears were only a breath away. Without risking more words, she turned her back on everyone and hurried out of the room.

Michael stared after her. Dr. Winter, bewildered-looking, set his glass down and said, "Hmm." Michael saw a look pass between his mother and his sister; some kind of understanding dawned in their eyes. He stood up. "I have to go." Remembering his manners, he added, "Excuse me," and made everybody a bow.

There was a ladies' lavatory at the end of the hall. He went toward it, thinking she might have gone there, distracted on the way by the sight of himself in the mirror-covered walls—very gentlemanly-looking in his father's black evening clothes. In the corner of his eye as he crossed the main corridor, he caught a flash of Sydney's yellow dress, just before she disappeared down a wide flight of steps to the lobby.

"Sydney!"

He veered left and ran after her, his feet sinking deep in the thick, silent carpet. When he reached the stairs, he skidded on the slippery marble and almost fell. He made a grab for the banister. Two women and a man coming up the steps delayed him—he dodged to his right at the same time they moved to their left; he shifted left, they moved right. It happened two more times. They started to laugh. Finally he got around them, and took the rest of the stairs three at a time.

The lobby was full of marble columns and fat velvet chairs and beautifully dressed people. But no Sydney. Could she have gone outside? He raced to the front desk, where the clerk was talking on the telephone.

"Did you see a woman," he panted, "just now, in a yellow dress? She just walked by."

The clerk said, "Excuse me," into the telephone and blinked at him, uncertain.

He straightened his shoulders and slicked back his hair, trying to look the opposite of a wild man. "I'm trying to find Mrs. Darrow," he said as calmly as he could. "I'm a guest in the hotel."

"Yes, sir." The clerk finally nodded, and Michael attributed his decision to trust him to his father's fine clothes. "She just passed through. I believe she went into the palm court."

"The what?"

"Through there, sir." He pointed to an arched doorway between two white marble pillars. Michael remembered to say thank you before he hurried toward the door.

The palm court had glass sides, a glass dome for a roof. The hot, heavy air smelled like the earth after a rain. Everything was green, like pictures of the jungle. Three brick paths fanned out from the entrance. He took one and followed it around trees and shrubs and a stone fountain until it twisted back to where it started. He tried the second one, and at the end of it he saw Sydney. She had her back to him; she was reading a sign, a little metal plaque on the ground in front of a tree. She didn't hear him until he came close enough to touch her. Then she turned. He was glad to see she wasn't crying.

As soon as she saw him, her face crumpled and she burst into tears.

He put his arms around her. "Don't." Her silky dress under his hands, her flower-smelling hair. The feel of her. "Don't cry. Oh, I missed you. You feel . . ." He squeezed her closer, surrounded her with his arms, wanting to take her inside himself. Her wet face looked so beautiful. "Shh," he whispered, putting his mouth on the tears, smearing her lips with them, and she stopped crying long enough to kiss him back. Oh God, the sweet, salty taste of her. She had desperate hands, holding his face, pulling in his hair. They pressed together closer, harder, until it was not enough and too much, they had to let go of each other to breathe.

He didn't know for sure, so he had to ask why she was so unhappy. "Is it because I'm going away?"

"Are you?" She wiped her eyes with her hands. "You are, of course you are. I want you to, you have to. Oh, Michael."

It started again, and this time he couldn't stop. Could they make love here? Behind this tree, *Hevea brasiliensis,* right on the damp ground. Or standing against it, "rubber tree," pressed together like animals mating, two turning into one.

A voice—"Look, isn't that pretty?" They jumped apart just before two people, a man and a woman, strolled around the corner and saw them. Michael made a shield of his body between them and Sydney, hiding her. The couple stopped. Looked. Turned around and walked the other way.

"Oh God, Michael, this is hopeless."

"No, it isn't." He was afraid she would leave, so he made her sit down on a bench at the side of the brick path. He gave her his big white handkerchief, thinking how much more women cried than men. She blew her nose and dried her face, taking a long time to pull herself together. He didn't care; he would have waited all night, he was so glad to finally be with her. "This is the first time we've been alone, Sydney, in so long."

She balled the handkerchief in her lap and took a long, deep breath. "I don't call this alone."

He had to touch her. He took her hand and kissed it and laid it against his cheek. She tried to smile, and he kissed her on the lips. "You look beautiful. You smell wonderful. The worst part of being in jail was not seeing you. Sydney, I'm never breaking the law again."

She laughed, a wet gurgling sound in the back of her throat. "I missed you so much. I knew they would let you go. Wasn't Mr. Osgood wonderful? When your parents came—oh, Michael, that splendid moment!—Mr. Merck almost slid right under the table. That's when I knew they'd let you go."

"I didn't know. I was afraid. I thought, if they make me

go to jail, it'll be even worse now, because I have a family."

"I love your family." Her cheeks turned pink; she looked away. "I'm sorry."

"Why?"

"I should be happy for you. I *am* happy for you. I am, but . . ."

"What?"

"I hate it that I have to let you go."

He frowned. When he put his arm around her, she twisted into him and pressed her face against his neck. "Why do you have to let me go?"

"Because you don't need me anymore. A different life is starting for you."

"Yes, a different life is starting." He couldn't see it, though; when he tried, it was like looking through fog. Today his father had spoken to him of his estate, his responsibilities; he had used words like *stewardship* and *birthright* and *prerogative*. "You'll be a gentleman," he had said, but Michael didn't know what that meant.

"I have to go to Scotland, Sydney." She nodded. He heard her swallow and knew she was trying not to cry anymore. "You come with me." She shook her head, and he said, "Yes. You come with me."

"I can't. You need to be with your family now."

"Yes, but I need to be with you, too. I always will. I love you, Sydney."

"I'll wait for you. It doesn't matter how long. Someday . . . But right now your real life is starting, Michael, your true life. You're Michael MacNeil, the Younger of Auldearn. I'm selfish, but not enough to keep you from that life."

He pulled away so he could see her face. "Do you love me?"

She closed her eyes. "Yes. I love you."

"Then why won't you come with me?"

"Because I don't belong with you now. Everything's changed."

"Everything's changed, yes, but not us. Aren't we the

same? I'm just more in love than before—that's all that's changed in me."

She put her hand on her throat. "It's not that easy."

"Why not?" She shook her head. "I'm not stupid, Sydney. Explain it to me."

"Of course you're not stupid—but—it's complicated. You have no idea how society works, and families, and—obligations. For God's sake, Michael, you're a *baron*."

"That's just a word."

"Listen to me. You know what my aunt is like, how much she cares about what people think. Appearances, rules, laws of conduct, how society has to be *regulated,* how—"

"Yes, yes," he cut in, impatient. He was getting angry, but not with her.

"Your father and my aunt—they don't have much in common," she said with a short, unhappy laugh, "but they agree on that."

"How do you know?"

"I know. He's an *earl*. You don't know what that means yet, but I do. Believe me: your father doesn't want me to go with you to Scotland."

"How do you know?"

"I know."

Was she right? She was so sure, and he didn't know anything.

They stopped talking. The silence grew, and he began to hate this hot, humid place. "We should go back," Sydney said, but neither of them moved. Water trickled from the invisible fountain; the sound was monotonous and maddening. What if she was right about his father? What if he had to choose between them?

But he had already chosen. "You won't come with me?" he asked her for the last time.

"Michael, I can't."

"Then I won't go." He stood up. "Come on, let's go tell them." He took her hands and pulled her to her feet.

"Wait—" He started to pull her along, even though she

hung back. "Wait, Michael. *Wait.*" He stopped. "What are you saying? You *have* to go."

"I don't."

"Yes, you do, you know you do."

"I'm not going without you."

"Michael, listen, this isn't the answer."

"What is the answer?"

"I don't know! I don't think there is one."

Not caring who saw them, he took her in his arms again. It didn't get them anywhere, but he felt better when they were touching. How could he be so sad now when he had been so happy an hour ago? Why did life have to be so complicated?

She leaned against him, pressing her cheek to his. "They'll be worried about us. We have to go." Stepping back, she brushed at his shoulder, and he pulled a strand of her hair out of her eyes. "Am I a mess?" He said no, but she looked doubtful and walked over to the glass wall to see her reflection. "Oh, dear God," she wailed softly, and started fixing her hair, her eyes, patting at her dress.

Nothing was decided, but she was right, they couldn't stay away any longer. They walked through the lobby, squinting in the sudden brightness, and went up the marble staircase to the mezzanine. At the end of the hall, the doors to the private dining room were closed, but he could hear the rattle of plates and glasses inside. Sydney gave him a shaky smile, for courage. He pushed open the door.

Except for a maid loading plates onto a tray, the room was empty.

"Uh oh," said Sydney.

"Maybe they went upstairs."

"Or out. What if they're looking for us outside?"

"Let's go upstairs and see."

They took the elevator to the fifth floor, both of them silent and grim, hiding their clasped hands behind her skirt. Michael had time to think, as the little car rose higher and higher, that he liked hotels. He liked them a lot, almost everything about them, and he wished the day would come soon when he and Sydney could stay in one together without hiding or being miserable.

At the door to the MacNeils' suite they drew themselves up again. "They're here," he whispered; he could hear voices behind the door. He almost knocked, but decided to try the knob first. It wasn't locked. They opened the door and went inside.

Nobody noticed them. Kate and Philip were leaning against the railing of the tiny balcony that overlooked the lake, talking, unaware of anything but each other. Across the room, the others were standing around the big table, peering down at something. A map?

"Now here, not half a league from Invergordon," his father was explaining while Sydney's father bent close to follow his pointing finger, "there's a large stone with an inscription in Ogam—which, as you know, makes no sense in any known Indo-European language."

"Quite," said Dr. Winter, sawing his pince-nez back and forth across his nose so he could see better. "Fascinating."

"Of course, even though there's evidence of descent in the female line, especially in the case of the Pictish royal family, we still don't know whether they were Aryans or non-Aryans."

"Yes, quite. We theorize that the Gaelic and Brythonic languages they spoke by the first century A.D. were imposed by Celtic-speaking invaders in some remote time, but we can't prove it. And you have a stone right there, do you? Remarkable. I should enjoy seeing that very much."

"Here is our little village, Miss Winter," Michael's mother said, pointing at something else on the map. "You will enjoy meeting the ladies in our horticulture club, I daresay. Of course, they'll try to impose on you—because I shall put them up to it—to give us the benefit of your expertise on the subject of roses at our fortnightly meeting."

"Oh," the aunt simpered, blushing, "how kind. Really, I should be delighted. Most honored."

"There's a fellow in Glasgow you'll want to meet, Winter. I knew him at school and we've kept up. Anthropology fellow, wrote a book about biology and ethics. Cutting edge sort of thing, very—"

"You don't mean McDuff, do you?"

"McDuff, that's the man."

"Good God. We've corresponded for years. I wrote a piece about his book in the *Times*."

"Well!" The two men clapped each other on the shoulders, beaming. "You'll be glad to meet him, then, won't you?"

"I should say!"

Sam, bored with the talk and finally bored with the map, swung around from the table. "Sydney! Michael!" He ran to them and grabbed his sister's hand. "Guess what? We're going to Scotland!"

"What?"

"Scotland! Dad's going to be a guest lectern at some university, and Aunt Estelle's going to talk about roses to a bunch of ladies." He took Michael's hand, too, and shook it. "The best part is, *your* dad says you can get married right on the boat if you don't want a wrong engagement!"

"Samuel!"

He glanced back at his aunt, worried. "Ma'am?" Philip was laughing; Dr. Winter kept clearing his throat.

Michael's mother came toward them, smiling radiantly. She kissed his cheek, then took Sydney's hands in both of hers. "Michael didn't tell us—we didn't know, and now I feel silly. Of course he would love you. My dear, I'm so very happy."

They kissed—and then Michael's father kissed Sydney and hugged Michael, and Dr. Winter kissed both of them, and Aunt Estelle kissed everybody.

"Did you ask her?" Sam demanded when the hugging and kissing were over. "What did you say? What did she say?"

Michael just grinned at him, confused.

"Samuel, for the lord's sake—"

"You have to ask her if she'll marry you! It's called *proposing*. I thought you knew that."

No, he didn't know that. While Philip laughed, the aunt clucked, and everybody blushed, Michael asked Sydney if she would marry him.

She said yes.

19

Aboard S.S. Alexandria
2 October 1893

Dearest Camille,
   I said I'd write every day, but I think we both knew when I made that rash promise I wouldn't keep it. But you forgive me, I'm sure, and take into account my special circumstances.
   Oh, Cam—I'm married. Captain Jordan performed the ceremony in the ship's chapel three days ago, with both families watching, everyone I love but you, and I missed you terribly. Michael looked unbearably handsome all in formal black, and I wore my Vienna green silk with lace trim and the little ivory train. We didn't really have attendants, but Michael and I both thought of Philip as our best man, Kate as bridesmaid (in your absence), and Sam as ring bearer. Yes, we had rings— Aunt Estelle and Elizabeth (how odd to call her that. But she's asked me to, and I'm trying to remember to do so)—Aunt E and Elizabeth somehow managed to get a jeweler to come to us at the hotel in New York on Friday, the day before we sailed—surely the maddest, most hectic day of my life! The actual sailing would've been an anticlimax under other circumstances. But not in my circumstances, because I was to be married the very next day!

*Oh, I am running on, and I sound like a perfect
ninny. But, Cam, I'm so very happy. It's a measure of
the strength of our friendship, isn't it, that I can say
that to you? I miss Spencer every day, and I always
will, but loving Michael takes nothing away from that.
I know you understand; otherwise I couldn't tell you
how happy I am for fear of hurting you. But I know
you rejoice with me.*

Sydney looked up from her letter and gazed across the
tiny desk at her husband fast asleep in their bed. She wasn't
being completely truthful with her friend, she realized. If
she told Cam honestly how happy she was, how could it
not hurt her feelings? Marriage to Spencer and marriage to
Michael . . . they weren't even—they didn't even— Words
failed her. One was normal satisfaction, ordinary good fortune, and the other was . . . out of this world.

*I think you'll rejoice when I tell you something else,
too. I believe Philip is falling in love with Kate. And
she with him, unless I've misjudged her completely
and lost all my powers of observation—not likely!
They've been inseparable from the moment they met;
they never stop talking and have eyes only for each
other. Of late there's a . . . I hardly know what to call
it. An atmosphere around them, impossible not to
notice, a sort of cloud of—well, desire, that's both
unnerving and fascinating to be near. (Which must be
the very thing people say about Michael and me, too.
Oh, Cam, isn't love the grandest invention?)*

*Anyway. Philip has loved you forever, of course you
know that, and it's always made me sad that you
couldn't love him back, not the way he wanted you to.
So: this is wonderful. I think it's wonderful (and needless to say Aunt Estelle is beside herself), but I can't
help questioning how wonderful the MacNeils think it
is. I don't know anything about the nobility and their
expectations and all of that, but it wouldn't surprise
me if the MacNeils had higher hopes for their only*

daughter than a titleless undergraduate from the colonies. On the other hand, the Winters aren't exactly poor, and we're about as respectable as Americans get. Best of all, Michael's parents truly seem to want nothing so much as the happiness of their children. Certainly they've never made me *feel anything but welcome and loved.*

So we will see what happens. Kate is lovely, by the way. She and Michael adore each other—it's really extraordinary how close they've become in such a short time. And she's very bright; I'm quite intimidated by her. But listen to this, Cam. Something good has already come of Philip's attachment to her. He's told Papa and Aunt Estelle that the spring term at Dartmouth was his last, and he means to give up science (which he's always loathed and been no good at, and only pursued in the first place to try to please Papa) and turn all his energies into becoming a writer. Hurray! "And I'm prepared to accept the consequences," he told Papa—and, of course, there were no consequences. Thank God it took Philip less time than it took me to learn that lesson—that our father's love and acceptance have always been there (hidden behind the vagueness and the pipe smoke), and we didn't have to rebel against him or try to be just like him in order to win them. Philip says I inspired him to take this step. I. *Because I took what I wanted and damned the consequences, he says. Well, if it's true, I'm doubly happy, but how can it be? All I did was take my heart's desire. No, if anyone inspired Philip, I'm quite sure it was Kate.*

Across the cabin, her heart's desire stirred and rolled over, his long legs tangling in the sheet. His naked backside presented a powerful distraction. She put her hand over her forehead, blocking the view, and continued.

The MacNeils claim Lake Michigan reminds them of their loch in the Highlands, which is called Rannoch.

This seems a little unlikely to me, but I suppose I'll find out for myself in a few days. At any rate, you'll never guess what they're thinking of doing, Cam; really thinking of, not just spinning fancies. They're talking of buying property on Lake Michigan and building a house on it, a sort of second home, to which they'd come often to visit, presumably, if Michael and I end up living in America.

Nothing's been definitely decided about that yet, of course; we aren't even talking about it, and whatever Michael wants to do I will do, without a single regret. Still, I can't tell you how glad I am to know his family won't be putting pressure on him to stay in Scotland. And frankly, I'm surprised. His father is very proud, very keen on duty and responsibility. Well, we will see what happens. My future is a complete mystery, but for once I'm not anxious about it. All I am is happy.

Sydney laid her pen down and stood up. Impossible to concentrate another minute with such a diverting temptation lying only steps away. The sun shining through their upper deck porthole had turned Michael's bare skin a tantalizing shade of tawny gold. They'd made love less than an hour ago, but she wanted him again. If she woke him up, he'd want her, too. She couldn't resist.

She sat down behind him and put her hand on his sun-warmed arm. Her weight sagged the mattress, rolling him gently against her hip. "Hey, sleepyhead," she whispered, and he smiled without opening his eyes. She tickled the tender skin inside his elbow, skimmed her fingernails down to his wrist and back up. "Wake uuuup," she teased. He groaned, pretending he didn't want to, but she happened to know he was wide awake already. She picked up his heavy hand and kissed each limp finger, then placed his palm on the side of her breast. His smile widened; all the lifelessness left his fingers. Both of them hummed at the same time, a soft, drowsy sound signaling the renewal of interest. "Are you awake?"

"I'm starting to be." He caressed her slowly, softly, through the cool, slick satin of her dressing gown. "What time is it?"

"Don't know." She closed her eyes, reveling in that delicious sinking sensation in her stomach. She leaned over to nuzzle his ear, a trick that never failed. He drew his breath in through his teeth, at the same time he slipped his hand inside her robe and brushed her bare, warming skin. They kissed.

"You always smell good and you always taste good. How do you do that?"

She shrugged, dreamy-eyed. He told her that so often she was almost ready to believe it. "I like the way you taste, too. In fact, I like everything about you."

He grinned, untying the bow in the satin tie at her waist. "Want to lie down beside me?"

"I don't mind if I do." But first she took off her dressing gown, watching his face while she did it. She was naked underneath. Michael was never lecherous exactly, but he was always so . . . *appreciative*. And she'd never felt so much like a woman as she had in the last three days. "Do you think we'll get tired of this some-day?" she asked, stretching out beside him.

"I won't."

The promptness of his answer made her smile. "Neither will I," she vowed. "Not even when we're fifty. Not even when we're *eighty*."

"A hundred."

"A hundred and twenty."

They started to giggle. He pulled the sheet over their heads, which was usually the prelude to a tickling contest, or sometimes a silly, sexy wrestling match he always let her win. This time they just rubbed against each other and rolled over, sealed together from top to bottom, mouth to toe. Michael's stomach growled. "I'm ignoring that," Sydney said, circling his neck with her arms. She turned her head to the perfect kissing angle. "You can nibble on me." He did, using his teeth on her lips and then her tongue, devouring her with wet, luscious kisses. His hands roamed, and she started to lose herself in the tender, seductive blur. Thoughts stuttered, stopped; she felt her brain disconnect from her body. Michael whispered something unbearably sweet as he slipped inside her, and the world fell away.

Soft and slow, sweet and easy. Long, lingering kisses and the leisurely caress of hands, bodies rolling and turning on the sun-warmed bed. He made a low sound, deep in his throat—and that fast, it changed. They rolled again, hands clutching, mouths greedy, and Sydney heard herself whisper a shocking, shameless thing to excite him, drive them both higher in a hurry. She let herself go.

Sheer ecstasy—she couldn't stand it. Sweaty, muscular, intense pleasure. Saturating satisfaction.

They collapsed. Sometimes they laughed after making love, just from happiness, a sort of giddy celebration of sex. Other times she cried—for no particular reason, a mere excess of feeling. This time they fell on each other and, for all intents and purposes, died.

Knocking at the door revived them, to a degree. "Did you hear something?" Sydney mumbled disingenuously; if one of them had to get up and open the door, she wanted it to be him.

Knock, knock, knock.

"No, I don't hear anything," Michael muttered into the pillow.

She swatted him on the behind and threw off the covers. "Yes?"

"Sydney, open up. Are you still *in there*?" Sam sounded incredulous. "It's time for lunch! Why are you still in there? Come on, open up."

She caught Michael's eye as he grabbed for the sheet and she wrestled with the arms of her dressing gown. "His timing could be worse," she reminded him, then went to the door and opened it.

Sam tumbled inside, followed by Hector on a leash. "You're still in *bed*?" He plopped down beside Michael, who had the covers tucked modestly around his chest. "Are you sick? Did you get seasick? You don't look sick," he decided, eyeing him critically.

"I was taking a nap," Michael told him, which was half true. He reached down to pet Hector, who was wagging his tail and sniffing the sheets with great interest.

"A nap in the morning?" Before they could think of an answer to that, he rushed on. "Well, hurry and get up because we're having a picnic on deck. Aunt Elizabeth said we shouldn't go below for lunch on a day like this, so she told the steward we wanted to eat right in our chairs. So hurry up and get dressed. Oh! I forgot to tell you— guess what?"

"What?"

"Captain Jordan said I can steer the ship."

"Really? That's exciting." Sydney caught sight of her-self in the mirror over the dresser. Wild hair, flushed cheeks; general blowsiness. She looked like a contented woman.

"Yeah! I get to do it this afternoon at three o'clock, right on the bridge with him and Mr. Addison. He's the first mate, and he's really nice. He came to our table this morning and talked about ships and everything—Hey, how come you didn't come to breakfast?"

"We didn't wake up in time," she said smoothly, "so we had it brought in on a tray. It was—"

"How come you had to have a nap if you slept so late?" That stumped her.

"What time is it?" she asked, to divert him. He had a new watch; he loved people to ask him the time.

"Twelve-fourteen."

"Goodness! You're right, we'd better get up. Hurry, Michael. Sam, run upstairs and tell them we'll be there in twenty minutes. No, better say thirty." She opened the door, which made Hector lunge for the hall, which pro-pelled Sam off the bed. She bustled the boy and dog out without ceremony and almost had the door closed when Sam whirled around to correct her. "Not 'upstairs,' Sydney," he said with seven-year-old superiority. "*Above.* How many times do I have to tell you?"

"Above. Go above. Go."

"I'm going, I'm going." He threw a suspicious look back over his shoulder as Hector yanked him down the corridor. "Boy, Sydney, sometimes it's almost like you're trying to get rid of me."

"Am I in heaven?"

Nobody answered; nobody heard the question.

No matter. Sydney knew heaven when she saw it, heard it, felt it, and this was definitely heaven.

She leaned back in her canvas deck chair and laid her book facedown on her chest. Who could concentrate on *The Magic of the Highlands,* fascinating as it was, when there were so many other things to do? Such as watch Michael and his mother paint seascapes on the quarter-deck at back-to-back easels, like two pianists in concert. Or listen to the tone—not the words; that would've taken too much energy—of the conversation between her father and her father-in-law on the subject of fossils. Philip and Kate had taken Sam off to steer the ship—she hoped they weren't heading for Brazil—and Aunt Estelle had gone below to have a nap. (A real nap, one presumed, nothing remotely resembling the kind of nap she and Michael liked to take.) A light, tangy wind blew. A few puffy clouds floated in an otherwise pristine azure sky. A waiter kept bringing her fresh cups of tea with thin sugar cookies that melted in her mouth.

Heaven.

"I'm finished," her mother-in-law announced, standing up and laying brush and palette on her chair. "For now." She picked up a rag to wipe her hands and walked over to Michael's side. "Oh, that's stunning." She leaned against him and put her arm around his shoulders, bending close to peer at his painting. *Mother and son,* thought Sydney. How beautiful they looked together. Elizabeth wore a paint-spattered smock over her violet gown, and a tartan scarf to keep her hair from blowing in her eyes. In the afternoon sun she looked her age, forty-five or so, Sydney reckoned; but sometimes, by candlelight or flattering gaslight, she looked like a girl.

Michael gave her waist a squeeze, then stood up to look at her painting. "Oh, it's beautiful," he exclaimed, earnest and delighted. "Yours is much better than mine."

"Oh, no, yours is."

"No, it's not." He laughed at the idea.

"Bring them both over here and let us judge," Lord Auldearn suggested—foolhardily, in Sydney's opinion; she wanted no part of this contest. "Call me Terence," her father-in-law had invited on the morning of her wedding, and she had thanked him and said she would. So far, though, she hadn't. Couldn't. *Terence?* No, no, no; impossible. So far she was calling him nothing at all.

They all had chairs on the quarterdeck, the Winters and the MacNeils. Lord Auldearn had reserved them for the whole voyage on the first day out, and the chairs were unquestionably the best situated and the most deluxe on the ship. How fortunate, Sydney often considered, that she liked her two families so much, the old one and the new one. It wasn't every bride who would happily share her honeymoon with her husband and seven other people.

It took some more urging, but presently Michael and his mother brought their paintings over to his father's deck chair. Auldearn looked and looked, but pronounced no judgment. Papa leaned over to peer at the canvases, hemming and humming, squinting through his pince-nez. Overcome with curiosity, Sydney made the ultimate sacrifice and got up to look, too.

They had both used oils—watercolors dried too fast in the breeze—but aside from that the two artists' depictions of the sea had nothing in common. A strong, confident line bissected Elizabeth's canvas where dark water met light sky, blue on blue. The painting was quietly dramatic and very pleasing to the eye. She had captured the tranquility of the sunny, lazy day and had avoided monotony by the addition of whitecaps and clouds and imaginary gulls. It was a lovely painting.

Michael's painting had no frame, no visual landmark

like sky or horizon to orient the viewer; he had painted the ocean and nothing else. The result ought to have been chaotic, a great blue muddle, but it wasn't. No one could mistake the energetic layerings and shadings of blue and green, umber, yellow, ochre, and ultramarine for anything but the moody, complicated sea. Where he had piled on paint in thick coats, layer after layer, he had even created a third dimension. Somehow the painting satisfied even as it unsettled.

"I teach art, you know," Elizabeth said mildly, perched on the edge of her husband's chair. She smiled, acknowledging what they were all thinking: there were still so many things they didn't know about each other. "Just a few students. They come to me—it's not an art school, nothing like that."

"They come to her *after* art school," Auldearn put in gruffly. "Don't be so modest, Lizzy."

She gave his cheek a brush with the back of her hand, absently affectionate. "I could teach you, Michael, but I'm afraid."

"Afraid? Why?"

"Your work has no discipline at all, none. It's pure imagination. I'm afraid I'd refine it. You'd learn the rules and lose the directness and emotion that makes your work unique. It's not a childlike quality. I've seen children paint with this much abandon, but not with this depth."

It was true, Sydney thought, with mounting excitement. Michael seemed to be *inside* the waves, inside *all* his paintings, because he had never been taught to take himself out of them. What if his talent was truly special? What if he could be a *real* artist, recognized for it, satisfied by it? She wanted it for him, she realized. It fit. She believed it was his calling.

"*Some* discipline, though," his father offered tentatively, deferring to the expert. "Don't you think, Lizzy?"

"Perhaps, but only a little. One would have to be so careful. Uninhibitedness is good, but not if it prevents an artist from showing us his vision. That's what rules are for, ideally—to make it easier for you to communicate with us. On the other hand, there's a danger that learning the rules might blur your vision, Michael. Cloud it. That's what frightens me."

"But you could teach me," he said cheerfully.

"No—but there's someone at the University of Edinburgh I know and trust."

"Frost?" asked Auldearn.

She nodded. "He would be careful. Respectful. Yes, I'd trust him."

Sydney's father took the unlit pipe out of his mouth. "The Art Institute in Chicago," he mentioned, "is one of the finest schools in the world."

Sydney could have kissed him.

"Yes, it is," Elizabeth agreed, nodding vehemently. "Indeed it is. Michael can study wherever he likes. Or nowhere."

There was a thoughtful pause.

"You know," Papa spoke up again, "these two paintings would make the perfect appendix to a paper I'm working on about human evolution."

Nobody actually groaned, but there was a subtle sagging all around.

"But then again, maybe not," he corrected himself, oblivious. "We could say Michael's painting, because it's 'wild,' is purely the product of heredity—pure nature, in other words—and Lady Auldearn's, the product of environment. Teaching."

"But my mother was an artist," Elizabeth protested. "Which means I must have acquired some of my talent, such as it is, from her. Heredity."

"Precisely," Papa cried, delighted. "And Michael lived in the wild all those years, not in a vacuum. In a sense, the wilderness was his school, as surely as . . ."

"The Royal Academy."

"The Royal Academy was yours. And who's to say which influence, even if you could separate them, produces a better artist in the end? Not I," Papa demurred.

"Not I," everyone echoed.

Not long after that, the MacNeils gathered up their

belongings and excused themselves, saying they wanted
to rest before dinner. They had all gotten so lazy; Sydney
realized it when nobody even thought of responding,
"Rest from *what*?"

Her father rose with them, but hung back for a moment,
letting them go ahead. He had been waiting to light his
pipe out of deference to Elizabeth. He fired it up now, and
the smoke and his thin white hair blew westward in a
stream, duplicating in miniature the ship's smokestack
overhead. "Not an art critic," he uttered, reverting to his
laconic classroom style. "Wouldn't know the first thing
about it. Just going on feel. Instinct, hm? Personal prefer-
ence, too. Wouldn't want this repeated."

"What, Papa?" Sydney asked, mystified.

"What I said about the better artist. Hm?" He pointed
with one discreet finger at Michael's canvas drying on top
of a vacated deck chair. "This is better. Not technically."
He screwed up his face. "Spiritually? Wrong word. *Heart,*"
he realized, sounding surprised. "That's it. More heart.
Don't tell your mother, hm?" He lifted his eyebrows con-
spiratorially, flashed his sweet smile, and tottered away.

Michael stared thoughtfully after him. What an interesting afternoon this had been. Sydney slipped her hand
through his arm and they wandered over to the railing.
"Sunfall," he told her, pointing to the horizon. "That's
what I used to call it, in my mind. Before I knew the right
word."

"Sunfall." She smiled up at him, and the reddish sunset
lit sparks in her pretty hair. Fox hair. Their deck was
deserted; he put his arm around her waist, inside her
shawl, and she put hers inside his jacket. He had been
wanting to touch her all afternoon.

"I'm so full, Sydney."

"Full?"

He looked out across the sparkling, darkening water
and thought that the depth and the vastness of it were like
his soul right now, his heart. "I'm full," he repeated; it
was as close as he could come. "And I've come around in
a circle."

"What do you mean?" She leaned against him, resting her cheek on his shoulder.

"I can remember the other ship. And I remember this ocean. It took me from my home when I was a child, and now it's taking me back."

"Home," she said softly.

"Are you sad?"

"No! Why would I be?"

"Because I'm going to my home, but you're leaving yours. We don't know for how long."

"Oh, well, I see you're not as smart as I thought you were."

"What? I'm not?"

"No." She glanced behind them, then stuck her fingers inside his belt and pulled him closer. Very daring—they were almost embracing. "There's no such thing as leaving home or going home anymore."

"There's not?"

She shook her head. Using her hat for a shield, she kissed him, just a quick, soft touch of her lips on his, but it stirred him. "Home is right here, silly," she whispered. "Wherever we are."

"Ah." Of course. "As long as we're together, we're home."

"That's it."

Beneath their feet, the ship's bow carved through the water like a sharp knife, cutting into the future. The past was its glittering white wake, and he and Sydney teetered above it on the thin line of the present. It should have been frightening—everything before them was unknown. It would have frightened the lost man.

But Michael was found. And he was already home.

If you loved *Wild at Heart*, be sure to look for Patricia Gaffney's next novel, *Outlaw in Paradise*, a stunning historical romance set in 1880s Oregon and filled with all the passion, humor, deeply felt emotions, and the kind of joy that Patricia Gaffney brings to her readers again and again. Turn the page for a special preview. . . .

Outlaw in Paradise

On sale this fall from Topaz Books

I

Some folks said it was a coincidence that the church clock got stuck at three o'clock on the day the gunfighter rode into Lazarus. Maybe so, but what about the leak that sprung in the water tower that same afternoon? And what about the grease fire at Swensen's Good Eats & Drinks? Not to mention the fact that Walter Rideout keeled over and died in his own outhouse that very day. Walter was pushing ninety, but still. It made you wonder.

Most people could tell you where they were and what they were doing the first time they laid eyes on the gunfighter. Chester Yeakes was sitting out in front of Wylie's brand-new livery stable, eating a green apple and reading the Lazarus *Reverberator*. "I see a shadow, I look up, and there he is, dressed in black and covered with guns. Two Colts in his belt, a Winchester in his saddle, another pistol in his boot, and I swear I saw a derringer's butt stickin' out of his vest pocket. Looked like a damn army'd rode into town."

"Stable your horse?" Chester inquired, and according to him, the gunfighter curled his lips under his long black mustache and sneered at him.

"I didn't come here for a haircut," he answered in that low, whispery voice you had to lean close to hear. Gave you gooseflesh, that whispery voice, and he talked slow, too, Chester said, like he wanted you to understand every word, and if you didn't he'd just as soon shoot you as repeat himself.

"This is Pegasus," Chester said the man said, introducing that big black gelding like they were all at a barn dance or something. "What he gets is whole oats in the morning and ground oats at night. Cottonseed meal and clover in the afternoon. Two ounces of salt. No timothy. You feed him timothy, I'm afraid I'll have to kill you."

Chester opened and closed his mouth a few times before he got out, "No timothy. No, siree."

"Pegasus better look good when I come around to check on him tomorrow. He better feel good. He better be singin'."

"S-singin'?"

"Some real happy tune. Like 'Little Ol' Sod Shanty on the Claim.'"

Chester kind of grinned at that. But then he saw the shine in the gunfighter's eye, the one that wasn't covered up with a black patch, and the icy cold in that steel-gray eye just about froze the blood in Chester's veins.

Floyd Schmidt and his brother, Oscar, were playing checkers outside the grange hall when they first saw the gunfighter. For once, Floyd, who's been known to stretch the truth to make a story tell better, didn't exaggerate when he said, "Feller didn't have on one stitch that weren't black. Black britches, black shirt, black vest, black coat. Black boots, black hat. Black cigarette. Looked like a walking one-man funeral."

"Friend," Oscar said the gunfighter whispered to him, making what little bit of hair Oscar's got stand on end, "What's the best saloon in this town?"

Floyd, who was drunk at the time and had more courage, answered when Oscar couldn't get his tongue to work. "Well, we got Wylie's Saloon, which you done passed comin' in. Then there's Rogue's Tavern up here at the other end. That's about it, saloon-wise."

The gunfighter squinted his eye on the Rogue, which you can just barely see from the grange hall. "Red balcony on the second story? Rocking chairs settin' around?"

"Yep. You can rent a room there, too." What possessed Floyd to say that, he never could explain afterward.

The gunfighter thumbed the brim of his Stetson up a notch and sort of smiled. "I got a hankering to set down in a rocking chair and watch the world go by." Floyd and Oscar both shivered when he whispered, "Never can tell who you might see passing down below. Ain't that right?"

They said that sure was right and watched him stroll on down Main Street real slow, spurs jingling, saddlebag on one shoulder and his rifle over the other.

Levi Washington, the colored bartender at the Rogue, almost dropped the whiskey glass he was drying when the gunfighter came through the swinging doors, quiet as a puff of smoke. "You could hear the head fizz on a beer," Levi claimed, "when he thunked his rifle butt down and said he'd take a double shot of bourbon, the best I got. Not many customers that time o'day, and what we had cleared off in a hurry, shot out the door like their pants was on fire. I was glad Miz Cady wasn't there in case trouble started, but kinda wishing she was there, too, 'cause she probably coulda headed it off. You know what she's like.

" 'House brand all right?' " I says, and he cocks his head and whispers, 'Talk into my good ear, friend,' just like that, like his voice is comin' outa the grave or a coffin or something. I begun to suspicion who he was, but I didn't know for sure till he says he wants a room upstairs lookin' out on the street. Corner room, he says in particular. He gives me four silver dollars, and says if anybody wants to see him I should send 'em right up. Somehow I got enough spit in my mouth to ask him his name.

"I swear the wind died down and some dog quit barking just before he says 'Gault' in that turrible whisper that makes your insides freeze. 'The name's Gault.'

"Well," said Levi, "I knowed we was in for it then, because I seen it happen before. Nothing's the same once a killer comes to town."

Cady McGill always took Friday afternoons off. Lately, now that April had come and the weather had finally dried out some, she'd taken to renting a buggy and driving out to the old Russell place by herself.

She'd unhitch the horse and let it graze while she wandered around the old going-to-seed orchard, running her hand over the scaly bark of the wild-blooming apples or down-at-the-heels pear trees. Butterflies fluttered through knee-high wildflowers, and the smell was so sweet she could feel it purifying her lungs, making her forget all the smoke she'd inhaled for a week at the Rogue. She'd stroll over to the big house and press her nose to the wavy front-door window, imagining what she'd be doing right now if she owned the place. She might be sitting in the parlor, which she could see about a quarter of from the door, drinking a cup of afternoon tea, maybe paging through a seed catalog and planning her summer garden. Or maybe she'd be reading a book—a novel, nothing serious—while she sipped a nice cold glass of lemonade. No, on second thought, not on a gorgeous day like today. If she wasn't planting flowers, she'd be working in the orchard alongside her men. Two men; three if she could afford it. This might be a daydream, but she was practical enough to put at least two sturdy day laborers in it.

La Valee aux Coquins. The Valley of the Rogues. Thirty years ago, after the Rogue Indian wars were over, that's what the Russell family had named their three hundred acres of orchard and pastureland on the cliff-edge of the river. Nowadays people just called it River Farm, all that French being too big a mouthful for honest Oregon tongues. But Cady liked both names; some nights she even fell asleep whispering them to herself, pretending she was standing on the high cliff and watching the blue-green Rogue rage from side to side in its half-mile-wide canyon. Her bit of the river. Her orchard. Her dark hills and pretty green pastures.

Well, someday, maybe. If everything worked out just right.

Time to go home now, though. It looked like rain in the west, and besides, she had work to do.

She hitched up the buggy, climbed in, and gave the horse a switch, thinking about Merle Wylie's latest offer for her saloon. If she combined it with her nest egg, it might be enough to buy River Farm, but not enough to do anything with it afterward, like put it in working order. Anyway, Wylie could kneel down, fold his hands, and kiss her butt before she sold him so much as a shot glass. Why did the one man, who could've helped her buy her dream place, have to be her worst enemy? Life sure was funny sometimes. Ha-ha. Life had been funny to Cady a few times too many, and she wished it would hurry and sober the hell up.

Not that she had much to complain about nowadays. Nothing like in the old days. Some might say she had it made: a few good friends, her own place to live, a business she owned free and clear. Why, she even had a gold mine. She had to smile as the buggy passed by the muddy, poky, weed-infested turnoff to the Seven Dollar Mine, the second thing any man had ever given her. (Third if you counted the tattoo.) *If it weren't for Mr. Schlegel, you wouldn't have anything at all, Cady McGill.* She reminded herself of that whenever she was feeling down on men. Which was pretty often. Being in the saloon business, she figured it came with the territory.

Riding past the entrance to the Rainbow Mine a few minutes later wiped the smile off her face. Merle Wylie's turnoff wasn't scraggly and overgown, and his mine wasn't placered out like hers. Which just went to show, there wasn't any justice in this world. If there was, a no-account rodent like Wylie wouldn't still be digging gold out of the ground, and a saint like Ed Schlegel wouldn't be moldering in his grave. He'd still be running Rogue's Tavern and hauling gold out by the bucket from the Seven Dollar Mine. And Cady would be . . . his mistress? Wife by now? She couldn't quite picture herself in those roles, although she'd wished for either one of them often enough when Mr. Schlegel was alive.

But that was all water under the bridge. You didn't get anywhere by cogitating on the past, which wasn't going to change, no matter how much you wished it would. You couldn't count on the future either, but sometimes you were allowed to dream about it. Paint yourself a picture of what you thought it would look like. For Cady, it always looked like an orchard farm in the Rogue River Valley.

Jesse almost set himself on fire lighting one of his damn black cigarettes. He was sitting in a rocker on the red balcony outside his room, doing his badass-sonofabitch-outlaw routine, when half an inch of red-hot ash fell in his lap. It's hard to look menacing when you're jumping up and down and slapping at your privates. Nobody was ogling him just then, though, which was a miracle, since about the only thing the good people of Lazarus had done since he hit town was stare.

He liked Lazarus. It didn't look like much, but with gold towns, looks could be deceiving. He was sure there was money under the wheel ruts in the dusty, unpaved streets; big money in the pockets of the rough-looking customers stumping up and down the wooden sidewalks; and buckets of money behind the yellow brick façade of the First Mercantile Bank & Trust Company. All an enterprising fellow had to do was be patient and wait for it.

Knock-knock-knock.

Well, shoot.

He got up, moving cool and slow in case anybody was watching. But he had to look down to hide a grin. This was getting so easy, it wasn't hardly even any fun anymore.

"Gault?" somebody mumbled through the door to the corridor. "Speak to you, Mr. Gault?"

Strapping on the gunbelt he'd hung on the bedpost, Jesse said, "It's open," in his creepy whisper.

"Mr. Gault?" *Knock-knock-knock.*

Which so often the trouble with creepy whispering. He cleared his throat and yelled, "The door's open!"

The knob turned and the door cracked open an inch, two inches. Three, four. Tired of waiting, Jesse yanked it all the way open, and a bow-legged, ginger-haired fellow with a smell on him like a dead buffalo half fell, half jumped into the room.

"Don't shoot, I ain't packin'!" he shouted with both hands in the air. He was built like a cob horse, short, round, and stocky, and if he'd changed his clothes in the last year or so, it didn't show. He didn't look like much, but Jesse had learned opportunity came in many different shapes and sizes.

"State your name," he hissed, flexing his fingers over one of the Colts, like a nervous habit.

"Shrimp Malone. Name's Shrimp Malone."

He looked like a shrimp, little and orange-headed. Then, too, he could've been *Chicken* Malone, because of the blond eyebrows and eyelashes. That and the fact that he didn't have any lips to speak of.

"I've been expecting you, Mr. Malone," Jesse said, and Shrimp's red face turned pale under the dirt and grime and gingery whiskers. "Close the door."

"You wouldn't shoot me here, would you?"

"Depends. Close the door and sit down."

Shrimp pretty much fell into a spindly ladderback chair by the door, while Jesse moved back as far as he could and still be heard in the creepy whisper, because the stink coming off his visitor was strong enough to kill a moose. Under the reek of booze and sweat lay the sour odor of clay-dirt, though, and that told him Mr. Malone was a prospector. Which made him as welcome as if he'd smelled like a lady's perfumed hankie.

The fastest way to make a man with a guilty conscience

talk is to keep quiet. Shrimp Malone stood the silence for about twenty seconds before blurting out, "Well, hell's bells, did you *see* 'er? God *damn*, that was the sorriest-looking female I ever clapped eyes on! I only poked her in the first place on accounta I was shitfaced drunk. Which she knowed, and so did her whole idiot family. They *trick*ed me. Any man woulda ran off if he'd saw the chance—you'd'a done it, too! God almighty, she looked like a goddamn possum, breath like a shut-up cave, and them two black teeth stickin' out like dominoes. Whuh!"

Jesse shuddered in sympathy, picturing the kind of woman Shrimp would scorn because of her personal hygiene. "That ain't worth two cents to me," he said, figuring it was time to bring money into the conversation.

It worked. "How much are those halfwits payin' you? Whadda they want you to do, drag me back to marry 'er, or just plug me right here and put me outa my misery? It don't hardly make a difference to me—I'd as soon be dead as shackled to that horse-faced hyena the rest o' my days." He looked cocky and resolute for half a minute. Then he caved.

"Okay, okay, here's the deal!" Jumping up, he dragged a filthy cloth bag out of the deep pocket of his brown, baggy, dirt-encrusted dungarees. "Here's sixty-four ounces of dust, all's I got in the wide world. Took me four month to sift and pick and scrounge it outa the river. You take it and tell the Weaver boys you done kilt me. Pocket what they give you an' this, too, and ride on. They'll never know, 'cause I don't aim to set foot in Coos County for the rest of my days, and that's the God's truth."

Jesse caught the bag one-handed. It hefted about four pounds. Gold was bringing twelve dollars an ounce these days. Twelve times sixteen, two sixes are twelve, carry your one is seven . . . seven hundred and fifty bucks. He didn't bother opening the bag to make sure it wasn't full of sand. In his short but profitable career, nobody had ever stiffed Gault yet, and Shrimp Malone didn't look like the man to start.

Jesse sent him his fiendish, one-eyed glare. "You wouldn't be trying to bribe me, would you, Mr. Malone?"

"What? No, sir! I'd never do nothin' like that."

"I hope not. Because I've got a reputation to uphold."

"Yes, sir. No, this 'ud be like . . . like a gift. This little bit o'gold for my life. A trade, like."

He looked thoughtful. "How'll I prove to them you're dead?"

"Huh?"

"The Weavers. They'll want proof. What'll I use to convince them?"

Shrimp looked baffled for a second, then crushed. "Aw, shit," he mumbled, digging down in the other pocket and pulling out something gray and nasty looking. "This here's the onliest thing that'd do it. My lucky pig's ear."

Jesse, who'd been hoping for a watch, took the bristly, petrified ear between two fingers. It appeared to be a hundred years old, so it must be his imagination that it still stank. "If you're trying to birdlime me, Malone—"

"I ain't, I swear I ain't! Anybody who knows me'll tell you, I'd ruther die than part with my lucky pig's ear. "

Jesse lifted the eyebrow over his good eye.

"Heh-heh," Shrimp said nervously, "leastwise, that's what I always use t'say. Ask anybody."

He pretended to think it over while the miner shifted from foot to foot. After a long time, he whispered, "I'm in a good mood today. Reckon I'll take you up on your offer, Mr. Malone."

Shrimp's knees almost buckled. "Oh, thank you, Mr. Gault. You won't regret it, I swear."

"I better not."

"You won't."

"Because if I do, that'll put me in a bad mood."

"Yessir. No, sir, you can rest easy." He started backing toward the door, smiling hopefully, tipping his chewed-up hat. "Well, I'll say adios—"

"I aim to stay in Lazarus for a while. I'd sure hate to hear any rumors about our little business deal."

Shrimp made an "X" over his chest with a black thumb. "Cross my heart, nobody'll ever hear about it from me."

"Because if they did, you know what would happen?"

Shrimp was smarter than he looked. "It'd put you in a bad mood."

"That's right. Folks say I get irrational when I'm in a bad mood."

"Yes, sir." This time he twisted two fingers in front of his mouth and vowed, "My lips're sealed."

Jesse could've pointed out that he didn't have any lips, but that would've been unkind. Besides, the smell was getting too bad. When Shrimp scrabbled for the knob behind him and finally got the door open, Jesse sent him one last steely-eyed glare and let him go.

Then he felt like letting out a rebel yell, or tossing his hat in the air. But the walls were too thin and the ceiling was too low. He settled for throwing himself on the bed and crooning, "Yee-ha," in a soft, celebratory tone.

LAZARUS—YOU'LL LIKE IT HERE, a sign said at the top of Main Street. Yes, sir, Lazarus was an all-right town. Gault liked it here just fine.

So did Jesse.

Cady had passed that sign so many times, she didn't even see it anymore. Today, driving by it, something else caught her eye anyway: Ham Washington, Levi's boy, flying straight at her down the middle of the street like wild dogs were chasing him. If she didn't know Ham so well, she'd have thought the saloon was on fire.

"Miz Cady, Miz Cady!"

The calm, slow-footed mare shied a little, halting just short of a collision with Ham. "Abraham, how many times have I told you not to run at a horse like that?"

He was too excited to apologize. "Miz Cady, a man—a man—" And too winded to make sense. "Guns, guns, a black horse—stayin' at your—place, and Poppy says—"

She reached her hand down, he grabbed it, and she hauled him up beside her on the seat. Ham was tall for eight, but skinny as a weed, all elbows and shoulder blades. "Slow down and catch your breath," she advised, handing the reins to him out of habit. Handling the mare calmed him down; Ham was crazy for horses.

"A man done rode in, Miz Cady," he managed all in one breath. "Bad man, Poppy say. He at the Rogue—done took a room. He have guns an' rifles all over, an' Poppy say he look like death walkin'. Just like death walkin'," he repeated with relish.

"What are you talking about? Why is he a bad man?"

"He a *gunslinger*. Look at him cross-eyed, he shoot you, Mr. Yeakes say. I ain't seen him yet—he up in his room, got the door shut. He name Gault."

They were almost in front of the Rogue. "Stop right here,"

Cady commanded, and Ham reined the mare in at the corner. "Take the buggy to the livery for me," she told him, jumping down, "and tell Mr. Yeakes I'll pay him later. You come straight back afterward and stay with your daddy, you understand?"

"Yes'm." If anything, he looked more agitated than before—her urgency had confirmed his worst, most exciting fears.

Watching him drive off, she noticed a knot of men across the street in front of the French restaurant. She recognized Stony Dern and Tom Blankenship; Gunther Dewhurt tipped his hat to her but didn't come over. On the oppostie corner, Livvie Dunne and Ardelle Sheets were talking to a third lady. Cady could only see her hat and the back of her gray dress. Like the men, all three were staring across at the small, red-painted balcony that ran across two sides of her saloon. Nobody was up there, though. Nothing stirred except the rocking chairs in the wind, and one blackbird flapping its wings on the railing.

She looked back at Livvie and Ardelle—who saw her and immediately turned their backs on her, the way they always did. If they'd had their children with them, they'd've gathered them up and herded them down the sidewalk, as if they were sheep and Cady was a big drooling wolf. She made her snooty, careless face, wishing they'd turn around so they could see how little their scorn mattered to her. Just then Levi poked his head out the swinging door. She picked up her skirts and hurried across the street toward Rogue's Tavern.

"Miz Cady," Levi greeted her, holding the door open. Over his shoulder, she noticed the saloon was almost empty, nobody but Jersey Stan Morrissey playing poker by himself, and Leonard Berg and Jim Tannenbaum, drunk and squabbling as usual. This time of day on a Friday, the place ought to be half full at least, and getting livelier by the minute.

"I just saw Ham," said Cady.

"Yep, I seen 'im fly by in the buggy."

"What's he saying about a gunfighter, Levi?"

The bartender smoothed one long-fingered hand back over his ear, feeling for bristles. Levi shaved his head every morning, shiny and smooth as an eight-ball. "Sho look like it to me, Miz Cady. He say his name's Gault. *Bad*-lookin' white man. Scared off all but these here," he said, nodding toward the three stragglers at the bar.

"You gave him a *room*?"

He ducked his head. "Didn't see no way not to. He look jus' like I heard he did, one good eye an' one good ear. Look like a killer to me. But he ain't *did* nothin' yet, an' plus . . . plus I was scared not to do what he say."

"It's all right," she said quickly, "I'd have done the same thing." Following his nervous gaze to the stair landing at the back of the saloon, she half expected to see Gault standing there, guns drawn. "Think Wylie hired him?"

He shrugged. "I don't know. I hope not."

She hoped not, too, but what else would a gunfighter be doing in Lazarus? "Where's Eric?"

Levi shrugged again, and added a roll of his eyes. Which meant, what difference does it make? She had to agree. Sheriff Eric Robertson (Rick-Bob, people called him for a joke) was either dutifully shuffling papers in his office or else mooning around Stella Shavers, Cady's best bargirl. Either way, if the man upstairs really was a hired killer, the sheriff wasn't going to be running him out of town anytime soon.

Cady looked back at the empty staircase. Looked around her mostly empty saloon. "I don't need this, Levi."

"No, ma'am."

She bit her lip for a while longer, scowling into space. "Well, I guess I'll go up there."

Levi sighed, as if he'd known that was coming. "Guess I'll go with you."

She looked at him doubtfully. Levi was tall as a telegraph pole, but he weighed about as much as she did. He never touched guns, and there wasn't a violent bone in his body. He kept the peace by talking men to death, reasoning with them in a calm, practically hypnotic voice that soothed the meanness out of the surliest customers. And if it didn't, Cady threw them out herself, with help from the little Remington five-shot she kept in her garter.

"No need for that, Levi. I can handle myself," she said.

"Prob'ly can, but I'm still comin'."

If she kept refusing, it might embarrass him. "Okay, but partway," she conceded. "Just see me into his room. After that, if you hear shooting, run for the sheriff." She said it with a smile, but she wasn't sure if she was joking or not.

* * *

Jesse was dreaming about women. Two women, a blonde and a brunette. The brunette was taking his boots off and the blonde was sitting on his lap, wetting the end of a cigar, fixing to light it for him. She wet it by running her tongue around and around the tip, making little humming noises. Somebody said, "Bet's to you," and all of a sudden he had three kings and a pair of aces in the hand that wasn't resting on the blonde's little round behind. "See that and raise you a hundred," Jesse said, and everybody laid down their cards. Slop everywhere—he won. The blonde kissed him on the ear. He reached for the pot—

Knock-knock-knock.

He opened his eyes, smiling, disoriented, unable to remember where he was. Big room, soft bed, yellow wallpaper—he sat up fast, going for his guns while he called out, "Who's there?" in a sleep-roughened voice.

"Cady McGill."

A woman. No need for weapons, then. In the mirror over the bureau, he noticed his eyepatch had slid over to his temple. Righting it, raking his hair back with his fingers, he padded over to the door and jerked it open.

And broke into a big, tickled grin—all wrong, not Gault at all, but he was just so glad to see her. She was a little thing, no more than about chin height, but she was real shapely. *Real* shapely. Shiny dark hair tied back in a ribbon, and eyes the same color as her hair. Green skirt and a yellow blouse, with a little piece of white lace at the front to draw your eye, just in case it wasn't there already. She had a man's felt hat on, hanging down her back by a leather strap, dark against the smooth white of her neck. He liked the thin, friendly line of freckles across the bridge of her nose. Most of all he liked her wide, sexy mouth, currently set in a nervous straight line.

"Mr. Gault?"

Gault, right, right. Jesse changed his smile into a leer. Pretty girls had guilty consciences, too, he knew for a fact, so he didn't say a word, just widened the door and stepped back. It was a fine line, though; he wanted her to come in, so he didn't want to look *too* dangerous.

She hesitated. After a glance down the hall to her right, she lifted her chin, like a stud player bluffing a flush when she's holding a pair of deuces, and stepped over the threshold.

Before he closed the door, he checked to see who was out there. Aha—the tall Negro bartender, on guard at the top of the stairs. He looked petrified, but he was standing his ground. Jesse liked that in a man.

Cady halted in front of the unmade feather bed. A black, bullet-studded gunbelt with twin holsters was slung over one of the posts, and a black Stetson hat hung at a rakish tilt on the other. Something, maybe the contrast between the rumpled, snow-white sheets and the dangerous-looking gunbelt, threw her off her stride. *So*, some frivolous part of her mind noted, *even outlaw gunfighters take naps. Under the covers, just like the rest of us. Maybe they even snore.*

Which was a ridiculous thing to be thinking right at that moment. With a mental shake, she pivoted to face the outlaw, and caught him staring at her rear end.

He was even meaner looking than Levi had warned her he'd be. He was taller than she was—who wasn't?—but not exactly a giant, maybe six feet or so. He wore his wavy hair long, and it was the same shade of dark brown as hers, only his was streaked with silver. Prematurely silver, though—he looked young, not even thirty. While she watched, he did up one button on his black shirt, but he didn't bother with the top button of his black denim trousers.

He folded his arms and leaned against the door, crossing his bare feet at the ankles. It was hard not to stare at the patch over his right eye. Was he horribly scarred under it? Maybe he had no eye there at all. That notion horrified and fascinated her about equally.

She knew his name, but only vaguely, mostly from unreliable barroom talk. She remembered something about him being wounded at Gettysburg before his gunfighter career started—but how could that be? In 1863 he wouldn't have been much more than twelve or thirteen years old.

"What can I do for you, Miss Katie McGill?"

"Cady," she corrected automatically.

"K.D.?"

"No, Cady. It's short for Cadence." *Oh, this is how you talk to hired gunslingers, Cady: You make sure they know what your name is short for.* "And you?" she said aggressively. "Have you got a first name?"

He narrowed his one eye, which was an eerie shade of silver gray, and didn't say anything for so long, she began to perspire. "I don't need one," he finally sneered, but by then she'd almost forgotten the question.

It wasn't like her to behave like such a peahen. She put her hands on her hips and said combatively, "I own this place."

"That so?" He nodded, glanced around. "Nice view. I'm real partial to a rocking chair."

"Yes, I—thought they'd be a nice touch." She waved her hand toward the low door that led out to the porch roof.

"Real nice touch."

Well, this was a pleasant conversation they were having. She caught sight of a Winchester .44-.40 leaning against the wall, and it brought her back to the point.

"What are you doing here, Mr. Gault? Who hired you?" He just stared at her until her palms began to sweat. "Wylie," she answered for herself, because it was so obvious. "Right? It was Wylie, wasn't it?"

"Why would Wylie hire me?"

"Maybe to burn me out, the same way he did Logan. How much is he paying you?"

Instead of answering, he started to walk toward her, naked feet slow and quiet on the carpet. She couldn't stop herself from stepping back, then sideways. Without even pausing, he passed her by and sat down at the foot of the bed.

It took half a minute for her heart to slow down.

"You listen here," she said when it did. "I'm not paying you anything, and I'm not leaving. Rogue's Tavern is mine, and Merle Wylie's never getting his dirty paws on it. He can't have the Rogue, he can't have the Seven Dollar, and he can't have me. And you can tell him I said so." Her anger had gotten hotter with every word; by the time she finished her little speech, her hands were shaking.

Gault stroked his shiny mustache thoughtfully, looking at her with more interest than menace for a change. "I'll tell him if you want me to. What's he look like?"

She blinked. "What?"

"Fellow Wylie. I don't know him, but I'll be happy to deliver your message."

"You're saying he didn't send for you?"

"Never heard the name 'til this afternoon. I stabled my horse at his livery."

"*His* livery. Hah. That's because two weeks ago he burned

Logan's down to the ground," she shot back, mad all over again.

"Now, why would he want to do a mean thing like that?"

Was he playing with her? "Because he wants the whole town to himself, that's why."

He stood up and started walking toward her again, but this time she didn't give way. "Greed'll do funny things to a man," he said in a low, rough, whispery voice that sent a little thrill across the tops of her shoulders. He was standing so close, she could smell him. Tobacco, bay rum, and leather. And danger.

"How long were you planning to stay in Lazarus?" she asked, sticking her chin out at him, glad when her voice didn't quiver.

He turned his head to the right, and she remembered he was deaf in one ear. "Long as it takes to get my business done, Miss McGill."

No need to ask what his business was. Professional gunfighter—he might as well have a sign across his chest. Who had hired him, though? And who could he be gunning for in Lazarus? No sense in asking; he wouldn't tell. "Well, you're welcome to stay here as long as you don't cause any trouble," she said firmly as she backed toward the door. "I won't stand for any trouble in my place."

"Sometimes trouble has a way of following a man, and there's nothing he can do about it."

So, the frivolous part of her brain piped up again. *It's not just in corny dime novels—gunfighters really do talk like that.* She hunted for the proper response, and finally settled for, "I expect that depends on the man, Mr. Gault."

"Yes, ma'am, I expect it does."

They stared at each other somewhat blankly until she said, "Well," and searched behind her for the door knob.

"You know what I want?"

The question made her nervous. Rather than ask what, which would've betrayed too much interest, she just lifted her eyebrows.

"I want a hot bath, a steak dinner, and a poker game."

For some reason—relief, probably—she smiled at him. "Sorry, there's no plumbing on the second floor—which Levi should've told you. But you can get a bath at the barbershop for a dollar. We don't serve meals, either, but Jacque's is right across the street. He says the food's French, but it's really Creole. Then there's Swensen's on Main Street, but I don't recommend it. Not unless your stomach's made out of cast iron."

That made *him* smile, the same infectious, almost sweet smile he'd greeted her with at the door. It hadn't lasted long, but she hadn't forgotten it. Now it struck her the same way as the rumpled bed and the six-guns—a funny contrast to the scary-looking rest of him.

"And the poker game?" he reminded her.

"Ah. Now there I can help you."

"Square game?"

"Absolutely. The fairest in town." Which definitely wasn't saying much. Gault smiled again, as if he'd read her mind. They shared a look, and just for a second she thought it was a companionable look, almost . . . conspiratorial. "Well," she said again, "see you."

He touched his index finger to his forehead in a cocky salute. When he took it away, the smile and the look, whatever it had meant, were both gone. He didn't say "See you" back; in fact, he didn't say anything. Oddly disappointed, Cady slipped out the back door and closed it softly behind her.

Levi was still waiting for her on the stairs. Walking toward him, she had the strangest sensation: That she'd just had a conversation with two men, not one, and she had no idea which one was real. Or which one interested her more.

WE NEED YOUR HELP

To continue to bring you quality romance
that meets your personal expectations,
we at TOPAZ books want to hear from you.
Help us by filling out this questionnaire, and in exchange
we will give you a **free gift** as a token of our gratitude.

- Is this the first TOPAZ book you've purchased? (circle one)
    YES   NO
  The title and author of this book is: _____

- If this was not the first TOPAZ book you've purchased, how many have
  you bought in the past year?
    a: 0 - 5   b 6 - 10   c: more than 10   d: more than 20

- How many romances in total did you buy in the past year?
    a: 0 - 5   b: 6 - 10   c: more than 10   d: more than 20 ___

- How would you rate your overall satisfaction with this book?
    a: Excellent   b: Good   c: Fair   d: Poor

- What was the main reason you bought this book?
    a: It is a TOPAZ novel, and I know that TOPAZ stands
       for quality romance fiction
    b: I liked the cover
    c: The story-line intrigued me
    d: I love this author
    e: I really liked the setting
    f: I love the cover models
    g: Other: _____

- Where did you buy this TOPAZ novel?
    a: Bookstore   b: Airport   c: Warehouse Club
    d: Department Store   e: Supermarket   f: Drugstore
    g: Other: _____

- Did you pay the full cover price for this TOPAZ novel? (circle one)
    YES   NO
  If you did not, what price did you pay? _____

- Who are your favorite TOPAZ authors? (Please list)

- How did you first hear about TOPAZ books?
    a: I saw the books in a bookstore
    b: I saw the TOPAZ Man on TV or at a signing
    c: A friend told me about TOPAZ
    d: I saw an advertisement in_____magazine
    e: Other: _____

- What type of romance do you generally prefer?
    a: Historical   b: Contemporary
    c: Romantic Suspense   d: Paranormal (time travel,
       futuristic, vampires, ghosts, warlocks, etc.)
    d: Regency   e: Other: _____

- What historical settings do you prefer?
    a: England   b: Regency England   c: Scotland
    e: Ireland   f: America   g: Western Americana
    h: American Indian   i: Other: _____

- What type of story do you prefer?
    - a: Very sexy
    - b: Sweet, less explicit
    - c: Light and humorous
    - d: More emotionally intense
    - e: Dealing with darker issues
    - f: Other

- What kind of covers do you prefer?
    - a: Illustrating both hero and heroine
    - b: Hero alone
    - c: No people (art only)
    - d: Other_____

- What other genres do you like to read (circle all that apply)
    - Mystery
    - Medical Thrillers
    - Science Fiction
    - Suspense
    - Fantasy
    - Self-help
    - Classics
    - General Fiction
    - Legal Thrillers
    - Historical Fiction

- Who is your favorite author, and why?_____
  _____

- What magazines do you like to read? (circle all that apply)
    - a: *People*
    - b: *Time/Newsweek*
    - c: *Entertainment Weekly*
    - d: *Romantic Times*
    - e: *Star*
    - f: *National Enquirer*
    - g: *Cosmopolitan*
    - h: *Woman's Day*
    - i: *Ladies' Home Journal*
    - j: *Redbook*
    - k: Other:_____

- In which region of the United States do you reside?
    - a: Northeast
    - b: Midatlantic
    - c: South
    - d: Midwest
    - e: Mountain
    - f: Southwest
    - g: Pacific Coast

- What is your age group/sex? a: Female b: Male
    - a: under 18
    - b: 19-25
    - c: 26-30
    - d: 31-35
    - e: 36-40
    - f: 41-45
    - g: 46-50
    - h: 51-55
    - i: 56-60
    - j: Over 60

- What is your marital status?
    - a: Married
    - b: Single
    - c: No longer married

- What is your current level of education?
    - a: High school
    - b: College Degree
    - c: Graduate Degree
    - d: Other: _____

- Do you receive the TOPAZ *Romantic Liaisons* newsletter, a quarterly newsletter with the latest information on Topaz books and authors?

    YES   NO

    If not, would you like to?   YES   NO

    Fill in the address where you would like your free gift to be sent:

    Name: _____

    Address: _____

    City:_____Zip Code: _____

    You should receive your free gift in 6 to 8 weeks.
    Please send the completed survey to:

Penguin USA•Mass Market
Dept. TS
375 Hudson St.
New York, NY 10014